Dear Reader,

Welcome to the wonderful world of *Scarlet*!

This month sees the launch of our exciting new romance series, offering you books I'm sure you'll enjoy reading as much as I've enjoyed selecting them for you. From June 1996 onwards, become a *Scarlet* woman and look out for four brand-new titles every month, written exclusively for you by specially selected authors we know you'll love.

At the back of this book you'll find a questionnaire and we'd be really happy if you'd complete and return it to us as soon as possible. Returning your questionnaire will earn you a surprise gift.

Scarlet is *your* list and we want *your* views on whether or not you like our selection of titles. So . . . feel free to drop me a line at any time, as I'd be delighted to hear from you.

Till next month,
Best wishes,

Sally Cooper

SALLY COOPER,
Editor-in-Chief – *Scarlet*

About the Author

Ann Kelly was born and raised in Sydney, Australia, but now relishes life as a 'country girl' in New South Wales' beautiful Hunter Valley; she resides there with her wonderful husband, active children, a rabbit and a temperamental Himalayan cat called Cloud. The whole family is sports mad.

'My need to write is an inherited idiosyncrasy,' she says. 'I've an uncle published in non-fiction, another who creates magazine comic strips and a Dad who dabbled in poetry and is now compiling the family history dating back to Eden!'

Ann, first published in 1993, enjoys creating character driven stories where the focus is on *people* – and of course her books always have a happy ending. She says, 'If people want the downside of reality they can get it in newspapers or by watching T.V. I like to balance things out a bit more and make people smile; life isn't *all* bad!'

Other **Scarlet** *titles available this month:*

DANGEROUS LADIES by Natalie Fox
FIRE AND ICE by Maxine Barry
THE MISTRESS by Angela Drake

ANN KELLY

PARTNERS IN PASSION

SCARLET

Enquiries to:
Robinson Publishing Ltd
7 Kensington Church Court
London W8 4SP

First published in the UK by Scarlet, 1996

A copy of the British Library Cataloguing in
Publication data is available from the British Library

ISBN 1-85487-468-3

Printed and bound in the EC

10 9 8 7 6 5 4 3 2 1

AUTHOR'S NOTE

Writing this book has been both a challenge and a learning experience which I've greatly enjoyed. However, in my bid for background authenticity I intruded unmercifully on the time and I'm sure patience of a number of people.

Special thanks must go to Helen Mateer and Howard Brown for their insights into how private investigators operate in Australia and the laws governing them. My thanks also to Heather Cleary, Kim and Valdo D'Ortona, Sharon Dzurynskij, Catherine and Rodger Garland, Dr Steve Hembry, Dr Michelle Kelso, Kath Macmillan and Karen Tiedeman.

Each and every one of these people has contributed to this book in some way, shape or form. Their knowledge, co-operation and friendship is greatly appreciated.

And lastly a *very special* thank you to my husband and children for being so wonderfully self-sufficient, supportive, understanding and tolerant of me during the writing of this book.

PARTNERS IN PASSION is about people, living, loving and learning; I hope you enjoy reading it as much as I've enjoyed writing it.

This book is dedicated to the late Frank Brennan. For providing an unpublished author with more encouragement and support than she could ever have imagined. No words can describe the measure of love and gratitude I feel for Frank Brennan.

Thank you, Wendy, for sharing him with me.

CHAPTER 1

December 1987

Feeling thirstier than she had in all her sixteen years, Tatum dragged herself up the airless stairwell thinking of nothing more than an icy cold drink. The worst thing about trying to escape Sydney's stinking summer heat and humidity by going to the beach was enduring the long trip home – in the same stinking summer heat and humidity. She'd kill for a dri –

Her hand froze halfway to the handle of the door displaying a backward '5'. Had anyone bothered to replace the missing screw from the aged numeral it would have read '2', but no one ever had – not in all the years Tatum had lived in the building. Fantasy had asked only once for it to be repaired. The landlord's response was that he'd been meaning to 'get around to discussing the matter with her. After all what was one little screw between friends?' To which Fantasy had replied, 'A matter of principle.'

Recalling the incident Tatum touched a finger to the numeral and set it swinging.

Fantasy and her ironic principles were gone now, and yet Tatum's life still seemed as upside down as the little

1

metal number. It had been months since she'd made the mistake of coming to the wrong door, but, tired from a day of lying under a hot Bondi sun, she'd lapsed into auto-pilot and old habits. For a moment she let herself remember the last time she'd walked into the apartment without it being a conscious decision. But only for a moment.

'Snap out of it, Tate!' she ordered herself, quickly turning to the opposite apartment, identified in new shiny brass as 'No 1'. *This* was her home now, and the ease with which her key slid and turned in the lock seemed kind of symbolic.

'I'm back, Lu!' Her announcement was greeted by nothing but the warring scents of incense, grass and the rarer perfume of the too large tinselled pine tree which dominated the tiny living room. Noting the door of the master bedroom was closed, she headed for the refrigerator. The kitchen, predictably, was empty, but her carry-bag and damp towel hit the floor when she discovered the fridge in similar shape.

'Ah, geez, Lu! I thought you said you were going shopping today,' she muttered, shaking a three-quarter empty bottle of Coke in the hope it would fizz with even minimum life. It didn't. Still, right now her thirst was willing to settle for anything even remotely cold and wet. It was dumb to think Lu might shop when they'd only been out of margarine for *two* days, she thought peevishly, plonking into the nearest chair. To Lulu's way of thinking, a person didn't need to go shopping unless they were out of soap, washing powder or shampoo. Oh, and sparkling wine, of course! Which was a cause for hope, since there'd been none of that in the fridge either.

2

'Haven't I told you not to drink out of bottles?'

Tatum started at the unexpected silent appearance of the redheaded Lulu, but recovered quickly. 'Wasn't worth dirtying a glass for the few mouthfuls that was left.'

'*Were* left, Tatum! The few mouthfuls that *were* left. I'll never comprehend how you can produce straight As in English when you're so lazy with grammar.'

Tatum didn't bother to correct Lu's misconception that the error had been unintentional. Mainly because Lu would then want such a comment explained and Tatum wouldn't be able to give her an explanation she'd understand. Actually, she couldn't really explain to herself why she used bad grammar whenever she was home – except that in some strange way it made her feel safe, more honest.

In the wake of Lulu's etiquette and grammar lesson, she was subjected to narrow-eyed scrutiny. 'You're burnt. I've told you to wear sunscreen. How long were you at the beach?'

Tatum fought down the desire to tell her to cut the maternal crap. It wasn't that she didn't appreciate Lulu taking her in, and all, but she was no more cut out for the Carole Brady role than Fantasy had been. Not that Fantasy had even bothered to fake maternalism.

'I left 'bout ten, I guess.' Her response went unacknowledged, the older woman's attention now devoted to filling the coffee percolator. Her actions were unusually awkward for a woman who seemed to make grace a fashion statement. Not for the first time Tatum wondered what, apart from their careers, her mother and Lu had ever had in common. What had happened in Lulu's past that she'd

3

managed not only to cross paths with Fantasy but to form a friendship with her, when it was plain to anyone who knew them they were as different as night from day?

She studied the woman, taking in the vivid russet colour of her hair and its sleek, stylish bob. The colour was natural, the cut the handiwork of a prominent eastern suburbs hairdresser – expensive handiwork. Its cost was only marginally overshadowed by the designer-label silver negligee draping her body. On most of the women Tatum had known over the years, her own mother included, the outfit would have blatantly screamed *sex* on Lulu it teasingly whispered *seduction*.

Her mother had envied her best friend's subtle sensuality, complaining that Lulu carried her airs and graces too far even as she'd tried desperately to copy them. But, having lived with Lulu these past months, Tatum realized the woman's perfect speech and understated elegance were as natural to her as breathing.

'Oh, shit!' Lulu's cultured tone was so at odds with the earthy swear word that it somehow lost all impact. Only Lu could swear with class.

'Tatum, I'm all thumbs because my nails are still wet; would you be a darling and fix the coffee for me, please?'

'Sure.'

That was something else Tatum admired about Lu; she didn't automatically expect her to fetch and carry for her, like Fantasy had. Of course, she didn't write herself off with booze and pills the way Fantasy had either.

The image of her mother lying unconscious across her unmade bed brought a strange stab of anger, pain and sadness. Blinking away unshed tears along with the ugly

4

memory, she set the percolator to brew and turned back to the woman seated at the table, blowing on long glossy fingernails.

'If you don't need the bathroom, I'll have a shower and get this sand off me.'

'Why not have a bath instead? Use my bubble gel; it's great for preventing sunburnt skin from peeling.'

'Lu, I'm half Italian. I don't burn or peel, I *tan*. Only you wimpy, lily-skinned Poms shrivel with a little sun.'

The redhead sent her a superior look. 'It's a medical fact that skin cancer doesn't discriminate between races. Besides, you're sixteen – it's time you started taking better care of your skin. Now *use* the gel.'

'Okay, okay. If it'll make you happy I'll use the bloody stuff!'

'And don't swear!'

'You swear.'

'Only when it's necessary.'

Tatum laughed. '*And*, as Zeta says, only if the client wants it, huh, Lu?'

'*What*?' The redhead was instantly on her feet. 'When were you talking to Zeta?' she demanded, both her face and body rigid.

The unexpected display of anger made Tatum slow to answer.

'Answer me, Tatum! When were you last speaking to Zeta?'

'A couple of days ago.'

'Did you go to the parlour? Haven't I told you I don't want you going down there? Haven't I – '

'I wasn't at the damn parlour! I bumped into her at the

shops! Geez, Lulu, what's with you? I've known Zeta since I was a baby. She used to babysit me after school – '

'Well, you don't need a sitter now. And I don't want you going down there – you hear me?'

'The whole of Darlinghurst and the Cross can probably hear you.'

As if only now realizing she'd been shouting, Lulu put an embarrassed hand to her throat. Bright red nails made a dramatic contrast against milky white skin, and Tatum saw fragility in a woman she'd always considered strong and in control.

'I'm sorry, Tatum. I . . . I didn't mean to yell. It's just that . . .'

'Lu, are you okay?'

'I'm fine. I'm fine.' The fact that she'd repeated the statement automatically seemed to weaken it. 'Really,' she continued, 'I just need a shot of caffeine, that's all.' She waved Tatum away. 'You scoot off and have that tub, honey. Off you go, now and remember to use plenty of gel. Oh, and try that new shampoo André recommended. It'll do wonders for that gorgeous black mane of yours.'

Forcing a smile, Tatum retreated to the bathroom, Lulu's uncharacteristic behaviour giving her an eerie sense of *déjà vu*.

Fantasy had been prone to sudden mood swings from about as far back as Tatum could remember. One minute she'd be all calm and civil, and the next ranting and raving about all kinds of imaginary stuff. At first it had only happened when she was coming off a bad trip or something, but it had got so Tatum couldn't tell the good ones – if there was such a thing – from the bum ones. And when

6

she'd mixed pills with booze . . . Well, those times it had been smarter just to stay out of her mum's way. Many a time in her primary school days she'd hung out at Lu's, watching TV or doing her homework till the worst was over and Fantasy had either passed out or gone to work.

As far as Tatum knew Lulu had never done hard drugs. In fact, if it hadn't been for the occasional smell of grass hanging in the air of the apartment, she'd have sworn the woman was completely straight; she'd certainly never smoked dope in Tatum's presence. Reflexively she sniffed the air, but now the only noticeable scent was that of the hundred-bucks-a-bottle bath gel, foaming beneath the tap.

'You're being paranoid, Tate.' She addressed her steam-obscured reflection in the mirror of the medicine cabinet as she pulled it open and extracted a packet of menthol cigarettes. Lulu was as clean as she was, tobacco and the odd glass of wine notwithstanding, and if she'd acted a little weird earlier it was probably because she had a difficult client scheduled for tonight.

'Yeah, that's all it is,' Tatum assured herself. After all, at sixteen she'd been around the business long enough to know the week leading up to Christmas was always a rough time . . .

Lulu was gone when Tatum came out of the bathroom almost an hour later, convinced she'd die if she didn't eat soon. Knowing the fridge was a lost cause, she dialled the number of Mario's Italian restaurant a block away and ordered a pizza with the works. Twenty minutes later, as she peered through the peephole her vain hope that Mario himself might make the delivery, as he sometimes did, was shattered at the sight of his nephew.

Giovanni-call-me-Jon-Grasso was twenty-one, insanely good-looking and a renowned ladykiller. He also turned Tatum's stomach. He might think he was God's gift to women, but she didn't, and she wasn't above using her friendship with his uncle to keep him at bay. Mario Grasso had always had a soft spot for Fantasy and he'd appointed himself guardian angel to both mother and daughter. Years ago he'd asked Fantasy to marry him, and Tatum had been heartbroken when her mother had turned him down.

'I didn't escape one old-fashioned Italian family to marry into another one! I'd sooner die,' she'd told her daughter. 'I'm not havin' my daughter grow up in a house that's so bogged down in old country traditions she can't even look at a man!'

Well, no one could ever have accused Fantasy of not living up to her promise to provide her kid with a more liberated lifestyle. And God knew she'd gone to her grave waiting for a white knight with anglo-Australian blood in his veins and a solid cash-flow to rescue her.

When Tatum opened the door Jon made no attempt to disguise his lecherous perusal of her skimpy shorts and top.

'Eating alone again, *mia bella*?'

'Just for a change,' she said drily. Then, with genuine surprise, 'Hey! This feels almost *hot*.'

He smiled. 'I rushed it straight from the oven to you.'

'Slow night, huh?'

He shrugged. '*Si*. Who wants pizza in thirty-degree heat, huh?'

'I'll eat anything as long as I don't have to cook it.'

8

'So why won't you let me take you out to dinner?'

'Because I'd hate to hurt you when I have to fight you off.'

'You know, for a *putana's* kid you sure think you're pretty good.'

Tatum wondered if his calling her a whore's kid was supposed to hurt her. If so he'd wasted his garlic-fouled breath; her own mother had used the term in the course of polite conversation.

'I guess I must be good, Jon,' she said with deliberate sweetness. 'Otherwise you wouldn't be standing there with a hard-on! Now, piss off, *Giovanni*, or I'll get you in all sorts of nasty trouble with *Zio Mario*!'

'Bitch!' he snarled. 'You'll get yours one day, Tatum Milano!'

'I know.' She gave him a dazzling smile. 'The meek are going to inherit the earth. *Ciao*, Giovanni.'

'Giovanni!' Lulu's voice surprised them both. 'Are you harassing Tatum?'

'Of course not, Signorina Grant. I delivered her pizza.' He flashed a smile as his hand came to rest on Lulu's forearm. 'Surely you don't expect a man my age would be interested in such a *bambino*.'

'What I expect, Giovanni – '

'Jon, please.'

'What I expect, *Jon*, is for you to remove your hand, before I push your smarmy *juvenile* backside down those stairs.' Spluttering and red-faced, he started backing down the stairs. 'Oh, and *Jon*,' she added, pleasantly, 'a word of warning. Don't touch what you can't afford nor hint at what you can't deliver.'

9

Tatum staggered back into the unit, giggling uncontrollably. 'Oh, Lu, that was brilliant! "Don't touch what you can't afford nor hint at what you can't deliver," ' she mimicked. 'That's priceless! I'll have to remember that line.'

'You'd be better advised to remember the line, Don't advertise what isn't on sale!' Lulu spat. 'Or *are* you thinking of doing a bit of part-time work during the school break?'

'Excuse me . . .'

'What do you think you're doing, parading about braless and in shorts that look like they've been painted on?'

'I'm wasn't *parading* anywhere! I thought I was going to be home *alone*. And I was hoping Mario would bring the pizza, not Hot-rod Harry. Sheesh! What the hell's got into you lately?' She frowned. 'How come you're home anyway?'

Lulu sighed and raked her hands through her hair, which immediately fell back into perfect place. Pulling off her spike-heeled sandals, she slid gracefully into the two-seater cream leather sofa. 'I told Zeta I was taking the night off.'

'*Four days before Christmas?* And she *let* you?'

'I didn't *ask* her; I told her. She needs me more than I need her.' Red-tipped fingers trembled slightly as she lit a cigarette. 'Look, why don't you get dressed and I'll take you out for dinner?'

'But I've just had a pizza delivered.'

'So? Put it in the refrigerator.' She smiled. 'When I last looked there was plenty of room.'

'Which is the only thing there ever is plenty of in there.'

'Don't bitch, Tatum,' she said mildly. 'Oh, and wear something dressy.'

'I don't own anything dressy.'

'Well, then wear one of Fantasy's dresses. But make sure it's something *I* picked – I don't want you looking like a trollop.'

She laughed. 'Why, afraid of the competition?'

Lulu visibly paled.

'Hey, Lu, c'mon – it was a *joke*. An old joke.'

'I know . . . but it doesn't seem that funny any more.'

The restaurant was the same one Lu had taken her to for her birthday last month. Located in Sydney's eastern suburbs, it served the finest seafood and offered well-dressed patrons a harbour view second to none.

'How'd you swing a reservation here on the spur of the moment?' Tatum whispered after they'd been seated. 'One of the owners a regular or somethin'?'

'Someth*ing*. And let's just say I have friends in high places.'

'Not to mention low ones.' The comment earned her Lulu's 'disapproving' eyebrow.

'That's quite right, Tatum – we *won't* mention those. Now, would you like the same wine we had last time or would you prefer to try something new?'

'Whatever.'

'Which, I *presume*,' Lu said in an exaggerated tone, 'is intended to mean, Why don't you choose? I'm sure your knowledge of wines is superior to mine.'

Tatum grinned. 'Whatever.'

11

For some reason since Fantasy's death Lulu had decided it was her responsibility to educate her friend's daughter in the ways of polite society. Perhaps if she'd seen some point to it Tatum would have been more obliging. Still, she co-operated as much as was necessary to keep the older woman relatively happy – which was why she was here all dolled up and not home eating pizza in front of the TV.

While Lulu chattered with the wine waiter Tatum amused herself by scanning the room. Dressed in a caramel silk strapless number that had been her mother's, she knew she looked good, and much older than her sixteen years, and she couldn't help smiling under the appreciative gaze from a man at a nearby table. Of course, having him return it was another matter, and quickly had her lowering her head and fidgeting with the cutlery.

It was one thing to trade insults with a dork like Giovanni, or flirt harmlessly with guys at the beach, but this part of town was a different story. These people, for reasons she didn't understand, made her feel threatened, exposed.

Carefully, when she was certain the man had stopped looking at her and gone back to eating his meal, she resumed her perusal of the room. Its expensively dressed patrons, the subdued buzz of well-bred conversation and elegantly appointed decor, made it seem light years rather than mere kilometres away from Mario's. Her eyes continued to glide aimlessly from one table to another, until shock and dread made her gasp, 'Oh, God!' What was *she* doing here?

12

'What's the matter?'

Ignoring Lulu's question, Tatum forced herself to acknowledge the curly-haired blonde waving at her.

'You know her?' Lulu asked, following her gaze.

'She went to school with me.'

'Which one?'

'Chelmsford Academy.'

'Were you close?'

'No – oh, shit! She's coming over.'

'Don't swear. It's not that bad.'

'Yeah, right.'

'Tatum! How fabulous to see you!'

'Er . . . yeah, you too, Nicola. Um, Nicola, this is my . . . er . . .'

'Aunt.' Lulu eased into Tatum's uncertain pause in her best British aristocracy tones. 'Louissa Grant. I'm Tatum's maternal aunt.'

'It's nice to meet you Ms Grant. I'm Nicola Ashton-Bradfield. My father's Gordon Ashton-Bradfield.'

'How fortunate for you. But please call me Lu. Tatum tells me you were at Chelmsford together?'

'Yes. Oh, gosh, Tatum, I'm so sorry about your mother. It must have been a dreadful shock for you.'

Tatum thought back to the day last Easter break when she'd come home and found Fantasy's comatose body. 'Yes. It was.'

'Of course, my mother always refused to ski, no matter how fashionable it was, because she considers it a dangerous sport. But just between us, Mother is a tad *boring*, if you know what I mean. I guess yours must have been a more sporty active type.'

To avoid meeting Lulu's eyes, Tatum focused directly on the bubble-brained blonde debutante. 'Yes, Mum certainly led an active life.'

'See! That's just what I mean,' Nicola said, as if she'd just discovered a cure for the common cold. 'My mother is so stuffy she'd die if I called her *Mum*. I mean, she'd simply perish right on the spot!'

If they'd ever introduced tact as a subject at Chelmsford, Tatum wouldn't have backed Nicola to get a passing grade. The few girls with whom she'd formed what could loosely be called a friendship at the school had all fallen into the 'quiet and studious' category. This babbling blonde hadn't been one of them, although surprisingly they did have something in common: a parent with an aversion to being called *Mum*. Tatum had never addressed her mother as anything but Fantasy. Not that she was about to tell Nicola that.

'Are they your parents at the table, dear?' Lulu asked, looking beyond the girl's shoulder. 'I think they're trying to get your attention.'

They were doing no such thing, and Tatum could only imagine they were grateful for even a momentary lapse from the inane, high-pitched drivel Nicola had been infamous for at Chelmsford.

'*My parents!* Good Lord, no! That's my godmother and her husband. Unfortunately I'm stuck staying with them until the New Year, then I'm flying to Paris to meet Mother and Daddy. They're in Europe, negotiating the purchase of an Italian film company.' She frowned at Lu with genuine concern. 'Actually I thought I'd *said* my father was Gordon Ashton-Bradfield.'

'Oh, you mean *that* Gordon Ashton-Bradfield! Heavens, what a small world!'

Nicola's face lit up even more – if that was possible. 'Do you know Daddy?'

'Well, of course, Nicola. We've crossed paths at several functions.' Lulu managed to look almost as thrilled as Nicola at the thought. 'Fancy you and Tatum being boarding-school chums and us not realizing it.'

Tatum wished Lu hadn't mentioned the bit about school, because immediately Nicola's attention pivoted back to her.

'I know you must have been upset about your mother, and all, but how come you didn't come back to school after the Easter break?'

'Er, well . . .'

'I felt it best that she be around family,' Lulu supplied. 'It was such a dreadful time for everyone, and to be honest I needed Tatum here to help *me* cope with things. Fortunately I was able to enrol her in a local school to finish the year.'

Nicola looked aghast. 'You mean she went to a *state* school?'

Lulu's eyes were wide with dread and her hand fluttered at her throat. 'Oh, good God, no, Nicola! What a ridiculous notion!'

As Nicola blushed with embarrassment at having made such a crass suggestion Tatum was struggling between not laughing and not wetting herself as Lulu went on to fabricate an elaborate tale about her 'niece' finishing the year at a notoriously exclusive private day-school.

'Actually, I brought Tatum here tonight to try and

15

convince her that going to a Swiss finishing school for the next couple of years would be in her best interests. But she's reluctant to leave behind the Ferrari I bought her for her birthday.'

'Oh, gosh! Tatum, I can't believe how *lucky* you are!' The blonde's high-pitched squeal drew the stares of several other diners.

'I don't believe it myself,' Tatum muttered, grateful that Nicola was too dim to realize she wasn't old enough to drive. She was beginning to think Nicola would never leave when a waiter approached the table and advised the blonde that her main meal was about to be served.

'Oh, drat. I was *so* enjoying catching up with you, Tatum . . . I know!' She looked positively gleeful. 'Why don't we get together while I'm staying in Sydney? I don't know another living soul here, and – '

'Oh, that would be wonderful . . .'

Tatum glared at Lulu. Like hell it'd be wonderful!

'But unfortunately Tatum is flying out to Tahiti tomorrow. It's my Chrissie present to her.'

This additional piece of bull subjected them to several more seconds of Nicola's inane chatter along the lines of how *lucky* Tatum was before the blonde mercifully returned to her table.

'I gather when you wrote to the school you told them Fantasy had died in a skiing accident?' Lu's tone rippled with an undercurrent of disapproval.

'I figured they'd relate more to that than a drug overdose. Besides, basically at least it's the truth – she *is* dead. On the other hand, a Ferrari and vacations in Tahiti are outright *lies*,' she accused. 'Did you have to pour it on

16

quite so thick, Lu? What am I supposed to say if I run into her again?'

'That's hardly likely, now, is it?'

'That's what you said when you told Fantasy to send me to Chelmsford.'

Four years ago, when Fantasy had been struck by the 'brilliant idea' of sending Tatum to boarding-school, Lulu had instructed her to choose one in South Australia, rather than risk Tatum ending up at one where she might possibly encounter the daughters of some of her mother's more affluent clients. And though the prospect of being sent to another state might have daunted some twelve-year-olds, for a kid who'd suffered years of taunts and gossip, not just from classmates but from teachers and parents too, it had been a promise of heaven!

Although at first she'd been intimidated by the school's strict military-style rules, Chelmsford had gradually allowed Tatum to feel safe, and for the first time she'd known what it was like to be treated as a 'normal' kid.

She'd enjoyed her three and a bit years at the upmarket girls' college. Free from the constant fear that someone might discover her background, she'd been able to concentrate on her studies and had done well both academically and in various sports. People there had accepted the story that her mother as was freelance public relations officer whose husband had been reported missing in action in Vietnam.

Of course, the only grain of truth in the bit about her father was the military angle. He'd been a Yank serviceman on R&R who'd convinced Fantasy he was going to take her home with him and marry her. By the time

Fantasy had realized he wasn't coming back Tatum had been a year old. Whether he was dead or alive hadn't mattered once it had become obvious that whatever *action* Fantasy had provided for him he wasn't *missing*!

Fantasy had rarely spoken of him to Tatum. On one occasion, though, she'd said his name was Ben and that his father was a Congressman. But on another his name had been Clint, and another time he'd been Ronnie, an Idaho farmboy.

'Are you going to eat those prawns or merely push them around your plate all night?'

Shutting down her thoughts, Tatum lifted her head to meet Lulu's eyes. 'Last time we were here you said it wasn't ladylike to scoff down my food.'

'One should at least make a token effort to look as if one appreciates a meal. What's the matter?'

'Nothing. I'm just hoping that if I drag the starter out long enough the main meal will be ready and Nicola won't get the chance to pop over for a chat between courses.' At that moment she recalled what Lu had said earlier. 'Do you really know her father?'

Lu laughed. 'No. But she obviously thought I should.'

'Yeah. He must be someone famous in the film industry.'

'More likely a cashed-up little nobody looking for a tax break. Now forget her. She's nothing but the clichéd dumb blonde, not to mention *nouveau riche*.' She made the term sound like an insult. 'Which was my reason for mentioning the car and trip,' she explained. 'Women like that are easily kept in check; trips, fashion and jewellery are the usually the sum total of their conversation and interests.'

'You say that like you're from, what is it . . .? *Old money?*' Again Tatum found herself curious about Lu's background. 'Are you?'

Lu reached for her wine glass, took a sip, then held it suspended as she sent a considering look across to Tatum. 'I can be, and I *am*, exactly who I want to be. Who one *was* or where one came from is utterly inconsequential. Always remember that, Tatum.'

The remainder of the evening passed without incident. Tatum was grateful that Nicola's godmother had been sufficiently anxious to leave the restaurant that she'd only allowed the girl time to slip an ornately gilded card bearing Nicola's name and Adelaide address to a waiter to deliver to their table. The message 'Do keep in touch!' had been scrawled across the back of it.

As she trailed Lulu up the stairs to their apartment Tatum wondered why a sixteen-year-old boarding-school student would need business cards. Then she grinned, recalling that Fantasy had always carried business cards too!

She was jerked from her bitchy speculation when Lulu swore for the second time that day. The sight of Lulu's boss waiting outside their door explained her succinct outburst.

As always, Zeta looked like the aging lead soprano in an opera: fat, with an over-abundance of bosom bursting from an overly theatrical evening gown. All that was missing was the horned headpiece, although getting one on over the heavily teased and lacquered blue-black hair would have been impossible.

'My, my, young Tatum! Don't you look stunning tonight?'

'Thanks. Er . . . it's an old dress of Fantasy's.'

Lu opened the door with a jerkiness that hinted at barely suppressed anger. 'Get changed and into bed, Tatum,' she ordered, before the three of them were barely inside. 'Sit down, Zeta, and tell me why you're here.'

'Really, darling, aren't you at least going to offer me a drink?'

It seemed to take an inordinate amount of effort for the redhead to reply, 'Tea or coffee, Zeta?'

'What, no wine?'

'No.'

Feeling obliged to soften Lulu's uncharacteristic rudeness, Tatum lifted the lid on the cigarette box on the coffee-table and offered one to the older woman before taking one for herself. That was another of the rules Lulu had implemented since Fantasy's death: Tatum wasn't allowed to smoke in public. For a moment she thought Lu was going to challenge the fact she was having one now, but instead she spun on her heel and headed to the kitchen.

'I'll have tea, dear,' Zeta called after her. 'White with two. So tell me,' she said to Tatum, depositing her large frame onto the leather sofa and patting the cushion beside her, 'how are you enjoying the school holidays?'

There had always been something about this woman that made Tatum hesitant to cross her, so, despite the suffocating smell of her perfume, Tatum sat down. 'Okay, I guess.'

'Not bored yet?'

Tatum shrugged. 'Not really. The weather's been good, so I've been going to the beach most days.'

'I thought you were trying to get a part-time job. Dorrie down at the dry cleaners told me you'd been in asking her about work.'

'I was. She didn't have anything for me, though. Mario sometimes calls me in to help in the kitchen, but with his nephew working there now it's not so busy.' From what Tatum had seen Giovanni wouldn't have worked if he'd had a three-pin plug and been connected to an unlimited supply of electricity, but his mother Rosa didn't like her, and what Mario wanted didn't seem to count in the overall running of the restaurant these days. 'I figured I'd wait until after New Year to have another crack at finding something more regular. Things might . . . you know . . . get better once Christmas is over.'

Zeta's chubby heavily ringed hand patted her on the knee. 'That's possible, darling.' She relaxed back into the sofa and drew hard on her menthol cigarette. 'You know, Tatum . . .' The words were delivered on a stream of smoke and with a half-hooded gaze. 'I understand how difficult this first Christmas without your mother is going to be for you . . .'

Most of the ones Tatum remembered hadn't been that easy *with* her!

'So I thought you might like to come to a small dinner party I'm having for some of the girls at my place on Christmas Night.'

'No!' Lulu's refusal hit the room with the force of a cyclone.

'Really, Lulu,' Zeta said. 'It'll be all female, and of course *you* are invited.'

'I've said *no*.' She all but shoved the cup of tea at the

other woman before swinging around to Tatum. 'Didn't you say you were going to bed?'

'No, you *told* me to go go bed. But I happened to feel like a smoke and a cup of tea.'

'Well, you've had the smoke, and if you still want tea you can pour yourself a cup *and then take it to your room*. I'd like a private word with Zeta.'

'Poor Zeta!' Tatum muttered, stubbing out the cigarette with undue force. 'Do me a favour, Zeet, don't let her have too many nights off. It kills her sunny disposition!'

Only the elder of the two other women found any humour in the remark. Despite Zeta's cackle of laughter Lulu's eyes remained icy cold, and Tatum, deciding not to bother with the tea, started towards her room.

'Tatum, wait. What are your plans for Christmas Day?' At Zeta's question she turned a questioning glance to Lu.

'We're spending the day at a friend's,' Lu answered quickly, looking at their visitor. 'Why?'

Again Zeta laughed. 'You're turning into an overbearing mother hen, Lulu, love! It's just that I've a small gift for Tatum, and I thought if you were going to be here I'd pop round and give it to her Christmas morning, but since you're not . . .' She opened the elegant gold envelope purse in her lap and withdrew a narrow gift-wrapped rectangle. 'For you, Tatum, dear. Merry Christmas.'

Excitement skittered through Tatum as she crossed back to the sofa. 'Thanks, Zeta.' She bent and kissed the woman on both cheeks. 'I'll put it under the tree.'

'Oh, nonsense! You're not a child any more! Open it now.'

She needed no second bidding, and spent no more than

22

a second admiring the beautifully wrapped package before tugging at its gold ribbon. She didn't think Zeta had ever failed to give her a Christmas or birthday present from the time Fantasy had started working for her.

Usually they'd been clothes or things she'd use for school, and Tatum had half expected the tradition would end now that Fantasy was gone. Yet last month for her birthday Zeta had surprised her by giving her a hand-carved music box. Surprised, however, didn't even come close to describing how she felt when she lifted the lid on the long leather box the wrapping had concealed.

'*Oh, my God!*' She didn't think she could breathe. 'Oh, Zeta! It's . . . it's beautiful. *Beyond* beautiful! Look, Lu! Isn't it *gorgeous*?'

Tatum hadn't ever seen such a beautiful gate bracelet, and her fingers trembled as she lifted the heavy glittering gold piece from its bed of satin.

'Oh, God,' she said on a half-sigh. 'It's . . . it's . . . Overwhelmed, she couldn't find adequate words. 'Thank you, Zeta,' she said finally. 'Thank you so much.'

'I'm thrilled that you're so pleased with it, my dear,' the older woman said. 'I know you're at an age where girls want to have nice things. Here, let me help you put it on.'

'It seems silly to put it on when you're going to bed, don't you think, Tatum?'

For the first time since she'd seen the bracelet, Tatum looked at Lulu. There was no sign of pleasure in her eyes and her perfectly made up face could have been set in concrete. *She's jealous!* The realization startled Tatum, although it shouldn't have; Fantasy had always said that Lu didn't like people having something she didn't. Perhaps it hadn't been a case of the pot calling the kettle black, as she'd always suspected.

'I can sleep in it if I want to,' she said defiantly, then looked at Zeta. Can't I? It won't get broken or anything, will it?'

'Of course it won't, darling. There!' she said, having completed the task of doing up the bracelet. 'I must say it looks fabulous against that exquisite olive skin of yours. I would kill to possess such skin!'

Tatum couldn't stop herself from grinning long enough to thank her for the compliment. She raised and lowered her arm so the cool weight of the gold could slip up and down it, sparkling in the light. Never in her wildest dreams had she thought she'd own something so beautiful, or so valuable. The few pieces of jewellery she'd inherited from Fantasy had been collectively valued at a little over a thousand dollars, but this . . . *this* weighed a ton! It was probably worth twice that *at least*!

Uncaring that Lulu would consider her behaviour undignified, she threw her arms around Zeta's thick neck and hugged her tight. 'Thank you, thank you, thank you! No one's ever given me anything so wonderful! Never ever!'

'You've grown into a beautiful young woman, Tatum,' Zeta said. 'You deserve beautiful things.'

CHAPTER 2

Christmas Day 1987

A refreshing sea breeze floated onto the balcony of the Manly penthouse, cooling Tatum's sun-warmed skin. Though her eyes were closed behind the designer sunglasses Lulu had given her for Christmas, her senses were alert to the delicious aromas wafting from the barbecue and the murmur of conversation taking place between Lu and their host, Christopher.

The idea of a small Christmas celebration with the two people she was closest to had been a welcome change from the crowded gatherings she'd had to endure in the past; so far it had been the most pleasant Christmas Day she'd ever had. She suspected she should've felt guilty feeling that way, since it was the first one she'd spent without Fantasy, but she didn't. Around Fantasy, Christmas had always been more of an ordeal than a celebration. If she'd been sober, which had been rare, she'd been contagiously depressed; drunk, stoned or, as had usually been the case, both, she'd been positively morose.

It wasn't as if her mother hadn't tried to make Christmas a special time – she'd always lavished Tatum with gifts and invited dozens of people over for parties right through the festive season. Yet her efforts had always been more show than substance. True Christmas spirit couldn't be faked.

'Tatum, darling, you're going to burn lying there.' Lulu's voice carried from the far side of the penthouse balcony.

'I put screen on earlier, Lu. Besides, I'm in the shade.'

'Lu's right, you know,' Christopher said. 'You've been there a while now. I don't mind you getting rid of your strap-marks with a little topless sunbathing on my patio, but I don't want Lu blaming me because you've got burnt tits.'

'*Christopher!*' Tatum smothered a giggle as Lu ticked her friend off about his language. Though the high back of the lounger she was on obscured them from her view as well as it worked in reverse, Tatum knew the objection would've been met with a boyishly cheeky grin. Christopher was good value, and Tatum had missed not seeing him since the school break had started. It wasn't that she couldn't have called over and seen him occasionally, but she'd figured she owed him a bit of space.

'C'mon, Tatum,' he called. 'Get something on. You don't want to end up looking like that lobster we're going to be eating.'

'Okay, okay.' With a resigned sigh she eased herself out of the sun lounger and slipped on a T-shirt that reached to mid-thigh, before strolling over to the barbecue.

'How long before this culinary delight is going to be ready?' she asked, her mouth watering at the sight of the sizzling garlic prawns and enormous stuffed bream covering the grill.

'Mere moments, my Italian princess! Mere moments.'

The claim sent Lulu hurrying inside to check whatever was in the oven, but Tatum was content simply to watch their host operate the barbecue tongs with controlled long-fingered movements. Tall, tanned, blue-eyed and naturally blessed with the tri-shaded blond hair women paid a fortune for, at twenty-nine Christopher Creighton was probably the most gorgeous male she'd ever met. And, in keeping with Murphy's Law, he was gay. Tatum considered the fact a tragic waste and had decided God either had a really warped sense of humour or hated women.

'So, you like that little creation I bought for you – or were you simply being polite?' he asked.

Since the 'little creation' in question was a hand-made satin nightdress with a matching robe, Tatum rolled her eyes. 'I love it and you know it.'

His grin showcased perfect white teeth. 'Good. Now, help me carry this banquet inside before Lulu does something diabolical to my wine-baked potatoes.'

Obediently Tatum picked up the tray he'd put the prawns onto. 'You know, Lu's a pretty good cook when she's motivated enough to actually go into the kitchen.'

'Ah, yes! She certainly has a way with toasted cheese sandwiches!'

'Hey, don't forget she roasted a chicken once.

'How could I, darling?' Christopher's handsome face contorted into an aghast expression. 'I was picking feathers from my teeth for a week afterwards. My dentist actually asked if I was "expanding my interests".'

Tatum giggled. 'He was probably jealous. What did you tell him?'

'Nothing!' Blond eyebrows wiggled mischievously. 'I invited him round for an intimate discussion on dental hygiene. And, much as I'd love to tell you the outcome of *that*, dear child, I daren't leave Lulu unattended in my kitchen a moment longer!' He shuddered theatrically. 'Still,' he said, 'not everyone can be a cordon bleu chef, like myself.'

Tatum gave a dry laugh. 'You're so conceited, Christopher Creighton!'

He shrugged. 'Can I help it if I'm bowled over by my own good looks, charm and personality?' He sobered. 'Did I mention I had a heart of pure gold?'

'Who's got a heart of pure gold?' Lu demanded as a giggling Tatum led the way through the glass sliding doors of the patio and into the decorated dining room of Christopher's apartment.

'You do, darling Lulu!' Christopher kissed her cheek as he passed her. 'You most definitely do.'

Tatum thought she caught an unspoken warning pass from Lu to Christopher, but in the face of the beaming smile the redhead bestowed on her she decided she'd imagined it.

'Take those – ' Lu motioned to the plate of prawns ' – through to the dining room, Tatum. I'll help Christopher fetch the rest of the food from the kitchen.'

The dining table was a picture of elegance. White linen napkins, blindingly bright silverware and three different types of crystal glasses were set at evenly spaced intervals around the circular table, and an arrangement of red and white native flowers supported by a flourish of greenery made a decorative and colourful centrepiece. Tatum carefully deposited the plate of prawns between two spectacular-looking salads.

By the time Lu and Christopher had brought in the bream, lobster, scallops and oysters Tatum figured they had enough food to feed the entire Australian Army. Christopher then darted back to the kitchen and returned with an ice bucket, complete with two bottles of French Champagne.

'Geez!' Tatum grinned. 'I wonder what the poor people are eating?'

Christopher paused in the act of easing the cork free, frowned, then shrugged. 'Who gives a damn? Merry Christmas, ladies!'

Tatum couldn't move. On second thoughts, she didn't want to move. Whatever she was lying on was the softest thing she'd ever known. Slowly she opened her eyes, blinking several times until her eyes adjusted to the dim light.

A large square box with a tiny flashing green light gradually came into focus, revealing itself as an elaborate sound system that by rights belonged in a recording studio. The flashing light indicated it was in use, but apparently sound couldn't permeate her clouded brain. Gently shifting her head, she encountered silver slimline venetian blinds – further evidence that she was still in Christopher's luxurious penthouse.

Okay, so where were Lu and – ?

'Ah, Sleeping Beauty stirs!'

Tatum swore as the words reverberated through her skull. Slowly she looked up the length of denim-clad leg which appeared only inches from her face, past the broad, naked chest and the headphones dangling around the neck into Christopher's incredibly handsome smile.

'Go away and let me die,' she muttered, closing her eyes again. 'Damn, my head hurts.' With enormous will power she managed to prise her lashes up far enough to squint at him. 'I think I've got a hangover.'

Clear blue eyes glittered with amusement. 'That would be my guess.'

'Shut up,' she said, struggling to sit up. 'It's not funny – Oh, shit,' she muttered. 'The room's spinning.'

'Only temporarily, princess. And though Lulu would probably tell you it serves you right, I, on the other hand, am far more sympathetic.' A hand grasped her forearm and gently assisted her to her feet. 'C'mon, princess. I'll provide as much aspirin and black coffee as you want.'

Tatum wasn't sure her stomach could hold anything as heavy as an aspirin, but, grateful for the strong, steadying arm around her waist, she willingly allowed him to guide her. 'Can I have them intravenously? I'm too sick to swallow.'

Christopher chuckled. 'French champagne can unfortunately produce such unpleasant side-effects if one overindulges, my Italian princess. But I assure you, you'll recover.'

Tatum grunted. Personally she had her doubts on that score. *God, how much of the stuff had she drunk?*

'Here, sit down and drink this. I'll get something for your headache.'

The steaming hot mug of percolated coffee thrust into her hands seemed like a life support system. At first sip the rich, exotic blend startled her, but then its bitter heat seemed to ebb into her veins and start her blood flowing again. As she drank she tried to recall what had happened between the time Christopher had proposed the first festive toast and her waking up on the sofa.

There'd been a lot of laughter, a lot of food and a hell of a lot more toasts! She'd stuffed herself stupid on every imaginable sort of seafood, salad and vegetable known to man and, if her head was any gauge, washed each and every mouthful down with imported champagne. And for dessert they'd had . . .

'We had plum pudding and liquored custard for dessert, right?' she asked hesitantly when Christopher returned to the kitchen and seemingly slammed a packet of aspirin on the table.

'You opted for ice cream on your second serving. Terribly common.'

Despite the brilliance of his smile, Tatum had to abort her efforts to raise a responding one. It hurt too much. She tore the foil off three tablets then looked at the sink. Could she walk that far?

'Stay.'

She obeyed Christopher's command, and within seconds he'd produced the necessary glass of water.

'Ta,' she said, then downed the tablets and water before reaching once more for her coffee-mug. 'Where's Lu?'

'She's gone home.'

'What?' Tatum blinked. 'And just left me here?' Even as she said the words she realized she must have sounded like a little kid. It wasn't as if she couldn't find her own way home.

31

'We thought it best to let you sleep for a while.'

'Why, so I could be wide awake for her lecture on overindulging in alcohol?'

Concern clouded the clean, sculptured lines of her friend's face. 'Don't sound like that, princess. Lu cares for you very much – surely you realize that?'

'Yeah. I guess.'

'No guessing about it. You owe her at lot, remember that.'

It was the closest thing to a reprimand Christopher had ever given her and it struck a nerve. She lowered her head to avoid meeting his eyes, finishing her coffee in silence then pushing the mug aside.

'More?'

There was no hint of remaining censure in the question, and, meeting his gaze, she encountered only a gently concerned smile in his eyes; relief rushed through her. Outside of Mario, Christopher was the only man she felt truly *liked* her; she didn't want to fight with him.

Nodding, she handed him the empty mug, then produced a cajoling smile. 'I could use a smoke too. You wouldn't like to go get them out of my handbag, would you?'

Despite lamenting the fact that Tatum engaged in such a disgusting habit as he refilled her mug, Christopher nevertheless did as she asked, returning with her cigarettes, lighter and a solid crystal ashtray.

'You're a real sweetie, you know that?'

'Of course,' he said haughtily. 'And flattery will get you everywhere with me.'

She paused in the act of flicking the lighter to her cigarette. 'Well, not quite *everywhere*,' she said.

'Hussy! No wonder you have poor Lulu at her wits' end!'

The shower helped. It wasn't a miraculous cure, but it definitely helped, Tatum decided as she towelled herself dry in the multi-mirrored decadence of Christopher's bathroom.

Well, she'd suffered her first hangover. And now knew she could have lived without the experience. No wonder Fantasy had been such a bitch to live with! The thought made her frown. How could anyone have found this blurred, disorientated feeling an escape? A rap on the door pulled her from her thoughts.

'You finished in there, Tatum?' Christopher asked.

'Just about. You mind if I use some of your aloe vera gel?'

A knowing chuckle came from the other side of the door. 'Let me guess – *burnt boobs*. We did warn you.'

'Yeah, yeah, all right. Can I use it or not?'

'Sure, princess. Come out to the patio when you're ready.'

Tatum sighed as she lavished the soothing balm onto her breasts. She hoped Christopher wouldn't tell Lu she'd got burnt or she'd *never* hear the end of it. Lu had such a phobia about being out in the sun, a person might've suspected her of being a vampire!

A bizarre image of Lulu in a black cape with fangs dripping blood popped into Tatum's head and made her giggle. Perhaps for some of her kinkier clients? Nah!

Tatum immediately dismissed the idea; Lulu didn't do kinky.

After finishing applying the gel she took advantage of the mirrors, studying her figure from all angles. Except for the pink tinge on her breasts and the minuscule white patch of flesh left by her bikini bottom, her skin was a deep golden brown. As long as her boobs didn't peel she'd end up as close to the perfect all-over tan as a body could get.

'Too bad no one but you can appreciate it,' she muttered at her reflection. It wasn't as if she was game enough to go topless on the beach or had a boyfriend – She clamped her mind shut on the thought. No more boyfriends! No more men of any description. She wasn't going to fall into the same trap as Fantasy. No way! Still, she did have a great tan and a good body –

'Damn it, Tate! What are you *doing*?' she demanded of herself, quickly snatching up her clothes. She'd *hated* Fantasy's obsession with her body, and now here *she* was, hung-over and acting just like her! She didn't want to be anything like Fantasy! Nothing at all! She was going to be a lady. Like Lulu.

'I am!' she told her reflection, brushing away the stupid tears blurring her vision. 'I'm going to finish school, go to university and I'm going to be a class act all the way!'

'Lulu!' she said with genuine surprise some minutes later, when she found the redhead out on the balcony with Christopher. 'There wasn't any need for you to come get me. I would've found my own way home.'

A quick, sharp glance passed between the two adults, but Tatum had no time to question it.

'I didn't come here to bring you home, Tatum. I came to drop off your things.'

'Huh? *What* things?'

'Your clothes, your books, your . . . everything. You're staying here, Tatum. Christopher agrees with me that it's the best thing.'

Tatum wondered if she was experiencing the DTs she'd so often nursed Fantasy through. There was no other explanation for what was happening. She shook her head simply to clear it, but Lu interpreted it as a refusal.

'You have to, Tatum. There's nowhere else you can go.'

'Nowhere safe, at any rate,' Christopher amended, and instantly drew Tatum's attention.

'What are you talking about, *nowhere safe*?' Her gaze swung back to Lulu. 'What the hell's going on? What d'you mean you've dropped my things off?' Yet even as she asked the question the answer came to her. 'I'm not *staying* here! I'm going home. And I'm going *now*.' But when she went to pivot towards the apartment door Christopher clamped a hand on her arm that tightened as she went to pull free. 'Let go!'

'No. Not until you've listened to what Lulu has to say.'

'I know what she's got to say! She's kicking me out onto the street!'

'No!'

As Lulu wailed the denial the man holding her arm shook it roughly. 'She's doing no such thing!' he said. 'She's trying to keep you off the effing street! We both are, which is why we want you to move in here with me.'

'But . . . I can't. I live with Lu. She's . . . she's my legal guar . . . guard . . . ian.' Tears that had previously only

blurred her vision now slurred her speech. 'I don't understand, Lu. Why don't you want me any more?'

The redhead started to speak, then stopped and, looking
skyward, drew a long, steadying breath. 'It's not that I
don't want you, Tatum . . . It's that other people do.'

Why was Lu doing this? She didn't understand. They
were supposed to be friends. Lu had looked after her,
taught her about how to dress and speak properly –

'Is . . . it because I . . . I swear, Lu? Is tha – that ww – ?'
In a flash the older woman was in front of her, cradling her
cheeks and futilely trying to brush the torrent of tears
away.

'Oh, no, baby,' she said, her own face tracked with tears
too. 'It's not that. It's just that you're too beautiful for your
own good. And too vulnerable. I love you, Tatum. I want –'

'I . . . l-l-l – love you t-t-t – too. I want to . . . stay
with . . . you. I want to be li – like you – '

Lu, fingers pressed across her mouth, cut off the
declaration.

'No, honey,' she said. 'You don't.'

There was a finality in her voice that triggered the same
feelings she'd had the afternoon she'd found Fantasy.
Emotions she couldn't identify seemed to be converging
on her from a thousand different directions with the force
of a hurricane. She tried to speak, but no sound came out.
And, though Christopher no longer held her, she didn't
have the strength to move. It was as if she was in a vacuum
– as if all the life had been sucked out of her . . .

Once more she woke to find herself lying on Christopher's
sofa, but this time someone sat at the end of it.

'Lu?'

'I'm here, honey.' The response was weak. Brittle. Tatum felt the same way. 'How are you feeling?'

In truth, Tatum didn't know. Visually she scanned as much of the room as she could, given her position. It was dark except for the soft glow of a lamp coming from somewhere behind them. They were alone.

'Confused,' she said eventually.

'You fainted. All in all you've had quite a day.'

'That's not what I meant, Lu.'

Her sigh was heavy. 'I know. Christopher is making some tea – '

'Good. His coffee sucks.' Tatum waited expectantly for a reprimand about her language. It didn't come.

'Tatum . . . I need you to understand why I've come to the decision I have.' Lulu sighed before continuing. 'It hasn't been easy for me.'

'I didn't think I'd been that hard to live with,' Tatum said softly. 'I tried not – '

'Oh, honey, I don't mean that!' Lu sounded almost amused. 'I mean *making* this decision hasn't been easy! I've loved having you stay with me!'

Tatum sat up and shoved her hair out of her face. 'Then why won't you let me come home? *Why, Lulu?*'

'Because if you're going to have any chance of making a decent life for yourself you've got to get away from Darling-hurst and the Cross – *now*. And *stay away*! You hear me?'

'Sh . . . *oot*!' Tatum just barely stopped herself from swearing as she blinked against the unexpected intrusion of light.

'Sorry, ladies, but I don't want tea-stains on my new

rug,' Christopher explained as he deposited a tray holding a silver tea service on the coffee-table. 'Now – milk, cream or lemon?' he enquired.

Despite Christopher's best efforts, the tea-pouring ceremony couldn't bring a smile to Tatum's face. And soon both adults ceased to try to amuse her.

'Tatum, Zeta's had her eye on you since you were barely in your teens,' Lulu surprised her by saying. 'But until a few months ago she wasn't quite so blatant about it.'

'*That's* why you spun out whenever I mentioned seeing her or stopping by the parlour.' At the woman's nod, Tatum laughed. 'But that's crazy! You know I'm not interested in going on the game! I'm still at school. Or I will be once it restarts.'

'I know, but Zeta can be very persuasive. Are you forgetting the bracelet she gave you a few days ago?'

'That was a *Christmas present*. She always gives me a Christmas present.'

'Oh, wake up, Tatum!' Lu snapped. 'There's a difference between a two-thousand-dollar bracelet and a T-shirt! She's setting you up for the kill. I know it and she knows I know it.' Lu paused and lit a cigarette. Her hands were less than steady. 'And that's why she's putting the word out that I'm dirty.'

Tatum could do nothing more than gape. The idea was ridiculous!

'It's true,' Lulu said. 'I heard it from one of the street girls. If it's on the streets, it's everywhere.'

'But . . . Lu, *why*? I mean, even if she got me I wouldn't bring her the money you do. Hell, even Fantasy said you were Zeta's biggest asset.'

Christopher opened his mouth to speak, then shut it again. But not before Tatum saw the warning glance Lu sent him.

'What?' she demanded. 'What is it you're trying to keep from me?'

'Nothing – '

'Bull!' Tatum jumped to her feet. '*Tell me!*'

'I'm going to Melbourne.' Lulu said.

It took a few seconds for Tatum to digest the startling announcement. 'Well, good!' she said finally. 'That way we won't have to worry about Zeta bothering us – '

'I'm going on my own, Tatum. You can't come. You'll be safe here with Christopher. You'll be able to finish school and – '

'Melbourne's got schools!'

'It's not about schools! Tatum, you're not going to be safe *anywhere* with me!' Lulu screamed at her. 'I gave the names of the guys who were supplying your mother to the cops!'

The crude four-letter word that fell from Tatum's mouth only drew a wry smile from the older woman. 'Yes. That about says it all.'

Tatum looked at Christopher, wondering if he was as stunned by the announcement as she was. Though he looked troubled, it was clear he already knew what his friend had done.

'Can't you ask for police protection? I mean – '

Lulu shook her head. 'You know as well as I do the cops are up to their eyeballs in the drug business.'

'But surely the Feds . . .?'

Lu smiled sadly as she took Tatum's hands in hers.

'Honey, I can't stay. Even if I wasn't on the downward slide professionally, I'm as good as dead if I don't get out of Sydney.' She brushed, Tatum's hair back from her face and tilted her chin up so she could meet her eyes. 'I made myself two promises when Fantasy died. One was to do my damnedest to keep you out of the business and the other was to get even with the bastards who killed her. I've done my best to keep those promises. I know *you* won't let me down . . . but, given my profession, I haven't ever been able to completely trust the cops.'

Terrified of losing the one person who'd been the only constant, stable thing in her life for the last twelve years, Tatum clung to her.

'Please,' she begged, tears streaming down her face. 'Please take me with you. We can change our names and no one'll ever find us. You . . . you can get a different job . . . or we . . . we could go live in the country. On a farm. Or in the mountains. You always said you wanted to live in the mountains, Lu. Please take me! We could . . .' Tatum kept up her loud, feverish pleas even as she fought the strong hands that tried to prise her free.

The sound of skin contacting against skin stalled her words, but while the palm connecting with her cheek forced her head sideways its sting was nothing compared to that burning her heart.

'Show some decorum, Tatum!' Lu commanded, lowering her hand. 'I'd like to think I'd taught you that much at least.'

With those words, she picked up her handbag and walked regally out of the front door.

40

CHAPTER 3

Christmas Day 1987

The bang of the screen door drew Judy Benton's attention from the turkey she was basting. 'Is it too much to hope that you're in here to offer your help?' she enquired of her son.

'Way too much, Mum.' He smiled. 'I'm just grabbing another beer for Grandpa Benton. Although Dad was wondering how far off lunch was.'

'Tell him fifteen minutes,' she replied, sliding the oven rack back into position and closing the door. 'But if he wants to come in and give me a hand with the gravy I can probably cut it down to ten.'

Jason shook his head. 'I think he'd rather wait. I know the rest of us would.'

The dry comment was followed by one of Jason's teasing blue-eyed grins, but Judy wasn't overly impressed by it, as most women would have been. She suspected part of her benign acceptance of her son's incredibly masculine good looks came from maternal immunity built up from having watched those looks emerge through almost twenty-three years – from the red-faced wrinkles of infancy through dirt-smudged boyhood to teenage rebellion. But, along with developing a slight resistance to both the smile and teasing tone, she'd also developed the knack of knowing when they were being forced. And they were now.

She watched as her raven-haired son leaned uninterestedly against the sink, opened the beer and, with an expression that said he was mentally miles away, took a sip.

'I thought that was for your grandfather.' Her comment brought first a puzzled frown then a vague shake of the head from Jason as he returned to the fridge and took out another beer. With a sheepish smile he again went out to the patio, the door banging on his exit.

Judy sighed. Jason's distracted behaviour of the last month was alien enough to cause her genuine concern, and not merely because of the tension it was creating between him and his father. He was taking the disappearance of Doug Russell far harder than she'd have expected.

While she understood why the sudden unexplained disappearance of his friend would be naturally upsetting to him, after seven weeks she'd hoped he'd have started coming to terms with the fact that everything that could have been done to find him had been. Instead he was becoming focused on Doug's absence to the exclusion of all else, and that in itself was extreme, considering that a shrugging 'shit happens' was his traditional response to everything from flat surf to parental criticism about his blasé approach to his university studies.

In recent weeks his lovable if at times infuriating devil-may-care attitude had vanished almost as completely as his friend, turning Jason from a cheerful extrovert into a silent, moody young man, who greeted all attempts at rational discussion on the matter with either indifferent shrugs or argument-provoking curtness.

Judy knew much of his distress stemmed from misplaced guilt. Jason believed that had he been more available to spend time with Doug, he might have realized something was bothering the other boy. Both she and his father had pointed out that it was an unreasonable expectation since not even Doug's mother, Mary, nor his long-time girlfriend Donna had sensed anything was troubling his friend. Jason wasn't convinced.

'Mum,' he'd said. 'Guys like Dougie don't just vanish for no reason! He was an ace student, a talented athlete, he had no family hassles and a terrific girl to boot!' Pursing his mouth he'd looked at them and shaken his head. 'It doesn't make sense.'

Brian Benton had tried to persuade his son that in all likelihood Doug, stressed from an arduous third year of pharmacy studies and the intensive training required by his budding rugby union career, had merely taken off somewhere to regroup. The trouble was that Jason had embraced *that* suggestion so enthusiastically he'd immediately cut his own university year short, thus missing two vital exams, and headed north to try and track him down.

Brian had been no more furious than Judy herself, but neither their ranting and raving, nor their pleas for Jason to wait at least until his exams were over had done one bit of good. Even Ethan had tried to convince his brother to curb his impulsiveness – without success. And since Jason's arrival home three days ago, it seemed the entire household had been walking on eggshells.

Fortunately, Brian had so far managed to refrain from pointing out that his son's excursion had been nothing but an exercise in futility, but Judy wasn't sure how much longer that would last. Jason's scathing comment last night that the New South Wales police force couldn't find their backsides if they were sitting on them had left his father apoplectic. As a senior officer with the police Internal Affairs, Brian Benton saw such remarks as personal insults.

And family relations hadn't been improved when Jason had learned that his twin brother Ethan had started spending a lot of time with Doug's girlfriend, Donna. Jason had made it abundantly clear he didn't buy Ethan's claims that he was only 'comforting a friend'. Neither did Judy, but with her sons only a week off twenty-three, it was no longer her place to oversee their personal relationships. However, her maternal instincts still led her to try and keep sibling disputes to a minimum, and she'd said it was only natural Donna would be missing Doug.

The sizzle of the peas bubbling over on the stove jerked Judy from her musings and back to the task at hand – Christmas dinner. But minor boil-over seemed almost like a symbolic warning. Up until now the day had passed without any emotional outbursts from either her husband or son; she only hoped it continued. Statistics showed that Christmas gatherings brought many a simmering domestic problem to boiling point.

She'd barely completed the thought when the back door again banged shut, but this time it reverberated in telltale evidence of anger.

'I cannot believe any one person could be that stub-

44

born!' her husband announced belligerently. 'If I'd stayed out there with him another minute I swear to God I'd have strangled him with my bare hands.'

'Oh, Brian!' Judy sighed, glaring at her husband. 'I *told* you I didn't want any arguing between you and Jason today. I expressly asked that you – '

'I'm not talking about Jason,' Brian Benton interrupted, looking injured by her assumption. 'Although his neck is on my list. I'm talking about Dad.'

'Ah,' Judy said, fighting a smile. 'I gather you've been trying to convince him to sell the house again.'

'Don't look at me like that!' he said, catching her amusement. 'Just because *your* father was sensible enough to move into a retirement village is no reason to gloat.'

'*Sense* had nothing to do with it, Brian,' she said, pouring the gravy from the large enamel baking dish into two bone china jugs. 'My father saw it as an opportunity to be close to an abundance of unattached women his own age. *Your* father, on the other hand, hasn't looked at a woman since your mother died forty-three years ago.' She grinned up at the man now standing beside her. 'This is one instance when the "sex sells" theory won't work.'

The only response was an ungracious masculine grunt.

'Look, let's not ruin your father's day by telling him he's getting too old to live alone,' she said, handing him a plate piled high with baked potatoes. 'We both know you'll be wasting your breath anyway.'

Again he grunted, before a slow smile emerged. 'At least we know who to blame for Jason's inherited stubbornness. It's no wonder he and the old man get on so well.'

Judy Benton bit the inside of her mouth. 'Guess I'm just lucky it skipped a generation in you, huh?'

'Yeah,' he said with absolute seriousness, carrying the potatoes into the dining room. 'Imagine if we were *all* that stubborn.

'Yeah,' she said aloud to an empty kitchen. 'Just imagine . . .'

'You're very quiet today, Jason. Don't tell me some girl's getting the better of you?'

'Gee, I hope so!' Ethan said before his brother could reply. 'That'd make my year.'

As three generations of Bentons chuckled at the comment Jace decided he'd better lighten his mood or his mother would be at him for spoiling everyone's Christmas. 'The only female who gets the better of me, Grampa Scorse, is Mum, and that's only 'cause you spoiled her rotten as a kid. You've got a lot to answer for, old man.'

'True, son, but you'll learn that spoiling women has it's own rewards.' He winked rakishly. 'And you've got to admit she cooks a damn fine turkey dinner.'

A loud throat-clearing noise from the end of the table drew everyone's attention. 'I think everyone here is overlooking the quality of the potatoes and pumpkin,' Brian Benton said. 'I'll have you know *I'm* responsible for them.'

'Be buggered! You cooked 'em, Bri?'

'No, Grandpa Benton, he *peeled* them.' Judy Benton patted her husband's hand. 'And he looked terribly cute in an apron.'

Forcing himself to get into the spirit of things, Jace grinned at his brother. 'Guess we'll have to get him to do the dishes after lunch so we can all get a look at him like that, eh, Ethan?'

'Oh, no, you don't!' their mother cautioned. 'You know how I embrace Christmas traditions. Particularly the one where the children clean the hot kitchen their mother's slaved in all morning while she has a well-earned drink and a siesta.'

'Actually, Mum,' Ethan said, 'some traditions are grossly overrated.'

'Well,' she said, 'if you boys really hate doing the dishes, I suppose the only thing to do is not to have a hot roast for lunch next Christmas. I'll do some salads, you men can do a barbecue and we'll eat off paper plates.'

There was a chorus of male protest at the suggestion.

'Not have turkey at Christmas!'

'Judith Scorse! Your mother must be spinning in her grave – '

'*Barbecue!* There's nothing traditional about a barbecue, Mum!'

Jace agreed with his brother. 'Couldn't we just get a dishwasher?' he asked.

'Why, Jason, what an excellent idea!' His mother beamed. 'Pure genius! Isn't that a wonderful suggestion, Brian?'

Brian grimaced, then looked at his son. 'Last Christmas you gave her the idea of having air-conditioning installed so the kitchen wouldn't be so hot. Now you come up with this?' He shook his head. 'Why is it your genius always costs *me* money?'

Once again witty responses and chuckles ricocheted across the table, and so the meal progressed. But Jace found it hard to stay focused on the seemingly mindless family merriment as again and again it highlighted the silent misery that had filled the Russell home when he'd called in this morning for his usual Christmas drink with them.

Where and how was Doug spending his Christmas Day?

He frowned down at his plate, surprised at how little impact he'd made on it. Christmas dinner was probably his all-time favourite meal, and in the past he'd have easily put away two helpings of his mum's roast turkey and been willing to crawl over crushed glass for a third before starting on the traditional pudding and brandy custard for dessert.

For a moment he cursed Doug's thoughtlessness for ruining his day. Damn it, surely it wouldn't have been too much effort to make a lousy phone call. A chill crept up his spine. Assuming, of course, he was able to make a call . . .

He knew the worry and fear gnawing in his gut had to be ten times as fierce for Doug's widowed mother and his three sisters, and he wondered how much longer they could endure it. Hell, Mrs Russell was only one Valium away from a nervous breakdown now, and the girls . . . Well, at fourteen and eleven Julie and Kate seemed more confused than anything else. But Suzy, who was a couple of years older than Doug, was taking refuge in anger.

She'd sworn a blue streak at Jace about her stupid, irresponsible brother and what she was going to do to him when she got her hands on him. The trouble was, Jace suspected that deep down she really didn't believe she'd get the chance to make good the threats, idle as they were. How many families were in the Russells' position today?

Sitting down to lunch with a vacant chair reminding them they had a family member whose whereabouts no one could account for?

'Will anybody mind if I excuse myself now? I'm not really hungry.' Five sets of puzzled eyes lifted in his direction before going to his plate.

'But you've hardly touched your food,' Grampa Scorse chided mildly.

'I've got a bit of a headache.' It was a lie, and his brother's expression told him he for one knew it. So did the silent exchange between his parents.

'Sure. Why don't you go lie down for a while?' his father suggested. 'We'll call you when it's time for dessert.'

'I think I'll skip it for now.' At the gentle concern in his mother's face he managed a smile and added, 'But that doesn't mean I don't want you to save me some.'

'Don't like your chances, son,' Grampa Scorse said. 'It's every man for himself when it comes to Judy's pudding.'

'Don't worry, Dad, there's plenty,' Judy Benton assured the balding man, before nodding to her son. 'Go on, Jason. I'll save some for you.'

'Thanks.'

'Hey, Jace!' Ethan called. 'I'll save you some of the dishes too!'

Three generations of Benton laughter followed him from the room.

It was almost twilight when Jace slammed the hood shut on the engine of his eight-year-old Torana. Cursing both the seized motor and his lack of success in fixing it, he wiped his grease-stained hands down the front of his you're-not-wearing-them-out-of-the-house jeans and left the garage contemplating a swim in the pool. All that stopped him from doing it was the thought of the exertion of going inside for his shorts and a towel; his mother wouldn't appreciate him skinny-dipping in broad daylight in full view of the neighbours.

Instead, Jason sat down on the patio steps and studied the Benton backyard's manicured lawn and sparkling pool – both the result of Brian Benton's devotion to his hobby of landscape gardening. Though he appreciated the results, Jace couldn't understand how his father could claim spending hours pushing a mower or digging in flowerbeds was relaxing. He smiled to himself. Sort of like he could appreciate that Brian Benton was a good father and a fine human being but he didn't understand how he could be so bloody-minded.

'Yer dad says there's still no word on your friend.'

Jace lifted his head at the sound of his paternal grandfather's voice. 'No,' he said. 'Nothing.'

'Mind if I join yer?' the white-haired man asked, indicating the step with his cane. 'Yer mother was getting that we-need-to-have-a-chat look on her face, so I thought I'd make m'self scarce.'

Smiling, Jace edged over to provide room on the top patio step. Though he loved both his widower grandfathers, he'd always felt a special connection with Bryce Benton. To Jace's way of thinking the old bloke was both as tough and as kind as a guy came. And as straightforward. A veteran of World War II and a dairy farmer who after the death of his wife had raised three sons alone, he valued honesty and loyalty above all else in life and wasn't impressed by fancy airs and graces; if people didn't like him calling a spade a bloody shovel, then it was their problem not his.

'Bri said the kid left without sayin' a word. That he just never come home after uni one day.' Bryce Benton's words were matter-of-fact. 'Said there weren't no family problems to speak of. No problems with his girlfriend or nothin'.'

'I don't get it, Gramps. He's never just taken off without telling anyone before.'

'Heard you an' that mate of yours, Taggart, missed a couple of exams when you knocked off uni early and went looking for 'im.'

Jace didn't detect an iota of disapproval in the remark. Unlike his parents, who'd been far from thrilled when he'd told them of his decision to cut the last few weeks of the semester to search for his friend, his grandfather was plainly accepting of the fact. Jace smiled at him.

'Thanks for sparing me the lecture on jeopardizing my education.'

'Huh! Never bin one to flog a dead horse. Besides, missin' a few exams won't hurt a bloke smart as you – just slow ya down a little.' The old man grinned. 'Told yer dad as much too, when he started in complaining about it to me. Told him what he could do with his fool idea 'bout movin' into one of them old people's homes too.'

Though he welcomed the switch of topic, Jace was torn between pointing out the practicalities of such a move and hurting the old man's pride. His grandfather lived only a couple of kilometres away and he was recovering well from his hip operation, but Jace, like everyone else, worried about him rattling about in his big house on his own. 'I don't think he meant a nursing home, Grandpa,' he said cautiously. 'I think he means something like the private villa complex Grampa Scorse is living in.'

'Pah!' A gnarled hand flapped with indifference. 'I'm not livin' in some pokey one-bedroom dollhouse, where I can reach out my window an' touch the next door neighbour's. I like having my privacy and room to move.'

There was little point in listing all the reasons why a seventy-eight-year-old man didn't need a four-bedroom house on a half-acre block of land. Bryce Benton had already stated long and loud that he regretted selling up his Taree dairy farm and moving to the city fifteen years ago, and how he wasn't compounding that mistake by giving up what little land he owned now.

'Car trouble, son?' the old man asked, motioning to Jace's hands.

'Yeah.'

'You get it fixed?'

'Nope. And I won't any time soon,' he grumbled. 'The whole gear box is rooted and the engine isn't much better.'

'Good thing yer dad lined up that job with his lawyer mate for yer, then. The cash'll come in handy.'

'Would if I was taking the job.' Jace gave the old man a rueful look. 'Thing is, I'm not going too. Tag and I agreed to spend the rest of our vacation trying to find Doug.'

The older man made a groaning noise. 'I reckon since you're still in one piece you haven't broken this to yer dad yet?'

'Nope. We only made the decision today, after we'd been to see the Russells. I didn't think I should wreck

52

everyone's Christmas with a full-scale domestic brawl then, though.'

A frown further concertinaed the old man's already wrinkled brow as he studied his grandson. 'Figured somethin' was botherin' you, lad. Yer bin lookin' as worried as a nun in a whorehouse since yer got back. Guess it was pretty depressing over there today.'

'That's one way of describing it . . .' Jace raked his fingers through his hair and swore. 'Hell, Grandpa, I don't think I've ever seen such hopelessness and desperation as I did in Mrs Russell's face. She's beside herself with worry and it seems like no one is *doing* anything! I mean, if the cops were *really* looking for Doug surely they'd have turned up something on him?'

'Son, you know better than anyone how much the police have on their plate. And the sad fact is that in the big picture your friend is simply another missing person.'

'Not to his family, he's not. Not to me.'

For several minutes they sat in silence, as if both were considering the pros and cons of Jace's decision. Although Jace suspected only *he* would readily see any sense in it. The pragmatist in him told him he was backing a long shot, with little chance of winning, but the emotional part of him told him that if he didn't do this he'd feel he was wimping out on a fourteen-year-old friendship. One that had started the day Doug had hauled him out of a fast-rising storm water canal.

'I can understand why you *want* to do this, son,' his grandfather said at length. 'Question is, can you afford it? You turn down this job your dad lined up, what are you going to do for money?'

'Well, Grandpa,' he started hesitantly, 'I was thinking if I got desperate I could cash in some of the bonds you gave me for my eighteenth birthday.'

'Ahh . . . I see.'

The response was annoyingly non-commital, forcing Jace to ask, 'Would you have a problem with me doing that?'

The old man shook his head. 'Son, that money was a *present* for yer coming of age; if you wanted to put it on a three-legged horse in the Melbourne Cup it wouldn't bother me. But if it helps you to do something that'll give you emotional peace, then I reckon that's all the better.'

The relief that flowed through Jace at these words was warmed by the enormous respect he had for Bryce Benton. 'Thanks, Grandpa,' he said. 'I wouldn't have touched those bonds without asking you first.'

'Good job I'm not dead yet, then, isn't it?' The old man laughed then added, 'Course, your father is gonna be madder than a cut snake when he hears all this, yer realize? Gets his temper from your grandmother – God rest her volatile soul.'

Jace sent his grandfather a wry grin. 'You want me to wait until you leave before I tell him what I'm going to do?'

The grey head nodded sagely. 'I'd appreciate that, son. Damn doctors don't like me gettin' overexcited these days. More's the pity. That's the only down side of living alone, you know? No domestics to spice things up a bit.'

Jace threw his head back and laughed. God, he loved this old man!

CHAPTER 4

Late February 1988

Jace checked his watch. Three-seventeen and still no sight of the sleazeball who was supposed to meet them. He flicked the handle of the empty cup sitting on the table and watched it spin on the gold-flecked formica.

'Want another?' Tag asked him.

He shook his head. He'd drunk that many damn cappucinos in the last few days, it was a wonder he didn't froth every time he opened his mouth. Once more he scanned the occupants of the cafe's other tables. Each and every one of them reflected the seediness and desperation of the area, but the guy he wanted wasn't one of them.

'He's over an hour late, Jace. You that certain he'll show?'

Jace wasn't, but after weeks of walking the streets of Kings Cross, flashing photos of Doug to every hooker, drunk and drug addict he saw, he wasn't giving up on the only solid lead they had. 'I've promised him a fifty if he can get me an address. He didn't look the type to pass it up.'

His friend looked around the room. 'None of them do.'

He shook his head. 'Much as I want to find Dougie, I don't want to find him here.'

'Yeah.' The trouble was, Jace thought, Doug hadn't been anywhere he should have been. Least of all home. Fourteen weeks and not a word from him. Tag and Jace were the only ones apart from his family who hadn't given up hope; even his girlfriend, Donna, was back dating.

'She's getting on with her life,' his brother had said. But then he would – he was the guy she was dating.

'Is this him?' Tag asked, and Jace immediately spun his head in the direction of the door.

A surge of adrenaline hit him as he recognized his acquaintance of yesterday. Even if the guy hadn't been wearing the same stained jeans and T-shirt *sans* sleeves, his dirty shoulder-length hair and exaggerated beanpole build were unmistakable. The first real lead they'd got! With forced patience Jace waited for the bloke, still blocking the doorway and peering expectantly at the customers, to spot him. He stood up in the hope of hurrying the procedure along.

Eventually the guy's sunken eyes settled on him. A moment passed before recognition showed on the heroin-ravished face and he acknowledged Jace with a curt nod. Then suddenly, for no apparent reason, the guy panicked, and before Jace could figure out why he'd bolted back out the door.

'Bloody hell!'

At first it was only the guy's beanpole height that enabled Jace to keep track of him as he wove his way through the afternoon shoppers, but as they started to thin Jace's natural speed and agility became a factor. By the time Beanpole had turned into a lane at the side of a popular nightclub, Jace had shortened the distance between them so that he was only a few metres behind. Jace knew he could get close enough to crash tackle the clown, but he wasn't sure he wanted to; yesterday he'd nearly choked on the stench of the bloke just talking to him.

'Hoy!' he yelled, opting to try and minimize physical contact if possible. 'You wanna play silly buggers or make fifty bucks?'

The man immediately paused and Jace did the same; something had spooked him in the café and it wouldn't do him any good to push it. The guy was panting and holding his side.

'I wouldn't count on entering this year's City to Surf if I was you mate,' Jace said, not prepared to let on that he was blowing a little hard himself.

'He a cop?' the guy asked.

The question threw Jace. 'Who?'

'*Him!*'

Jace started to turn at the same instant Tag's voice rang out from behind him. 'Relax! I'm not a cop. I'm a law student.'

'Oh, that'll impress him,' Jace mumbled, then said aloud, 'He's a mate of mine. Mate of Doug's too,' he added. 'You know, the guy in the picture . . .'

'Dunno no Doug. Fella I met's called Russ.'

'Bingo,' Tag said under his breath. 'Doug Russell – Russ.'

'Sounds like the same guy,' Jace went on, having made the same connection as Tag. 'You got that address where we can find him?'

57

Beanpole made a cackling sound. 'I can give ya the name of a couple streets, but he ain't got no *fixed address*, as the cops'd say.'

'Seems good enough to me.' Jace reached for his wallet.

'Seems like fifty down the toilet to me,' Tag muttered, his eyes everywhere. 'And we're sitting ducks to get rolled in this bloody alley.'

Jace hastily looked back the way they'd come. *Damn!* Why hadn't he thought of that? He had firsthand experience that even in broad daylight this part of town was bad news. Again he addressed the guy midway down the lane. He wasn't back pedalling now. 'So, you gonna tell me where I might find old Russ?'

'Not till I get me fifty.'

Jace laughed. '*Right!* Like I'm dumb enough to hand over a fifty on *your* word.' A noise from behind spun him around. Tag responded in kind.

'Well, looky here! Aren't you two just too cute?' The observation came from a heavily made-up blonde in a pink-checked halter mini that looked as if it had been painted on. Combined with her stiff, teased shoulder-length hair and gold stiletto evening shoes it made her look like a badly co-ordinated Barbie doll.

Tag swore. 'Hell, they're just kids.'

Fifteen – sixteen tops, Jace figured. The second of the two had long black hair and wore cut-off jeans and a crop top – *almost*.

'We can do a real good deal for a hundred,' she advised, then flicked her hair behind her shoulders. 'Interested?'

'Maybe,' Jace said. 'Our mate here – ' he jerked his thumb towards the guy down the lane – 'is on a promise of

58

a fifty for some information, but if you girls can help us out with it, I'll make it as even hundred.'

The girls exchanged a quick couple of words, then the blonde spoke. 'You sayin' you'll give us a hundred for some information?' Jace nodded. 'What kinda information?'

He pulled out the photo of Doug taken at their high school graduation and held it up. 'You seen this guy around?'

'Can't tell from here, sweetie. You're gonna have to get closer,' the brunette told him.

Jace glanced back at Beanpole. 'Sure you don't want that fifty?' he asked. 'You got first call on it.'

'Yer offerin' them a hundred!'

'Yeah, but there's two of them,' Jace told him, 'Besides, they're prettier.' Behind him the girls giggled. 'Okay then.' He shrugged. 'If you don't want it . . .'

'I do! I do!' he shouted. 'The guy ya lookin' for, Russ, he hangs out down The Wall.'

'*Shit!*'

Jace was amazed Tag could get the word out. He felt too physically sick to speak. The Wall was a stretch of street were young male prostitutes plied their trade in desperation. He and Tag hadn't bothered to check it out simply because the possibility of Doug being there had been beyond the realms of their imagination. For Jace it still was!

His hand curled into a fist and he'd already taken one angry stride before Tag's restraining hand clamped on his shoulder. 'Easy,' his friend whispered. 'Don't do anything dumb.'

Jace nodded and drew a steadying breath. 'You're lying!' he said, needing to believe it.

The druggie shook his head. 'I ain't!'

'Yeah, you are!' accused a high-pitched female voice. 'Russ ain't queer!' the blonde went on. 'No effing way!'

Tag closed in on her. 'You know Doug?'

'Doug? Who's Doug?' Her eyes squinted, as if she was standing in the glaring sun rather than a shabby, shaded lane.

Jace shoved the photo under her nose. 'This guy – you know him?'

'What's it to you?'

'Don't get cute,' he told her. 'We can haul your under-age ass down the cop shop and get you busted quick smart!' Jace wasn't entirely sure about this, but it sounded good, and having an old man in Internal Affairs ought to count for something.

'You want to hope they know something, Jace.' Tag jerked his head towards the back of the lane. ''Cause the other bloke just shot through.'

Jace turned just in time to catch a glimpse of Beanpole running for the alley. He swore.

Just great! You should've settled for the bird in the hand. Benton, he told himself, studying the two girls. This pair could be making it up as they go along. Still, right now they were all he had left.

'Okay, girls,' he said. 'You know him? Yes or no?'

The two shared an uncertain look, then the brunette shrugged. 'The guy's name is Russ.'

'We already know *that*. You know where we can find him?'

60

'Depends why ya want him?'

'We're friends of his,' Tag said.

The girl looked pointedly at their clean jeans and T-shirts. 'You don't dress like no friends Russ'd have,' she accused.

'Yeah, well we've let ourselves go since we last saw him. Now, are you going to help us out here or what?'

Smirking at Tag's challenge, the brunette suddenly looked more like a hardened forty-year-old than a kid playing dress-up. The summer heat had caused the heavy make-up to run into tiny creases around her thickly mascaraed green eyes. Schoolgirl smile lines gone wrong, Jace thought. With her long-limbed fairness and long dark hair, she could have been striking; instead, the faint yellowing on her jaw suggested she'd been struck. Probably more than once.

'What's ya names?' The blonde's question startled Jace. In the weeks he'd spent flashing Doug's photograph, no one had so far bothered to ask who *he* was. He was still trying to ascertain the wisdom of identifying himself when Tag took the decision out of his hands.

'I'm Lee Taggart and this is Jace Benton.'

The blonde's eyes widened to reveal deep blue irises highlighted by a cobweb of red lines framing them. '*You're* Tag?'

Her knowledge of Lee's nickname almost put Jace onto his backside. *Finally they'd found someone who knew Doug!* For a moment he could do nothing but wait until the rush of elation soaring through him had subsided; his heart was thumping at light speed. The look on Tag's face said he, too, was reeling from the implication of the blonde's question. Jace recovered first.

'Yeah,' he said, clearing his throat to dispel the strained quality of his voice. 'He's Tag. And if you know that, you must know Doug . . . er . . . Russ pretty well.'

She shrugged. 'Maybe.' As if seeking leadership she glanced at the brunette. The latter's vermilion mouth twisted into a sneer as she shook her head.

'Too late to backtrack now, Kel,' she said. 'They ain't dumb.'

'She's right, Kel,' Tag chipped in. 'You may as well tell us where we can find him.'

Jace hadn't realized he was holding his breath until it came out in a relieved sigh at Kel's nod.

'I'll take ya there.' She looked at the still unidentified brunette. 'You comin'?'

'Nah,' she said, holding her hand out to Jace. 'I'll take the fifty now.'

'I'll give it to Kel when we find . . . Russ,' he told her.

'I get *my* fifty now, pretty boy, or Kel won't be takin' you anywhere.'

There was enough uncertainty in the blonde's face for Jace to realize she took her cues from her friend. He handed over the note. She crumpled it in her hand, her smile smug. 'Catch ya later, Kel,' she said. 'An' don't let pretty boy con ya out of ya fifty.'

The blonde nodded and stood watching her friend exit the lane the way they'd entered, then turn left. The moment she was out of sight Kel rallied to action. 'C'mon,' she said, starting in the opposite direction.

Tag exchanged a quick look with Jace, reminding him

that it was the same way Beanpole had disappeared earlier. They were probably being paranoid, but paranoia beat getting mugged hands down. Jace knew. He'd been rolled the first week he'd started asking around about Doug and he'd learned not to carry cash he didn't need; which was why he hadn't been able to pay the druggie for his info yesterday and had set up the meeting today. And though the chances that the girls and Beanpole were trying to scam them were probably slim, Jace preferred to err on the side of caution.

'Can't we go that way?' he asked, indicating the direction the brunette had taken, where the population of the main drag would offer at least token security.

'Yeah,' the blonde replied. 'But it'll take longer.'

'How much longer?'

'Coupla minutes.'

Jace grinned at her. 'We've got the time.'

She looked uncertain of what to do. Then she shrugged. 'It'll cost ya another twenty.'

Tag laughed. 'Geez, you must be better than you look!'

'Shut yer face, smart – '

'Kiddies! Kiddies!' Jace said. 'Be nice.'

Roughly seven minutes later they entered a darkened three-foot square lobby that stank of urine and vomit. The only escapes on offer were the door they'd just come through leading to the street and a narrow staircase rising at an eighty-five-degree angle. The sole evidence that it had once been carpeted were the rows of tiny nails in each wooden step while the rotting timber implied they hadn't been safe for the last fifty years; the place was a fire waiting to happen.

The blonde started up the steps, unperturbed by their creaking and the ready sway of the banister. 'Up 'ere.'

A chill skated down Jace's spine when he realized Tag had quietly started humming 'Stairway to Heaven' in perfect time with his own mental rendition. The eerie thing wasn't so much the sight of the tragic Kel climbing the stairs, but the fact it was Doug's all-time favourite song.

'You fellas comin' or what?' Kel demanded from half-way up the stairs as she leaned dangerously against the banister to let an old lady past.

Jace nodded, but waited until the crumpled old woman reached the bottom before easing aside and holding the door open for her. His chivalry went unacknowledged. 'Whores,' she muttered under her alcohol-foul breath. 'Whores 'n' trollops, all of em!'

The landing at the top of the stairs wasn't much bigger than the entrance and housed three doors. On the wall a peeling red arrow with 'fire exit' written on it pointed to the stairs. The tragic irony of it filled Jace with an anger his twenty-three years in middle-class suburbia hadn't prepared him for.

'Which one?' Tag asked, and the blonde indicated the door beside the arrow.

'At least he'd get a head start on the others,' Jace said drily, shaking his head to dismiss the comment at Tag's confused frown.

'Russ!' The girl leaned her head near the door as she knocked. 'Russ, it's me. Kelly.' She knocked again, more heavily this time. 'Russ! You in there, babe?'

Babe! She couldn't mean . . . Nah! This girl was as far

removed from Donna as night was from day. Hell – further! No guy could go from Donna to this.

'He oughta be here,' she said, seemingly reasoning aloud. 'He was sick this mornin . . . He couldna gone'

'*Sick?*' Jace echoed, dread nibbling at him. 'How do you mean, *sick?*'

The blonde wrapped her arms around her waist and shook her head.

'Tell us!' Tag demanded pulling her round to face him. '*What was wrong with him?*'

'He was . . . just sick you know. Strung out. But he weren't bad or nothin', not like before! Not – '

No longer listening to the girl's tearfully incoherent babbling, Jace thumped on the door. 'Doug! Doug! It's Jace, Doug! Open the door!' Closing both fists, he pounded them against the aged timber. 'Doug! Dammit! Open the friggin' door!'

'Where can we get a key?' Tag wanted to know. 'Who'd have a spare?'

Jace turned in time to see the blonde head shake. Hell! How were they going to get in? His mind was racing in a hundred different directions, and none of them led through this bloody door! *Think*, he ordered himself. Damn it, *think*, Benton!

'See if you can find a beat cop in the street,' he told Tag. 'Otherwise go to the station and drag one back. He – '

The door at the bottom of the stairs opened, the outside sunlight momentarily outlining a spindly male form before the gloom of the building disguised it again.

'Terry!' Kel shrieked. 'Somethin's wrong with Russ!'

'Who're they?'

'It doesn't matter! You gotta open the door for me!'

It was the hesitation in Terry's reaction as he lowered his head that gave Jace the few seconds' start he needed to be halfway down the stairs before the guy realized what was happening. But it could only have been lunacy combined with an act of God that enabled him to *dive*, without injury, over the remaining steps and grab hold of the bastard's shirt before he got entirely out the door.

'Get here!' Jace sneered, reefing the sleazeball by the collar until he gagged.

'Lemme go, man. Yer chokin' me!'

'Too bloody bad!' Jace manoeuvred him back into the minuscule lobby, kicked the door shut and shoved him onto the stairs. 'You get up there and open that door!' This time holding him up by the front of his shirt, Jace frogmarched him backwards up the stairs, grateful that the idiot was small and too drugged out to try putting up a fight. Three steps from the top, Tag grabbed an arm to help him unceremoniously up the rest of the way.

'Open it!' he ordered, shoving the weedy body against the door with a thud. '*Now!*'

For the first time Kelly was regarding the two of them with genuine fear. Whether because of their treatment of her mate Terry or because of what she was afraid they'd find behind the door, Jace couldn't tell.

The click as the barrel in the lock retracted sounded like an explosion within the silence of the stairwell. Jace met Tag's visual message of strength, then nodded. Would it be better or worse than they expected? He tried to fortify his nerves with a deep breath of musty air as Tag muscled Terry out of the way and pushed the door open.

It was worse. Much, much worse. It could have been used as the set for an episode of a New York crime show. Or a garbage dump.

What little light there was came not from the exposed bulb hanging from the paint-chipped ceiling, but through an unopen, grime-coated window at the far end of the room. Battered lino of indeterminable colour covered the floor, along with too many years' worth of filth. Cartons depicting the logos of various international fast food franchises created a maze for lethargic cockroaches on both a small battered table and an equally battered sink. Stuffing erupted from an old couch stained by substances Jace wasn't game to think about for fear that, combined with the stench emanating from what was presumably the bathroom – although only a large sheet of floral plastic sectioned it off from the main room – it would cause him to heave.

'Oh, my God . . .' Tag managed, but shock rendered Jace physically and vocally numb. Paralysed. It took Kelly, pushing her way between them, calling 'Russ! Russ!' to reactivate him.

He was right behind her as she hauled the plastic room-divider aside. So close that as she reeled back with a demonic scream she collided with him. Instinctively he steadied her, at the same time he sought the cause of her distress. And in that split second of time he started questioning the existence of God even as he invoked His son's name.

There was no trace of the talented rugby player in the naked bony body sprawled across stiff grey sheets. The good-looking graduation smile was long lost behind a scruffy, vomit-splattered beard. And there was only the faintest beat of life beneath Jace's fingers as they sought a pulse in the wrist of the arm not flagged by a crudely tied tourniquet.

'Get an ambulance!' he roared. 'Get a fucking ambulance *now*!'

CHAPTER 5

Late March 1988

Jace braced himself as he stepped from the warmth of his grandfather's cosy house into the biting cold of an unseasonably premature winter.

'Brrrr!' the old man said from behind the screen door. 'Brass monkey weather, fer sure. Why doncha come back inside an' I'll phone ya mum to come getcha? You'll catch yer death walking home in this.'

Jace fought down a grin. Grandpa Benton might always generously remember his birthdays, but even after twenty-three of them there were times he tended to treat his grandsons as if they were still ten.

'She'll be all right, Grandpa. I need the exercise.' Actually, what he really needed was a new gearbox, but until Tag and he got paid for their current job, he wouldn't get it.

'Yer know, boy, it wouldn't kill yer to ask for a loan,' Bryce Benton said, as if he could read minds. 'Just 'cause everyone else in this family thinks yer a fool fer chuckin' in yer law studies an' playing Sam Spade, don't assume I do.'

The revelation snapped Jace's head up. '*You* don't think I'm a fool?' he asked, surprised.

'Nope. Crazy, maybe . . . but not a fool by a long stretch.' Bryce Benton's grin displayed aged, yellowed dentures.

Never immune to the old man's kindness, and feeling well overdue for a bit of sympathy, Jace slumped against the brick wall of the entrance porch, shoving his hands into the pockets of his leather jacket. 'That's somethin', I guess,' he said. 'Every time Dad sees me he gets this look of disbelief on his face and starts shaking his head; Mum's not much better, but at least *she's* speaking to me. The old man just grunts.'

His grandfather cackled with amusement. 'He'll get over it, son. I did.'

Though now he wasn't exactly sure what his grandfather was talking about, he knew he soon would. With Grandpa Benton even the simplest statement was followed by an explanation, an anecdote or both.

'When yer dad announced he didn't wanna be a dairy farmer – ' he started, then stopped again. His disappointed expression was given added impact by his slowly shaking bushy grey head. 'I didn't mind so much when the two older boys took off ta the big smoke, 'cause I still had young Brian. But when your dad turned his back on the farm . . . I was dirty with him somethin' fierce. Knew me last hope of establishin' a farming dynasty was up in smoke when yer father decided he wanted ta become a copper.'

For a fleeting moment there was genuine sadness in the old grey eyes, but it was gone in a blink, replaced by what Jace considered a perpetual twinkle. 'But I got over me disappointment, son,' he went on. 'An' now I'm proud as punch of all me boys. Same thing'll happen with yer dad,' he assured Jace. 'Yer just gotta be patient, son.' A wickedly amused grin doubled the creases in his old face moments before a chuckle erupted. 'Kinda gives me a kick to see Brian become the stubborn old man he used to accuse me of being!'

Laughing, Jace pushed away from the wall. 'Thanks, Grandpa,' he said. 'You always were good for a bit of inspiration.'

'I'm good for a small loan too . . . Ifin' you need one, young Jason.'

Though the offer was as tempting as it was touching, Jace shook his head. 'Thanks, but Tag and I aren't exactly in over our heads yet. We can manage.'

The grey head nodded in understanding. 'Fair enough. But if yer get too wore out treadin' water, you be sure an' come see me. Yer hear?'

'Gotcha,' he said, then added sincerely, 'And . . . *thank you*.'

Never one for drawn-out displays of sentiment, the old man waved the gratitude aside and again started issuing warnings about the health risks Jace was taking in walking home. Taking the hint, Jace said goodbye and stepped out into the damp street.

By the time he reached the first corner a niggling rain had started falling. It wasn't enough to encroach upon the protection of his leather jacket, but it quickly dampened his jeans, lowering the temperature a few more uncomfortable degrees. For a moment he looked up and down the the street, uncertain whether to go left or right.

Left would mean a two-kilometre walk home in weather that was only going to get worse. A right turn and he'd

71

reach the rowing club in a few moments and possibly bum a lift home with either Ethan or any one of a dozen guys he knew would be there. On the other hand he could have a few beers and a couple of games of pool and start breathing some life back into his social life before rigor mortis claimed it.

He turned left and started walking. Solitude and the night's cold dampness were more appealing than the thought of running into Donna Browne. It was hard to believe he'd once thought Donna the hottest thing on two legs and even envied Doug the relationship he'd had with her. These days it was all he could do to be civil to her when Ethan brought her home and, although in the last few weeks her visits had thinned, Ethan made no secret of the fact he was still seeing her.

Well, Jace just hoped she was as good a lay as everyone believed and that Ethan was getting plenty of her action, because God knew he'd never get anything else out of the shallow little bitch! He swore as Donna's words replayed in his head.

'In a way it's better he died; I could never have taken him back knowing how he'd lived all those months. I could have ended up with herpes or even AIDS! It's easier for everyone that he died.'

Who the hell was 'everyone'? Jace wondered. *Not* Doug's widowed mother, who'd been so heavily sedated for her grief at the funeral that she'd been little more coherent than her son had been when they'd found him. *Not* his older sister, who, crying hysterically, had thrown herself onto the coffin and had had to be dragged off. And it certainly hadn't been *easy* for anyone who'd been at the cemetery and seen a distraught eleven-year-old Kate Russell collapse and almost tumble into the grave her big brother's coffin was being lowered into.

But of course Donna hadn't been at the cemetery, her parents having taken their beautifully tearful daughter home after the funeral service, claiming she was 'too emotionally sensitive' to take any more. Ha! The selfish little bitch didn't possess one iota of sensitivity; but oh, boy, was she an expert when it came to taking emotionally from others! She had Ethan so tied up in knots he couldn't see straight.

Absorbed in his own angry thoughts, it was only the blast of an airhorn that stopped him from walking into the path of a truck as he started across an intersection against the flashing 'DON'T WALK' sign. Jumping back onto the kerb, he automatically fingered the driver's offsider as he graphically questioned his eyesight, then patiently waited for the lights to change in his favour.

Guess that proves the statistics are right, Benton, he told himself. Most accidents *do* happen within a close radius of the home.

The near miss had alerted him to the fact that the rain had become heavy enough for it to have started dripping from his hair down the neck of his jacket. Adjusting the collar, he started to jog the remaining couple of blocks home.

The landscaped front garden of the Benton house was only partly illuminated by the metre-high lampposts on either side of the upwardly sloping driveway, but a sensor light on the porch was designed to activate once the infra-red beam aimed at the approach to the front veranda was crossed. Moving in that direction, Jace made a mental note to remind his mum she'd left her car in the driveway.

Light flooded the front yard, but a startled gasp followed by a movement in his peripheral vision yanked his attention back to the car. Through the rain he saw an unidentifiable figure backing out of the driver's door.

'Hey!' At his yell the person nimbly darted clear of the car and raced down the drive.

The head start the guy had got on a momentarily stunned Jace might have been enough to get him into the street had he not slipped on the rain-slick pavement of the drive. That fault in his stride cost him dearly.

As tackles went, Jace figured he'd probably pulled off better ones, but it was results that counted, and the thief's grunt as he hit the ground was indicative of its effectiveness. But unlike in football, where the 'tacklee' usually just got up and politely played the ball, this one took advantage of Jace's lapse into smug satisfaction to fight back. Twisting, the would-be thief lashed out with elbows, feet and fists – one of the latter cuffing Jace across the top of his eye.

He swore, inadvertently providing the opportunity for angry fingers to gouge the inside of his mouth. Instinctively he bit down, and a shriek of pain was his triumphant reward. Seconds later, though, he was more grateful that a vicious knee which had rammed into his inner thigh had missed its intended mark.

Quickly estimating that he had more than a few kilos of weight working in his favour, Jace rolled them onto the grass island in the centre of the drive, pinning his opponent face-down by driving an his elbow – hard – onto his back. When grunted obscenities continued flowing from the writhing form, he moved quickly to sit on the kid's backside and shove his face into the soggy grass. He was bending the guy's left arm into a half-Nelson when he was blinded by headlights swinging into the driveway.

The vehicle braked, its driver out the door almost before it came to a complete stop.

'What the hell – ?' Ethan started, studying the scene before him.

'Caught him . . . trying to . . . steal Mum's car,' Jace said between hard-fought breaths. The culprit was still struggling, so he exerted more pressure with the hand that held his face into the ground. 'Gimme a hand getting him inside and we'll call the cops.'

'He must have a helluva punch,' his brother said as Jace gingerly eased himself to his feet. 'He opened up your right eyebrow again. Looks like it'll need stitches'

Jace swore. There was nothing he hated more than needles. 'Bastard!' he muttered, giving the bloke's pinned arm a vicious jerk as he dragged him to his feet, coughing and spluttering mud.

'Er . . . Jace,' Ethan said warily. 'You'd better go a bit gentler – '

'*Go a bit gentler?*' he roared in outrage. 'I'm thinking of breaking his bloody arm!'

'Well, you'd better think again,' Ethan advised. 'Unless you want a reputation as a *woman*-beater!' He followed his amazing announcement by pulling the wet woollen ski cap from the thief's head. A mass of long dark hair dropped out.

Shock loosened Jace's grip, and, though Ethan was

75

quick to counter the girl's spontaneous burst for freedom, it took their combined efforts to subdue her second wind.

'Feral little thing, isn't she?' Ethan said, pulling his face out of the way a whisker before it met with a vicious clawing.

'Tell me about it – dammit, quit fighting, you little fool! We're twice your size and you're going to wind up getting hurt!'

They were trying to manoeuvre the struggling wildcat across the lawn to the house, but Jace's well-intentioned advice was greeted with a screaming barrage of profanities in both English and Italian.

His brother laughed. 'Does that translate to, Yeah? Then how come you're the one bleeding?'

'Shut up, Ethan! And dammit, you too!' he said, shaking their captive. She ignored him. 'Geez, at this rate we won't have to bother calling the cops; the neighbours will've already done it.'

Judy Benton appeared on the front veranda, her nightgown and rumpled hair indicative of her having been in bed. 'What on *earth* is going on out here?'

'Call the cops, Mum,' Jace said, skipping out of the way of a flying foot. 'We just caught this kid trying to pinch your car.'

'I wasn't stealing it you dickhead! Ow! Quit yankin' my hair!'

'Quit fighting!'

He tightened his grip on her arm to steer her around his slightly bemused-looking mother. 'She's a girl! For heaven's sake, don't be too rough with her . . .'

Honing in on the female sympathy, the kid turned an imploring face to her. '*Please* hel – '

'Don't let her con you, Mum,' Jace cut in. 'If she was any tougher you'd have to rust-proof her.'

'No! They're hurting me! I swear – '

'Geez, a liar *and* a thief! You're a regular little charmer, aren't you?'

She swung her head back to face him, but instead of the abusive retort he'd expected deep, deep brown eyes that threatened to explode with hate simply stared into his. If there was even the remotest chance looks *could* kill, Jace figured this one of hers would do it. A whimsical part of him fleetingly wondered if she was trying to put some sort of a hex on him. I guess you'll know if you wake up sitting in a lily pond and croaking, Benton, he told himself.

He realized Ethan was staring at him as he asked, 'What's so funny?'

He shook his head to dismiss the question. 'Nothing. Let's just get her inside.' But of course the would-be thief-cum-witch wasn't about to get co-operative, immediately stiffening her body and bracing her feet on the veranda's dry concrete, her stubborn resistance as heartfelt as her ongoing string of Italian curses.

Well, Jace assumed they were curses – had she been praying that fervently an army of angels would have ridden to her rescue. Then again, considering how successfully her scrawny five-five build was managing to withstand two six-foot-plus males' attempts to get her through the door, perhaps she did have access to supernatural aid! He and Ethan were on either side of her and holding her by the forearms, and they were getting

77

nowhere fast. Jace was reluctant to resort to any more force. Hell, she was just a kid, and female to boot, why didn't she just give in gracefully?

Sighing, Jace considered the merits of tossing her over his shoulder, but visualization of that idea put her vicious little Reeboks too close to his groin for comfort. He opted for the physically safer plan B. With nothing more than a wink at his brother, he quickly but firmly pressed his knee into the back of hers; she buckled, and he used the moment to lift her over the small front doorstep and into the house. 'Oops, careful,' he said cheerfully. 'Nearly *tripped*.'

'Smartass bastard!'

For all her bravado, she looked like a muddy drowned rat, and as the victor he could afford to be generous. He smiled. 'I've been called worse.'

'Gee,' she sneered. '*Big surprise!*'

'In here?' Ethan motioned to the archway of the lounge room.

'Nah, the kitchen. Otherwise we'll track mud – '

'*Take her into the family room and turn up the heater this minute!*' They turned at their mother's overriding tone. 'In case you haven't noticed, the poor child is drenched to the bone.'

'Yeah, but – '

'*Do it,*' she insisted. 'I'll get some towels. Oh, and by the way, Jason,' she added as she disappeared down the hall, 'your eye is bleeding.'

He was about to say, Blame the *poor child*, when the person in question suddenly went limp in his grasp. 'What the – ?'

'Ah, hell! She's blacked out.' Accusing blue eyes the

78

same shade as Jace's own glared at him. 'How bloody hard did you hit her?' his brother demanded.

'Hey, I don't hit females!'

'You didn't *know* she was a female till I told you!'

'Yeah, but I hadn't hit her!'

Their joint efforts to move her from the hallway to the family room were clumsy, and Jace told himself it was expediency not guilt that prompted him to pick her up and carry her the remaining distance to the sofa. He waited until Ethan tossed scatter cushions to one end of it, then lowered her gently down so her head was supported by them. His stomach tightened as Ethan brushed matted dark strands of hair from a face that was deathly pale beneath smatterings of mud.

'Well, whether you hit her or not, one thing's for sure – she's out cold.' There was still a hint of censure in his brother's voice.

'Listen, *I didn't hit her*, okay? I figured it was just a young kid an' I didn't want to hurt him . . . her. All I did was try and restrain her.'

'Okay, okay, I believe you.' For a moment they simply stared at her inert form. 'Did she seem drunk to you? Or doped up?'

Ethan's question hit like a blow to the guts! Still raw from the memory of watching Doug die after arriving too late to do a damn thing to save him, Jace dropped to his knees, immediately grasping her thing, limp wrist.

'What's happened?'

He left it to Ethan to answer their mother's question. 'I think she fainted,' he heard him say. 'She just kind of . . . crumbled.'

He found her pulse at that the same time his mother crouched beside him. Relief gushed through him. 'A strong pulse,' he said. The softness in his mum's eyes told him she knew his fears. 'Slow, but definitely strong.'

Gently his mother placed the back of her hand on the girl's forehead, then frowned and felt her hands. 'She's burning with fever, but her hands are like blocks of ice. Ethan, get a couple of blankets out of the linen cupboard. Here,' she said to Jace, retrieving an ice packet from an end-table piled with neatly folded towels. 'Hold that onto your eye and phone Kevin Prendergast. Ask him to come up here.'

Kevin Prendergast was both a family friend and a doctor, who lived a convenient four houses away. 'Okay. I'll call the cops while I'm at it.'

'No, you won't,' she corrected, not pausing in her task of tucking towels around the bedraggled figure on the sofa. 'The last thing this poor girl needs is the police hassling her.'

'*Mum* . . . she was trying to steal your . . .' He paused in the face of her why-must-male-offspring-be-such-a trial? expression.

'Jason,' she said. 'The car is still in the driveway. This poor girl is one step from pneumonia and in no condition to *sit up*, let alone make a dash for freedom. And *you* are dripping wet and bleeding profusely.' The smile she gave him belonged on a Madonna. 'Now, go and call Kevin before *you* collapse as well and we have bloodstains on the carpet to contend with . . . Oh, good, Ethan! You've got the blankets.'

Brian Benton arrived home twenty minutes later,

although, sitting in the family room, Jace and his brother heard him long before he walked in the front door.

'A man builds a three-car garage and because no bugger uses it he's still got to park in the street and get wet when it rains!' he complained from the vicinity of the front veranda. 'Ethan!' he bellowed, his voice now coming from the hallway. 'You left your door open and your headlights on!'

'Damn!' Ethan sprang to his feet. 'If the battery's not flat the damn car'll probably be flooded!'

'It is,' Brian Benton confirmed. 'But since I've switched off the lights and locked it, at least it'll still *be there* in the morning.'

'Thank – ' Ethan's attempt at gratitude was pushed aside as Brian Benton caught sight of his eleven-minutes-younger son. 'What the hell happened to you?'

'Long story, Dad,' Jace said.

'Well, I'll shorten it! Ethan,' he said, pivoting back to the older twin, 'have you and him been arguing about Donna Browne again?'

'Hardly likely since *he* hasn't got a mark on him, Dad.' Jace's pointed comment earned him a droll look from his brother, who then answered their dad's question.

'It had nothing to do with Donna. And, *no*, I didn't do it. Jace can explain; I want to check out the car.'

Brian Benton marched his six-foot uniformed frame over to stand in front of the sofa where Jace was slumped. 'So,' he said, 'what the hell happened?'

Exchanging the bloodied towel for the ice pack, as he'd been doing for the last fifteen or so minutes, Jace winced. 'I think it was a right, but I wouldn't swear to it 'cause her left was pretty busy too. Kevin's going to take a better look at it after he finishes reviving my assailant. He's in your room doing his stuff now.'

'Your *mother* did this!'

Amazement brought Jace's upright, the sudden movement causing him to bang the ice pack against his wound. He swore, then stared at his father. 'Of course not! Why would you think that?'

'Because you just said *her* left was pretty busy and that Kev was in our bedroom reviving her! Now, either Judy hit you or she didn't!'

'Why would *Mum* want to hit me, Dad?'

'I can think of plenty of reasons! Starting with your idiotic behaviour of late and going on down to your inability to answer a simple question! Now, what happ –' He broke off as his wife entered the room.

'Brian! I'm glad you're home.'

'Well, that's one of us,' Jace's father said, bending quickly to kiss her cheek. 'You want to tell me what's going on? Why Jace looks like he's been rolling in the mud with Muhummad Ali and why Kev Prendergast is reviving someone in my bedroom?' He paused. 'Actually, *start* with who is in my bedroom.'

'We don't know her name. But she collapsed when the boys dragged her into the house – '

'They *dragged* her into the house?'

'So I thought I'd better call Kevin. Jason wanted to call the police, but I wanted to wait for you. After all, she didn't steal the car and Jason wasn't seriously hurt -- '

'Hey, stitches are serious . . .'

'*Didn't steal what car?*'

'Er . . . Judy . . . Brian . . .?' Kevin Prendergast's entrance into the room drew all attention. If he wasn't the only doctor who still made house-calls, Jace would bet he was the only one who made them in his PJs and dressing gown! But he could have been dressed in suspenders and tights tonight and it wouldn't have bothered Jace as long as he was *finally* going to do something about his eye!

'How is she, Kevin?'

'*Who* is she, is what I'd like to know.'

Kevin Prendergast held up his hand for silence and answered Judy's question first. 'She's conscious, but feverish and too incoherent to get any sense out of at the moment. *But*,' he went on, 'as far as I can tell she's simply pathetically run down and suffering a viral infection, nothing more. As for *who* she is, Brian – ' he shook his head ' – I've no idea.'

'I do.'

Four sets of eyes went to the doorway where Ethan stood wearing a smug grin and holding up a battered backpack. 'Her name's either Francesca Milano or Tatum Milano. She left this in Mum's car. There's a wallet with a Medicare card in those names, fifty-five cents, two doorkeys and a collection of papers I haven't looked through yet. But you want to know what's really interesting . . .?'

'Just give us the bloody bag and stop being a hero!' Jace snapped. Hell, he was bleeding to death and every other bugger wanted to grab the limelight!

Undaunted, his brother went on. 'What's *really* interesting is that Ms Milano has a collection of jewellery the royal family would envy . . .'

CHAPTER 6

With his head angled over the back of the kitchen chair, Jace was in a better position to have his throat cut rather than his eye stitched, and in all honesty he'd have happier with the first prospect. Regardless of how many times he'd been through it, he simply couldn't get comfortable with the idea of sharp bits of metal piercing his flesh. Right now, though, the pyjama-clad doctor was going through some sort of pre-op cleansing and probing of the wound. And it stung like all hell!

'Sorry, Jason,' he muttered, sounding anything but.

'You'll have coffee, won't you, Kevin?'

Jace opened his good eye at the sound of his mum's voice, only to shut it quickly again as the light from the desk lamp which Kevin Prendergast had set on the table nearly blinded him.

'Tea if you've got it, Judy. I'm just starting to get back that nice drowsy feeling – don't want to get home and find I can't sleep.'

Great! The guy's sewing me up half-asleep! Jace thought. Deciding it would be better to spare himself the bizarre conversation going on around him, he visualized a blank television screen. Then the needle pierced his flesh and he found himself picturing the incision in Technicolor and changed his mind. On second thoughts, any sort of conversation would be a pleasant distraction!

'It's not serious is it, Kevin?' he heard his mother ask with concern. Better late than never, Mum, he thought, recalling how his assailant had commandeered all her maternal instincts with her fainting act.

'Nah, same old story,' the doctor said. 'Actually, how many times *have* you opened up this eyebrow now, Jason? This must be the third or fourth time *I've* patched it.'

His mother jumped in before Jace could calculate an answer. 'Lord, Kevin, we've lost track of the number of times he's come home with a bloody bleeding face!' She laughed. 'With Ethan it varied from skinned knees to the odd broken limb. But *Jason*! It got so we worried if his eye *wasn't* bleeding.'

Well, gee, Mum you don't have to sound so cheerful about it!

He could hear her moving about the kitchen as she continued. 'The first time it happened he was only six. A neighbour's kid was showing off on a skateboard and it flew up and hit him in the face. You've never heard such a racket as when we took him down to Casualty and they tried to stitch him up! Cried and screamed at the top of his lungs. It took his father and two nurses to hold him down.'

You omitted to tell him the sadists forgot to use any anaesthetic before they started!

'After that it pretty much opened up at least once every football season. Isn't that right, Brian?' she asked.

'Near enough to every season,' his father agreed. ''Course, all those fights he got into didn't help any either. I'm convinced the kid must *lead* with his face!'

The joke drew general laughter from all but the patient.

That's right, Dad! Make the guy laugh while he's plying a sharp object around my eye!

All went quite for a couple of minutes, and Jace had the feeling everyone was standing around watching the embroidery in progress. Then the kettle whistled and he recognized the sound of cups being placed on the table and chairs being scraped back.

'Could you stir two sugars into mine, Judy?'

'Certainly, Kev. You'll have cake, of course?'

'Need you ask?'

Geez! Surely he wasn't going to take high tea while he was doing, this? But then, why not? he mused. No one seemed to think stitching up good old Jace was any big deal.

'So, Brian,' again it was Doctor Dare-Devil who spoke. 'What have you managed to find out about our would-be thief?'

'Not much.' Dissatisfaction coated the response. 'According to the documents in her bag, she's *Tatum* Milano, sixteen-year-old daughter of Francesca. But there's nothing with an address or phone number on it. I've called the local station and one of the desk boys is checking to see if she's listed as a missing person.'

'You think she's a runaway?' Prendergast asked.

'Probably. One thing's certain, though, she's definitely a light-fingered little miss,' Brian Benton said. 'At a guess I'd say she has about three grands' worth of jewellery stashed in that bag of hers.'

'Wha – ?'

'Shh, Jason! Keep your face still,' the doctor chided. 'I'm trying to concentrate on this needlework.'

Well, that's good news! You're trying to concentrate! I wasn't sure with the way you're yapping to my old man.

'How long do you think she'll sleep for, Kev?'

'Hard to say. I've given her something for the fever, so that should help. But she's not going to be up to answering police questions for a least a day. Maybe two.'

In other words, Dad – Down Boy! You'll have to wait for the joy of giving her the third degree.

'Well, that's damned inconvenient. She can't be held in a detention centre until she's been interviewed and charged.'

'Meaning?'

'Meaning if the mother can't be located a place will have to be found for her to stay until then,' his father grumbled. 'Judy, call the refuge. See if they know anything about her, and if not ask them to arrange somewhere for her to stay till she's up to going to the police station.'

'I've already called them. No one there has heard of her or seen anyone answering her description. Nor can they take her in. They're full up because of the weather. And – '

'All done, Jason! Good as new.'

Sighing with relief, Jace cautiously opened his eyes, blinking as he readjusted to the kitchen's fluorescent lighting. He pursed his mouth at the mild discomfort the action brought.

'It'll be a little sore for a day or two,' Prendergast advised. 'But the scar shouldn't be any worse than what was there before. Fortunately there isn't much swelling. Try and keep it dry, though.'

Raising his hand, Jace gingerly felt the wound. 'How many stitches?'

'Six. Two just for good measure.' He peeled off his gloves and started packing his gear away. 'They can come out in, oh . . . ten days. Pop in home and I'll whip them out for you.'

'Thanks.' He smiled up at his mother as she placed a mug of coffee in front of him. Boy, could he use that. Sheesh! What a night!

'So, Dad,' he said, stretching for a slice of chocolate sponge from the centre of the table. 'Our little car thief's got a more successful sideline in jewellery, huh?'

'So it seems.'

'*Seems* being the operative word,' Judy Benton said pointedly. All three men rolled their eyes. 'Don't give me that!' she told them. 'I see kids like her every day. People like you lot are all too quick to believe the worst of them before you know the facts.'

'*Mum . . . I caught her getting into the car.*'

'You have to admit, Judy,' Kevin Prendergast said reasonably, 'that's as close as it gets to being caught with your hand in the cookie jar.'

'Intent to steal. Pure and simple,' Brian Benton stated. 'Probably go close to getting an assault charge to stick too,' he added, motioning towards Jace.

'Oh, don't be ridiculous!' his wife told him. 'We've just agreed Jason's eye opens easier than a book! And besides, she's only a slip of a girl! They'd take one look at the poor, fragile little thing, one look at Jason and laugh you out of court!'

'That's okay, Mum, *you* might as well bruise my ego.

That "poor, fragile little thing" did a good job on every-thing else,' Jace said, drily.

'Huh! Your ego's indestructible. Anyway, there's no need to press *any* charges. There's been no real damage done.'

'Not press charges!' Brian Benton exploded. 'She was breaking the law. Her success or lack of it notwithstand-ing, the thing is she trespassed with intent to steal. It's my job to see people who thumb their noses at the law face the consequences.'

Glaring at her husband, Judy Benton pushed her chair back. 'Well, all *you* – ' her look encompassed all three at the table ' – fine, law – abiding *men* may see yourselves as her judge and jury. But it's *my* job to consider the extenuating circumstances.'

'What *extenuating circumstances*?' her husband asked. 'We know nothing about the kid!'

'*Exactly*! And until you do she deserves the benefit of the doubt and a little human compassion!'

Jace met his father's here-we-go-again look with a shrug. To say anything would only encourage his mother to climb up on her soapbox. Not that she ever needed much encouragement. Ten years younger than her police-man husband, and a firm supporter of women having careers outside the home, she'd gone back to university when he and Ethan had started high school. Then, having graduated with a first class honours degree, she'd started full-time work as a social worker.

Eighteen months ago, after leaving a long-time position with the education department, she'd taken a job with the local government health service, which had brought her into contact with an increasing number of street kids. Deeply moved by their plight, she'd begun volunteer work at the local youth refugee, and since then her commitment had grown to crusader proportions.

But Judy Benton wasn't silly enough to believe she could right the world on her own. So she'd turned her relentless determination and persuasive personality on her husband, until she'd coerced him into getting the various sporting and recreational activities at the nearby Police Citizens' Youth Club expanded. Jace and his brother had also been railroaded into helping out down there on more than one occasion.

'I guarantee you wouldn't be feeling quite so compassionate if you were missing your damn car,' Brian told her. 'And how about a little compassion for the poor buggers whose jewellery she's knocked off, huh?'

'You don't know for certain she st – '

The shrill of the wall-phone intruded on the argument. Jace's mother answered it then held it at arm's length to her husband. 'Burwood police station.'

His father took the phone, turning his back on the rest of the room's occupants.

'With him everyone's guilty until proven innocent,' his mother complained, moving into the chair her husband had vacated. 'Everything's black and white – no shades of grey, no middle ground.'

Tell me something I don't know. Jace wisely kept the comment to himself, although he noticed Kevin Prendergast dip his head to hide a smile. Probably if the doctor hadn't been a family friend he'd have prudently excused himself and gone home by now, but this wasn't the first Benton domestic the man had sat through and World War III would have to break out before Kev would leave when there was homemade cake sitting on the table.

'Ethan gone to bed?' Jace asked, realizing he hadn't seen his brother since he'd gone up to change into a dry sweatsuit.

His mother gave a distracted shake of her head, her eyes on her husband. 'Er . . . no. Donna rang a little while ago. Her car broke down.'

So good old Ethan had raced to rescue his distressed damsel, huh? Wasn't *he* being a regular superhero tonight!

'Well,' his father said, hanging up the phone, 'she's not listed as missing and there are no warrants out on her – '

'There, see!' His mother looked triumphant. 'Her only crime is being sick.'

'There's still the question of the jewellery,' her husband reminded her. 'And where the devil she's going to spend the night.'

Pushing her chair back, Judy Benton said, 'She's spending the night right where she is now.'

Father and son spoke as one.

'Like hell!'

'Mum, I don't think – '

'She's sick. It's after midnight. And there's no ready alternative,' his mother said quickly. 'Now, you can all argue to your heart's content, but I won't be responsible for turning that child out in the street! And *that* – ' she thumped the table ' – is final.'

She left the room with her husband hot on her heels. 'Now, just one minute, Judith – '

Kevin Prendergast was chuckling with undisguised amusement. 'I should have warned him. I saw this coming a mile off.'

With twenty-twenty hindsight Jace realized he should have too, but for the first time in months he was on his father's side. It was one thing to feel sorry for the kid, but his mother was letting herself get personally involved. In her line of work it wasn't advisable to take the job home with you, not if you wanted to stay sane. And especially not if you wanted to keep your silverware!

Sunlight blazed cruelly through the kitchen windows, causing Jace to squint, then swear as his stitches pulled.

'Good morning to you too.'

He turned to find his brother still dressed in the clothes he'd worn the night before and holding a box of cereal.

'Just getting home?'

He nodded, pulling a bowl from the cupboard. 'You want some?'

'Yeah. So what'd you have to do?' he asked snidely. 'Rebuild her motor?' He set a carton of milk and orange juice on the table and sat down. Though he'd have appreciated another twenty-four hours' sleep, Tag was picking him up in forty minutes.

'No.' His brother's response was terse. 'She'd run out of petrol. Now, if you don't mind I'd rather not have to eat breakfast defending Donna. *Again.*'

A million comebacks raced through Jace's mind, but he kept silent. Talking about the treacherous Ms Browne would only ruin his appetite anyway.

'How'd last night finish up?' Ethan enquired, dropping two spoons onto the table.

'Let me put it this way,' Jace replied, reaching for a spoon and waving it. 'We're lucky we're not having to eat breakfast with our hands.'

'Huh? Come again.'

'Remember how when we were kids and we brought that stray kitten home Mum wanted to keep it and Dad didn't?' His brother was frowning at him. 'Do you remember who won?'

'Mum, I suppose. We got to keep the cat. But what's that got to do with last night?'

'Dad is now *none from two*.'

Through half-closed eyes she watched the woman standing in front of the dressing table applying lipstick. She wasn't old, but she wasn't young either, despite the blue jeans and sweatshirt she wore. Forty-something, Tatum guessed. She put down the lipstick and, picking up a small tortoiseshell brush, began brushing her wavy fair hair, grimacing when she encountered a tangle and –

Tatum, too, grimaced as a sudden cramp hit her. She clutched her stomach as the pain bit into her, groaning before she could stop herself. Oh, God! *Not now*. Not this too! When the pain eased she again opened her eyes to find the woman standing over her.

'You're awake. Good.' Her smile, designed to be reassuring, wasn't and Tatum jerked away from the hand that touched her forehead. 'You're still a bit hot, but the worst is over, I'd say.'

'Who are you? And what am I doing here?'

The woman sat down on the edge of the bed and took a glass of water from the night table. 'Here, the doctor said you had to drink plenty of fluids.'

Tatum frowned at her. 'What doctor? Who are you?' she asked again.

Another smile curved the freshly glossed lips. 'I'm the person whose car you tried to steal last night. Remember?'

A vague recollection of a nightgown-clad woman edged into her mind as she said, 'I wasn't going to steal the bloody car!'

'My son thought you were.'

'Your son's a dickhead.'

The woman laughed. 'Maternal pride forces me to disagree.'

Tatum shrugged and looked around the room. It was neat as a pin and decorated in a cute country cottage style. 'What am I doing here?' she asked, feeling both so tired and confused it was hard to sound angry. 'I mean, if you're so convinced I was going to pinch your stupid car, didn't you call the cops?'

'Firstly I'm not convinced you were trying to steal the car – '

'I wasn't!'

'And secondly when you passed out I thought a doctor should be the first priority.'

'I *passed out*?'

The woman nodded. 'How much do you remember?'

'Everything up to the part where two goons dragged me into the house. I don't remember any doc – ' Another cramp grabbed her. She swore.

94

'What's the matter?' Concerned hands held her shoulders.

'My . . . my gut hurts.' The pain easing, she drew a long, slow breath.

'When did you last have a decent meal, Tatum?' Her surprise must have shown because the woman said, 'You had ID in your backpack.'

'You had no effing right to go through my things!'

'And *you*, miss . . .' a huge greying man said from the door, 'have no right to speak like that to my wife nor try and steal her car!'

'I wasn't stealing the bloody car!' Tatum yelled back. 'I just . . . I was ju – ' To her utter mortification she burst into tears.

'Now look what you've done, Brian! Honestly! Was it really necessary to come barging in here like a bull in a china shop?' his wife asked crossly. 'For goodness' sake, *go away*!'

'*Barging in*? Damn it Judy, this is *my* bedroom! I need to get dressed.'

'Well, then, hurry up and do it. And then go and get Kevin Prendergast back here.'

It seemed to Tatum that once the tears started they wouldn't stop, and not even the comforting embrace of the woman called Judy could nullify the trembling of her body. A loud sob turned to a gasp of pain as yet another cramp bit, and it was far too easy to surrender to the urge to turn her head into the shoulder of the woman holding her and simply lose herself in the softly soothing chants of, 'Hush, hush, pet. It's all right . . . Everything is going to be all right . . .'

* * *

95

'What happened to *you*?' Tag asked, when Jace climbed into the front seat of Tag's father's new Holden Commodore.

'A feral brown-eyed witch.'

Shifting into gear and peeling away from the kerb outside the Benton home, Tag laughed. 'If that's the result, your pick-up technique really needs overhauling, mate.'

More like his whole life needed overhauling. He was beginning to feel as if he was in an episode of the *Twilight Zone*. Buckling his seat belt, Jace slumped lower into the seat and proceeded to related the entire story.

'So what do you want to do?' Tag asked when he'd finished. 'Spend a bit of time checking her out?'

Jace shook his head. 'Dad and his police buddies can handle that. I'd rather spend my time on things that'll bring us in some money.'

'Glad to hear it, 'cause that ad we ran in the paper last week has paid off.' A broadly grinning face turned to him. 'We're about to get our second official case.'

The week after Doug had been buried Jace, like Ethan and Tag, had recommenced the new university year and their fourth year of law studies. But in the wake of what he'd seen in the months he'd been searching for his friend the routine, insulated environment of academia had suddenly struck him as pointless. He'd gone through the motions of attending lectures and tutorials only to find that he spent more time doodling than taking notes and that he was unable to resume easily the carefree student lifestyle he'd practised before. People whose company and ideals he'd once shared suddenly seemed self-centred and

96

naïve. He'd had no interest in or energy for socializing – either on or off campus.

He'd felt restless and dissatisfied with his life, but unsure of what to do about it. Then one evening he'd got a phone call from a woman called Truman. She'd said she was the sister of someone who knew Doug's mother and that she'd heard he'd been responsible for finding Doug when the police hadn't be able to. Then to Jace's utter amazement she'd offered to pay him if he'd try and locate her runaway fourteen-year-old daughter.

Initially he'd said no, that it was a matter for the cops. But he hadn't been able to argue with her statement that the police didn't really *look* for people, that they tended to wait for them to turn up. For three days he'd resisted the idea of calling the woman back and telling her he'd help her for nothing, but common sense had told him if he wanted to do the job properly he'd have to apply himself to it full time, just as he had with Doug. That meant it was going to cut into his limited cash supply and his time at uni; the latter wouldn't be a hardship, the former definitely would.

Deciding he needed a sounding board, and since Ethan had no time for anyone but Donna, he'd sought out Tag and told him about the woman's offer and that he was seriously considering taking her up on it.

'You mean, you're thinking of dropping out of this semester to work full-time finding the kid?' he'd asked.

'No. Actually I'm considering dropping out *altogether* and making a career out of finding missing kids.'

Tag had just stared at him for a few minutes then said, 'You mean become a private investigator?'

'Well, yeah,' he'd replied, surprised. 'I guess I do.'

Until that moment he'd never thought of what he wanted to do in a professional sense. But he realized then that what he was contemplating was exactly what was commercially known as private investigating. And the term implied that he didn't necessarily have to limit himself to tracking down missing persons. He could sub-contract his services to insurance agents, legal firms and earn a living doing it. The more he'd thought about it the more certain he'd become that he was making the right decision.

'Your old man is a cop,' Tag had reminded him with a wry smile. 'He's gonna go ape when you tell him.'

Jace had nodded. His old man was going to be positively rabid, all right, but he'd grinned and said, 'True . . . but it won't be the first time he's disowned me.'

Then Tag had floored him by saying, 'So? You want a partner?'

That day, six weeks ago, Bentag Investigations had been conceived . . .

'Jace, am I talking to myself here, or what?'

'Sorry!' he said, quickly bringing his mind up to speed. 'I was daydreaming.'

'Well, snap out of it,' Tag told him, swinging the car into the driveway of a prestigious-looking two-storey home. 'This is the Perelli place and they're willing to pay big bucks to find their son.'

'Well, that explains why you're driving your old man's car and not your rust-bucket,' Jace said as they pulled to a stop in the circular drive.

'Hey, at least mine runs, mate!'

'My transport problems will be rectified as soon as we get paid for finding Cassandra Truman.'

'We have been,' Tag informed him. 'There was a cheque in the post office box yesterday. Although that in itself creates a problem.'

'Oh, good, I needed another one.'

'We're going to have to find someone to do our book-keeping for us. Someone who knows about keeping business records. Any suggestions?'

In theory, six weeks ago, everything had sounded so easy, but it seemed to Jace that every time they turned around they had some legal hassle to deal with. 'My mum could probably help out – there's always someone at the women's refuge she volunteers at looking for work. I'll tell her to ask around.'

'Just make sure she tells them the pay's lousy,' Tag warned as they went up the steps of the house. 'We've got to watch our overheads.'

'We'd be better off watching our butts . . . Take a look at our welcoming committee.'

Jace wondered how long it had been since the two salivating Rottweilers eyeing them had been fed.

'Tea will be ready in fifteen minutes, Jason,' his mother announced as he let himself in the back door. 'Oh, hello Tag. I didn't see you there.'

'Hi, Mrs R. How's things? Still running the best juvenile detention centre in the state?'

'By that I gather Jace has told you about Tatum?' She cast an irritated glance at her son.

'Well, hey,' he said, taking a beer from the fridge and

99

tossing another to his friend, 'you never said it was a secret. Besides, Tag was too shrewd to buy my story about walking into a door. So . . .' He pulled out a chair and sat down. '*Is* she still here or has Dad tossed her out of his bed and into maximum security at Long Bay?'

Tag laughed. 'Gee, now, *there's* a headline.' He used his hand to indicate huge print. 'SENIOR POLICE INTERNAL AFFAIRS OFFICER SHARES SHEETS WITH JUVENILE DELINQUENT!'

'I'm glad you find it so amusing, *Lee*.' Brian Benton's tone and expression clearly said *he* didn't. Jace laughed anyway. 'Judith,' his father went on to say, 'she refuses to say anything to me. Now, either she starts co-operating or I'm hauling her smart-aleck little mouth down to Burwood police station right now!'

'Maybe it's your bedside manner, Dad? Did you say *please*?'

'I've had a gutful of her lip; I don't need yours. Go in and talk to her, Judy. I want some facts and I want them *now*.'

'Fine! But *you* stay outside this time, okay? Things were going fine until you stuck your bib in last time!' Judy Benton banged the lid onto a huge pot of what to Jace smelled like spaghetti sauce and stormed from the room.

'I guess that puts dinner on hold,' Jace observed. 'You want a beer, Dad?' At his father's weary nod he leaned the chair onto its back legs and pulled open the refrigerator.

'I take it the perpetrator isn't being co-operative, Inspector Benton.'

'Don't push it, Tag,' the man warned, accepting the beer with a nod. 'It wouldn't be hard to arrange to get a newly issued private investigator's licence pulled.' All three knew the threat was an idle one. Brian Benton had no time for coppers who used their position to settle personal scores.

'So what *is* the latest with little Miss Slugger, Dad?'

'Well, she's told us next to nothing. Except that she *wasn't* trying to steal the car and the jewellery belongs to her.'

'You believe her?'

'When she's this uncooperative? When pigs fly! Anything we do know hasn't come from her. The birth certificate had her mother as being Francesca Milano, father unknown. The local boys have confirmed the mother died from a drug overdose almost exactly twelve months ago. Apparently she's been living on the streets since then. At least, that's what she's led Judy to believe.'

'But most street kids don't carry three grand's worth of jewellery around with them.'

Brian Benton grunted in agreement with Tag's comment. 'Not honest ones, at any rate.'

'Curiouser and curiouser,' Tag said, pushing himself to his feet. 'Well, I better get going. I'm hitting the Cross to look for a runaway tonight.' He looked to Brian Benton. 'You want me to ask around about this kid while I'm at it?'

'No thanks, Tag. The police can handle it.'

Jace got to his feet and shot his mate a you-must-be-crazy look. 'The cops think private investigators are more trouble than they're worth – don't they, Dad?'

'Huh! If they didn't before they will now you two have joined the ranks!' Then he rose and accepted Tag's farewell handshake. 'Good luck at any rate, son. Try and keep out of trouble.'

'Oh, I should be okay, sir. Jace won't be with me.'

'Gee, thanks, *partner*!'

Tag had been coming to the house for too long for Jace to stand on ceremony and see him to the door, so with no more than a casual 'See ya later!' to his friend he rejoined his father at the table.

But the faint hope that his dad might have asked how he and Tag were faring in their business endeavour, or even initiated a trite conversation about the weather faded when the man got to his feet grumbling that he needed to water the garden; after three days of almost relentless rain only a fool wouldn't have recognized it as a deliberate avoidance tactic. While the older man was prepared to assume a façade of semi tolerance when others were around, the message to his son was still being made loud and clear – *Don't expect my encouragement or blessing for this folly.*

CHAPTER 7

'Mind if I come in?'

From her prone position in the bed Tatum gave a facsimile of a shrug. 'It's your house.'

'Yes.' With precise movements Judy Benton closed the door. 'It is.'

Tatum groaned. 'The tough cop struck out so now it's the social worker's turn, huh? You're wasting your time –'

'No, *you're* wasting *my* time! I'm a patient person, Tatum, but I don't like being played for a fool. I believe you when you say you only wanted somewhere to sleep when you got in the car,' she said, 'but I'm not going to swallow the fact that you've survived on the streets for twelve months with thousands of dollars' worth of jewellery.'

'It's true –'

'It's *bullshit*!' Judy felt momentary satisfaction in knowing she'd jolted the girl, but her wide-eyed surprise didn't last long.

'So,' she sneered, 'this is where Mrs Middle Class Respectability gets down and dirty, huh? Is swearing some kind of pyschological ploy to get me to identify with you?'

Letting the accusation go undefended, Judy moved to sit on the edge of the bed. 'Tatum,' she said, keeping her voice calm, 'I see kids like you all the time. They come in all different shapes and sizes and a variety of backgrounds – fifth-generation Australian, migrant, poor and rich. In fact the only common denominator is the story they tell.'

There was a determination in the older woman's tone that told Tatum it was vital not to let her guard down. Nothing as obvious as the loud, gruff hostility of her cop husband, but a subtle firmness that seemed even more dangerous.

'Yeah, *so*?' she said, reinforcing the lack of interest in her voice by rolling on her side and pulling her hand away from the one that attempted to grasp it.

'*So* . . .' The woman addressed her back. 'I know how tough it is on the streets. Even in the refuges. And I know what it takes to get by. A kid with anything of value will hock it within the first few months just to survive . . . That is if someone even more desperate hasn't already stolen it from them.'

Tatum hated the cocksure certainty of the woman's tone, and the reality it washed over her. For a little while, lying here on clean fresh sheets, in this clean, pretty blue and white middle class bedroom, she'd been able to forget where she'd been, where she'd come from and what was waiting for her. Biting down on her trembling bottom lip, she wished she could shout, Liar! It's not like that! It's not like that at all!' But it was . . . and *she'd* lived it . . .

On the one occasion when she'd been hungry enough to think about hocking one of Fantasy's rings she'd made the

104

mistake of selecting a reputable pawn shop where they'd demanded proof of ownership, then tried to detain her when she'd had none. Except that the stalling tactics of the man behind the counter had been so transparent she might have still been pleading with him when the police had arrived; fortunately she'd picked up on the guy's impatient glances at the door and hightailed it out of there before he could stop her.

At the time she'd been crashing in a squat at Annandale, in Sydney's inner west, and when she'd returned and tried to find out from a few of the other kids where she might be able to sell some jewellery, they'd claimed they didn't know. That night she'd woken to find a stoned thirteen-year-old going through her stuff. Tatum had won the ensuing fight only because of the other girl's drugged out lethargy, and she'd quickly fled. But the incident had taught her not to let on what she carried in her backpack.

'Tatum . . .' Judy's voice broke gently into her thoughts. 'Where did you get the jewellery from?'

She turned angrily. 'I told you! It was my mother's.' She didn't explain that the gate bracelet was hers or how she'd come by it. It was hers and that was all that mattered! 'Damn it, why won't you believe me? I'm not a thief! I haven't stolen anyth-' She faltered. *But you have*! her conscience taunted. *You are a thief*!

'No . . .' The word broke on a half-sob as the memory surfaced of how a couple of weeks ago her hand had whipped out and snatched a bag of six bread rolls from an unattended bakery van. She hadn't meant to . . . it wasn't as if she'd *thought* about doing it . . . not really. But . . . but she'd been so hungry . . .

105

It wasn't until she felt the arm around her shoulder that she realized she was crying. To her own ears the noise she made was sickeningly pitiful, and the tears pouring down her cheeks burned just as hard and fast as they had the night Lulu had left her. For an endless time she was aware of nothing but an utter sense of isolation. It was an isolation she didn't understand, yet it was so crazily familiar it was almost as comforting as it was frightening.

'Tatum . . .' She heard the voice from a long way off, yet the word brushed her ear. She shivered, trying both to breathe and suppress the sobs racking her body.

'Tatum, love . . .' The voice, still gentle, seemed to penetrate both her blurred mind and vision; a face devoid of make-up, but with a concern wrinkled brow was almost directly in front of her own. 'Tell me what happened to you, Tatum.'

'I . . . I thought I'd . . .' Oh, God what *had* she thought, beyond getting as far away from Robin's lurid suggestions and wandering hands as possible? That she could really survive on her own? That she'd be able to get a job? That with no experience, no references, no skills someone would hire her? Say, Well, sure we'll take you on – even though you've got no clean clothes, nowhere to wash, nowhere to even live!?

'*What* did you think, Tatum?' the woman asked. 'That running away would be better than what you were leaving?'

Knowing what she did now, the question seemed designed to highlight her naïvety. It was all very well for this pillar of suburban motherhood to pass judgement

106

on what she'd done, but she had no idea how insulated her existence was from *life*. Real life.

'You haven't been on the streets for a year, have you, Tatum?'

Since there was little point in continuing the pretence, she shook her head, pulling a fistful of tissues from the box placed on her lap.

'How long has it been?'

For ever, she thought cynically, but the bitter laugh she tried for was overpowered by a hiccuped sob. 'A-about . . . f-f-five weeks,' she said finally, then gave her nose a healthy blow.

'Where were you living?'

'N-n-nowhere. Everywhere. S-sometimes I'd c-crash at a re-refuge or a . . . a squa – squa . . .'

'Squat?'

'Yeah . . . You know, an e-empty house or building . . . that's . . . waiting to be dem . . . ol . . . ished.'

'I know what a squat is. What I meant was where did you live *before* you were on the streets?'

'W-w-with a fr – friend.' Her tears were abating, but she was struggling to get her breathing back to normal.

'Here.' Judy handed her a glass, then filled it from the plastic water jug on the bedside table before getting to her feet.

'I . . . I don't suppose I . . . I could have a smoke?'

For a moment the woman looked confused, then shook her head. 'I've given up. Anyway, Brian won't allow smoking in the bedroom.'

That bit of information only made Tatum want one more. Brian Benton was the epitome of the tough, arrogant cop who thought his uniform made him God. She wondered what had made this woman marry him. Sure, he was good-looking, in an 'old' kind of way, but he was a pig in more ways than one as far as she could tell. He'd practically smirked when he'd told her that he'd discovered her mother had been on the game at one time. It had taken all Tatum's will power not to retort, *Ha*! Shows what you know! She was on the game *all* the time!

The woman walked to the end of the bed and began pacing back and forth, trailing her hand along the carved bedframe. After a few moments she looked up and ran a frustrated hand through her hair before speaking. 'Tatum, I *can* help you. I can find you a place to stay where you'll be safe, get you enrolled in some sort of skills training programme. You *can* turn your life around.'

'Yeah, right!' She didn't have to work at looking sceptical. In the time she'd been on the streets she'd heard all about what those rehabilitation schemes promised; she'd also seen their failure rate. 'And it's because all these *programmes* of yours are so successful that there are so many kids still in my position!'

'I won't insult your intelligence by arguing *that* point. I'm not suggesting these schemes are the perfect solution. As a social worker, I know more needs to be done, but right now they're all we've got, and for them to be any use at all takes effort from *everyone* involved.' Her expression turned to one of challenge. 'I *can* help you, Tatum. I *want* to help you. But you've got to want to help yourself. And you have to be honest with me. I want to know who this "friend" was and how you came to end up on the streets.'

Tatum looked down at the tissue she was shredding

onto the bedspread. Why, when the people she'd known and trusted all her life had let her down, should she believe a total stranger wanted to help her? And why, *why* did she so desperately want to put her faith in this woman? An ironic half-laugh slipped from her lips. Why? Because she didn't have any faith in herself any more; it was becoming harder and harder not to crawl back to the Cross and ask for Zeta's help.

'Tatum?' The tone sounded both patient and insistent. 'Who was this friend?'

'A . . . a guy called Christopher. He was a . . . a friend of . . . of my mother's.' Tatum wasn't sure when she'd decided that she wasn't going to mention Lulu, only that she had. If what Lu had said about the police being involved with the pushers who'd supplied Fantasy her junk was right, then telling anyone about her, especially the wife of a cop, was asking for trouble.

'Boyfriend?'

The absurdity of the suggestion made her laugh. 'No.'

'But he took you in when your mother died?'

'Yeah,' she said. 'Christopher let me move in with him. If you don't believe me, you can check out the records at the high school near where he lived.' It was a safe challenge. When she'd been unable to return to Chelmsford, Lulu had suggested she use Christopher's Manly address to get into a school on the other side of the harbour, where there was less chance anyone would learn about her background. Sometimes, to spare herself the cross-town trip back to Darlinghurst, she'd stay overnight at Christopher's.

'You attended school while you were living with this

109

Christopher?' The quick upward motion of the woman's eyebrow was enough to show the admission was unexpected. 'Okay,' she said quickly. 'And what did he do? Did he have a job or was he on social security?'

Judy Benton was so quick to assume her background was financially disadvantaged that Tatum decided to tell the absolute truth – just for the satisfaction of taking her down a peg or two.

'He's a sound expert for a recording studio. Actually, he's an *executive* of EarWell Recording.'

'How old is this . . . Christopher?'

'Twenty-nine.'

'I see. Were you . . . er . . .?'

'Were we sleeping together?' Tatum inserted. The woman's discomfort made her feel the playing field was evening out. She smirked. 'Let's see . . .' she said in a taunting voice. 'Since that bloodhound hubby of yours has already ferreted out the fact my mother was on the game, I wonder which would shock you the most – a yes or a no?'

Judy sighed. With tears now spent, aggression again came to the fore. She'd lost count of the number of kids she'd seen try and mask their despair behind a façade of toughness, little knowing how transparent the action was.

'I'm not interested in anything you gave your consent to, Tatum. I was going to ask if Christopher had abused – '

'No! In his own way Christopher *loved* me.' That she was desperate to believe that was evident from the intensity of her words.

'Plenty of men claim to love the women they abuse. It's what keeps them victims. It's also one of the reasons

110

abused women are slow to seek help from refuges. And . . .' She paused. '*The main reason they do.*'

'Christopher wasn't like that! He was always good to me.'

'So good you preferred to take your chances starving on the streets?'

'It wasn't him! I . . . It wasn't his fault not . . . not really . . .' Frustration was etched in her face and actions as she combed her fingers through her mass of thick black hair.

'If not him then who?' Judy asked, knowing that to back off now would give the girl time to secure her emotional guard. 'Who frightened you so much that you ran?'

'His lover.' The response was given with a bent head and came in a rush. 'Robin. Robin . . . didn't like me; said Christopher had to choose whether he wanted me or he wanted Robin.'

'This Robin . . .' Judy prompted. 'She imagined there was something going on between you and Chri – ?' She broke of in the face of Tatum's laughter.

'God! You are so middle-class *wholesome*!' she accused. 'Robin was a *bloke*, not a girl! Christopher is *gay*!'

'I . . . I see.'

'No! No, you don't *see*. Christopher loves me in his own way but he has no sexual interest in me or any other female! Robin, however, will screw anything that moves regardless of sex. He wanted both Christopher *and* me.' Tatum didn't bother gauging what effect her revelations were having on the older woman; she wanted only to purge herself of the guilt she felt.

'At first I thought I was imagining the way he would

find excuses to brush up against me or . . . or touch me. I . . . I didn't feel threatened by him because . . . well, because I considered myself *safe*. Then one day I was sunbathing out on the balcony alone, when Robin came home early. He offered to rub more oil into my back and I said okay. I mean, it was like having Christopher or another woman do it, you know?' The question was a rhetorical one. 'The next minute he was kissing my back and . . . and his hands were – ' She broke off with a shudder of distaste.

Judy moved back to sit beside her. This time she met no resistance when she took hold of her trembling hands. 'Did he rape you, Tatum?'

The girl shook her head.

'Christopher arrived home while I was fighting him off. Robin said there was no point telling him what had happened because he'd deny it and Christopher would believe *him*.' She paused and turned to Judy with confused brown eyes. 'It was true. Christopher was crazy in love with him. He'd already told me that he'd do whatever it took to hang onto Robin.'

'So that's when you decided to leave?'

'No. I thought if I managed to avoid being alone with Robin things would be okay.' She paused, seemingly to collect herself, before continuing. 'I tried to work it so I was only at home when Christopher was there too, but one night they were having a party. Everyone was pretty out of it – Christopher could barely stay awake, you know – and they thought it was funny when Robin started coming on to me.' Her eyes narrowed hatefully. 'He was acting like it was a real big joke, except I knew he wasn't just fooling

112

around. After a while Christopher flaked out and people started to leave, but Robin just kept . . . watching me and . . . and saying things . . .' She looked at Judy. 'You know, things like . . . uh . . .'

'Sexually suggestive remarks?'

'Yeah. But sicko stuff, you know. Anyway, I started getting real scared. I went into my room, but there weren't locks on any of the doors. Nowhere I could hide until morning, or until Christopher surfaced again.' Tatum paused, recalling how completely helpless she'd felt. How her stomach had rolled with fear and dread at the thought of Robin carrying out his perverse threats. Shaking her head to dispel the ugly images in her mind, she hurried to finish the story.

'I realized then that even if I could find a way of avoiding Robin that night, he wasn't going to stop hassling me. And that's when I decided I had to get away. For good. So I shoved some stuff in my backpack and snuck out while there were still enough people around to keep him occupied.'

As memories of her time on the streets rolled through her mind like a fast-forwarded video hatred rose swift and bitter inside her. She'd escaped one hell only to land in another. The irony of her life made her angry, and she lifted her head to glare at the woman who stupidly thought social workers were the modern-day equivalent of fairy godmothers.

'So now you know. Satisfied?'

Judy was more sickened than satisfied, the fact of girl's escape before she was physically violated providing only minuscule relief. Instinctively she wanted to spare the youngster further pain, but there was still the matter of proving ownership of the jewellery.

'If I contacted Christopher,' Judy went on, 'would he back up your story that the jewellery belongs to you? That it was your mother's?'

Alarm raced through Tatum. 'No! I mean, he knows it's mine, but you can't contact him!'

'Why's that? I'd have thought you'd *want* to prove you can support your story.'

'Because . . . because . . . Robin might answer and deny they knew me!' Tatum said quickly, realizing only as she said the words that this was a real possibility. Robin was the type of scum who'd get off on revenge. 'He hates me,' she said.

The girl could merely have been trying to avoid having her story shown up for a lie, Judy reasoned, but what she said made sense, and she wanted to give her every opportunity to prove her honesty.

'What if I offered to take you to see Christopher when Robin wasn't there? Would you agree?' Silent suspicion was Tatum's only response. 'The way I see it, Tatum,' Judy continued, 'it would be the simplest way of confirming your story.'

'Christopher won't believe anything bad about Robin.'

'Then more fool him. But all I'm interested in is that he unconditionally agrees the jewellery belongs to you.' Seeing the resistance in the girl's face lessening, she pressed onward. 'We wouldn't have to go until you felt a better . . . Say the day after tomorrow.'

'What day is that?'

Judy frowned. '*You don't know?*'

'Hey, I didn't have much need to keep an appointment diary recently! On the streets it's hard to tell where one day ends and the next begins!'

'Today's Saturday,' Judy responded, feeling chastened. 'We could go Mon – ' She stopped in the face of the girl's shaking head.

'If we go tomorrow there's less chance Robin will be there,' she said. 'He goes sailing nearly every Sunday.'

'I'm not sure Dr Prendergast wants you up and about that soon. Perhaps we could see Christopher at the recording company?'

'No. Robin works there too.'

Judy considered her options for a few moments as she studied the girl's still less than healthy pallor. 'All right,' she said finally. 'If I think you're well enough, we'll go tomorrow.'

Apprehension skated along Tatum's spine as the elevator doors slid shut on the basement car park and she pushed the button that would take them up to the penthouse. For the entire drive from the quiet inner-western suburb of Strathfield to the beachside Manly development her mind had played out various possible scenarios of what would happen when they reached the door of Christopher's apartment. None of them filled her with hope. And none of them had prepared her for the overwhelming urge she had to cry at the split second of disappointment she saw in Christopher's eyes before he pulled her into an enthusiastic bear hug.

'Tatum! My darling, darling girl! Wherever have you been? You've had us so worried!'

'But not worried enough to file a missing person report?'

At Judy's words Tatum felt Christopher stiffen with resentment, or perhaps it was guilt. But she was too worried he'd say the wrong thing to analyse his body language now.

'Er, Christopher,' she said hurriedly, bringing his indignant eyes from Judy and back to her. 'This is a . . . a friend of mine, Judy Benton. She's a social work-er, her husband is a *cop* . . .' She accompanied her words with an intense go-with-me-on-this look. 'I told her how I've been living with you and going to school locally *ever since Fantasy died.* She wants to . . . er . . . ask you some things.'

Tatum didn't dare look at Judy Benton to see if she'd heard the cryptic warning in her words to Christopher, but the gregarious smile that started to spread across Christopher's handsome face told her he'd gone into full-on suck-up mode.

'Well, good!' he said. 'That means I'll have the company of two gorgeous ladies at least long enough to treat you to some of my special blend coffee. Do come in, Ms Benton. I'll be more than happy to answer any enquiries you have. Tatum darling will take you through to the living room while I whip the kettle on.'

At forty-four Judy was still young enough to appreciate Christopher Creighton's incredible good looks and mas-culine physique, but even had she not been married and already aware of his sexual preference she knew he'd never have been capable of stirring her on either a physical or emotional level. She'd sensed an insecurity in him that hinted at a self-centred 'clinger' rather than a strong, independent adult. And even seeing the obviously expensive furnishings and art that shouted at financial security didn't alter her opinion but merely added to his plastic 'Ken Doll' image rather than that of the successful businessman Tatum had portrayed him as being.

After being caught off guard initially, he'd displayed a genuine fondness for Tatum – genuine, but not very deep. A few hours ago she'd toyed with the idea that perhaps Tatum had overreacted and misinterpreted Robin's interest in her, and that there might have been some way of resolving the issue. But now Judy had no intention of trying to re-establish Tatum's residency here. When she left here this afternoon Tatum would be with her, and so would as many of her remaining possessions as Judy could cram into her car!

When Jace arrived home, shortly before dinner, his parents were debating the merits of half a dozen snapshots scattered on the kitchen table.

'These are photos Christopher Creighton had,' his mother said. 'They show Tatum's mother wearing some of the jewellery.'

Jace's curiosity led him to inspect the shots of a stunningly attractive brunette standing with a young girl in school uniform; obviously Tatum *before* she'd hit the streets.

'*Some* of the Jewellery,' his father put in pointedly. 'And that doesn't prove the stuff wasn't hot anyway.'

'She doesn't look like a hooker.' Jace's casual observation brought a grunt from his father.

'Francesa Milano, or *Fantasy*, as she called herself,

wasn't your regular street prostitute. She was a *big bucks* call-girl with a high-glass clientele.'

'*Which*,' his mother said, 'only makes her ownership of the jewellery seem all the more valid! Especially since the police don't have any record of pieces fitting their description listed as stolen property!'

Again his father grunted. Brian Benton had grunts down to an artform, so that his meaning was clear even to people who, unlike Jace, hadn't grown up interpreting them. His last one had been of the that-doesn't-prove-anything variety, tinged with a reluctant trace of I-suppose-I-*could*-be-wrong. But at his wife's triumphant smile he demanded to know what she intended doing *now* with *her* 'house guest', because he wanted his damn bed back!

'I've spoken with Father Cleary down at the youth refuge,' she explained. 'He thinks he'll be able to take her in tomorrow for a couple of weeks while I get her social security entitlements sorted out and find somewhere more permanent for her to stay. I'll also take her down and have her checked out at the women's clinic. For tonight, though, she'll sleep in the spare room. 'Oh, and by the way, she'll be joining us at the table for dinner tonight, and I don't want *anyone* saying *anything* that'll make her feel any more uncomfortable than she already does.' Much of his mother's attempt at generalization was defeated by the way she glared at her husband during the issuing of the terse warning.

Not even the tense silence and the four pairs of eyes Tatum felt watching her could distract her from the meal which had just been set before her. It was so long since she'd seen so much food, much less had the opportunity of eating it, that the plate of mashed potatoes, carrots, beans and crumbed lamb cutlets swimming in thick dark gravy seemed like manna from heaven.

Holding her breath, as much from reverence as disbelief at her good fortune, she picked up her knife and fork and cut off a generous piece of the meat. It took all her will power not to moan with pleasure as her mouth closed on the hot, succulent lamb; nothing, *nothing* – not even Christopher's fabulously exotic meals – had ever tasted so good! Even before she'd swallowed, her fork was loaded and poised to deliver a second serving of bliss.

Watching the kid eat made Jace feel guilty for having accepted a lifetime comprising three meals a day as unconsciously as he did breathing. Being aware that there were people living in twentieth-century Australia who went without even one regular meal a day was entirely different from being confronted with evidence of it. Just as reading about the fatalities of the heroin epidemic hadn't had the crippling impact that having it encroach on his safe, sterile existence had done.

He wondered how long Doug had gone without a decent meal before he died; how long he'd been addicted before the need for his next fix had taken priority over the need for his next meal. And he wondered if Antony, the spoilt, pampered son of the Perelli family that he and Tag were currently trying to locate, was at this minute regretting his decision to run away.

'Jace, pass the pepper, please.'

As he responded to his brother's request Jace noted the silently tense eye contact bouncing between his parents.

His mother was visually saying, See, you were wrong. The jewellery *is* hers. The old man, however, clearly wasn't convinced, or at least wasn't prepared to admit he was wrong, despite the evidence. So far Brian Benton had kept his mouth occupied with his meal and nothing else, but if the waif-like brunette opposite him wasn't feeling uncomfortable with the awkward, unnatural silence around the dining room, she was the only one who wasn't.

Tatum glanced up and found herself under the intense gaze of Judy Benton's dark-haired son. The one who'd caught her in the car. 'You got a problem?' she asked him.

'Heaps. If you've got a spare day or two I could give you a brief rundown.'

'Like I give a damn!'

'*Jason.*' His mother's warning not to respond was evident to everyone. Surprisingly, though, his father elected to spring to his defence.

'Jason was merely answering a question.'

'It was more a challenge than a question, Dad,' Jace said. 'But that's okay, so long as she doesn't decide she wants to start throwing any more punches my way.' His fingers touched his eyebrow and he grimaced theatrically, trying to coax a smile from the kid. 'Might marr my good looks permanently.'

'What looks?' she snapped. 'I've seen better bloody faces on the south end of northbound camels, you arsehole!'

Well, so much for a bit of light-hearted stirring! Jace thought drily, not needing to look at his father to know he was red-faced.

'Now, just one minute, young lady! I won't put up with that kind of language in – '

120

'Stop it now!' Judy Benton's voice rose voice above the outraged one of her husband. '*I will not tolerate this barbaric behaviour at the table*! Not from *anyone*.' Her glare moved over both her sons and her husband before settling on the sullen-looking girl to her left. 'Everyone appreciates you aren't entirely comfortable being here, Tatum, but there's no need for you to be deliberately rude.'

'Who's rude? I was being *honest*.' Her deadpan reply drew a muffled chuckle from Ethan.

'*That's enough, Tatum*! Either you agree to be civil for the remainder of the meal or leave the table now. I'm not about to put up with you insulting my family while you're sharing our dinner table. Is that understood?'

As three sets of arrogant male eyes watched her expectantly, Tatum wished she had the will power to get up and walk from the room. But Judy had promised that dessert would follow the main meal and she wasn't going to cut her throat to save her pride! Hating herself for being so weak, she shrugged and picked up her fork. 'Sure,' she said, then mumbled, 'It's not like I haven't eaten in *worse* company'

The angry glare she sent Jace left no doubt as to whom her comment was directed at.

With the surly-faced departure of Tatum Milano from the Benton home the following morning Jace assumed it would be the last he saw or heard of her, but that wasn't the case. His mother continued to keep the family monitored on how the kid was faring with life at the refuge, Yet after three weeks, while Judy Benton was confident the girl had the potential to be 'turned around', few others shared her conviction.

'I just can't understand it!' she complained one evening as she hung up the phone in the family room. 'I was *sure* things were going to work out for Tatum with the O'Connors.'

Jace looked up from the shot he was about to make, which would sink the last of the red balls and put him a few points up on his grandfather. 'What's happened *now*? Did she poison a pet dog this time?'

Grandpa Benton chuckled. Like everyone else, he'd heard how the first family who'd agreed to take Tatum in had changed their minds when she'd overfed their tank of exotically expensive tropical fish.

'That's not funny, Jason,' his mother chided. 'She was trying to be helpful.'

Having made the shot, he grinned at his grandfather. 'Kinda makes you wonder how dangerous she'd be if she *wasn't* trying to help, doesn't it?'

'You gonna chatter or take your next shot, son? I'd hate to die of old age before I beat you *four* times in a row.'

'Dream on, old man.'

'Honestly, can't you pair stop clunking those stupid snooker balls while I'm trying to think?'

At his daughter-in-law's frustrated outburst, Bryce Benton frowned at Jace and racked his cue. 'How 'bout fetchin' yer old grandpa a beer, son? We can finish this later,' he said tactfully.

'Sure. Mum, you want a glass of wine or something?' She nodded distractedly, and, replacing his cue, Jace moved to the pine bar in the corner of the room as his grandfather guided his mum to the sofa.

'So what did this infamous Tatum I've heard so much about do this time?' he asked.

'That depends on whose story you believe, Bryce. According to what Mrs O'Connor told Father Cleary, Tatum punched her son Keiran in the face for no reason and broke his nose.'

'Well, gee, Mum,' Jace interrupted, 'I personally don't find *that* scenario too difficult to believe.' The comment earned him thin-lipped disapproval as his mother continued.

'Tatum claims both Keiran and his brother have been trying to, in her words, "hit on her" ever since she moved in a week ago, and that Keiran bailed her up in the laundry yesterday afternoon while they were home alone and tried to kiss her and – '

'Let me guess,' Jace said, handing his mum a glass of red wine. 'And she socked him one in self-defence?'

Judy bit her lower lip. 'Er, no, she said she didn't punch him – '

'Yeah, right. The guy busted his own nose!'

'She *said* – ' Judy Benton spoke over her son's scorn ' – that she *head butted* him.'

Riotous laughter burst from both Jace and his grandfather at the same time. Jace could just picture the little hellcat belting her forehead hard into some guy's face, and he was willing to bet a stream of vitriolic Italian had followed the action. Nothing so tepid as a slap in the face and an indignant How dare you! for that feral female.

123

'It's no laughing matter.' Concern was etched deep into Judy Benton's brow.

'Surely if what the girl says is true, Judy, she should be allowed to go back to the refuge.'

'Father Cleary can't keep finding a bed for her at a moment's notice. His programme is only set up for short-term accommodation until someone in the parish can provide something permanent. When a kid is placed with a family, such as Tatum was with the O'Connors and before that with the Wangs, someone else takes their bed at the youth centre; actually it's just a big old Victorian house.'

She paused and sighed despondently. 'Peter Cleary and the other volunteers do a good job, but it's only a small, privately operated project supported by a trust fund set up by one of Peter's former parishioners and two local Catholic churches.'

'But surely there someone else who'll take Tatum in?'

'Maybe,' Judy Benton conceded. 'Although it looks doubtful; unfortunately Tatum is rapidly getting a reputation for being a wilful, irresponsible troublemaker.'

'Not to mention *violent*,' Jace added.

'She is *not* violent!'

Raising his scarred eyebrow in his mother's direction, Jace said, '*Right*.'

'Seems to me this girl's got yer more bothered than most, Judy,' Bryce Benton said sagely. 'What's so special about her?'

Jace watched a dozen different expressions cross his mother's face; she took a thoughtful sip of her drink before answering. 'I'm not sure. It's just that there's *something* about her. Something that makes me feel she's worth that extra bit of effort.' She shook her head and smiled at her father-in-law.

'I'm not saying she's not a prickly, smart-mouthed little thing, but in lots of ways she seems almost naïve. But she's really bright! She wanted to go back to school rather than start one of the youth training programmes . . .' The enthusiasm in his mother's voice was reflected in her face. 'I checked out her record at the high school she finished at last year and the boarding-school she went to in South Australia. She was a top student at both!'

Not surprisingly Bryce Benton frowned. '*Boardin'*-school? I thought Brian said she was the daughter of a hooker?'

'She is. Apparently, though, her mum wasn't your garden variety prostitute,' Jace explained. 'From what I've heard round the Cross, those high-class call-girls earn really big bucks. I guess rather than have a pretty young thing who was bound to eventually create competition under her feet, it was easier for Mother Milano to pack the kid off to a swish private school interstate.'

Bryce Benton nodded. 'The sort where as long as yer pay the fees they don't ask questions. Or leastways they're prepared to believe whatever lies they're told once the cheque's cleared.'

Jace grinned. 'And I bet Tatum Milano batted those big brown eyes of hers and told them some whoppers! She struck me as the type who could shovel bullshit until you were neck-deep in it and still convince you the earth was flat.'

'Jason Benton! You have no reason to say such things

about Tatum. Everything she's said so far has turned out to be *true*. Despite your father's best efforts to prove otherwise!'

'Big brown eyes, eh?' His grandfather smirked. 'Guess you private investigators have got a real good memory for takin' in minute details like that.'

'Yeah.' The response was out before Jace thought to question the amusement lurking in his grandfather's eyes. By the time he did the old man was again addressing his mother.

'Is the girl going to school now?'

'Yes,' Judy said. 'The local high. I've talked with the councillor there, but her grades are only average. She's barely completing half her set homework and isn't mingling well with the other students.' She frowned. 'Still, it can't be easy going to a school made up of upper middle-class families and having everyone know you're a charity case.' Again she sighed. 'I guess that's what I find most frustrating – *knowing* that given the chance of an equal footing Tatum would probably outstrip ninety per cent of those kids academically. And she's naturally athletic as well.'

'In that case, Mum, maybe you ought to get her involved in the sport programme down at the youth club,' Jace suggested. 'After all, Dad reckons the boxing team only needs one kid who can throw a halfway decent punch for them to take out the regional championships.' He laughed. 'Hell, with Tatum they'd probably have a shot at taking the nationals!'

'You know, Jason,' his mother said, '*sometimes* what you say can be quite brilliant!'

* * *

126

Tatum completed filling out the registration card, signed it and aggressively shoved it back across the desk. 'There!' she said. 'Done.'

The man on the opposite side picked it up and scrutinized the details before flipping it back on the desk and leaning back in his chair. Staring at her with intense blue eyes, he folded his arms.

'Let's get one thing straight, young lady,' he said. 'I'm no more thrilled at having you here than you are to be here, so don't think your being objectionable is going to ruin my day any more than your presence already has, okay?'

Tatum made no response except to fold her arms in mirror likeness to his.

'Now,' he said. 'If you'll tell me what sport you're interested in doing, I'll take you down to the course instructor.'

'What makes you think I'm interested in doing any? I might've changed my mind. And once you leave the room I could walk out of the class and be gone before you could do anything to stop me.'

The man's smile was genuinely amused. 'Trust me, I wouldn't even *try* to stop you. I'm accepting you into the sport programme only because Judy asked me to, not for any other reason. Which is the same reason *you're* here – to impress my wife.'

'Hey, I don't have to impress *anybody*! If I'm here it's because *I feel* like being here! Okay?'

Brian Benton grinned. 'Good. Then what is it you *feel* like doing? Today being Tuesday you have a choice of basketball, squash, badminton, aerobics, weights and jazz ballet for beginners. Wednesdays there's – '

Tatum groaned. 'Spare me the rundown of the week's activity roster; Judy already told me. I want to do aerobics and judo.'

'Why?'

'Because.'

'Because why?'

'Because I've always wanted to wear one of those really skimpy Lycra suits they wear doing aerobics!' she said. 'You know, the kind that are cut so high across the bum they look like a G-string?'

'I see,' Brian Benton said, giving Tatum the first real smile she'd seen form on his face. 'And I suppose you chose judo because you like white pyjamas?'

Tatum clamped her teeth shut so she *would not* smile and stared him down.

'Well, while we can oblige with the pyjamas, most of the kids here wear bike shorts and T-shirts to do aerobics. You might feel a bit conspicuous in a pseudo G-string.'

'I'll try not to let it worry me.' Determinedly she held his gaze without blinking, wanting him to be the one to look away first. She won.

'It wouldn't hurt you to let your guard down occasionally,' he said, in a gruff attempt at gentleness. 'Not everyone is out to get you.'

'Right.' She was relieved when Benton's square jaw tensed again. In his tough cop mode she knew what to expect; she didn't trust his attempts at civility.

'You know, Tatum, attack isn't *always* the best defence. There are some situations where passive resistance is a person's best option.'

'Not where I come from. There you either go down fighting or you go down *hard. And fast.*'

The flash of sympathy in his eyes made Tatum wish the words back. They'd come out only because he'd caught her off guard. It was the first time he'd addressed her by name rather than the term 'young lady' which he usually managed to make sound like an insult. But she didn't want anyone's pity – least of all a judgemental cop's!

'Well, are you going to take me down to the instructor or not? I didn't come here to sit in this crummy office all afternoon.'

After studying her with narrowed eyes for several moments the man got to his feet, once again showing from where his overgrown sons had inherited their height and bulk.

'After your class come back up here to the office,' he said, leading the way to a flight of stairs that descended to a lower level. 'Judy thought you might like to come home for dinner. If not, I'll drive you back to the refuge.'

Tatum paused on the stairs. 'Why?'

'Because it'll be dark and it'll be safer than you walking alone.'

'I mean *why* does Judy want me to come to dinner?'

'Probably because she enjoys your warm personality and scintillating conversation.'

Tatum again found she had to fight a smile, so she lowered her head and let her hair hide her face.

'So what's it to be?' Benton asked. 'A home-cooked meal or hit and miss at the refuge?'

Tatum refused to surrender too quickly. 'What's Judy cooking?'

'Since it's Tuesday, it's bound to be a roast dinner.'

God, how long had it been since she'd had a baked dinner? she wondered, swallowing fiercely as her mouth watered. Aware that Brian Benton was waiting with amused indulgence, Tatum lifted her chin and in a barely interested tone asked, 'Chicken or lamb?'

'Beef, I think. But I couldn't guess at dessert.'

Hell, it wouldn't matter to Tatum if there *wasn't* any dessert! One serving of roast beef and she'd die happy!

'Well . . . *okay*,' she said, as if making a sacrifice. 'I guess I'll come.'

The unexpected laugh that came from the cop startled her as it bounced off the walls of the otherwise empty lower level lobby. 'It's too bad those eyes of yours are so expressive, Tatum,' he said, holding open a door so she could pass through ahead of him. 'Otherwise you'd make a hell of an actress!'

CHAPTER 8

May 1988

At the sound of her husband's car in the driveway Judy stopped placing the serviettes around the table and handed them to her father-in-law.

'They're here. I'll start bringing in dinner. And remember,' she warned, 'not a word to Tatum until I say so. If you spring it on her the moment she's in the door she'll instinctively buck at the idea.'

'Yer worryin' 'bout nothing, Judy, me girl.' The comment was accompanied by a confident, knowing nod. 'I talked Brian round to agreein', didn't I?'

Recalling the battle royal which had taken place in her kitchen a fortnight ago, when Bryce had first voiced the idea of Tatum going to live with him, Judy limited herself to non-commital response. Like her husband, she, too, had initially rejected the suggestion as ludicrous, although *she'd* refrained from shouting that the idea was proof positive that Bryce should be committed! *How*, Brian had demanded, was a seventy-eight-year-old man with an artificial hip going to look after a rebellious sixteen-year-old girl?

'Won't have to,' Bryce had replied. 'She's old enough to

look after herself. Sounds to me like she's been doing it most of her life anyway.'

It had been a valid point, but even Judy hadn't been swayed by it. Because of her past, Tatum was instinctively self-centred – not maliciously so, but more than enough to prove a difficult housemate for even the most laid-back individual; the concept that she and Brian's stubborn, elderly father could coexist in the same house seemed far-fetched at best. A point Judy had tried to get across to Bryce between her husband's less rational rantings and ravings against the idea.

She might as well have saved her breath, because typically neither Benton male had been listening to her – Brian roaring that his father had no idea what he was suggesting and Bryce deliberately goading Brian by calling him 'sonny' and 'kid'. By the time both had wound down enough to let Judy get a word in edgewise, Bryce had been frowning so deeply at all the negative aspects of the notion she'd raised that Brian became sympathetic to him.

'I can understand that you want to help the girl, Dad,' he'd said gently. 'And your offer is a generous one. But, like Judy pointed out, it's not simply a matter of finding her a place to stay. Emotionally the girl needs a lot of support.'

Of course, Bryce had a cunning, manipulative streak, which he employed when he wanted to get his own way, and it was at this stage that he'd played his trump card.

'Yer right, Bri,' he'd said, in a tone that hinted he was surrendering. 'But how 'bout we make a deal . . .? What if Tatum came and stayed with me on a trial basis, like. Say . . . oh, three months – '

'Damn it, Dad! Haven't you heard a word we've said? Tatum wouldn't last three days with you! She didn't last more than a week with those other two families, and they were better equipped mentally and physically to deal with a teenager!' Brian had retorted. 'With your age and recent health record you'd be buying nothing but trouble. In fact the smartest thing you could do would be to sell that great useless house and move into a retirement villa, like the family want you to!'

'I will,' Bryce had said smartly. But even before Judy and her husband had stopped reeling from the shock of the words, the old man had been adding a condition. 'If Tatum moves in with me and it doesn't work out I'll sell up and do what you've all been hounding me to do. *But* if Tatum and me *do* get along, then you've all got to drop this retirement home crap. Agreed?'

'It'll never work, Dad!'

'*Agreed*?' the old man had repeated.

Seeing the determined look in her father-in-law's eyes, Judy had only been able to shrug when her husband had appealed for input from her. The old man was more worked up over this than he'd been about anything else for years – except, of course, the idea of moving to a retirement complex – and, given his age, Judy was reluctant to make matters worse. Besides, she'd thought, maybe, *just maybe*, the arrangement *could* work. If so, it would have dual benefits; Tatum would have somewhere permanent to live and it would ease the family's worries about the elderly Bryce being alone in his house.

Tentatively she'd said as much to Brian, but, realizing he'd need time to cool down and consider the issue more fully, had suggested all three of them think the idea over for a while longer. 'It's probably best to wait a couple of weeks before putting it to Tatum anyway,' she'd said. 'Give her a chance to settle into school and everything first.'

Well, Judy thought, D-day was now upon them.

'Reckon she'll say yes?' her father-in-law asked, looking as eager as a kid on Christmas Eve about broaching the idea with Tatum.

Judy shrugged. 'Who knows? Trying to anticipate what Tatum's reaction to *anything* will be is crystal ball stuff. If there's one thing I've learned about that girl,' she said, smiling, 'it's that she's as unpredictable as an earthquake and potentially as destabilizing.' The admission prompted her to ask, 'Are you sure about this, Bryce? It's not too late to change your mind, and Brian's still only lukewarm about the whole thing.'

'I'm sure. Hell, I really like the kid!'

Judy shook her head. 'You like strawberries too, and *they* give you hives.'

Tatum had come to look forward to the twice-weekly dinners she had at the Benton house – and not merely for the food! The first night Brian had brought her home from the youth club, his father, Bryce, had also been there for dinner. Although Tatum had initially felt uncomfortable with his presence, he'd had her laughing, *really laughing*, within a few minutes of her sitting down. He was bright, witty and didn't bullshit. Tatum liked him. She liked him a lot.

'What was it tonight?' Bryce asked, passing her the

platter of baked vegetables. 'Aerobics or judo?'

'Judo.'

'Neither of the boys going to be here for dinner, Judy?' Brian's question was directed at his wife.

'Ethan's over at Donna's and Jason . . .' Judy shrugged. 'Well, who knows *where* he is?'

Brian grunted with disapproval at the response, but Tatum was relieved. Ethan had been friendly enough the first time she'd come here for dinner, but, while he hadn't been the primary bully the night she'd first 'met' the Benton family, he reminded her of an incident she'd sooner forget. As for Ethan's twin brother, the dark-haired Jason . . . Well, revenge didn't have a use-by date; still, she counted herself lucky that he'd so far been absent each time she'd visited.

'So how's life at the refuge, Tatum?' Bryce enquired casually. So *casually* that Judy wanted to throttle her father-in-law!

'Okay. A new girl came into our room last night. She's from the country somewhere.'

'Reckon things must be gettin' pretty cramped over there, eh?'

Tatum rolled her eyes. '*Getting*? I've felt like a bloody sardine ever since I moved in there.' Though the old man chuckled, both Judy and Brian were frowning. Brian at her, presumably because she'd sworn, and Judy at her father-in-law for . . . Well, presumably because he'd *laughed*.

'Must make studyin' hard,' the grey-haired man said, his eyes sparkling with mirth, as if the notion pleased him. 'I mean the noise an' all.'

135

'It's no big deal,' she lied. Finding somewhere quiet was impossible.

'Have you – ?'

'Tatum,' Judy said, abruptly cutting off her father-in-law, 'How's . . . er . . . how's your meal?'

The hissed chuckle Bryce emitted and the subsequent glare Judy gave him caused Tatum to look from one to the other. 'Great,' she replied, confusion overpowering any enthusiasm in her tone.

'Oh, good. I'm glad you like it.'

''Course it's great!' Bryce was still cackling. 'What were you 'spectin' her to say?'

'Have you pair been getting into my good Scotch?' Brian asked, eyeing the two suspiciously.

'I don't drink Scotch. You know that,' Judy said defensively.

'I do though, son. And now that you mention it I wouldn't mind a wee drop.' Tatum giggled at the impish wink the older man directed at her. He was a sweet old rogue.

'Nice try, Dad,' Brian said. 'But Scotch's one of the things the doctors want you to limit.'

'*Limit*. Not *ban*,' the older man muttered. 'Bloody doctors only want people to live just so as they can be miserable.'

Amusement lifted the edges of Brian's mouth. 'I'll give you one before I drive you home,' he promised. 'In the meantime, if you want a glass of wine with your dinner I'll get you one.'

The older man grunted. Tatum decided it was a family thing.

'Thanks, but I'll wait for the Scotch. Don't know how a man can drink that damn wine! Tastes like piss mixed with vinegar.'

'No, it doesn't,' Tatum objected. 'It's nice.'

'Is that a fact?' Bryce said. 'Aren't you a little young to be drinking.'

'*Yes, Dad, she is.*' Though Brian Benton addressed his father it was Tatum who received his visual disapproval.

'Yeah, well . . .' she mumbled. 'I've only *tried* it a few times.'

'Well, you drink piss mixed with vinegar and then tell me they don't taste the same!'

'*Dad.* That's enough. From you too,' Brian added, when Tatum's laughter got the better of her. 'Honestly, you're both as bad as each other.'

'No, they're not, Dad. Grandpa's never split my eye open with a right hook!'

The intrusive voice had every head pivoting to the six-foot-plus leather and denim-clad male grinning from the archway to the hall.

'Actually, that's something I need cleared up,' he went on, amusement lurking in his eyes as they stayed on Tatum. '*Was* it your right or your left that did the damage?'

Embarrassment at being ridiculed in front of everyone brought heat to Tatum's temper as well as her cheeks. 'Put your face closer and I'll give you a definite answer.'

'Ah, good one, Tatum!' Bryce cheered. 'The kid always was too cheeky for his own good.'

'Thanks, Grandpa. Whatever happened to your "blood's thicker than water" ideal?'

'Runs a poor second to a good fight these days, son.'

Easy male laughter reverberated in the room, the late arrival saying, 'In that case maybe I can talk Tatum into hitting *you*? What about it, Tate? Think you could get the better of the old codger?'

'Ha!' his grandfather retorted. 'If she does she'll be the first ever.'

'Don't be too cocky, Dad,' his son cautioned. 'You're a mite slower since you had that hip operation. And Tatum here's been taking judo lessons for three weeks, now . . .'

'Oh, for heaven's sakes, you lot, cut it out!' Judy said. 'You're embarrassing Tatum and what's more I don't care to listen to a load of macho bull. Now, sit down, Jason, and I'll get you something to eat.'

'Stay put and finish your own meal,' her husband told her. 'He's big enough, smart enough and ugly enough to help himself to whatever he wants.'

'Which, dear husband, is *exactly* what I'm afraid of! He's likely to help himself to *everything* that's left.'

Smiling unrepentantly, her son remained propped in the archway, and as Judy departed for the kitchen Tatum had to bite her tongue to stop herself from asking Brian Benton if he'd picked out a name for a guide dog. True his son was *big*, and a smartass jerk, but not even *she* could lie well enough to call him *ugly* – and she had reason to hate his guts! Not only had he been rough and smug when he'd caught her that night at the car, but he rubbed her the wrong way just by *breathing*.

If she hadn't thought slugging the guy a second time would backfire on her, he'd be unconscious in a heartbeat! She smiled, enjoying the mental image, then quickly lowered her head over her plate so none of the bantering males noticed. No, pleasurable as the thought of drawing more blood from pretty-boy Benton was, Tatum knew she couldn't risk screwing up again or she'd find herself back on the streets quick-smart. Father Pete had already said any more trouble and she was out the door – like it had been her fault that dickhead O'Connor was on hormone overload!

She decided then that if she kept her head down and ate fast she could avoid meeting those amused blue eyes from across the table, then escape to the kitchen with the alibi of starting the dishes for Judy. But what seemed a good plan crashed and burned as the chair alongside her was pulled back from the table. He was *supposed* to sit next to his grandfather.

She jerked her leg away as a long, denim-clad one brushed against it, causing her stomach to roll. She didn't like this guy. She really didn't. And with him sitting right beside her it would be a miracle if she could swallow another bite without throwing up. Then again, if she was going to embarrass herself by chucking, she'd make damn sure she spewed all over *him*.

Jace detected the girl beside him stiffen, then edge her chair away from him, making him wish he'd been a bit more sensitive to the kid's feelings and not mentioned their first meeting. But he'd been surprised at seeing her sitting at the family table and reacted instinctively, saying the first thing that came into his head. Which wasn't something he did much these days, and definitely not something to be encouraged in his line of work.

Though he'd known his mother and more recently –

surprise, surprise – his father had taken a personal interest in the girl's welfare, he hadn't realized the extent of it. Ethan had mentioned she'd been to dinner *once*, but the familiarity of the conversation he'd heard as he'd walked into the house suggested it was a fairly regular occurrence. That being the case, it hightlighted how seldom he was home long enough to do more that snatch a few hours' sleep and change his clothes.

'Well, son, I'm glad to see you're still alive,' his grandfather said. 'Seems like ages since you been round for a chat.'

Jace grimaced. 'It is, Grandpa, and I'm sorry,' he said with genuine regret. 'Tag and me have been flat out in all directions. I've spent the last four days doing an insurance job.'

'Does that mean you've decided to leave the *real* police work to the *real* police?'

Trust his old man not to be able to resist having a dig at him. 'No, Dad, it means that in the twelve months Tag and I are acting as sub-agents to Mac Gregory, we're supposed to learn all aspects of investigation work.'

'*Acting* is right!' his father snorted. 'Mac Gregory might hold a current investigator's licence, but he hasn't done a scrap of work in the field since he won the pools ten years back.'

'Doesn't matter. He's *licenced*, so he's qualified to take on sub-agents. Anyway, he knows his stuff, and it's unlikely any active investigator would have been prepared to take on *two* sub-agents at the same time.'

'Sounds like you're enjoying the work, son?'

Jace considered his grandfather's question. Was he

enjoying the work? No, that wasn't the right word. He liked it, he found it challenging and rewarding, but there had been no enjoyment in having to confront the parents of the Perrelli boy and tell them their son was lying on a slab in the morgue. The memory of the experience was enough to chill him. The knowledge that it probably wouldn't be the last time he'd have to perform the task was too disturbing to think about.

He shook his head and forced himself to smile at his grey-haired grandfather. 'It's interesting,' he compromised. 'And at the moment *profitable*. That's another bonus of having Mac take us on; while he oversees everything we do, he insists on letting us keep every dollar we make. Elsewhere, subbing to an active agent we'd only be pulling a wage and a fraction of what we're earning now. Thanks to Mac, Tag and I are going to be more cashed up than most just licensed private investigators are – '

'Most what?' The amazed interjection from the girl beside him was so unexpected he wondered if he hadn't imagined it.

'He's a private investigator,' his father answered before Jace got a chance. 'He sacrificed a promising law career, where – '

'Dad, I'd rather not get into – '

A volley of hysterical giggles erupted from the chair beside him. 'A *private detective*?' Tatum gasped, before laughter again overwhelmed her.

'Oh, God!' she managed amid uncontrolled hilarity, which apparently everyone bar he found amusing. 'What a scream! What an absolute . . . bloody scream I thought

141

you were just a dickhead!' she laughed, wiping tears from her amused face. 'Instead you're a dickhead who thinks he's *Magnum*!'

'Very funny!' Jace's irritation wasn't helped by the fact that he'd had a bummer of a day or by the sight of his father laughing nearly a hard as the witch next to him.

'Hey, Jason, this mean you'll be buyin' one of them red Ferraris?' his *former* favourite grandfather asked.

'No, but I know who I'd like to run over in one,' he muttered, leaning towards the gradually calming girl sitting beside him.

'Leave her be, Jason,' his mother said, not entirely successful at keeping her face straight. 'She was only joking. You have to admit the term private investigator doesn't exactly inspire the same respect as say . . . oh, *lawyer*.'

'I hope you're satisfied?' Jace said, scowling down at Tatum. '*They* – ' he used the knife in his right hand to indicate his family ' – *had* started to restrict their disapproval of my career choice to silent suffering mode. Thanks to *you* they're all verbalizing again.'

Tatum met his accusing gaze with the brightest smile she could produce. 'You're welcome.' She gave herself bonus points when he stabbed his fork into a baked potato, muttering viciously under his breath.

'Judy,' she said, picking up her not quite empty plate and deciding she'd rather finish eating in the kitchen. 'Would you like me to start dishing up dessert now?'

One glance at her husband and Judy knew he was biting the inside of his mouth as hard as she was at Tatum's exaggeratedly demure tone. 'Er, yes . . . thank you,

142

Tatum. That way my son may be able to resist the temptation of choking you for a little while longer.'

Hampered by a mouthful of food, Jace's response was limited to a low growl and a narrowed-eyed glare at his mother.

'Oh, goodness!' Tatum lifted a shocked hand to her throat. 'You mean I've *upset* Tom?'

'The name,' he mumbled, 'is *Jason*.'

Feigning confusion, Tatum shook her head. 'I thought . . . Oh!' she grinned, as if having discovered world peace. '*That's right*!' she said. 'Silly me! I was getting you confused with Tom Selleck! But he *does* have a Red Ferrari!'

Laughter accompanied her smiling exit from the room, and Jace, reminding himself she was just a kid, relaxed enough to let his lips twitch. 'Dad, are you *sure* the police don't have some unsolved felony you could pin on that kid?'

'She's not so bad once you know what makes her tick.'

'Knowing what makes something tick is one thing,' Jace retorted, more than a little surprised by his father's changed attitude towards the girl. 'Being able to *defuse* it before it blows you to kingdom come is another. I can't believe you're encouraging her to take judo lessons. Talk about asking for trouble . . .'

His grandfather frowned. 'I thought judo was a nonaggressive martial art.'

'It is, Dad,' Brian said. 'What we teach at the youth club is purely designed for self-defence.'

'Ha!' Jace scoffed. 'She'd make Tai Chi aggressive.'

'What yer got against poor little Tatum?' his grandfather asked.

'You mean apart from the fact she was responsible for me having to have stitches? And her warped sense of humour?'

'Look who's talking!' Judy said. 'When I think of some of the things you've done, Jason Benton . . .' She shook her head. 'I remem – '

'Never mind his sense of humour!' his grandfather interrupted. 'I want him to tell me why he don't like Tatum.'

'It's not that I don't *like* her. Actually I feel sorry for her, having to live in the refuge and all, but you've got to admit she's a feral little thing. And her mouth needs a good soaping. It's not hard to see why no one's keen to take her in.'

No one admitted to any such thing. In fact a leaden silence seemed to fall momentarily about the table as his parents and grandfather exchanged uneasy looks.

'He doesn't know?' His grandfather's frowned question was directed to his son.

'Know what?' Jace asked automatically.

'Er, no, Dad,' Brian Benton said.

'Neither of the boys do,' his wife added.

'I repeat,' Jace said, looking from one to the other. '*What* don't I know?'

Judy Benton was quickly on her feet. 'Pass me your plates,' she said, motioning to the two older men. 'I'll go and help Tatum with the dessert.'

'Good idea, Mum.' Jace leaned back in his chair and surveyed the two older men. 'You go ration how much arsenic she's sprinkling into mine, while Dad and Grandpa tell me what's going on.'

It was impossible to miss the questioning look that passed between his father and mother. 'Oh, I don't suppose it'll hurt to tell him,' Judy said, sounding annoyed by the fact. 'Just don't let – '

'Tatum's coming to live with me.'

'*What*?'

'Bryce! Not so loud; *she'll hear you*.'

Even though their combined expressions confirmed that Jace had indeed heard what he thought he had, he was hard pressed to believe it. 'Are you all crazy? That's the most stupid thing that's ever been said in this house!'

'Really?' his father said. I think, 'Dad Mum, I'm giving up law – I want to become a private investigator' beats it hands down for stupidity!'

'Knock it off, Dad! You know bloody well one has nothing to do with the other. You're talking about putting some street kid we don't know anything about – '

'That's not true. In the last month we've all got to know a lot about her,' his mother objected. 'And she's – '

'Not the sort of kid you inflict on a partially crippled elderly old man – '

'Who you callin' crippled an' old, you upstart! That any way to speak to your grandpa?'

'Shhh! She'll hear!' Brian hissed to his father. 'Keep it down.'

'Jason, this really has nothing to do with you,' his mother informed him.

'Like hell! It's my grandfather you're putting at risk – '

'Rubbish! The only risk is that it won't work out – '

'*It won't*. I can tell you that *now*.' Jace was amazed his father was going along with such a hare-brained idea. For

145

months he'd been saying that at seventy-eight his father was too old to live alone and had been hell-bent on convincing him to go to a retirement complex. While Jace had sided with his grandfather over that issue, and made a point of trying to spend more time with the old man so his dad wouldn't push the issue, this was a whole different ball-game!

'Jason,' his mother said, 'this isn't a spur of the moment decision. We've *all* given it a great deal of thought and discussion. Apart from solving the problem of Tatum finding a permanent place to live, it means your grandfather will have someone to keep him company and – '

'Mum, this isn't Pollyanna or Tammy you're dealing with here. She's not some sweet, wholesome kid who's going to be falling over herself to mow the lawns by day and stay home and play rummy with him at night!'

'We're aware of that, Jason,' his mother said. 'Naturally, Tatum will be told there are certain rules she has to obey if she accepts Bryce's offer. It's also possible she won't.'

'You want to pray she *doesn't*. Because rules or no rules, with her track record she'll probably have God knows what kind of weirdos dropping in on her at all hours, and more than likely if she doesn't help herself to anything that isn't nailed down they will! What's more – '

A stunned gasp coincided with something cold and wet landing on his head. Seconds later an upturned plate of peaches and ice-cream slid into his lap.

'*You bastard*! You effing lying bastard!'

'Now look what you've done!' his mother accused, folding his assailant into a comforting embrace. 'Honestly, Jason!

146

Sometimes I think you're the most insensitive person I know!'

'It's me. Can I come in?'

Having just finished his much needed shower, Jace was caught literally with his pants down by the rap on his bedroom door. Though the ice-cream might have been out of his hair, anger was still flowing pretty freely through his blood, and it was on the tip of his tongue to refuse his father's request. He'd come home expecting to share an uncomplicated meal with his parents, for the first time in weeks, and instead found himself in a war zone.

'Jason?'

Sighing, he tossed the towel he was wearing onto a chair and snagged a pair of underpants from the drawer. Hurriedly he stepped into them. 'Yeah, c'mon in.' His already testy mood wasn't helped by his father's smiling appraisal.

'Hell, son, I think it's the first time you've been so eager to *wash up* after a meal.'

'Not funny, Dad.'

'Well, you have to admit young Tatum puts new meaning into dishing up desert. And you were worried about a little arsenic!'

Letting his father laugh alone at his pathetic joke, Jace slid the door of his wardrobe open and pulled out the first pair of jeans his fingers touched. Crossing to the dresser, he picked up his wallet and shoved it into the back pocket even before he put them on. It was a habit he'd gotten into as a schoolkid after a week of being put off the bus for not having his travel pass. Pocketing his wallet before putting

147

his trousers on reduced the chances of him forgetting it. The action wasn't lost on his father.

'You going out? *Now* – after all the commotion you caused?' There was no missing his old man's disapproval.

'I'm due to relieve Tag on a surveillance at midnight.' He zipped his jeans with a dry laugh. 'Unfortunately I'm a bit light in the psychic powers department and I stopped home hoping for a decent meal and a few hours' sleep first. Believe me, if I'd had the ability to foresee what was going to happen I wouldn't have bothered.'

His father rubbed a hand wearily across the back of his neck before sitting down on the foot of the bed. 'I suppose we should have said something to you boys . . .'

'It would've helped,' Jace agreed. 'But it wouldn't have made a difference to how I feel about things.'

'Meaning you don't think Tatum deserves a chance? That she shouldn't be given the benefit of the doubt?'

'Don't put words into my mouth, Dad. Sure she deserves a chance. From what little I know I'd say she's had a rotten life – '

'She has.' The statement came swiftly and with a superior glare. 'And you don't know the half of it.'

'And you and Mum only know what she's told you. What she *wants* you to know.'

'Maybe. But I know for a fact she doesn't have a criminal record. And despite her home life she's got an excellent school attendance record – no wagging, no expulsions. I'll admit I was against the idea when Dad first suggested it . . . so was your mother. But since she's been coming down to the youth club after school . . . well, I've seen a different side to the kid that makes me view her in a different light.'

'Believe me, you'll get another view again from under a plate of ice-cream,' Jace told him, sorting through his T-shirt drawer until he found one that suited his mood: all black. Before pulling it on, he turned back to his father. 'You've just seen again how volatile she is; do you seriously believe Grandpa is capable of dealing with her?'

His father grinned. 'Doesn't seem to me that *he's* the one having the problems.'

Unamused, Jace reached for his leather jacket. He swore as his hand encountered the sticky residue of ice-cream and peach juice. 'If I didn't think she'd probably use acid, I'd make the little bitch clean this.'

'Take it easy on her, son,' his father said. 'She might've overreacted, but you hurt her feelings calling her a thief.'

'*Might've over reacted?*'

His father chuckled. 'Sorry, mate,' he said, with little sincerity. 'But it's pretty funny in hindsight.'

'Really? I'll let you know in ten years or so if I agree.'

'You looked like a stunned mullet when that plate landed on your head. And then when she tossed the second one in your lap . . .' Hearty laughter punctured his account of the incident. 'Oh, Lord, you should've seen yourself!'

The realization that this was the first occasion in a long time his Dad had been so relaxed in his company evaporated much of Jace's anger, and he ceased trying to the fight the tiny smile tugging at his mouth. His father noticed it and began laughing harder.

'Yeah, okay, Dad,' he said. 'I get the picture. But I've had a hard enough time getting life insurance as it is,' he complained. 'If the insurance company hear about my run-ins with Tatum they're going to hike my premiums sky-high.'

'Stop provoking that Italian temper of hers and your life expectancy will look a lot healthier,' his father suggested.

'I never *meant* for her to hear what I said. I thought she was in the kitchen.' It was the truth. For all he was against the idea of his grandfather taking her in, he hadn't intended to deliberately hurt the kid. 'I was simply trying to talk sense into the rest of you. This is not what I call a smart move.'

'Look, son, if it'll make you feel any better, I'll admit I'm not as confident as the others that it'll work. I've only really gone along with them because they're so keen.'

Jace considered this bit of information. It wasn't like his father to be easily coerced into anything. In fact he could be as stubborn as a Mallee bull if it suited him. No sooner had the thought popped into his head than he worked out what his father was up to.

'You're counting on her saying no to the whole thing, aren't you?' He grinned. 'You're betting she'll run a mile at the thought of living with Grandpa.'

His father stood up, shaking his head. 'If I was, son, I'd have done my money. She's already said yes. More to spite you than anything else, I'd say.'

'What? You're kidding, right?'

'Nope. Your mum and Grandpa have taken her to the refuge to pick up her stuff now.' Amusement again wrinkled his face. 'Guess family dinners are going to be real worry to you for a while, eh?'

CHAPTER 9

Tatum sighed with relief as the bell signalling the end of her biology class rang. Quickly she flipped her note folder shut with one hand while gathering her pens in the other; if she hurried she could make the two twenty-eight bus. Without bothering to put the folder into her bag, she shouldered her way past the slower moving students out into the corridor and headed towards the science blocks' main exit.

'Hey, Tatum! Wait up!'

Though she didn't recognize the female voice, the urgency in the request automatically caused her to turn around, frowning. From the throng of grey and lemon-clad teenagers a slim, pretty girl approached, her quick springy step making blonde curls bounce around her shoulders. Tatum vaguely placed her from one of her classes, but couldn't imagine why she'd want to speak with her. What was her name . . .? Kelly – no, Kylie something.

'Hi, I'm in your Ancient History and maths class,' she said pleasantly. 'My name's – '

'Kylie. I know. What's up?'

151

'Actually it's *Kay*lee.'

More worried about missing the bus than getting the name wrong, Tatum forced a smile. 'Sorry, I was close.'

'No sweat. People always make that mistake. Kaylee's a combination of my mum and my brother's name, which is why I wanted to talk to you.'

Fascinating! Tatum thought. 'Look . . . er . . . Kaylee. I'm in a bit of a rush. I've got – '

'I'm Kaylee *Taggart*,' she announced. This time her grin was wide enough to show off her shiny metal braces. 'Lee's my brother.'

'*Lee?*'

'Yeah. You know – Lee *Taggart*.'

Tatum was mutely staring at the girl, wondering how such a dimwit could be doing top level maths, when it suddenly occurred to her that if the look Kaylee was giving her was anything to go on, the other girl thought *she* was the stupid one. 'Am I supposed to know . . . er . . . Lee?'

Kaylee laughed. 'You should if you're a friend of Jace's.'

'I don't know – ' She swore. 'You mean Jason Benton?'

'Bingo!' Excitement intensified the brightness of the girl's brown eyes, then she gave an exaggerated sigh of relief. 'For a minute there I was beginning to think I'd made a mistake.'

'You did,' Tatum told her. '*Jace* Benton isn't a friend of mine. The guy's an up-himself jerk. I wouldn't spit on him if he was on fire!'

Kaylee looked poleaxed. 'You don't think Jace is a total *hunk*? You're kidding, right?'

'A total hunk of shi – '

'What are you girls doing out here? Why aren't you in class?'

Great! Now she'd been sprung by a teacher!

'Oh, er, Tatum's sick, Mr Longly.'

Caught off guard by the lie, Tatum opened her mouth to protest it, but the other girl's look eloquently told her to *shut up*.

'She's been sick all through last lesson, sir,' she went on as the man strode towards them. 'I was just about to take her to sick bay.'

The teacher's red puffy face peered into into Tatum's. His proximity allowed her to register that she definitely wasn't in any of his classes and that he didn't practise the use of deodorant.

'She doesn't look sick to me, Miss Taggart.'

On cue, Tatum grimaced and clutched her stomach. 'Cramps,' she gasped, then bit the inside of her mouth until her eyes watered.

'It might be appendicitis, sir,' Kaylee said helpfully. 'If it ruptures she'll die.' The comment drew the man's sceptical gaze back to her. 'Well, that's what happened to my next door neighbour.'

'Oh, dear! You don't think it's appendicitis, do you?' The teacher was seeking a negative response from Tatum. Obligingly she gave it to him.

'N-no, sir.' Keeping her voice feeble, she grimaced again. 'Period pain . . . sir. Sometimes when this happens I just start gushing red all over the place.'

The man paled. 'Oh! Oh, dear. Er – perhaps I'd better call someone to come and take you home. I – '

'Oh, there's no need for that, sir,' Kaylee put in

hurriedly. 'My brother is picking me up in about ten minutes. He wouldn't mind giving Tatum a lift home.'

Longly frowned. 'In ten minutes? But school isn't due out for another forty minutes.'

'Um, I've got a dental appointment sir. I've got this abscess. See?' Moving closer, so her face was almost against Longly's, she opened her mouth and stuck a finger in.

Longly backed away. 'Yes, I'm sure you do . . . Are you certain your brother won't mind dropping Miss . . . er . . .?'

'Milano,' Tatum supplied, sounding as if she was close to drawing her last breath.

'He won't mind at all, sir!' Kaylee assured him. 'As a committed Christian, my brother loves people being sick so he can help them! Er, I mean he loves helping – '

'Yes, yes, Miss Taggart, I understand.' His brusqueness faded under another groan from Tatum. 'Perhaps it'll be best if you take Ms Milano straight out to the car park,' he told Kaylee. 'I'll take care of signing you out on the early leave sheet in the office and keep an eye on you until your brother arrives.'

'Oh, thank you, Mr Longly! Here, Tatum, give me your folder and bag and hang onto my arm. Gosh you really look *awful*! Do you think you can walk to the parking lot?'

Head bent, Tatum nodded as she slipped her arm through Kaylee's. With small, hesitant steps the pair shuffled towards the exit.

'Keep up the act until we make the car park.' Kaylee spoke softly. 'And whatever you do don't laugh.'

Don't laugh! Hell, Tatum was close to wetting herself!

And she could feel the silent, shaking amusement of the girl she was leaning against all the way out of the building.

'Don't recover yet,' Kaylee said as they started towards the student parking area. 'Old Longly'll be watching from the window.'

'Was all this really necessary? We're only cutting scripture classes, for God's sake. They're not compulsory.'

'I know, but Longly's a born-again. He'd have given us a sermon on why they *should* be compulsory. Oh, good, there's Tag!'

Recognizing the nickname from having heard the Bentons use it, Tatum halted. 'Your brother really is picking you up?'

'Yeah. We're going shopping to get Mum a birthday present. He supplies most of the money and I supply *all* the good taste.' She grinned. 'But we can drop you off on the way. You live at Jace's grandfather's, right?'

Tatum nodded. 'But it's okay, I can get the bus.'

'Sure you can,' Kaylee agreed. 'But why would you want to?' A light, easy laugh burst from her. 'C'mon Tatum,' she urged. 'Hobble over to the car and I'll introduce you to my big brother. Just *don't*,' she cautioned, 'tell me he's gorgeous! I get sick of hearing it!'

Ensconced in the back seat of Lee Taggart's car, Tatum decided that even though Kaylee's brother *was* terrifically good-looking, the warning not to say so hadn't been warranted; with the blonde chattering at warp speed Tatum could barely get a word in edgeways. After a rapid introduction of, 'Tatum, this is my brother Lee –

but call him Tag. Everyone else does. Tag – Tatum Milano,' she'd barely given the pair time to exchange greetings before telling her brother they were dropping Tatum home and launching into an account of their run-in with the teacher as they'd been cutting out early.

Having reminded herself to smile in all the right places, Tatum found that Kaylee's account was so comical that her amusement didn't have to be fabricated. Tag's reaction to the tale ranged from disbelieving groans to dry sarcasm and unrestrained laughter. His sister, however, didn't draw breath between that story and a scathing attack on a girl in her drama class whose acting ability was only slightly less than that of a brick.

'Trust me,' the girl said, looking over the front seat-back at Tatum. 'If *she'd* been in the hall with us when Longly arrived we'd be doing detention for the rest of our lives!'

Tag smiled at Tatum via the rearview mirror. 'You'll have to forgive Kaylee. She's been painfully shy like this all her life.'

A sisterly punch hit his arm. 'Ignore him, Tatum. He thinks he's got a sense of humour.'

Initially suspicious when Kaylee had stopped her at school, and subsequently bemused by what had followed, Tatum was surprised to find she didn't feel awkward in the company of Kaylee Taggart or her brother.

It had been no secret when she'd started at the local high school that she was 'one of the refugees', as the handful of kids who lived at the refuge and were enrolled there were called. In some sort of unspoken 'safety in numbers' theory, or perhaps simply to avoid running the risk of being excluded by the other students, the refugees socialized only among themselves.

If they were fortunate enough to be placed with a family, and once Father Peter was convinced the arrangement was stable, they were offered the opportunity of changing schools to one where their background wasn't general knowledge and they could mix more easily with other students. But, more interested in keeping her education on a steady path than starting a fresh social life at yet another new school, Tatum had decided to stay where she was, and thus had found herself accepted by neither group.

She'd told herself the situation didn't bother her – she'd survived without a gaggle of close girlfriends all of her school life, so another twenty months of it wouldn't be a hardship – yet being treated like a 'regular' person, not just by Kaylee but by her brother, was like eating forbidden fruit. Still, common sense quickly told her not to develop a taste for it. While Kaylee might only have a limited knowledge of her background, Tatum had no doubts that Jace Benton would have filled in *all* the blanks for Tag, and she didn't have the slightest doubt that once she was out of the car Kaylee would get some brotherly advice about taking care who she associated with in future.

By the time Tatum registered that Tag had spoken to her they'd stopped in Bryce's usually empty driveway behind an unfamiliar white car.

'Looks like Jace's here,' Tag said.

Bloody hell! Tatum thought, before immediately calculating her chances of slipping around the back way without being seen by Bryce and hiding until his grandson left.

Given the depth of *her* annoyance at finding him here, it seemed bizarre that Kaylee looked so fabulously pleased by the idea.

'Let's go in and say hi,' she said, her seat belt already retracting. 'I haven't seen Jace in ages. *Or Bryce!*' she added quickly, reddening under the amused look Tag sent her.

Praying the guy wouldn't pander to his sister's crush, Tatum got out of the car. If they went in she'd have to go in too, giving Jace yet another opportunity for publicly embarrassing her.

'Not today, kiddo. We've got shopping to do. I'm sure Tatum won't mind you coming home another afternoon with her to, er, *visit Bryce*.' He directed an appealing smile towards Tatum and asked, 'That okay with you?'

Relief had her nodding before the implication of the words fully registered. *Tag was encouraging his sister to spend time with her?*

Yet as she stood mute with confusion from Tag's suggestion Kaylee, smiling her satisfaction, proceeded to rebuckle her seat belt while eagerly instructing Tatum to meet her at the milk bar around the corner from school the next morning.

'Try and get there by eight,' she yelled from the window as the car reversed down the drive. 'So we get a good table. See ya!'

Jace deliberately kept his approach silent. There was only one entrance to the small corridor that separated the shed from the fence dividing the two properties, unless a person wanted to climb through the compost heap at the other end. Holding his breath, he moved to block the more savoury route of escape, quickly absorbing the scene before him.

Shoulders hunched and her back to the wall, she sat on the ground with feet braced against the fence. Her knees, bent to compensate for the length of her long black-stockinged legs, acted as a resting place for the book she held.

'Getting a bit dark out here for reading, isn't it?'

Shock jerked Tatum's head back against the aluminium wall of the garden shed, it's dull thump more muffled than the swear word which hissed into the grey autumn dusk. Swearing softly, she dropped the book she held to touch the back of her head.

Stepping into the narrow unlit area, Jace bent and picked it up. His lightening reflexes snatched it beyond her reach when, anticipating him, Tatum tried to beat him to it.

'Give it to me!'

For a moment Jace considered refusing the demand. He glanced at the title, then back at her. Though anger and irritation flared in her face, the knowledge that she'd been sitting out here alone for nearly three hours made her seem not so much aggressive as forlorn. Forlorn and vulnerable. Both to him and the rapidly decreasing temperature.

The oversized lemon sweatshirt bearing the school crest might have been effective during the day's mildness, but it wouldn't be much protection against the early evening dampness; nor would the short grey and blue tartan skirt she wore. The notion that she'd rather freeze than face him made him feel worse than the revelations his grand-father had treated him to since his arrival. He sighed and held the book out to her.

'Bryce said to tell you dinner was ready.'

Her expression told him she'd assumed his grandfather hadn't known she was home before it became stubborn. 'I'm not hungry.'

'Strange. My grandfather said you're always starving when you get in from school. He figured you'd be ravenous by now.'

Her eyes travelled his length, from head to foot and back again. 'The thought of some *things* will kill my appetite real quick,' she said. 'If I tried to eat and had to *look* at them at the same time I'd projectile vomit.'

Jace leaned against the fence, studying her. 'Would you feel better if I said I wasn't staying for dinner?'

Shoving the book in her hessian backpack, she quickly stood up and brushed her hands across the back of her skirt, then flicked her hair over her shoulders in an exaggerated manner and stared at him.

'If you want to make me feel better,' she said, 'hand me a loaded gun.'

He fought a smile.

Snatching up her bag, Tatum went to pass him, but he quickly straightened, blocking her way. Instinctively she took a step back from his solid imposing bulk, before reminding herself to stand her ground. '*Move.*'

'Not yet,' he said. His chest rose on a heavy sigh. 'Tatum, I owe you an apology.'

She spared him only a brief mutinous glare before spinning in the other direction.

160

'Unless you want to tramp through a damp compost pile, you're going to have to hear me out.'

It was on the tip of Tatum's tongue to tell him she'd rather *eat* compost than listen to anything he had to say – except she'd have to back up the words by walking out the other end. Knowing he'd *enjoy* seeing her knee-high in rotting God knew what had her clamping her reckless tongue between her teeth.

'Tatum,' he said softly, 'I apologize.'

She refused to turn around and face him.

'I was wrong about you and I'm sorry.'

Jace hadn't expected she'd be easily won over. Instead he'd anticipated very earthy instructions on where and how far to stick his apology. He didn't get them. The silence that followed his words could have been measured on a sun dial. The thought had him lifting his arm so he could see his watch in the dim light; mentally he cursed.

'Look, I don't have time to stand around here all night, so I'll say what I need to and it's up to you whether you listen or not. Okay?' He sighed. A corpse would have shown more response.

He went on regardless. 'While I never meant for you to hear what I said at dinner that night, I still had no right to say it. I was prejudging you without really knowing you and I'm sorry. It's just that I care about my grandfather a great deal; in some ways he's more important to me than anyone else in my family.' It was an admission he'd never made to anyone before and he was surprised to hear the words aloud. What was it about this sixteen-year-old kid that he was desperate to have her accept his apology?

'I was afraid you'd take advantage of him. After talking

161

to him, I realize you've been good to the old guy, Tatum; good to him and *for him*. Having you here seems to have given him a new lease on life.'

Jace wasn't exaggerating. They'd been a bright, healthy glow in his grandfather's eyes, and the limp he'd had a few weeks ago now seemed more like a spring in his step.

In the past the only things he'd seen his grandfather produce in the kitchen had been burnt toast, canned baked beans and boiled water, so walking in today and discovering he was not only *making pikelets* but thoroughly enjoying the task had rendered Jace momentarily speechless. When he'd recovered enough to pass comment, he'd been blithely informed that Tatum was always starving when she got home from school and that pikelets were one of her favourite foods.

Of course Jace had immediately jumped into a spiel about how Bryce was a fool for waiting on the girl hand and foot, but *that* argument had been shot down in flames when his grandfather had whipped the lid off a slow cooker, allowing the aroma of bolognese sauce to seduce the atmosphere. Tatum, he'd informed his grandson curtly, had prepared it before going to school, and would make the spaghetti to accompany it for dinner when she got home. All that had happened within a few minutes of him arriving at his grandfather's house, and had merely been the start of a litany of praise for Tatum Milano.

Though curious as to the circumstances that had led to Tag dropping the kid home, his partner had driven off before Jace had a chance to go out and speak with him. So he waited in the living room, mentally composing the apology he owed to Tatum. Waited. And waited. *And waited*.

'Go *outside* and talk to her.' His grandfather had said when after two hours Tatum still hadn't put in an appearance.

'Look, I don't want to hassle her any more, okay? Besides, it's getting pretty cold; she's not going to want to hide out there much longer.'

'Don't bet on it! You're both so damn stubborn you'll be sitting in that chair at midnight,' his grandfather had warned.

Jace had shaken his head. 'Not me. I've got a date with a hot blonde horse trainer that I'm not about to miss.'

'Fine! But is it too much to ask you not to leave your poor old grandfather with a frozen brunette on his hands?' his grandfather had demanded testily. 'Now, either go see her or leave, so I can get her inside before she gives herself pneumonia.'

It hadn't taken him long to find her, but it was, he realized, going to take more time than he had to spare to get through to her.

He tried again. 'Look, I know I was rough on you, but I really am sorry. Now, either you accept my apology or you don't, but I'd appreciate it if you'd at least acknowledge you've *heard* it.'

Just as he made the discovery that statues didn't stand as still as she did, the wind kicked up and she shivered. Frustrated to the point of wanting to shake her, he swore. Then he said wearily, 'Okay, you win! I'm going. Which ought to help restore that appetite of yours. But even if it doesn't I advise you to get your stubborn hide inside before you end up sicker than you were that night I found you! If you don't care about your own health, at least consider the strain your getting sick'd have on Bryce; *he* thinks the damn sun rises and sets with you.'

He was turning to go when she spoke. Her voice, softer and more uncertain than he'd ever imagined it would be, stopped him in his tracks.

'If you want to stay for dinner . . . stay.'

'Does that mean you've accepted my apology?' he asked, trying to defeat the almost total darkness of the evening to read her equally dark eyes.

'Bryce *is* your grandfather.'

He fought a smile at her evasive answer. 'True. Although at the moment I think you're more likely to inherit the family's secret pikelet recipe. You've made quite an impression on the old guy, and he's shrewd enough not to be easily impressed. For what it's worth, Mum, Dad and Ethan have been singing your praises for weeks.'

Tatum's blood was so warmed by the sincerity of his words that she felt herself blush, and was immediately grateful that it was too dark for him to see her reaction. While she was prepared to go along with a mutual ceasefire for as long as he was, she didn't want to give him the idea she was in any way vulnerable to anything he said, did or thought. Nor did she want him treating her with pity.

'Is that why Kaylee Taggart has suddenly become pally with me?'

'*Huh?*'

Her question appeared to have genuinely blindsided him. 'Did you ask Kaylee Taggart to try and make friends with me?'

'No. Why?'

She shrugged. 'Seems strange the sister of the guy you work with comes up and speaks to me for the first time the same day you apologize. And she used you as the excuse.' The demon in her demanded she put him on the spot, so she said, 'I suppose you know she has an enormous crush on you?'

He surprised her by laughing. 'Kaylee's got a crush on any male with a heartbeat! She's a terrific kid, but I'm way past the point where a sixteen-year-old could hold my interest.'

'Not even one as pretty as Kaylee?'

'Not even one as pretty as you,' he said easily. 'Now, why don't you hop inside before you freeze. I've got to dash.'

'You aren't staying for dinner?'

'Can't. Much as I have a weakness for Italian food, I've a bigger one for leggy blonde racing fillies.' White teeth flashed behind a roguish grin. 'I promise the next time I come I'll stay for dinner, okay?'

His tone was friendly in the manner of an adult placating a small child. Tatum resented the fact, but refused to justify it with a juvenile remark.

'C'mon, I've got to say goodbye to Gramps. If we walk in together he'll be more inclined to believe we've sorted things out.'

Shrugging, she fell into stride with him, and they entered the kitchen together.

'Tatum,' he said, stopping her at the back door with a light touch on her arm. 'I meant what I said . . . *I really am sorry*.'

165

Quit while you're ahead, Kaylee, she thought, looking up into the bluest of blue eyes set in a Hollywood-handsome face. Even if the guy did take you seriously, you'd get trampled in the stampede!

Tatum discovered that developing a gradual friendship with Kaylee Taggart wasn't an option for her, because the other girl was determined to haul her into it at full speed! She had no reservations about sharing her opinions, her secrets, her laughter or her family and friends, and Tatum, despite initially being suspicious of the girl's enthusiasm, found herself with a 'best friend' for the first time in her life.

'You do realize,' Tatum said to her a week after they'd met and Kaylee was still being so nice to her, 'that my mother was a prostitute who died of an overdose?'

'Yeah,' she replied awkwardly, looking down at her shoes. 'But listen . . .' She lifted her head and gave Tatum a shy, sad smile. 'If you ever want . . . you know . . . to talk about her or . . . want someone to go with you to visit her grave or something . . . Well, just ask me. Okay?'

Utterly floored by the offer, and the sentiments behind it, Tatum could only respond with a slow nod. Kaylee gave her a bright smile. 'Good.' And then in her next breath said, 'God! Isn't Daniel Crosby just *the* biggest hunk on two legs? I swear I hyperventilate every time I see him! C'mon, let's head to the milk bar and see if he's hanging out down there . . .'

A month later, Tatum went to Judy's forty-fifth birth-day barbecue wishing she'd had the money to buy a gift that better expressed her appreciation of what she'd done for her than a scabby box of chocolates!

'Hey, Tatum,' Brian said from behind the sizzling barbecue. 'Could you do me a favour, love? Ask one of the boys to bring me out a beer?'

Smiling, she got up and went to get it herself. She returned to find a stunning-looking blonde in skin-tight jeans and an expensive leather jacket holding a huge gift and laughing with Brian. Smiling, she handed the beer to Brian.

'Oh, thanks, love. Tatum, this is Donna Browne, Ethan's girlfriend. Donna, Tatum Milano.'

'Hi, Tatum! I've been looking forward to meeting you. Ethan's mentioned you.' She smiled, making herself look even more beautiful. 'Well, I'd better get this present into Judy and find Ethan before he thinks I'm not coming! We'll talk later, Tatum, okay?'

'Sure.' Watching her walk to the house, Tatum didn't find it hard to understand why Ethan was so seldom at home.

Tatum was helping to clear away the dishes after a delicious but laid-back meal when Donna came into the kitchen. For the first time since her arrival, Ethan wasn't attached to her arm.

'Ah, Tatum! Scored kitchen duty, have you?'

'I thought I'd start clearing up a bit before the birthday girl decides to do it herself.'

'How *nice* of you. I'll bet you spend a lot of time thinking up cute ways to ingratiate yourself with your benefactor, don't you?' she sneered. 'But then so you should. If it weren't for Judy's do-gooding little heart you'd have ended up like the rest of the scum up at the Cross.'

Though she wanted to throw the plates in the bitch's face, Tatum held onto her temper. 'I'd left the Cross long before I met Judy.'

'Ah, yes, you were a *street kid*!' Her eyes hardened. 'Well, trendily pathetic as that is, don't expect *me* to have any sympathy for you!'

'I'd die before I'd accept your sympathy. So why don't you just piss off?'

The blonde smirked. 'Typical. You're exactly what I expected you to be the minute Ethan told me about you. Foul-mouthed, cheap and common.'

It was a struggle for Tatum not to show her exactly how foul mouthed, cheap and common she was, but she was determined not to. Instead she gave her a sickly sweet smile. 'How intuitive of you, Donna,' she said, trying to imitate the cool, controlled superior tone she'd often heard Lulu use. 'But you're *nothing* like I expected. It's a good thing Brian introduced us, because when Ethan told me I'd recognize you the second you arrived because you were tall, beautiful and friendly, I didn't realize he was using euphemisms for a bow-legged, trout-mouthed bitch who wore too much make-up.'

The older girl gave her a droll look. '*I'm* too well bred to care about what a *junkie whore's daughter* thinks of me.'

'That's enough, Donna.' Jace must have been somewhere inside the house, because Tatum hadn't heard him enter the kitchen. Nor, from the surprised expression on Donna's face, had she.

'Mum wouldn't be happy to know you were upsetting

168

Tatum,' he told her. 'I know I'm not. So why don't you go find Ethan and ask him to take you home, before you make anyone else unhappy, hmm?'

With a narrow-eyed look of hatred, she spun on her heels and hurried to the door.

'Either she's dynamite in the sack or Ethan's got a warped taste in women,' Tatum said.

'Donna's the one who's warped,' Jace said, before giving her a reassuring smile and saying, 'Don't let her worry you, Tatum. She's just got a grudge against the Cross.'

She frowned. 'You obviously heard most of what was said. But I'd say she worries you more than me,' she said. 'Why?'

'I've got my reasons.'

'Knocked you back, huh?' Tatum teased.

The handsome face hardened. 'Once. But we were seventeen at the time and that's not what I've got against her.'

Tatum, when she'd asked the question, had not really expected him to answer at all, unless it was with a smart come-back. She'd certainly never expected what, judging by the bitterness of his tone, was the truth.

'She's a cold-hearted bitch with no sympathy for anyone. Not even old boyfriends who die tragically.'

Jace remembered the pain he'd seen on Tatum's face when Donna had referred to her mother as a junkie. Whether Donna knew the kid had been the one who'd discovered her mother's body or not didn't matter, her malicious words were inexcusable. He knew that the memory they would have prompted in Tatum's mind would have been every bit as ugly as the one they'd prompted in his. Maybe it would help the kid if she knew someone understood exactly what she'd experienced.

'Can you play pool, Tate?' he asked, clearly surprising her with the question.

'No.'

'Well, you're about to get a lesson.'

'*You want to teach me to play pool?*'

'Yep. And,' he said, taking a can of Coke and a beer from the fridge, 'While I'm doing it I'll tell you about the guy who taught me to play . . . Doug Russell.'

That night, Tatum discovered that Jace hated Donna Browne's guts as much as she did. Obviously the guy had some redeeming features.

CHAPTER 10

July 1988

'Oh, Tatum, please? *Please* say you will?' Kaylee clenched her hands as she continued to badger Tatum. 'I'll *hate* doing it on my own, but Mum's got her heart so set on it there's no way I'll talk her out of it.'

Tatum again shook her head, and hurriedly began peeling off her sweat-drenched exercise gear. 'I can't, Kaylee, so quit begging.'

After a solid hour of circuit work Tatum normally found the hard, hot spray of the gym shower relaxing; of course, normally she didn't have to listen to Kaylee's heartbreaking pleas from the next cubicle.

'Oh, c'mon, Tatum! I let you talk me into joining the aerobics class.'

'Bull,' Tatum replied. 'You joined because you heard Daniel Crosby hung out down here.'

'Okay. Okay. And now I want a good excuse to ask him out,' Kaylee went on, undaunted. 'The deb ball is perfect.'

'The deb ball is a drag. At least that's what you said a few weeks ago.'

'I know. And I still think *that*,' Kaylee stressed. 'But unfortunately Mum doesn't, and I can't stand the thought

171

of having to put up with all those stuck-up little bitches like Melanie Porter and Libby Dixon on my own.'

'You won't be on your own. You'll have Daniel hunk-of-the-year Crosby with you.'

Tatum was drying herself off when Kaylee stepped from the shower. 'Need I remind you,' her friend said in a superior voice, 'that Daniel hunk-of-the-year Crosby was once an item with Libby bitch-from-hell Dixon?'

'*Was*. Past tense.'

'Sure, but Ancient History is Libby's favourite subject!' Kaylee continued. 'She'll be all over Daniel like a rash. I *know* she will! Oh, *please* come, Tatum. I really need you there. No one puts a person down like you do. And you know how much you love cutting Libby to shreds.'

Halfway into her jeans, Tatum burst out laughing, but her amusement soon died at the genuine worry on her friend's face. 'Oh, Kaylee, you're worrying about nothing, but even if you weren't I couldn't go to the ball. I can't *afford* to make my debut. I'm on Austudy, remember? And the pittance I pick up for helping out with the tiny tot judo class here is gone before I even get it!' Tatum didn't add that she'd been trying unsuccessfully to find a casual job after school.

'I'll lend you the money!'

'*Right*. And how am I supposed to pay you back, huh?' She shook her head, telling herself she was glad to have a valid excuse for not going. 'It costs hundreds for a debutante's dress, and besides, who would I take?'

'Are you kidding?' Kaylee exclaimed. 'You mightn't be top of the popularity list with our female classmates, but that's only because every guy in the school drools at the

172

mention of your name! Take your pick – ask any of them!'

'Even Daniel Crosby?'

'Do and I'll shoot you,' Kaylee vowed with a smile. 'But seriously, getting a partner isn't a problem for you – all the guys are dying for a chance to go out with you.'

'No, my problem is all the guys are dying for a chance to get into my pants and – '

'Geez, Tatum! You call *that* a problem? *I* should have such problems! Unfortunately the whole world seems to think I'm a committed virgin!'

'You are. I've never known anyone more committed to losing their virginity.' Tatum had only known Kaylee a week when the other girl had 'confessed' that she was sadly lacking in sexual experience, but that she was taking positive steps to solve the problem before her eighteenth birthday.

'Which is exactly the reason I intend asking Daniel to the ball. He's good-looking, popular *and*, if the rumours are to be believed, a great lay!' She grinned with lustful anticipation. 'But since I've never been one to believe groundless rumours, I'm going to have to verify the fact for myself.'

'Such a noble sacrifice! But *what*, given your, let's say limited research in the field, are you going to compare Daniel's performance to?'

Kaylee shrugged. 'A girl's got to start somewhere. With Daniel at least I'll be starting at the top.'

'What, and work your way down?'

'Yeah.' A broad grin accompanied the word. 'And then back up and down and up and – ' Both girls' laughter echoed through the empty changing room.

'See, I *do* know what I'm doing. Even if my knowledge does only come from biology books and *Cosmopolitan*.' The curious look that suddenly crossed her friend's face had Tatum groaning and quickly focusing her gaze on the shoe laces she was tying.

'Oh, c'mon, Tatum, *tell me*. Have you done it or not? I'm your best friend, you can tell *me*. I'm not going to blab if you say yes. I'd *never* do that! You know I wouldn't!'

Tatum sighed. Ever since they'd known each other Kaylee had been desperate to know whether Tatum was a virgin or not. School rumour had it that she wasn't, based on her background and looks rather than any proof.

'Look, I *know* you said you hadn't done it with any of the guys at school,' Kaylee went on. 'But you usually go out with guys you meet *here*.'

'So go ask *them*,' Tatum teased.

'Oh, right! Like I'm going to walk up to Greg Flecher or Peter Chapman and say, Excuse me, but have you slept with Tatum Milano? Heck, you've gone out with the entire basketball team at least *once*. Not to mention some of the guys in your judo class. I don't have that much spare time!'

Tatum merely smiled at the gross exaggeration and remained silent, knowing from experience that Kaylee would wind down more quickly without encouragement.

'Besides, for all I know you might have lost your virginity before I even met you. Oh, go on, Tatum, put me out of my misery and tell me and I promise I'll put you out of yours by not badgering you any more.'

'Nice try, Kaylee, but one of us will only be *more* miserable no matter what I say.'

Her friend frowned. 'How do you figure that?'

'Easy. If I say I'm *not* a virgin, you'll be *convinced* you're the last one on the planet! And if I say I *am* one, you'll be as worried about me losing my virginity as you are about losing your own!' She patted the other girl on the back and, manufacturing a gentle smile, said solemnly, 'Trust me, it's better you don't know.' Then, snatching up her bag, she hurried to the doorway.

'I know you wouldn't say anything to anyone else, Kaylee, but it's hard enough putting up with you badgering me about going to the ball. I sure don't want you on my back about my sex life!'

Laughing, she ducked the wet towel thrown at her. 'Hurry up and finish getting dressed. I'll meet you in Brian's office.'

Since Kaylee had started doing aerobics she often joined Tatum at the Bentons' for dinner after the Tuesday evening class. The initial invitation had been issued unexpectedly by Brian one evening as the girls had waited for him to drive them home.

A week later Tatum was at the Benton house, helping Judy sort through some clothes from a charity drive she'd held for the refuge. Even though winter was still officially weeks away an unexpected cold snap had seriously depleted the organization's supply of warm clothing.

'I appreciate you helping me with this, Tatum, but I thought you and Kaylee were planning to hire some horses and go riding somewhere in the Blue Mountains.'

Tatum paused in the act of taping one of the huge plastic clothing bags shut. 'We were, but she got a better offer. Daniel Crosby asked her to the movies.'

'Ahhh! I see. I take it this is the same *Daniel* – ' Judy said the name with a theatrically breathy sigh. ' – she's going to ask to be her partner at the Rotary Debutante Ball.'

'Gee, Judy! How'd you work that out?' Tatum said, being equally theatrical. 'It's not like she's been raving about him or anything.'

Judy laughed and shook her head ruefully. 'Kaylee's a lovely kid, and I've known her practically all her life, but if marriage isn't that girl's first priority in life I don't know what is.'

'Losing her virginity before her birthd – ' Tatum cringed. 'Forget I said that!' she ordered, scrambling to get her foot out of her mouth. 'Or if you can't forget it at least don't tell Kaylee I told you. And for God's sake don't say anything to her mum!'

Judy Benton's mouth was pursed in a tight line, and Tatum immediately jumped to her friend's defence.

'Judy, don't think Kaylee's slack or anything, because she's not! I mean, just because she wants to . . . well . . . you know, *do it*, doesn't mean she's suddenly going to become a slut or something! Hell, it's not like sex is a big deal or anything.'

'Sex is sex and physical love between two people is something else again. But *neither* should be taken lightly!' Judy said firmly.

Well, Kaylee sure wasn't doing that! Tatum thought drily, but refrained from saying so.

'I hope you'll pass that on to Kaylee. Of course, I'm not so naïve as to think girls your age aren't sexually active,' she told Tatum. 'But I'd like to think you'd be sensible enough not to undervalue it.'

An ironic laugh erupted from Tatum. 'If anyone knows the market value of sex, it's me!' she said bitterly.

'I'm talking about its emotional and spiritual worth, Tatum,' Judy said softly. 'From personal experience I can tell you that the ultimate . . . *high*, if you like, of a physical relationship between two people who love each other is so *spiritual* it transcends the mere act of sex in ways you can't imagine until you experience it.'

For the life of her Tatum couldn't imagine Brian in the role of super-stud! Sure he was nice, and not bad looking, but he was *old* – he'd turned fifty-five just a few weeks ago. Still, Judy was obviously satisfied, if the dreamy smile on her face was anything to go by.

'Do you understand what I'm trying to say?'

Having read just about every sex manual Lulu and Fantasy had kept in what they'd referred to as their 'Trade reference library', Tatum nodded. 'The ancient Chinese and – '

'And what are you two discussing so seriously out here?' Ethan enquired as he and Jace came in.

Tatum smiled. 'Tantric sex.'

'*What?*' Jace and Ethan exploded in unison.

'You know, the Eastern lovemaking technique that's supposed to incorporate spirit – '

'For heaven's sake, Tatum!' Judy's face was several shades of red. 'That's not what we were talking about at all!'

Ethan laughed at his mother's obvious embarrassment. 'I always figured there were only *two* types – good and bad. How about you, Jace?'

Jace shook his head. 'All I can say is I must lead a

sheltered life. I've only ever come across *one* type – good.'

With the exception of Judy, everyone laughed. 'As usual, you've walked in on the tail end of a conversation and grabbed the wrong end of the stick – ' She broke off, blushing under another roar of laughter.

'Poor choice of words, Mum,' Ethan said gleefully.

'I give up! If you must know were discussing the joys of love and marriage – '

'Ouch! Four-letter-word alert!' Jace held crossed fingers out in front of him and Tatum laughed.

'Relax, you're safe,' Ethan told him. 'No thinking woman would tag you as husband material.'

'Thank God!' He wiped his brow. 'The last thing I'm interested in is a *thinking* woman. With or *without* her eye on matrimony.'

'Speaking of which, Ethan,' Judy inserted. 'How's Donna's sister's wedding plans coming along?'

'Was that which as in w-i-t-c-h?' Tatum muttered, so only Jace heard. Jace slanted a quick look across to where his mother and brother stood talking before licking his finger and chalking up a point in the air. But the conspiratorial smiles vanished as Ethan's voice reached them.

'. . . but since she's on her way over . . .'

At the announcement of the girl's imminent arrival Tatum was on her feet. 'Listen, Judy, I think I'll head home now. Kaylee'll probably be trying to phone me and tell me how things went at the movie.'

'All right, love. Thanks again for helping me pack those things. And you be sure and tell Kaylee not to rush her fences.'

'Uh? Oh! Yeah, right. I will. See you guys later.'

'Wait up!' Jace was immediately beside her. 'I'll drive you. I want to see Bryce.'

Tatum knew seeing Bryce was less a priority for him than avoiding Donna. She was about to accept immediately, but couldn't resist making life just a *little bit more difficult* for someone who claimed he didn't know *bad* sex existed!

'I'll walk and save you a wasted trip,' she said generously. 'Bryce is at the club.'

'Oh. Well, I'd better drive you home anyway. It looks like rain.'

She ignored his go-with-me-on-this expression. 'It's been cloudy all afternoon. It's not going to rain.'

'You don't know that for certain – '

'Well, even if it does I'm not going to melt. I can walk – '

'*Why would you want to walk?*' he said tersely. 'When you don't have to?'

'It's kind of you, Jace . . .' Her tone and smile were sugar-sweet. She opened her eyes in exaggerated innocence. 'But I'd feel *awful* putting you to that much troub – '

'It's no trouble!' Jace himself flinched as his raised voice cracked the air, surprising even him and bringing startled attention from his mother and brother. Tatum, though, smart-aleck brat that she was, could barely control her mirth.

'Jason,' his mother said, 'for heaven's sake stop bullying Tatum. If she prefers to walk, let her.'

Tatum decided it was time to call a halt to her fun. She was sure the Geneva Convention listed leaving people to the mercy of Donna Browne's company a cruel and inhumane act. If not they should.

179

'On second thoughts,' she said, 'I think I will take Jace up on his offer.' At Judy's bemused expression, she offered a brief, apologetic smile. 'I'll get home quicker that way.'

'See how long it took her to work that out, Mum?' Jace said, looking rueful. 'Any wonder why I don't want her roaming the streets alone?' Deftly his hand captured the elbow Tatum had intended for his ribs and he steered her through the back door.

'Can I expect you for dinner?' his mother asked as he stepped onto the patio.

It was Tatum who answered, and did it in a tone of awed disbelief and raised eyebrows. 'On a *Saturday night*, Judy?'

'You're right,' his mother said, nodding. 'Silly question!'

By the time Jace had stopped for petrol and then decided to put his car through the autowash it actually took Tatum longer to get home than if she had walked. A point she made as they pulled into Bryce Benton's drive.

'Yeah, but look on the bright side,' Jace responded. 'At least we had the chance to spend some quality time together.'

Rolling her eyes, Tatum climbed out of the car, frowning when he did likewise. 'Bryce really is at the club,' she said. 'I wasn't making things up earlier just to be difficult.'

A wry smile twisted his mouth. 'No. You can be difficult even without using your imagination.'

She gave him a droll look. 'What are you doing?'

'Locking the car.'

'Why?'

'So no one steals it.'

'I mean why − ?' She stopped as he began walking around to the back door, then hurried to catch up with him. '*You're staying?*'

All the Bentons had a key to the house, and after using his Jace stood back and waved her inside ahead of him. 'You don't seriously think I'm going to go back and share milk and cookies with Donna, do you?'

Tatum sighed. 'Not even *you* deserve that!'

'Only fools like my brother.' His tone and face were grim. 'I know he's not the first bloke to be bowled over by Donna's looks, but I'd hoped that by now he'd have realized she's all packaging and no substance.' He looked at Tatum. 'So, you going to offer me coffee or what?'

The question only highlighted Bryce's absence. Previously Jace had only been here when his grandfather was home, and Tatum usually left the two males to amuse themselves. Now it seemed Jace expected her to play host and it unnerved her.

'Er . . . all right. I . . . I'll make some.' Realizing she still had her handbag slung over her shoulder, she quickly put it on the table. As she filled the kettle and got out the cups she was conscious of every move Jace made behind her. For some reason her senses seemed more finely tuned to him than usual.

She heard the refrigerator door open and turned to find him surveying the contents with concentrated interest.

'The milk's in the door rack,' she told him.

'I know. I'm trying to guess what's on the menu for dinner.'

She set the kettle on the stove and turned it on. 'Stir fry beef.'

Blue eyes registered their surprise. 'You're kidding? You've actually got the old guy eating Asian food? Hell, I thought you'd made a monumental breakthrough with the spaghetti bolognese!'

Tatum had to laugh. Bryce's refusal to eat anything other than 'good Aussie tucker' was the only thing they'd disagreed over since she'd first moved in. It had taken a while, but he'd gradually started to allow her to expand their menu beyond meat and three vegetables.

'Oh, he's still pretty picky, but stir frys are one of his favourites.'

'Mine too. What time do we eat?'

'*We?* You want to *stay* for dinner?'

He propped himself against the refrigerator and folded his arms. 'Well, since you jumped in and ruined any chance I had of eating at home, the least you can do is feed me.'

'But it's Saturday . . . don't you have a date?'

''Course I've got a date!' His tone suggested only a moron would have to ask. 'But it's not for dinner.'

'Oh. Well, I suppose you can stay.'

He grinned. 'How could I possibly turn down such a gracious invitation?'

The whistle of the kettle saved Tatum from responding, and she was grateful for Jace's announcement that he was going to watch the last half-hour of the rugby on TV.

As she busied herself in the kitchen she focused on trying to *relax*. It was stupid to feel so self-conscious just because she was on her own with Jace. They'd been getting along fine for months now, there was *nothing* they could possibly get into a fight over and it was only their fighting that bothered her – well, not the fighting itself, but the after-math. While she enjoyed trading verbal blows with Jace, regardless of whether or not she finished with the upper hand, she always felt, well . . . *edgy* afterwards; kind of wired, chock-full of adrenaline and unable to use it. It wasn't easy to describe and she doubted she could put it in words herself, but it was weird. *Definitely weird.*

A few minutes later she carried the tray of cake and coffee into the living room to find him sprawled full-length on the sofa in a pose reminiscent of a Levi commercial. He began straightening as she set the tray on the low table in front of him. 'Hang on, I'll make room – '

'No!' she said quickly, feeling uncomfortable all over again. 'I'd rather sit in an armchair.' Snatching up her cup, she did just that. 'Er . . . who's winning?' she asked, for something to say.

'Gordon by three. What team do you follow?'

'Huh? Er, no one really. I'm not much of a Rugby League fan.'

'Tate . . . this is Rugby *Union.*'

'Oh . . . right.' The chance that she sounded less ignorant than she felt was probably so slim it was razor-sharp, but rather than showcase her bizarre lack of knowledge about rugby in general she turned towards the television and quietly sipped her coffee. After watching the two rampaging sides, the second of which, according to the commentators, was Randwick, for several minutes, her only summation of the game was that Randwick had more cute players than Gordon.

'Hey, Tate, this cake is great! Who taught you to cook like this? Your mum?'

Jace knew he'd said the wrong thing by the way her head swung around and she stared at him, but she didn't give him any chance to retract the words.

'My *mum's* idea of teaching me to cook was to hand me a cookbook and enough money to buy the ingredients for whatever recipe she thought I could manage to read.' Her eyes were hard before she looked back at the television. 'Sara Lee made the cake.'

'Tat – '

'Shut up!' she ordered. 'I'm trying to watch this.'

Letting the lie go unchallenged, Jace too turned his attention back to the screen, but despite the drawn score-line and the commentators emotive call of the game his eyes kept drifting to Tatum's silent presence.

With most people the question would have been harmless, but Tatum Milano wasn't most people. She'd been raised not just by a woman whose maternal qualifications would have been labelled 'unfit' had they ever come under legal scrutiny, but in an environment 'most people' considered depraved. A few months back Jace hadn't had any trouble remembering that, nor the pitiful sight Tatum had been when he'd caught her at his mother's car. But now . . . He glanced across at the profiled figure in the armchair.

She looked like an ordinary sixteen-year-old girl, sitting there relaxed in jeans and sweatshirt, with her legs curled up under her watching television. Except he could see she wasn't relaxed; she was stiff as a board. And she wasn't watching the TV she was staring right through it, her lips pursed.

'Tate . . . I didn't mean to upset you.'

184

'You didn't.'

'So how come you're crying?'

'I'm not.'

'I'd say you're close to it.'

'Then you'd be wrong.'

'All right,' he conceded. 'So turn around and prove it.'

'I'm watching the rugby.'

'What's the score?' She shrugged. 'Aw, hell, Tate, don't sulk. Look, I'm sorry I said what I did, but it wasn't *personal*. Well, not deliberately,' he qualified. 'Men just *assume* that women who are good cooks learnt from their mothers. I didn't – '

She flew out of the chair. 'Shut up! Don't mention my mother again!' she yelled at him. 'You're as bad as everyone else!'

'Whoa! Settle down.' She wasn't crying, but her eyes were liquid bright and flashing with anger. She went to rush past him and he only just managed to snag her wrist. She tried to tug free, but his size advantage was enough to haul her down onto the sofa next to him.

'Let . . . *me go*!'

'Not till you tell me what the hell's got into you! One min – '

She gave a harsh, ugly laugh. 'Believe *half* the rumours round school then every male who's ever breathed has gotten *into me*! And why? Because bloody men *assume* girls are good at whatever their mothers were good at!'

'I don't understand . . . Ah, shit!' As the light came on in his brain he felt like an absolute bastard, merely for being male.

'Let me go, please.'

185

This time the request was barely audible as she sat, head bent, her face hidden by a curtain of glossy dark hair. Hating to see her so dejected and forlorn, Jace searched his brain for the words to try and make her feel better. Obviously this must have been what she and his mum had been talking about when Ethan and him had interrupted them. He wished now they hadn't. Discussing sex with a sixteen-year-old girl had been hard enough when *he'd* been sixteen too, but now he was twenty-three the thought of it was daunting!

But the simple fact was he could see someone had to talk to Tate. Now. Unfortunately he was the only one here.

He breathed deeply and hoped for the best. Keep it general and light, he told himself.

'Tatum,' he began. 'You shouldn't let what the kids at school say bother you.' He knew it was clichéd advice, but, hey, clichés only became clichés because they were true, right?

'I mean, just because they *think* something or even *say* it doesn't make it so. And smart people never believe rumours anyway. Right, Tate?'

There was no response from the girl beside him. He sighed. 'Tate, people who know you won't believe those rumours. I bet Kaylee doesn't believe them, does she? Does she, Tate?'

Applying gentle pressure on her chin, he lifted her face to his, but at that precise moment a solitary tear slipped from her thick closed lashes onto her cheek. His chest tightened with pain for the poor kid, and of its own volition his other hand released her wrist and rose to brush it way.

186

She flinched and opened her eyes. For a moment he thought she was going to bolt, but instead she drew a deep breath and, blushing, drew an embarrassed smile. 'You're right. I'm being stupid and overreacting. You must think I'm a real dork.'

'I don't think you're a dork. I think you're a very pretty girl who's more than tough enough to rise above locker room bragging and a hundred times smarter than any idiot who believes it.'

It amazed Tatum that one minute he could make her angry and the next – Damn! She was getting that weird feeling again! She was going to have to teach herself not to lose her temper with this guy. Trying to disguise her discomfort, she forced a smile.

'I don't know why I exploded like that. I mean, it's not like I think my mother was a horrible person or . . . or anything. It's just . . .' She shook her head, trying to get the right words into the right order.

'Just what, Tate?'

'Until I started school, I really didn't understand how Fantasy supported us, you know. She'd just get all dressed up, tuck me into bed and go out to work. It wasn't until I was in third grade that I knew her "client meetings" weren't the same as the ones Sophie Peterson's father went to. Sophie said her dad was an accountant, but that my mum was a whore.'

Jace knew this time that a cliché like, all kids can be cruel, wouldn't cut it. 'What did you say?'

'Nothing. I didn't know what a whore was.' She smiled at the sad irony of the statement. 'I went home and told Fantasy what Sophie said and she proceeded to give me a talk on the facts of life and a lecture on the reality of ours. So I went off to school the next day and told Sophie my mother *wasn't* a whore, she was a public relations liaison officer and that she earned a lot more money that *her* father! It's okay,' she added. 'You can laugh.'

Obviously she'd noticed Jace was struggling to hold back a smile, but the poignancy of her words stripped him of the urge to do so. 'What did the precious Sophie say after that?'

'Nothing. She wasn't allowed to play with me any more.' She lowered her head and studied her fingers as she twisted and untwisted them. 'It'd be an understatement to say I wasn't the most popular kid in the school. That's why I jumped at the chance to go to boarding school. I liked it there. On the school records Fantasy, or should I say *Francesca*, was still listed as being a PR executive, but at least there everyone believed she worked in an office.'

'Dad said she died of an overdose. How long had she been on drugs?'

Tatum frowned. 'For ever, I think. I know I was hospitalized when I was about five because I accidentally swallowed some uppers – '

'Shit, Tatum!' Jace couldn't believe any *adult*, let alone a mother, could be that careless! 'Why the hell didn't social services take you away from her?'

'Because Fantasy had friends in high places,' she said simply. 'And she always maintained that it was Vince who'd left the pills on the dresser.'

'Who's Vince?'

'One of the guys Fantasy fell in love with and thought

188

would marry her. There were a *lot* of those, but Vince was the only one she ever let move in with us. He got the shove after the pill incident. For a long time I thought it was my fault for stealing "treats", so to punish myself I stopped eating sweets.' She laughed. 'It didn't last long, but even now I still can't bring myself to eat too many.'

'I take it you've never experimented with drugs?'

'I once had a couple of tokes on a joint when I was at boarding school, but in the back of my mind I was terrified I'd end up like Fantasy, so I never did it again. I smoke cigarettes occasionally, but not as much as I did before I came here.' She frowned. 'Don't tell Judy I said that. She thinks I've given up completely.'

He laughed. 'Your secret's safe with me. At least until *I* catch you doing it!'

Tatum groaned. 'God, don't tell me you're anti-smoking too?'

'No,' he said, deciding that since she'd been so honest with him he'd reciprocate. 'Actually, I've been known to smoke myself, on odd occasions.'

'Let me guess!' she said. 'At parties and . . . after sex.'

He grinned. 'Sometimes at parties. But after sex? I'm not – '

'Not sure – I've never looked!' she finished in a sing-song tone. 'That's a pathetically old joke, Jace.'

'Yeah, but you're smiling again so that excuses me using it.'

She sighed. 'I know I shouldn't let what people say bother me, but . . . Sometimes it feels like no matter how hard I try to fit in, there's always someone reminding me that I don't.'

'Is that why you don't want to make your debut?'

She looked at him dumbfounded. 'How do you know about *that*?'

'Tag. He said Kaylee was trying to talk you into making your debut, but that you didn't want to.'

'It's not so much that I don't want to, it's that I can't *afford* to.'

'What if you could? Would you do it then?'

She shrugged. 'Maybe. No. Oh, I don't know! It seems a bit pretentious, don't you reckon? I mean, all that "coming out" stuff. I thought the only ones who "came out" these days were gays! And bowing down to the Mayor or the Bishop, or whoever they've got lined up, seems sexist to me – ' She stopped when she realized Jace was shaking with silent mirth.

'Hey!' She punched his arm. 'What's so funny?'

Wordlessly he shook his head as he tried to recover. 'Tatum, *no one* takes deb balls seriously any more. They do it for the fun of getting dressed up, that's all; although I must admit my date had to drag me there kicking and screaming when she did it.'

'You went to a deb ball? What was it like?'

'Very formal, seriously snobby and boring – '

'That's what I thought.'

'To begin with,' Jace continued over her interruption. 'Then it degenerated into being a lot of fun and a bloody good piss-up!' He smiled. 'You really would enjoy yourself if you went.'

She thought about it for a few minutes. 'Nope. No way. I couldn't afford a dress.'

'What about all those dresses you left at Mum's place.

The ones you said belonged to *your* mother?' Jace knew of them because he'd taken at least a dozen out of the car at his mother's request. 'Aren't any of them white?'

'Some are. But doesn't it strike you as being just a tad tacky to wear one of Fantasy's working dresses to something as pristine as a debutante ball?'

'No.'

'*Oh, c'mon –* '

'No, seriously, who's going to know it was Fantasy's besides you?'

'Well, no one, unless I told them. But . . .'

'Which of course you wouldn't,' Jace said reasonably.

'Ah, but you're wrong. I *would* tell them!' A malicious grin came over her face. 'I love it! Oh, God, it's so utterly, perfectly bizarre! A hooker's daughter, wearing a hooker's dress to a debutante ball!' She threw her head back and laughed.

'Oh, Jace, can't you just see it? Some spiteful little stuck-up bitch like Libby Dixon comes up to me and says, My, my, Tatum! Don't you scrub up well for a hooker's daught – And then she pretends to be shocked, like she's made a slip of the tongue or something . . .' Tatum continued with the imagined scenario, acting out the role of Libby.

'And that's when I'll say, Why, thank you, Libby you two-faced, rumour-mongering little bitch! It just so happens this dress was one of my mother's. You know her–Fantasy Milano. Actually, I think I recognize your father as one of her regulars!' She broke off, laughing. 'Oh, God it's perfect! I love – '

'*Tatum, are you nuts?* You pull a stunt like that and

you'll end up getting a smack in your pretty little mouth.'

Her huge brown eyes positively sparkled with devilment as she laughed off his concern.

'No worries. I've been taking judo lessons, remember, and you for one know I pack a pretty good punch myself.' Grinning, she raced to the phone and started punching out numbers. 'You're a genius, Jason Benton. I'd never have thought of wearing one of Fantasy's dresses myself.'

'Oh, good. Blame me.'

'Kaylee! It's me. Guess what? Cinderella's going to the ball! And boy,' she said triumphantly, 'is *she* gonna kick butt!'

CHAPTER 11

September 1988

Judy Benton had spent her normally prized Saturday morning in the hairdressers with two vibrant teenage girls whose laughter and chatter dripped with excited anticipation as they went through the ritual of preparing for their first 'formal'.

Tatum and Kaylee's youthful enthusiasm had infected even the most reserved of the salon's clients, drawing out tales of long passed but fondly remembered debutante balls amid shampoos, sets and manicures. After that Kay Taggart, Kaylee's mother, had suggested the foursome have a quiet lunch at her place. The girls, however, had favoured Kaylee's suggestion of lunch at a nearby restaurant – a noisy, crowded restaurant that by some 'totally mega coincidence' had been packed with dozens more giggling, talkative debutantes.

A long two hours later Judy had left the restaurant with a severe headache and a longing for a conversation with someone who didn't use the words 'hunk', 'dishy' or the phrase 'to die for' in every second sentence. As the mother of two sons, the excursion had been an entertaining and enlightening experience, but she was still undecided as to whether not having a daughter was something she'd missed or been *spared*!

Now, watching a robe-clad Tatum carefully surveying the various palettes of eyeshadow on the dressing table of her simply furnished room, Judy felt a rush of pride that was almost maternal. Someone seeing the attractive, healthy, bright-eyed teenager would be hard pressed picturing her as the bedraggled waif-like creature she'd been six months ago. Yet the social worker in Judy was more interested in Tatum's emotional state rather than her physical one.

The very fact that she was preparing to make her debut was indicative of positive advancements in that area, but the protective forcefield Tatum armed herself with was still in evidence, albeit reset from automatic to manual operation. Judy knew it would be a long time before the the youngster felt secure enough to switch it off and discard it all together, but the last couple of months had given her hope that it *would* happen. More than anything Judy wanted Tatum to learn to look towards the brightness of her future rather than back at the shadows of her past.

The shrill of the phone roused her and she looked up to meet Tatum's eyes in the mirror.

'Jude, will you grab that? And if it's Kaylee – '

'*Again?*'

The teenager grinned. '*Again*. Find out what she wants.'

Making her way down the hall of her father-in-law's home, Judy smiled. She couldn't object to playing personal assistant to Tatum today, simply because she'd been too moved when the girl had asked if she and Brian would like to use the 'parent tickets' issued to each deb.

'You don't have to say yes,' she'd said awkwardly. 'I mean, I'd understand if you *don't* want to come. 'Cause, well . . . you know you aren't my folks or anything, and it'll probably be a real hassle an' all, getting all dressed up and everything. And it's not like I won't know anyone there – not that it'd worry me if I didn't!' she'd assured them, rapidly adopting a confident expression. 'It isn't as if I'm a little kid or anything, but . . .'

Judy recalled how her big tough husband had silenced the babbling teenager by gently placing his hand over her mouth and saying, 'Tatum, we'd *love* to go.' That he had done so without needing to look at Judy indicated not only how sensitive he was to *her* feelings, but how comfortable he'd grown in his relationship with Tatum.

Still smiling, she picked up the phone and started reciting Bryce's number. After two digits the caller cut in.

'Honey . . . There's been a slight hitch . . .'

Judy's grandmother's pet saying had been 'Think of angels and hear the flutter of their wings', but there was nothing celestial in her husband's tone. This was his now-don't-get-all-het-up one, which always pre-empted a disruption to her plans. Traditionally Brian followed it up with a sheepish apology and a promise that he'd make up for her disappointment. After twenty-five years of marriage to a police officer she'd heard a veritable plethora of excuses, and the work-related ones she'd learned to accept as being beyond Brian's control. However, he *wasn't* on official duty today!

'Brian Benton, if you're going to tell me you're going to

be late because the judo championship is running over-
time, you can start looking for a divorce lawyer,' she said
coolly. 'I don't care if the Pope is personally presenting the
trophies. The ball starts in a couple of hours and I want
you there.'

A heavy sigh met her ear. 'Oh, I'll be there. But young
Chapman isn't going to be a starter – he's just broken his
arm in two places!'

'*What*?' Tatum leapt to her feet so fast she knocked the
dressing table and sent cosmetics tumbling to the floor.
'Tell me you're joking!' As a joke, Judy's news would have
come under the heading of terminally ill rather than sick,
but the sheer relief of knowing there was no truth in what
she'd said would have been enough to make Tatum laugh
with appreciation.

'My God, Judy, you've *got* to be joking! This is too
bizarre to be true! *A broken arm*? I'm being stood up
because the idiot broke his *arm*! I can't believe Chapo
would do that to me!'

'I doubt it was *deliberate*, Tatum.'

'Is that supposed to make me feel *better*? Because it
doesn't! Of all the rotten, lousy – ' Stopping abruptly, she
kicked the white satin pumps she'd bought to wear, but
despite the force she put into the act, the thick carpet made
the effort look futile. Muttering under her breath, she
threw herself onto the bed. She should've known better to
think someone like her could pull off the role of Cinderella.

'Tatum, honey, it's not as bad as it seems. You can still
make your debut.'

'Oh, no! No bloody way!' She shook her head resolutely. 'If you think I'm walking into that place without a partner you're crazy! I cop enough flak from those stuck-up little prima donnas at school as it is. No way am I going solo tonight!'

'But that's just it – you won't have to go solo. Ethan said he'd be happy to stand in for Peter.'

'Ethan as in your *son*?' The affirmative nod only made Tatum more bemused. 'But . . . but *why*? Why would he want to go to a deb ball, for God's sake? *With me*.'

'Probably because like the rest of us he's beginning to think of you as *family*. And the Bentons always come through for each other in a crisis.'

The notion that *this* constituted a crisis in the Bentons' middle-class world might have made her laugh had the sentiment behind the softly spoken words not sounded so sincere. Tears pooled in Tatum's eyes and she had to blink hard to clear her vision.

The next hour and a bit passed in a flurry of activity that almost rivalled the one the butterflies in Tatum's stomach put on. She was glad she'd listened to Kaylee and asked Judy to help her get ready because the woman's cool efficiency was a Godsend, not least because her steady hand was adept at taking over the task of applying eyeliner when Tatum's own shaking one threatened to inflict blindness.

Bryce arrived back from the club with two mates who were staying to share dinner with him twenty minutes before Tatum was due to leave.

'Tatum, me girl, you look absolutely beautiful! Don't yer think so, boys?' he demanded of his two elderly companions, speaking over their chivalrous murmured agreement. 'Pretty as any princess. If I didn't have a gammy hip, I'd tell the young fella who's escorting yer to bugger off and I'd take yer meself.'

Tatum smiled. 'If not for Ethan you might've had to.' As she was explaining what had happened Judy appeared brandishing a camera which she thrust into her father-in-law's hand.

'Take some shots of Tatum and me together,' she instructed, running her hands over the hips of the peacock-blue Thai silk pants suit. 'Then I'll get a few of her on her own and a couple of her with you. When Ethan gets here we'll take some more.'

During the next ten minutes Tatum decided it was a good thing Judy had pursued social work and not photography as a career, because otherwise most of the world's top models would have quit their jobs to work as check-out operators. Figuring she owed it to the woman to humour her without complaint, Tatum allowed herself to be directed through various poses and facial expressions. She only hoped she looked calmer on the outside than she felt on the inside, both physically and mentally.

While it was a safe bet every girl who would be there tonight would probably be experiencing a touch of nerves, Tatum doubted any of them would be suffering the doubts and confusion she was. Was she selling herself out? Two months ago she'd decided to go to this simply as a show of bravado, and to prove a point to others; now she wanted to go for herself.

Somewhere along the way she'd changed her mind about wearing Fantasy's slinky white sequinned dress with the leg-length split and opted for a more subtle velvet one, with a fish-tail back to provide ease of movement. Lacking the frills, ruffles and kilometres of tulle that most of the girls talked of wearing, it couldn't be classed as a traditional debutante dress, but Tatum felt comfortable in it. No, she conceded silently, she felt *beautiful* in it. More beautiful than she'd ever felt before.

Displaying only a shadow of cleavage, it had one long, close-fitting sleeve that finished in a point on the back of her right hand, leaving her left shoulder and arm bare. Tatum was grateful for her naturally olive skin which, despite the fact that it was winter, provided a contrast to the snowy purity of the velvet.

At Judy's request she raised a hand, straightening the three-strand faux pearl choker she wore so that the engraved gold disk in its centre was perfectly aligned. The choker had been one of Fantasy's cheaper pieces of jewellery, but only an expert would know it wasn't every bit as genuine as her teardrop earrings or the matching pearl bracelet on her left wrist.

'How many rolls of film are you plannin' on usin'?' Bryce asked drily when Judy had rearranged Tatum and him for what seemed like the twentieth time. Winking at Tatum, he squeezed the arm he had around her waist, causing her to sag a little. 'See, Jude!' he said. 'Poor girl's so exhausted she can barely stand!'

'Stop it. A couple more and –' The doorbell cut into her instructions. Stifling a relieved sigh, Tatum moved to answer it.

'Tatum, no! Not you.' Judy looked horrified. 'You're supposed to make an entrance. Go into the formal lounge, close the door and stand elegantly by the fireplace. It's the best we can do, given the absence of a staircase.'

Rolling her eyes, Tatum went into the rarely used room and pulled the door shut, but she drew the line at posing by the fireplace. Hovering midway between the window and the sofa, she crossed her fingers, hoping Ethan would know how to waltz. Peter hadn't – at least not before the three compulsory practices they'd had to attend – and even now he wasn't so hot. Still, she hadn't asked Peter Chapman to escort her because of his affinity with Fred Astaire. She'd asked him because, of all the guys she knew from the youth club, he was the best looking, and as they were both attempting to get officially qualified as aerobic instructors, they had become friendly.

A few of the things he'd revealed during their conversations had hinted at the fact that he was questioning his sexuality, and even though he hadn't come out and admitted he *was* gay, to Tatum, the possibility only made him *more* suitable as a partner rather than less. Ethan, though, was an eminently safe understudy, and, apart from being better looking than Peter, his age and law studies made him even more perfect for parading in front of Libby Dixon's crowd.

She turned at the sound of the door opening, then gasped at the sight that greeted her.

'What are *you* doing here?' Even though she hadn't seen Jace since he'd moved into an apartment of his own six weeks ago, it was a dumb question. It wouldn't have taken a three-figure IQ to work it out, since he was dressed in a tuxedo.

'Donna spat the dummy when she heard Ethan was

subbing for your partner. Now *I'm* filling in for Ethan.' His smile was devilishly handsome, and Tatum felt a wave of apprehension at the thought of the evening ahead.

'Don't look so bothered, Tate,' he said. 'I'm not used to coming off the reserve bench, but I'm pretty sure I can bluff my way through the game. I *have* done this before.' Holding open the door into the hallway, he executed an exaggerated bow.

Kaylee's slack-jawed amazement when she sighted Tatum and Jace was on a par with Libby Dixon's, but Kaylee's was friendlier.

'Quick, Jace,' she muttered through the side of her mouth. 'Check my pulse, I've just taken the full impact of a lethal glare.'

'From whom?' he asked, following her gaze from the entrance of room where the debutantes and their partners were to assemble.

'The sawn-off blonde in the Scarlet O'Hara number.'

'And she is?'

'Libby Dixon.'

'Ah! The girl behind your vengeful decision to be here.'

'I swear, she says one word to me to try and put me down and I'll punch her lights out.'

'No, you won't, Tatum.'

'Wanna bet?'

Jace's hand tightened on her forearm. '*You won't,*' he said, turning her to look at him. 'You look breathtakingly beautiful tonight, Tatum. Every inch a perfect lady. If she's stupid enough to shoot her mouth off, ignore her – it'll be plain to everyone in the place she's firing blanks.

The only one who'll convince anyone otherwise is *you*.' Lifting his hand, he gently righted her choker, which had slipped askew again. 'Now, turn around,' he ordered. 'I'll see if I can tighten this a bit.'

Mentally scrambled by his praise, Tatum mutely did as he asked. Then, to avoid being further unsettled by his fingers moving against her nape as they worked on the clasp, she concentrated on Kaylee, who was rapidly approaching with Daniel in handclasped tow.

'My God, Tatum, you look *absolutely stunning*! Your dress is *gorgeous*.' Though she said the last word in a reverent whisper when she looked at Tatum there was a flicker of hurt in her eyes. 'It's not the one you showed me.' Her tone, too, implied that Tatum had been deliberately secretive.

'I decided you were right. The other one was a bit . . . over the top. So I changed my mind.'

'All right,' the blonde said, folding her arms with pseudo-superiority, her good humour clearly restored. 'That explains the *dress*. Now . . .' She jerked her thumb at Jace. 'I didn't say *Peter* was over the top, so why the staff changes?'

Jace replied before Tatum could explain. 'Tate thought if she was going to be understated with the dress, she could afford to be a little risqué with the accessories.' His voice was thick with wry humour. 'By the way, Kaylee – ' he gave the girl a very appreciative look ' – you look extremely pretty.'

Tatum was glad Jace hadn't said her friend was 'breathtakingly beautiful' too. And it had nothing to do with jealousy! Judging from the way Kaylee had blushed and stumbled over her introduction of Daniel in the wake of the more understated compliment, Tatum figured she'd have started hyperventilating at being told she was 'breathtakingly beautiful'! And Jace had more than enough women swooning over him!

Slipping her arm through Jace's, Tatum suggested it was time for them to get into the line-up for presentation to the Mayor. Though she tried to sound eager, inside she was a quivering mass of nerves.

'With my luck, I'll probably fall flat on my face,' she muttered to herself. Surprised by the male hand that closed reassuringly over her forearm, she looked up and met Jace's encouraging smile.

'You'll do fine, Tate. Have a little faith in yourself. I do.'

'Why didn't you tell me you couldn't waltz?' Tatum hissed through a false smile as she stumbled over Jace's feet for the fifth time in as many seconds.

'Because I *can*. I'm just not used to trying to do it with a plank of wood. Geez, loosen up, will you?' The arm he had around her back pulled her closer.

'*What* are you doing?' She glanced around nervously. 'At practice we were told to keep a discreet distance between us.' His body vibrated with suppressed laughter.

'Tate, they could put a Mack truck through your idea of discreet! *Relax*.'

Jace had no trouble identifying the exact moment she decided to follow his advice. The tension in her body vanished on one soft sigh and her left hand, which had been literally clamped to his shoulder, was repositioned so that it gently rested against his shoulderblade, allowing her to move much closer to him.

The top of her head didn't quite reach his chin, so that when she spoke her words were muffled somewhat by his body.

'Thanks for bailing me out. I appreciate it.'

'No problem. So how long have you and this Peter guy been an item? I haven't been home much lately, so I'm not up on your latest escapades.'

She tilted her head to look at him. 'Peter and I *aren't* an item. He's a friend, that's all. And what do you mean, *you're not up on my latest escapades*?' Her eyes narrowed with hostility. 'You still think I'll rip off your family fortune?'

'Settle down,' he said. 'I merely meant I haven't heard much about how you're getting along. Still having problems at school?'

'My grades have improved. And my English teacher wants me to try for the senior debating team.'

'That's good to hear,' he said. 'But it wasn't what I was talking about.' His expression sobered. 'Are the kids still giving you a hard time about your mother?'

She lowered her eyes, away from his too perceptive ones. 'I'm handling it.'

He moved their joined hands as one, and placing them under her chin nudged it up. 'Are you?'

At that moment she noticed Libby Dixon staring at them. The desire to irritate the snooty bitch prompted her to dip her head a fraction and kiss Jace's hand.

Libby's eyes widened in astonishment.

Jace reacted as if she'd bitten him. He jerked his hand away. '*Tatum*! What do you think you're doing?'

'Feeding the rumour mill.' She gave him a smug smile, then turned an even smugger one on the couple dancing beside them. Jace recognized the girl as Tatum's despised nemesis.

The music stopped and, with the announcement that dinner was about to be served, everyone started back to their tables.

'It'll be fun to see how Libby embroiders a simple kiss on the hand.'

'Didn't you learn as a kid that playing with matches is dangerous?'

Tatum laughed. 'Don't worry, Jace. I'm a big girl now; I know what I'm doing.'

As they rejoined his parents at the table they'd been assigned, Jace wasn't sure he found her assertion reassuring.

Later, watching her and his father laugh their way around the dance floor in the Dads 'n' Daughters waltz and seeing the genuine pleasure his mother took in visually following the pair, Jace realized exactly how deeply the gypsy brunette had woven her way into the hearts of his parents.

'I've admitted I was wrong to her.' Jace directed his comment to the woman beside him, though his eyes stayed on the dance floor. 'I guess it's time to say the same to you and Dad.'

'The words aren't necessary. Stepping in for Ethan like you did, so she wouldn't be disappointed, was enough.'

A more noble person, Jace knew, would have admitted that the initial reason he'd offered to go in Ethan's place was to prevent Donna scoring a victory over Tatum. When

205

he'd called at his parents' home late that afternoon it had been to pick up some stuff he hadn't previously had time to transfer to his apartment. Instead he'd walked into an argument between his brother and his girlfriend.

'How can you claim to love *me*,' Donna had been screaming, 'and take another woman out? *How*?'

'Oh, for God's sake, Donna! She hardly qualifies as *another woman*; she's a sixteen-year-old kid!'

'A sixteen-year-old slut, you mean! People like her don't belong at functions like that. Hell, her mother was a pro and *she's* lived on the streets and done Lord knows what with God knows who! She might have your parents and grandfather fooled, Ethan, but believe me I know her type! She's a selfish user who's out for what she can get. And I'll be damned if I'll let her get *you*.'

That had been the point where Jace could no longer stand in the hall and keep silent. 'I've got to agree with Donna on this one,' he'd said, walking in on the startled pair.

His brother knew him well enough to identify the facetious tone in his voice. Donna, working on the 'any port in a storm' theory, grabbed victory prematurely.

'See!' she'd said. 'Even Jace thinks I'm right.'

'Oh, definitely. If anyone has the personal insight to recognize a selfish female who's out for all she can get, it's you, Donna.'

With an outraged gasp and spontaneously produced tears, the girl had run from the room, sobbing that she'd be in the car.

Ethan had lunged to grab Jace by the front of his shirt. 'I ought to slam your teeth down your throat for that, you bastard.'

206

'Go ahead. But it won't change the facts.'

The air had been heavy with barely suppressed anger as they'd stood nose to nose, staring into each other's eyes. Neither had spoken, nor taken a backward step.

If it came to blows Jace favoured himself to finish on top, if only because his work kept him active, where as Ethan spent the bulk of his days in lectures. Presumably Ethan must have come to the same conclusion, because it was he who had averted his glance first. Releasing his hold on Jace, he had put the width of the room between them.

'I presume it was Tatum she was bad-mouthing when I came in?' Ethan said nothing.

'Ethan, forgetting the fact, just for a minute, that you're too old for Tatum,' Jace had gone on, 'I really have to question your judgement in telling a woman you're involved with you intend two-timing her. Not that I've ever done it, but somehow I don't think it's something you advertise like that.'

'Don't be a smartarse, Jason. Dad rang a while ago and said Tatum's deb partner had broken his arm at a judo competition. Since the ball's tonight, I told him I'd fill in for the guy. I know how much she's been looking forward to it. I thought it fair to let Donna know.'

'But dear, liberal-minded Donna doesn't think people of Tatum's ilk should mix in polite society, huh? Surprise, surprise.'

'I'd can it, if I were you, mate, because until *you* butted in I at least had a show of talking her round. But now Tatum is definitely going to be without a partner, because I'm going to have to spend the night with Donna, minimizing the damage *you* caused.'

'Minimize it tomorrow. Take Tatum to the ball.'

'Much as I like Tatum, my first priority is Donna.'

'Ah!' Jace had exclaimed. '*That's* what you have in common; Donna's first priority is Donna too. And her second, third, fourth – '

'Fuck off, Jace.'

'Sure,' he'd said pleasantly. 'Can I borrow your tux first?' At Ethan's narrow-eyed query he'd added, 'I can't very well take Tate to a ball in jeans, now, can I? And if she doesn't go, I'll feel like Donna's won.'

For several silent seconds they'd held each other's gazes. It was Ethan who had spoken first. 'Make sure you bring it back *dry cleaned.*'

Jace was startled back from his reverie when fingers were snapped in his face.

'You haven't heard a word I've said,' his mother accurately accused. 'I asked how the apartment was going.'

'Fine. *I think*. I'm hardly ever there. The work's really starting to roll in now.'

His mother frowned. 'It wouldn't hurt you to drop in for dinner occasionally, you know. Even if you're busy, you have to eat. Since you moved out it seems your father and I are lucky to see you for five minutes. Not that we saw that much of you when you *were* living at home.' She sighed, then produced a sheepish smile. 'I sound like a domineering mother. I'm sorry.'

'I'll forgive you, if you dance with me.'

Their arrival caught the attention of his father, who whispered a smiling aside to Tatum, making her laugh and look in their direction.

'Brian's really taken a shine to Tatum,' his mother said, her gaze watching the pair. 'I have to confess, I have too.'

'The daughter you never had but always wanted, huh?'

She shook her head. 'I'd be happy if Tatum came to think of us as family, but to be honest I've never felt the need for a daughter.'

'So you're satisfied with your perfect twin sons, huh?' he teased.

'Perfect! That'll be the day! It was so hairy raising you and Ethan, I doubt your dad and I would've survived a stubborn, headstrong daughter as well.'

Jace laughed. 'Yeah, Tate's that, all right.' The comment was barely made before the girl they'd been discussing and her partner danced alongside them.

'*Psst!*' Brian stage-whispered to his wife 'Tatum was saying the kid has a bit of trouble co-ordinating his feet once they're out of his mouth. I thought you might appreciate it if I cut in.'

'How thoughtful of you, Mr Benton. I'd appreciate that very much.'

'I swear your dad made that up,' Tatum told her new partner. 'Truly,' she added, at his sceptical expression. 'He was trying to spare my feelings, but he was sick of me trampling all over his toes.'

'So how come you aren't trampling on my toes?'

'You've got smaller feet . . . Must be shrinkage from all that saliva.'

'Brat!' He pulled her closer. 'To think I sacrificed a night of writing up reports to be here.'

'You mean you put off work to partner *me*?' The thought of someone inconveniencing himself on her behalf staggered her. 'If I'd known I'd never have asked you – '

'You *didn't* ask. I volunteered.'

'I know . . . but I assumed you were doing it because you had some spare time on your hands. Hell, I'm sorry. I don't know how to thank you. I'm used to getting what's left over of people's time; they don't make it for me.'

It didn't seem right to Jace that someone as young as her should feel that way. Hadn't she ever felt secure enough to expect people to want to be with her, to want to help her if she really needed it? Didn't she realize that was all part of caring for and being cared about?

No, he thought sadly, she didn't. Because one learned from experience, and for the last sixteen years Tatum's experiences hadn't been good. Jace vowed to start changing all that.

'Tate,' he said, 'you can thank me two ways. The first is by telling me you've enjoyed tonight.' The brown eyes that met his seemed puzzled by the simplicity of the request. 'Well?'

She nodded. 'I didn't expect to. Well, maybe a bit. But the main reason I wanted to come was to piss off people who didn't think I belonged here.'

You and me both, Jace thought, smiling.

'I was going to,' she continued. 'You know, shock them by turning up in something really inappropriate . . .' Dipping her head, she let the words die.

'What changed your mind?'

There was genuine confusion in her eyes when she looked up. 'I'm not sure. The more I thought about it, the less funny it seemed. In the end I decided it was a smarter move *not* to live down to their low opinion of me.'

'It was. You've blown them right out the water tonight. You're easily the most beautiful deb here.'

The smile she gave made him realize he'd just made a massive understatement.

'You tell nice lies, Jace Benton. But I wouldn't have come without a partner, though. I owe you a big favour.'

'Which brings me to the second way you can show your gratitude.'

She gave an exaggerated sigh. 'I've heard that line before. This better not require me to be flat on my back with – '

'*Tatum!*'

Only an idiot could have misinterpreted his anger. Immediately she wished the words back. 'Jace, I was only kidding.'

'Well, don't! Jokes like that aren't funny. Hell, they're bloody insulting! *To both of us*. If – '

'Tatum!'

Kaylee would probably never make a more timely intrusion in her life, Tatum decided as the girl appeared at her elbow. 'I want us to have a photograph taken together. But if you don't hurry up the photographer will have packed up his gear.'

'You're a sight for sore feet, Kaylee,' Jace said, releasing Tatum with a subtle push towards her friend. 'I could use some time out.'

As he strode quickly from the dance floor Tatum wondered if she was the only one who'd noticed his teasing tone was forced.

* * *

In many ways Tatum regarded making her debut as the turning point in her life. While it didn't stop her enemies from continuing to treat her with disdain and spread new rumours about her, it seemed to reduce the number of people taking notice of them considerably. She found herself suddenly invited to social functions by people who'd previously given her little more than a tight smile when she'd caught them watching her. Initially pride prompted her to refuse, and she resented the fact that she was being treated like a new puppy who was allowed inside once everyone was certain she was house-trained. But then she recalled something Lulu had said . . . 'I can be, and am, exactly who I want to be. Who one *was* or where one came from is utterly inconsequential. Always remember that Tatum.'

And so she started accepting the shyly offered invitations to beach parties, barbecues, and finally requests for dates from guys at her school. After all, she reasoned, if she could get away with infiltrating something as snobby and quaintly old-fashioned as a debutante ball without being burned at the stake, she was more than capable of taking anything and anyone on and emerging unscathed. Not least the clumsy, inept attempts at seduction from boys who *thought* they knew all about sex!

But while Bryce was vocal in his approval of the increased activity in her social life, he was vocally disapproving of every guy she went out with.

'Dump him Tate, the bloke's spent too much time surfing; his brain's waterlogged!' he said of one.

'Never did trust a fella who couldn't play cards!' he complained of another.

And, naturally, he couldn't resist passing on his opinion of Tatum's dates to his grandson, which meant she had Jace riding shot gun on her social life too!

'Will you pair *please* butt out of my love life!' she screamed one evening, when she'd arrived back from a date to find Jace visiting with Bryce and received the thumbs down from both of them on her current boyfriend. Who, Jace had discovered through the sources available to him, was driving without a licence! Both men ordered her not to get in a car with him again.

'I'm nearly seventeen years old!' she told them. 'Stop treating me like a child!'

'We're only watchin' out fer yer cause we care about yer, love,' Bryce said. 'Don't want to see yer settling for less than yer deserve.'

'I'm not *settling* for anything! I'm *playing the field*!' she retorted.

'In that case . . .' Jace grinned. 'Think of us as merely coaching you from the sidelines.'

Tatum wanted to throttle both him and the sweet, chuckling old man sitting next to him. Instead she stormed into her bedroom and slammed the door. Loudly. Twice.

In between all this, she worked towards her aerobics instructor's certificate and studied. *Hard*. Her Higher School Certificate was a little over twelve months away and she was determined to get the marks necessary to get into university. Unlike most of her fellow students, and much to Judy's obvious concern, she had no real idea of what she wanted to study, but that wasn't important.

What *was*, was having a career that required more qualifications than merely having a female anatomy. For a long
time she'd regarded going to university as her dream; now
it was her goal.

CHAPTER 12

Boxing Day 1989

For several seconds Jace watched Tatum and Kaylee giggle and wrestle with each other from their positions atop the shoulders of two teenage guys in the Taggart family pool.

He recognized Kaylee's team-mate as the same bloke she'd made her debut with, Daniel Something; the one Tag was worried she was getting too serious about. Maybe she was, but from where he stood things seemed pretty bloody cosy between Tatum and the tall, tanned blond whose hands were wrapped around her thighs. Even with the assistance of his sunglasses and narrowed eyes, Jace couldn't place the bloke, but then Tatum played a field bigger than the cast of the Old Testament.

At the precise moment Tatum's gaze fell on him Kaylee connected with a sweeping arm motion against her shoulder, and with a startled shriek she tumbled backwards, flailing long tanned limbs into the water.

'Jace!' Kaylee called. 'I haven't seen you in yonks! Merry Christmas and all that stuff!'

Tatum surfaced, pushing wet hair from her face, and glared at him. 'If you hadn't distracted me, that wouldn't have happened!'

'Sure it would've. You weren't gripping hard enough with your legs. In shoulder wrestling, you're supposed to wrap your legs around your partner's back.'

'And that doesn't just apply to shoulder wrestling, does it, mate?' The unidentified guy's comment might have been directed at him, by it was Tatum he aimed his lewd grin at. The old Tatum would have taken a swing at the jerk, but now she merely rolled her eyes; Jace momentarily missed the old Tatum.

'Is your brother around?' he asked Kaylee as Tatum started swimming towards the pool steps.

'Nope. He took off a while ago, like the devil himself was after him.'

Jace frowned. 'Know where he went?' She shook her head. 'If he gets back before six, get him to give me a call.'

'Sure.'

Peripherally he noticed Tatum standing on the pool deck, pulling her hair over her shoulder and wringing water from it; the action destroyed what little decency the hip-length hair had lent to her bikini. Uttering a general goodbye, he turned to leave.

'Jace, wait!' Tatum called. 'Can you hang on a second, while I get dressed?' she asked. 'I could use a lift home.'

'Hey, no problem!' her wrestling partner put in. 'I can take you.'

'No, it's okay, Lachlan,' she said quickly. 'It's out of your way and Jace is going right past my place. Aren't you Jace?'

Her look was so pathetically desperate Jace had to hold back laughter. It would serve her right if he left her to the lecherous Lachlan, but he wasn't about to do *that* cretinous little creep any favours. Whatever other reservations Tag had about Daniel, at least the kid could be trusted to look after Kaylee. Jace wouldn't have trusted Lachlan enough to let him walk Tatum to the front gate.

'You're a lifesaver, Jace!' Tatum grinned as she buckled herself into the front of his car.

'Having second thoughts about the latest boyfriend, huh?'

'Yeah, and they're just as bad as the first ones I had. And he's *not* my boyfriend. I have much better taste than that!'

'That's a relief. So who is he?'

'Daniel's cousin.' She pulled a face. 'After today, I *know* one of them's adopted; the guy's got the arms of a drunken octopus!'

'You weren't exactly fighting him off when I arrived. Or if you were your smile disguised it well.'

The implication that she'd been leading Lachlan on angered Tatum. 'Things aren't always what they *appear* you know! It so happens I was conserving my physical strength for a possibly bigger battle if he drove me home.'

Jace laughed. 'If Lincoln had known that, he mightn't have given me such a filthy look when we left.'

'Lachlan.'

'What?'

'His name is *Lachlan*, not Lincoln.'

'Does it matter what I call him?'

'Well, no – '

'Good.' His wink was wicked. 'We'll nickname him Dickhead and save future confusion.'

'Jace, will you teach me to drive?'

217

'No.'

'No? Why not?'

'My doctor told me to avoid undue stress.'

'Oh, Jace! *Please*. I don't want to waste money paying a driving school and there's no one else I can ask.'

'Sure there is. You could ask Ethan.'

'Yeah, right. And have Donna come after me with an AK47.'

'What about Dad.'

She gave him a droll look. 'The guy's a *cop*.'

'Exactly. Think how well-versed you'll be in road safety and – '

'And he'll lecture me over and over and over on every little thing. God, I'll be a pensioner before he even lets me out of the driveway! *And don't*,' she cautioned over his chuckle, 'suggest your mother. Judy is the sweetest person in the world, but as a driver she sucks!'

Her dark eyes took on a pleading expression. 'Aw, please, Jace? I really need to get my licence. I've been saving up to buy myself a cheap little car so I can get to uni next year, but I can't buy a car if I can't drive, can I? No! And if I get my licence, you won't have to waste time driving me about – '

'Tate, I *occasionally* have to drive you between Mum's and Grandpa's. That isn't – '

'Yes, but what about today?' she countered. 'If I'd been able to drive I wouldn't have needed to beg a lift from you to escape what's-his-face's groping.'

'Yeah, you would've. You don't have a *car*, remember.'

'But only because I can't drive! If I learned to drive I – '

218

'Enough! All right!' Jace said loudly, then sent her a bemused look. 'Sheesh, Tate, they could've used you to extract information from enemy prisoners during World War II.' He sighed. 'Okay. I'll teach you.'

'Oh, Jace, thank you!'

Before he knew what was happening she was out of her seat belt and throwing her arms around his neck. 'What the – ?' Surprise sent the car drifting towards the gutter. He scrambled to correct the steering, grateful they were in a quiet backstreet. Safely stopped at the kerb, he yanked the hand-brake on.

'Don't *ever*,' he roared, 'do that when I'm driving! You could've caused a bloody accident!'

'I'm sorry . . . I . . . I didn't think . . .'

There were a thousand biting responses he could have made, but his emotions were so scrambled he didn't trust himself to speak. He drew a deep calming breath.

Common sense told him that, given the absence of traffic in the street, the dry weather conditions and a speed of only sixty kilometres an hour, the *worst* case scenario would've had them mounting the gutter and *maybe* giving the telegraph pole, some ten metres away, a small nudge. And, had that happened, Jace would have been demanding a refund on the ridiculous sum of money he'd recently paid to do a defensive driving course under the tutelage of a champion racing driver.

The reality was that his reaction, complete with shaky hands and thumping heart, exaggerated the bare facts: caught unaware by Tatum's enthusiasm, he'd veered slightly to the left and braked with more gusto than was necessary. Even accepting that, he still decided he needed a few more minutes to stabilize his pulse and fraught nerves. He knew what the problem was, he told himself. He needed a vacation. Working sixteen hours a day, six days a week, for nearly two years would leave anybody easily rattled.

He sighed. Bali? Fiji? A blonde? Yeah, definitely a blonde or a redhead! Ever since Tatum Milano had barged into his life he'd taken care to avoid the added complication of *more* brunettes!

Tatum called herself every sort of fool for acting so stupidly. Jace had every right to be furious with her. She could have killed them both! The thought made her shiver.

'You okay?'

Too embarrassed to look at Jace, she nodded. Beside her he sighed heavily and shifted in his seat. Her peripheral vision told her he'd pulled one leg up under him and twisted towards her. A sixth sense told her his blue eyes were slowly taking in every inch of her, from her wet hair to her bare feet.

'You got shoes with you?'

Her head came up at the unexpected question. 'Yeah. Why?'

'Put them on.'

The resigned flatness of his tone was more than a clue to his intentions. Guilt alone prompted her to retrieve the hessian bag at her feet and pull from it a pair of cheap canvas espadrilles splattered with red, yellow and orange paint. She quickly slipped them on. There was a strange tightness in her chest she wanted to attribute entirely to anger at how unfair he was being, but she felt more like crying than swearing. She reached for the doorhandle with one hand and her bag with the other.

'The bag'll be all right where it is,' Jace told her.

'I'd rather take it with me.'

'Take it – ?'

Jace's words were cut off as she shut the door, but she'd gone only three steps before he yelled her name. When she turned back his door was open and he was standing with an arm resting on the roof of the car looking totally confused.

'*What*,' he said, shoving his sunglasses up onto his head, 'do you think you're doing?'

'What you wanted me to do!' she snapped. '*Walking home*!'

'Tate, you idiot!' He laughed, taking all the sting from the insult. 'I didn't tell you to put your shoes on because I was going to make you walk home. I told you to put them on because it's not a good idea to *drive* barefooted! Now, do you want a driving lesson or not?'

'You mean it?' she asked. 'You'll still teach me?'

'I've obviously got a death wish, but, yeah. I'll still teach you.'

Her squeal of delight caused a kelpie at the front of a nearby house to start barking. 'Oh, thank you! Thank you! And I promise I'll never hug you like that again. Okay?'

'Tatum,' he said impatiently. 'Shut up and get in the car, before I change my mind.'

Tatum got her license, a cheap multi-owner orange VW and acceptance into university all in the same week of January 1990.

By August the same year she'd quit the tedious, frustrating grind of her arts course and taken a full-time job as an aerobics instructor at a local gym. The work was fun, the money more than adequate for her needs, and the guys she met there were hunks.

'Pass all your rejects my way,' Kaylee told her, depressed over the break-up of her relationship with Daniel. 'I need a man, but I'm not motivated enough to get my own.'

'For God's sake, Kaylee, stopping looking so grim! So you got dumped. Big deal!' Tatum decided she'd poured out sympathy for long enough. 'I dump guys all the time. As far as I know none of them have died! You won't either!'

Kaylee sent her a scathing look. 'So says a professional *dumper*. You wouldn't say that if you were the *dumpee*. I promise when it happens to you – if ever you go out with a guy more than three times! – you'll understand how painful it is. And, like me, you'll cry buckets.'

Recalling the tears Fantasy had shed over various men, Tatum shook her head. 'No way. If the day comes that I cry over a man . . .' She looked her friend squarely in the eye and said, 'I want you to get a gun from Tag or Jace and shoot me. My motto is death before dishonour.'

Kaylee laughed. 'Dishonour being caring about a guy, huh?'

'Nope. Crying over one.'

By the end of the year Kaylee's love life was back in full swing, and to celebrate, she threw a New Year's Eve party at her parents' house.

Tatum arrived late because she'd been helping Judy

prepare for the barbecue she'd planned for the next day for Jace and Ethan's twenty-sixth birthday.

'Hi, Tag!' Tatum spied Kaylee's brother among the crowd. 'Don't tell me your parents are *still* making you play chaperon.'

He looked horrified. 'Are you kidding? That was hard enough to do when she was sixteen. It'd be a nightmare now! C'mon. I'll get you a drink.'

She followed him through the throng, responding to the cheerful, if slightly inebriated greetings of her friends. She was looking forward to partying through the last two or so hours of this year and welcoming the new one. She had a feeling 1991 was going to be a great year for Tatum Milano!

Jace was in a lousy mood even before he spotted the bright yellow dress Kaylee had said Tatum was wearing. Who the guy she was with was, Jace didn't know; it was hard to recognize his features when his face was welded to Tatum's!

It took him probably twenty seconds to work his way through Kaylee's well lubricated guests, and when he reached them they still hadn't come up for air. Clamping a heavy hand on the guy's shoulder, Jace cleared his throat.

'I hate to break this up, but my wife has to come home now,' he said, smiling as the jerk let her go. 'Sorry, honey,' he said as she blinked in confusion. 'But Bradley just stabbed the babysitter.' He shrugged. 'Guess it's right what they say about the terrible twos.'

'Jace!' She smiled up at him. 'Happy New Year!'

'Don't bet on it!' he snapped, grabbing her hand and dragging her back the way he'd come.

'*Jace*! Damn it, let go! You can't keep dragging me out of parties every time I kiss somebody, you know!'

Ignoring her protests, he kept going until they were in the less populated front yard. 'Sit down,' he told her, nudging her to the low brick wall.

'I don't want to sit down!'

She flicked her hair behind her shoulders, jutted her chin and put her hands on her hips. Hips accentuated by the skin-tight short dress she wore.

'Jace Benton, I'm not sixteen any more. If I want to give a guy a kiss to wish him luck for the New Year, I'll damn well do it!'

'From where I was standing you were wishing that guy luck into the next century!' he snapped. 'But if you think your lip powers really work then go kiss Ethan, because he's going to need all the luck he can get! I've just left Mum and Dad's . . . Ethan has announced he and Donna are getting married!'

Tatum sank to the wall, grateful for its presence. 'Bloody hell.'

Jace grunted. 'My reaction was stronger.'

She turned to him. 'Is it official? Or – '

'The big announcement is being made at the barbecue tomorrow.' He gave a bitter laugh. 'Or should I say today? It's after midnight.'

'Daylight saving. It's not really tomorrow yet,' Tatum said despondently. She wasn't superstitious, but a disaster right at the start of the year seemed a really bad omen. *Really bad.*

'I'm sorry, Jace,' she said, putting her hand on the arm he braced on the wall. It was tight with muscle as well as tension. She sighed. 'Looks like you're going to have a lousy birthday.'

'Yeah, but Ethan's setting himself up for a lousy life.'

In October, a month before her twentieth birthday, Ethan and Donna tied the knot. Jace told Tatum he'd refused to be best man on the grounds that he couldn't bring himself to be that hypocritical. In the church he sat beside Tatum in the second pew.

In November, a week before her twentieth birthday, he sat beside Tatum in the front pew. He practically had to hold her up as she did something she'd sworn never to do, cried over a man.

If that made her a hypocrite, Tatum didn't care. Bryce Benton was dead . . .

CHAPTER 13

October 1995

Jace stood for a moment staring at the discreet brass indentification plaque to the right of the frosted glass door that concealed the inner sanctum of Bentag Investigations and waited for the familiar tingle of success and pride he always got from it. Today it didn't come. Sighing, he turned the handle and walked in.

His entry instantly drew the attention of the firm's middle-aged secretary, Dawn. Almost immediately her expression went from professional interest to relief.

'Thank God you're back. The phones have been running hot all day.' She waved the a message pad in evidence. 'And your distinguished partner has phoned *three* times since lunch.'

Jace groaned. Tag was currently in New Zealand doing the ground work required prior to them opening a branch of Bentag Investigations in Auckland, and so far he had encountered problems with everything from slow-moving builders to bad press from incompetent local investigators, who saw Bentag's expansion as a threat. Hardly daring to imagine what might be causing this latest spate of trans-Tasman telephone calls, he headed to the coffee machine.

'That stuff is going to kill you,' Dawn observed.

'After four hours with the Iluilano family I can think of worse addictions.'

The older woman nodded in understanding. 'How'd they take it?' she asked quietly.

'How do *any* of them take it?'

It was a purely rhetorical question. Lucy Iluilano had been a fourteen-year-old runaway who'd been missing for twelve months when her distraught parents approached Bentag to try and track her down. Jace had handled the case from day one, finally getting lucky three weeks ago when he'd come across someone who recognized a picture of the pretty young teenager. This morning, though, when he'd viewed her addict-thin remains at the city morgue, she'd looked neither pretty nor young.

Telling parents their child had become one of society's statistics was the hardest thing Jace could imagine he'd ever have to do, and it seemed the more he did it, the harder it got. Unfortunately he seemed to be doing it more and more often. He didn't delude himself that he knew exactly what the parents felt, but to an extent their gut-wrenching pain was contagious.

The burr of the phone intruded on his thoughts, reminding him that his day was hours away from being finished. He had reports to write up and a surveillance scheduled for tonight; with Tag away he'd been putting in forty-eight hour days. Moving to his secretary's desk, he picked up the message pad and skimmed its contents. It contained the time and name of each caller, a contact number and the reason for the call. As usual, the most common reason was 'strictly confidential', few people

227

being prepared to reveal why they needed the services of a private investigator, even to the highly skilled, utterly discreet Dawn.

She'd been with them ever since the early days when, desperate for someone to do their bookkeeping, Jace had asked his mum if she knew any one who might be interested. She'd produced Dawn Sutcliffe, a mother of three and long-time victim of domestic violence, who'd finally sought help at the women's refuge where Judy did counselling.

During the first twelve months, when Jace and Tag had officially been sub-agents for Mac Gregory, Dawn had kept their books working from her home, an arrangement that had been fine even after they'd moved into their first office; a shabby set-up above a butcher's shop in Ryde. Once they'd become fully licenced, however, the investigators had found their workload dramatically increased, demanding a full-time secretary, and with her youngest kid starting high school Dawn had jumped at the chance of getting out of the house and into full-time employment.

She'd proved an efficient, capable and practical woman. Jace knew he'd miss her when she left, and not merely from a professional standpoint. Over the years she'd become a second mother to him and Tag, providing everything from advice on the decor of their two subsequent offices to home-made cakes for morning tea. Jace smiled. Not to mention her unsolicited advice on their private lives. Just then the voice of his highly valued, but all too soon to be *ex* employee claimed his attention.

'I've got a woman here, wants to speak to you about her missing sister. She says it's urgent. You don't have any appointments for the rest of the day; want me to tell her to come on over, or slot her in tomorrow?'

It was on the tip of his tongue to say, make it tomorrow, and use what little free time he had before the surveillance to grab a feed and a quick nap, but the still fresh memory of the tragic Lucy Iluilano stopped him. Checking his watch, he mentally assigned time-frames for what he had to do.

'Can she be here by six?'

Dawn repeated his query into the phone and nodded.

'Tell her okay.'

'Well?' he prompted, with a questioning eyebrow, when his secretary had replaced the receiver.

Dawn prided herself on being able to judge the personalities of prospective clients from their voices alone, and Tag enjoyed putting her to the test. However, her assessments were usually so close to the mark that after six years Jace was more surprised when she was *wrong* rather than right.

'She's a Pom; very strong accent. Name's Phyllis Worthington. *Ms* Phyllis Worthington.' Dawn's tone reflected her disapproval of the title. 'She sounds about mid-thirties and strikes me as being well educated, earnest, a tad pushy and probably used to getting her own way.'

'I suppose it's too much to hope she also has a work visa, brilliant secretarial skills, a pleasant phone manner and a lifelong ambition to work as a personal assistant to a couple of private investigators?'

'You wish!'

Jace assumed his most wounded expression. 'Dawn,

don't you feel the *slightest* bit guilty about deserting me in my hour of need for anything as inconsequential as true love? Where are your priorities? Where's your loyalty and devotion to your boss?'

'Jace Benton! You've known for months I was leaving. Besides, if you and Tag can't find *one* secretary, in a country with nearly a million people unemployed, then perhaps you're in the wrong business.'

'Secretaries we can find,' he retorted. 'It's intelligent capable ones that are as scarce as spots on a zebra.' He sighed

'That's because,' she said, folding her arms and giving him a knowing look, 'few secretarial colleges produce graduates with minimum eighty words a minute typing skills, a degree in psychology and a first dan black belt in one of the martial arts!'

'Very funny,' he grumbled. 'We never stipulated a *black* belt.'

'Hmm. Might as well have. God couldn't fill *your* list of qualifications.'

'Maybe not, but we're getting desperate, so if He turns up for an interview send Him through.' He propped himself on the corner of her desk. 'What did Tag want?'

'The first two times he said he wanted you to call him back ASAP . . .' She let the sentence hang.

'And the third?'

'To ask, quote, "Why the bloody hell have we gone to the expense of buying mobile phones when Jace never bothers to turn his on?"'

Jace grimaced. 'I hope you pointed out that getting the mobiles was *his* idea, not mine.'

'No. You'll have to get used to doing your own dirty work. I finish up in two weeks.'

'Right,' he said drily. 'Thanks for nothing.'

'Hey, you're the one who's been telling me for years I should get married again,' she accused.

'Yeah, but I didn't think anyone who worked for a private investigator would be foolish enough to actually marry one! What's more,' he said giving the older woman a chiding look, 'read any of the classic PI novels and you'll see the secretaries are supposed to be dedicated and long-serving.'

'After working for you and Tag, I'd say they have to be *demented* and *long-suffering*!'

'Now, now, Dawn,' he placated glibly. 'You'll miss us both and you know it.'

'Well, just remember I won't accept *any* excuses for either of you missing my wedding!'

Winking, he patted her cheek. 'We'll be there with bells on; promise! Now, can you try and get hold of my illustrious partner and switch him through?'

'Will do. And remember I'm leaving early today; anything you want typed urgently?'

He paused at the door of his office and shook his head. 'Nothing that can't wait till tomorrow, but you *can* order me in a pizza for dinner.'

'*Again*? Jace, that'll be the third time in as many days!'

'Tell me about it.'

On entering his private office, he tossed the message pad on his desk then moved to the window and adjusted the vertical drapes to shut out the afternoon sun. Of a morning his view across to the Darling Harbour complex was impressive, but by late afternoon it was distorted by the lowering sun and reflected glare from both the water and the architect's liberal use of glass. He remained standing and rolled his shoulders in an effort to ease the tension clawing his body. Even after seven years what he'd had to do today was still the one aspect of his work he couldn't treat as routine, the one part of tracing a missing person he hated . . . and the only part he wouldn't delegate.

With a sigh he walked into the small room separating his office from Tag's and unlocked the filing cabinet housing their current cases. Opening the second drawer, he pulled out a standard buff-coloured folder labelled *Iluilano – Lucy*, carried it back to his desk, scanned the contents and began to scribble a final summary of the case. He'd barely sat down when the phone on his desk buzzed.

A cacophony of excited background chatter hit his ear the minute he released the incoming call from hold. 'Mum?' he asked, puzzled.

'Oh, Jace! *Tatum's home!*'

'She's coming home? When?'

'No! She's already home! *She's here, now*! At the house! Oh, I was just so surprised! Hang on a minute – '

Jace struggled to comprehend his mother's excited words as they faded to merge with various background conversations. After dropping out of university in her first year as an arts student, Tatum had worked full-time as an aerobics instructor before deciding to become a personal fitness trainer. Then, out of the blue, she'd announced she was going to Europe for a few months backpacking; those *few* months had turned into thirty-three.

Though she wrote and called his parents regularly, he'd

232

received only the occasional postcard and two gifts each December to cover Christmas and his and Ethan's January the first birthday. Recalling the elaborate hand-carved walking canes she'd sent them when they'd turned thirty this year, he grinned. Regardless of whatever other changes three years in Europe might have wrought on her, it was a safe bet her sense of humour was still as warped as ever! So, evidently was her knack for being totally unpredictable – the last he'd heard, via the family grapevine, she'd been living in Greece and planning to go to the States for Christmas.

'*I'm baaack!*' The eerie tone Tatum injected in to her voice was so good it created a tingle down Jace's spine as it reached his ear.

He laughed. 'And just when we were starting to think we were safe. What country deported you?'

'I'll have you know my departure from Greece was declared a day of national mourning!' she retorted. 'Which is why I came back unannounced. I didn't want to be responsible for causing traffic jams at Sydney airport as thousands came to welcome me home.'

'Judging from the noise in the background, there's a few hundred at Mum's as it is.'

She laughed. 'I think Jude's phoned everyone she knows and invited them over, but so far the Taggarts are the only ones here. Kaylee's still OS, but they're desperate for a firsthand report on her.'

'From what Tag told me of the week he spent in London with you both, I hope you're going to give them an edited version.'

'Tag exaggerates.'

233

Yeah, right! Jace thought. His friend was the most pragmatic person created. He thought about asking her to explain the friendship she'd established with the student son of an Arab oil sheik, but decided it was safer not to know how her temper mixed with jet lag. The silence between them became so long that Jace figured she must have put the phone down and gone to get his mother again. He could still hear the background voices.

'Tate?'

'Yeah?'

'I thought you must've gone.'

'No. I'm still here.' They laughed together at the obvious inanity of her response.

'So,' he said, when the laughter had died and another silence seemed imminent. 'Does Dad know you're back; have you spoken to him yet?'

'Judy rang him the minute I walked in the door. He said he'd missed me so much he was coming straight home!'

Again there was was a long silence, but this time it was Tatum who broke it. So,' she said, 'How long will it take *you* to get your butt over here, Benton?'

Jace sighed. 'There's no way I can get over this afternoon, Tate. Tag's in New Zealand and I'm drowning in work.'

'Oh. Well, that's okay Judy's offered to let me stay until I can find an apartment. We can catch up tonight.'

'You better not count on seeing me tonight either,' Jace warned. 'Unfortunately I've got an insurance surveillance scheduled.'

'Can't you delegate it to someone else? Judy says you've got dozens of guys working at Bentag these days and – '

'Hardly *dozens*. And they don't work *at* Bentag, we sub-contract them.'

'All of which means . . .'

'That reorganizing my plans for tonight will be a monumental hassle.'

'I see. Well, I wouldn't want you to go to any trouble on my account – '

'C'mon, Tate, don't go getting upset about it. You know I'd come over if I could, but with Tag aw – '

Her laughter cut him off. 'Chill out, Jace! I'm not upset. If you're busy, you're busy. I understand. It's not like you knew I was coming home, and after all it's been nearly three years since we've seen each other – what's another couple of days between friends? It's nice to talk to you, though . . . Well, look,' she said quickly, 'I don't want to take up any more of your time at work, so I'd better go. Um . . . See you when I see you, I guess. Bye!'

The dial tone reached his ear before he could respond and Jace immediately became reaccquainted with the urge to reach out and strangle her. A succinct four-letter word burst from his lips, just as Dawn opened his door.

'Trouble?' she asked, with a concerned frown.

'Tatum's back.'

As far as Jace was concerned, *that* said it all.

Even as she replaced the receiver, Tatum wanted to kick herself for sounding so petulant. Of course Jace couldn't just drop everything at a moment's notice, she reasoned, so why was she so disappointed because he'd said as much?

Because, dammit, *he* hadn't sounded the least bit disappointed about it! In fact he hadn't even said he was glad she was back, or asked how her flight was, or made any of the polite, cliched comments he should have. He'd acted as if she'd only popped out to the Seven-Eleven for a few minutes rather than spent thirty-three months on the other side of the planet. Not that he'd approved of her going overseas in the first place, she reminded herself. Everyone else had been saying they'd miss her, had been excited for her and encouraging her to go. But not Jace. Oh, no! Jason Benton had acted as if she was committing the crime of the century . . . .

'What is it with you, Tatum?' he'd asked one night. 'Are you frightened of getting in a rut or what?'

'What are you talking about?' she'd asked, genuinely confused by the force of his seldom seen anger.

'I'm talking about your inability to see anything through! How after nearly studying yourself into a nervous breakdown working to get a HSC result in the top fifteen percent of the state and guaranteeing you acceptance at *any* university to study practically any course you wanted, you go and pick a prissy, any-idiot-could-do-it Arts course! *Then chuck it in after barely two semesters!* Two semesters in which you topped the friggin' class, I might add!'

'You should talk! *You* dropped out of *fourth year law!*'

'Yeah, but I chose a career, stuck at it and established a business! *You* got a job where you run around in Lycra instructing bored housewives and steroid-stuffed bodybuilders on how to lose weight and smear on baby oil!'

'Oh, I get it! You're ticked off because I kept seeing Tiki Larsen when you didn't like him!'

'The guy was a steroid junkie!'

'Bull! Despite your best efforts, you couldn't prove that. And I *still* don't believe you. Tiki Larsen is a nice guy who looks after his body.'

'Tiki Larsen is a brain-dead Neanderthal who associates with questionable types of similar intellect. He's obsessed with his looks, getting laid and his car – in that order.

'And you're so obsessed with sticking your nose into other people's business you made a career of it! I don't need you checking out my boyfriends' backgrounds! And I don't need you telling me what I should or shouldn't be doing. I'm twenty-one-years-old and if I bloody well want to go overseas I will!'

'And support yourself doing what? Doing step classes? Waiting tables?'

'Why not? Believe me, I can think of worse ways to earn a living.'

Tatum knew it had been her rare, but deliberate reference to her background that had been enough to make Jace pause. When he'd spoken again it had been in a calmer, if patronizing tone.

'All I'm saying, Tate, is that you've got certificates to prove you're a bright, intelligent girl. If you took the time to back them up with a bit of *practical* evidence you'd be better credentialled to get work overseas. Why not put the trip off for a year or so and in the meantime do a computer course, or something that will enable you to get a decent job? I run into a lot of backpackers when I'm trying to trace an MP in the inner-city, and at least fifty percent of them are scratching for money because they can't get jobs. Not because they don't have work permits, but because they lack the qualifications or a good grasp of English. I don't want you to end up in a foreign country in the same position.'

'I won't. After twenty years of speaking English, I think I'm finally getting the hang of it.'

'I'm being serious, Tate.'

'No, you're being your bossy, arrogant, interfering self. In case you've forgotten I'm a qualified aerobics instructor and a certified personal fitness trainer. Now, that may not be your idea of a prestige profession, but then again, according to the old saying, an acorn doesn't fall far from the tree, and in my family earning a living from one's body is a tradition!'

That had been the last conversation she'd had with Jace before she'd flown out three weeks later. Though he'd phoned the night before she'd left to say goodbye, unlike the rest of the family he hadn't come to the airport to see her off, saying he couldn't spare the time off work – although Tag had been there to farewell Kaylee.

Three years later it seemed nothing had changed, except that without the excitement of making her first overseas trip to distract her, Jace's absence left her feeling empty. Because, despite the warmth and tears of joy Judy had greeted her with, and Brian's unfettered happiness when he'd identified her voice on the phone, Tatum hadn't felt she was truly home until the instant she'd heard Jace's voice.

The sound of his deep, dry tones had touched her heart as nothing else had, and it hurt that he could represent such a vital part in her homecoming when to him her return was merely an inopportune disruption to his professional snooping!

'Ms Milano, I presume.'

Tatum turned and discovered Brian Benton smiling at her from the doorway. As his huge arms opened wide she threw herself into them, feeling as if she'd never needed a hug more desperately.

A week later, Jace let himself into his apartment wondering if everyone wasn't playing some huge joke on him and Tatum was really still overseas, because on each of the four occasions he'd called past his mother's with the intention of seeing her, she'd been absent.

'You've just missed her Jason,' his mother had said, mid-morning on the day after her unexpected return. 'She's gone down to register with the CES for a job.'

He'd then called that evening. 'Sorry, mate,' his father had said. 'She's out catching up with some friends.'

And so it had gone on. Between job-hunting, catching up with friends, working out at one gym or another – she wasn't going to the one which she'd favoured three years ago because he'd checked – and going shopping, Tatum was either immune to jet lag or didn't slow down enough to let it catch her! After a week of trying to chase her down, he leaned heavily towards the latter.

For someone who'd seemed eager to see him when he'd spoken with her, she wasn't exactly making it easy for them to connect. While she did return his phone messages, not once had she tried to ring him at the office; instead she left a string of annoyingly bright, cheerful messages on his answering machine at home:

'Got your message, Jace, but obviously you're working. Geez, with the hours you put in you must be richer than God!'

'Hi, me again. Judy said you wanted to see me. Let me know when you're free and we'll get together. See ya!'

'Got the message you left about meeting you at the club Thursday evening. Sorry, but I've got a date that night. Can I have a raincheck?'

'Boy, Benton! You sure have a hectic schedule. Aren't you *ever* home?'

Now, as Jace glanced at the flashing six on his answering machine, he wondered what she'd have to say to him today. He'd phoned his parents' place twice today, leaving messages for them to have Tatum phone him *tonight*, and, by God, he was going to sit beside that phone and not move until he heard from her!

With Tag having arrived back yesterday, Jace had self-indulgently decided to give himself an entirely free weekend. Two operatives were handling the only case Bentag needed to be active on for the next two days and if anything urgent cropped up it could be referred to Tag, because *he* was bound and determined that in the next forty-eight hours he'd succeed in establishing face to face contact with Tatum even if he had to stake out her bedroom to do it!

He flicked a switch on the machine and went to get a beer while the tape rewound. The torment of Tatum aside, all in all it had been a good week for him. He'd nailed two insurance defrauders and AllComp Insurance, a new but rapidly expanding company, had been impressed enough to promise Bentag first shot at any future work they needed done. They'd also located one runaway and re-united him with his parents, and got solid leads on two others that should enable them to tie those cases up pretty quickly. An added bonus was that Tag's report from the New Zealand office had been more promising than either of them had dared hoped at the beginning of the week.

He was still in the kitchen as the machine automatically began replaying the calls. Typically there were two irritating hang-ups, followed by a request from a woman he'd dated recently to give her a call. Jace smiled. While Sonia had been a pleasant and extremely attractive diversion, Jace wasn't in any hurry to follow up on their first date. She might have had the body of a porn star, but her strongest desires ran full speed in the direction of marriage, mortgages and motherhood. In Jace's opinion he'd encountered her ten years too early on his life chart; right now he had about as much interest in marriage as –

'Just me, Jace . . .'

He stilled as Tatum's voice suddenly filled the apartment.

'I know I was supposed to phone you tonight, but I can't. Sorry. I'm having dinner with Tag. Talk to you soon though. Bye.'

Jace didn't hear the messages that followed. He was too busy trying to make sense of what he'd just heard.

She was having dinner with Tag! Why the hell would she be having dinner with Tag? And how had Tag, who'd only arrived back in the country himself *yesterday*, managed to get in touch with her when Jace hadn't been able to all week?

If he'd been at all paranoid, he'd have thought Tatum was deliberately avoiding him. That she was – 'You bloody idiot, Benton!' he muttered aloud, then laughed at his own stupidity.

That was exactly what the little witch was doing! Ticked off because he hadn't gone over to see her the minute she'd arrived home, this was her way of getting square! Three years of peace had duped him into forgetting that Tate's favourite pastime was inventing ways to get him back when he'd done something to annoy her. Sometimes it had been nothing more than not speaking to him, on other occasions she'd been more extreme. Such as the time she'd had one hundred business cards made up listing his home phone number and reading: *Benton Private Liaisons. Discreet Personal Services. Reasonable Rates*

That had been her revenge on him checking into the background of a body builder she'd been dating. Though Jace hadn't been able to get anything solid against the bloke himself, he'd uncovered enough murky stuff on some of his mates to tell Tatum to dump him. His advice had gone down like an atom bomb in a fish bowl. The cards had been her way of telling him that if he was going to mess with her social life, she was going to do the same to his.

Another example of the planning she put into her pay-backs had come as the result of him intervening in a heavy necking session between her and some guy at one of Kaylee's parties. Jace had thought the incident long forgotten until one night, a month later, when he'd been wining and dining a particularly co-operative blonde and Tatum had turned up at his place, belting on the door like the Vice Squad.

In a bizarrely brilliant portrayal of a sobbing hysterical teenager, complete with pigtails and a pillow shoved under her sweatshirt, she'd stormed inside, past his stunned form, stating that if he wasn't prepared to attend pre-natal classes with her then there was no way she was going to remain living with him!

Even after he'd explained the stunt to his horrified-looking guest, the night was beyond redemption.

After all these years he could see the funny side of the incident and appreciate the daring and creativity Tatum had put into her revenge. But back then he'd been livid, and his reaction had pleased Tatum no end. This time he wasn't going to give her that satisfaction. If she was hoping her deliberate evasion of him would work like some form of slow torture, she was going to be disappointed. When they did eventually see one another, it was going to be because *she* initiated the contact.

He laughed again. There was something comforting in knowing she hadn't changed.

Jace had always joked that the good thing about working in a job where you were often on duty weekends as well was that Monday mornings didn't seem any worse than any other morning. And when he'd climbed out of bed after a rare and restful weekend of complete leisure, he'd been certain he was well prepared for any eventuality. He'd been wrong. *He hadn't been prepared to hear that Tag had hired Tatum to replace Dawn!*

Yet even as he stood in mute disbelief, praying he was merely suffering some hearing impairment, his partner continued to utter the impossible.

'Because Dawn's got the morning off, I told Tatum not to bother coming in until lunchtime, but for the rest of the week they'll both start at eight so Dawn can bring her up to speed on how things operate here. She's done a fair bit of office temping and data entry while she was overseas, so once she gets used to Bentag's idiosyncrasies she should be fine. Of course – '

'Are you completely insane? Shit, Tag! At least tell me you're on drugs!'

He sent Jace an evil smile. 'You're supposed to say, Thanks for solving our staffing problem so quickly, Tag.'

'Like hell! If you think I'm going to agree to this . . . this lunacy, then you *are* friggin' nuts! There's no way I'll have Tatum working here! No bloody way!'

'Why not?'

'*You have to ask*? Hell, Tag! You know how dangerous this business can be at times – '

'She's being employed as a *secretary*, not a field agent! Dawn saw more danger when she was married than she ever saw in this office.'

'Tatum isn't Dawn. And she's a lifetime away from passing as a competent secretary. She doesn't even come close to any one of the five thousand applicants I interviewed and rejected last week!'

'Ah, yes,' Tag said, nodding as if Jace had raised a valid point. 'Mentioning all those interviews . . . You may recall that on Friday you dumped the job of finding a new secretary squarely in *my* lap. Your words were, "I've had a gutful. *You* handle all interviews from here on. And if *you* can find someone who's even *half* capable of meeting our requirements, I'll shout you a dinner for two at the Hilton."'

Jace stared at the ceiling as his own words came back to haunt him.

'For your information, Jace, I happen to think Tatum's a lot more than halfway capable. But because I'm such a sport, I'll hold off on accepting the dinner until *you're* convinced.'

'Then they won't be seeing you at the Hilton again in this lifetime.'

'Give her a chance. She needs the job. Besides, what's the worst thing that can happen?'

Jace looked at him. 'One of us will end up killing the other. Do me a favour . . . If I turn up slumped over my desk with the back of my head smashed in and holding a typed suicide note and a bloody paperweight, don't automatically assume it's suicide.'

Tag laughed. 'Don't worry, mate. Our partnership insurance is paid up.'

'Thanks very much,' he muttered, then paused before speaking in a direct, almost accusing voice. 'Tell me one thing. How'd she find out we were looking for a secretary?'

They was a wry twist to Tag's mouth. 'I happened to mention it when we were having dinner the other night.'

'And just *how* did you come to be having dinner with her in the first place?'

'Through the most bizarre set of circumstances. I asked if she had plans for the evening, she said no, so I asked her to dinner. Weird, huh?'

CHAPTER 14

Jace couldn't get a lick of work done all morning.

In an office usually buzzing with the ring of telephones, the clicking of keyboards and the tuneless singing of Dawn, the uncanny silence that descended once Tag had left reminded Jace of the quiet eeriness that preceded a violent storm.

He wore a path from his chair to the coffee machine. He removed the clock from his wall when he couldn't stop watching it and laid it face-down on the credenza; he removed the batteries from it when he found himself counting each tick and every tock.

His office door was open, allowing him to monitor the entrance to the firm's outer office. Chest tight, stomach uneasy, blood and adrenaline humming around his body, he watched and waited for the tempestuous Tatum to storm once again into his well-ordered life.

The precise neatness of Dawn's desk would have been enough to announce the secretary's absence even if Tatum hadn't already known the woman wouldn't be arriving for eighty-five minutes. Tatum was early. Extremely early.

But she'd not been able to wait any longer. Over the weekend her urgency to arrive at this moment had been tempered somewhat by the diversion of having other people around, yet last night alone in her bed, all she'd wished for was the morning. She'd felt as she had as a small child on Christmas Eve, wanting desperately to sleep so tomorrow would come sooner, but kept wide-eyed by both joyous anticipation and the insidious, niggling doubt that Santa might not come, that perhaps there would be no presents to greet her in the dawn.

Now that her craved moment was within reach, she felt a sudden need to stall it off; procrastinating, she turned and closed the door with slow, concentrated thoroughness. When she turned back he was standing in an open doorway, on the right of the reception desk.

Neither time nor distance had diminished the impact of those blue, blue eyes; they still had the ability to sharpen her awareness of things she otherwise never noticed. The loudness of her pulse, the susceptibility of her knees, her brain's ability to take in every little detail of him in a timeframe so small it was immeasurable. He looked older, harder, more handsome. Different. And he looked exactly the same. Confident, strong, dependable. Sexier than any man breathing.

Only a few metres of carpet separated them, but Tatum felt as far from him as she had those last six months in Europe. With everyone else, Judy, Brian, even Tag, she'd had no hesitation in running and throwing herself into their arms, yet when it came to the person she needed most to touch, she couldn't.

From across the room his eyes acted as a surgical laser,

reaching beneath her skin and altering her internally, creating major disruption to her heart's electrical system, short-circuiting her brain and completely shutting down her lungs. The tightness of her throat would have made uttering a greeting impossible, even if she'd known a suitable one; hello or any of its equivalents were too generic, given the emotions churning through her.

Once Jace would have laughed at anyone who applied the word *fragile* to Tatum, yet looking at her now that was one of only two words that aptly described her. The other was beautiful. Then again, *beautiful* hardly did justice to the woman standing across the room. The whipped-cream smoothness of her olive skin and her classic even features gave her a natural beauty, but it was the vulnerability and innocent sensuality she projected when she lowered her lashes and nibbled uncertainly on her bottom lip that elevated her above what was traditionally classed as beautiful. *Ethereal*. Yes, that suited her far better.

His eyes took in the thick shiny waves of her shoulder-length hair, then drifted to the tailored tan jacket worn over a dress that, at mid-thigh, ended both too early and too late on her shapely tanned legs. Strappy high-heeled sandals displayed toenails painted a burnt red, and that in itself seemed to signify the extent of the changes she'd undergone; that she no longer took the time to paint each individual toe a different colour said more than the absence of her trademark blue jeans.

Her metamorphosis was so complete not even the familiar scent of the *Charlie* perfume had survived, instead Jace's nostrils were teased by some more adult, musky, erotic potion. And while his body was all too male not to tingle appreciatively at such an abundance of beauty and feminine sophistication, his chest tightened with disappointment that all that remained of the old Tatum existed only in his memory.

Embarrassed under his lengthy silent perusal, Tatum fought down the desire to rush back out the door. 'I . . . I thought I should make an effort to look . . . businesslike. If I'm overdressed, don't be afraid to say so.'

He raised a mocking eyebrow. 'You *have* changed. The old Tatum wouldn't have *invited* criticism, she'd have told me to get stuffed if she thought I was even hinting at it.' His mouth twisted. 'Might as well come through to my office,' he said, moving with one stride from the doorway he'd been blocking and inclining his head.

She swallowed, then nodded, hoping her legs would carry her the distance. 'I . . . I brought you a present,' she told him, rummaging through the satchel hanging from her shoulder rather than looking at him as she stepped past him into the room. The brush of her arm against his abdomen brought her to a jerked stop; flustered, she turned and shoved the package at him before he was fully through the door.

With a slight frown he accepted the oddly shaped turquoise-wrapped gift and she watched mutely as he swapped it from one hand to the other, testing its weight.

'Must've gone close to putting you over the allowed luggage weight just by itself.' The dry comment wasn't accompanied by a smile.

For a few moments the sound of paper being removed deafened Tatum to the thumping of her heart. But only until blue eyes were raised questioningly from the solid mass he held in his hands to her.

She had to swallow hard before she could answer them. 'It's a crystal. I bought it from a gypsy in Hungary.'

'Relative of yours, was she?'

'Huh?'

Giving a dismissive shake of his head, Jace studied the glacier-like object in his palm. His parents had received Italian leather wallets. Tag an elegant pen. He got a rock.

'Clear crystal is supposed to generate clear thinking. Well? What do you think?'

'I think . . .' He paused and wryly shook his head. 'I'm glad you're home, Tate.'

The radiant smile his admission sparked made him want to repeat it a thousand times if she'd never stop looking at him like that. Never go away again.

'Me too.' Tatum couldn't contain the resigned sigh that slipped from her. 'I missed you, Jace.' His searching eyes trapped her gaze even before his free hand lifted to ensnare her chin.

'Did you?' he asked softly. 'How much?'

Her first instinct was to say something witty and dismissing, but at some point she had to be honest with and to herself. Determinedly she lifted her head, freeing herself from his hold.

'*Too much*,' she said. With self-destructive tenacity she maintained direct visual contact. 'More than I wanted to. More than I understood. More when I got back and heard your voice than at any time I was overseas. A hundred times more in this last week when . . .'

'When you've been *avoiding me*?'

She shook her head. Scowling, he set the crystal on a bookcase and stepped closer. Only inches separated them.

'Tell me you were avoiding me, Tatum.'

In the confusion, his proximity caused her body and mind she thought the words sounded almost like a plea. Again she shook her head, but this time in an attempt to reorientate her senses; this close she was drowning in him. 'I wasn't avoiding you.'

It was the truth. If she'd been avoiding anyone, it had been herself, by refusing to place herself in a position where she'd be forced to admit she was attracted to Jace Benton. Sexually attracted to him. She suspected she always had been, but in the past she'd been more fascinated by the novelty of having people, male and female alike, respect and care for her. For a sixteen-year-old girl who'd grown up in an emotional isolation chamber, those things had been far more mysterious and valuable to her than sex had ever been.

But she wasn't sixteen any more. Or even twenty or twenty-one. She was a woman who understood the wants and needs of her body. Hearing Jace's voice the other day had been enough to alert her to the fact that it was specifically *his* body she wanted and needed. The realization scared as much as it excited her. There weren't many things Fantasy had told her that stuck in her mind, but one that did was, 'Good sex ain't that hard to come by kid, but good friends? Now, they're rare as a virgin in a brothel. Screw a friend and you screw a friendship.'

Not that she could explain any of that to Jace, who was quite clearly waiting for an explanation. She gave what she hoped was a suitably apologetic smile, before saying, 'I've been busy. I wanted to get my life organized. Find work, somewhere to stay . . . I've had a million things to – '

'*Bull* . . .' he leaned closer '. . . *shit*! You were avoiding me, Tatum. You were pissed off with me for not coming and seeing you right away and we both know it! And you're a liar if you deny it. Go on,' he dared her. 'Deny it.'

'Okay! I *was* pissed off, all right!' she retorted. 'But at *myself* for caring so damned much! After three years away I'd forgotten what a bloody arrogant jerk you – '

He grabbed the wrist of the hand she poked into his chest and tugged her to him, grinning. 'Welcome home, Tatum Milano . . .'

If Jace thought of anything as he lowered his mouth to hers it was that he'd wanted to do this a thousand times before, but hadn't realized it; perhaps the crystal did work. But from the moment her lips parted beneath his he thought of nothing bar the woman in his arms.

Driving his fingers into her hair, he angled her head first one way then the other, desperate to taste all of her. Her honey-sweet mouth was pliant and willing, and the eager innocence of her throaty responses stoked his sexual ego. But the notion that he was in control was shot to hell when she nipped his bottom lip, and before his startled growl had passed his throat her agile little tongue was stroking the roof of his mouth.

Jace was lost. Lost in the whirr of his own blood as it raced at light-speed through his body. In the soft purrs and muffled moans of a woman who held him as if she'd never let go. Lost to everything but the absolute conviction that the white-hot desire she generated would incinerate him from the inside. He'd been with his share of women over the years, but none had sparked him as quickly or as intensely as Tatum did; it was a fact, not a surprise.

From the first night she'd slugged him one, this volatile, feral little witch had had him off balance. From the reactions she'd caused in him over the years he'd come to accept that she made him angrier, happier, sadder and flat-out crazier than any other person alive. If it had taken longer to discover that she also made him hornier, it didn't matter a damn. Not now. Not now when he could taste the honeyed sweetness of her tongue against his. Not now that her long, elegant nails were grazing his scalp and sending the chill of goosebumps down his spine, while her breasts burned hot through the too many layers of clothing separating them. Devoid of logical thought, he dragged her closer, even as his hands feverishly worked to peel her jacket off.

Tatum had gone limp the moment Jace's mouth had descended on hers, and from that point on the heat in his passionate kisses rose until she was certain every bone in her body had liquefied. She seriously doubted she was capable of standing, but, since the only way of being certain meant letting go of the strong male body currently bearing all her weight, she had no wish to verify her suspicions. Actually she had no wish for *anything* beyond this moment lasting for eternity.

The potency of her need to touch him exceeded any-thing she'd even known. Her hands moved over his body with the same jerky frantic actions as his explored hers; sliding, stroking, squeezing. Their kisses were equally manic, but punctuated with breathy, panted prayers to

God and broken, unintelligible expressions of their jumbled thoughts and unfettered emotions.

The scent and sounds of passion and desire muffled the sounds of buttons bursting, seams splitting and zippers releasing. The practicalities of time and place were immersed in the power of lust, longing and need.

Tatum became obsessed with the contrasts her fingers and mouth discovered as they played over Jace's body; the hard, contoured muscles of his shoulders and back, the sensuous, furred coarseness of his chest and the damp, salty-smoothness of his skin. But, as a woman, it was the skill of his multi-textured hands that fascinated her most. The calloused toughness on the pads of his fingers as they rolled her engorged nipples set off showers of sparks in her blood, brain and belly. The sensation of his palm stroking against her abdomen made the muscles there jerk in response. And the feel of the strong hands grasping her buttocks, pressing her hips to his so that his arousal nudged against her, heated every millimetre of her bare flesh.

Ensnared in a mesh of sensuality, she was unaware that Jace was lifting her onto his desk until something crashed to the floor; but nothing could tempt her attention from the man holding her. With infinite gentleness he touched a finger to her lips, and with a sensuality that made her gasp he slipped it in and out of her mouth without his eyes leaving hers. A trillion questions could have been asked and answered in that long suspension of time, but only one was. Wordlessly raised, silently answered, and then accepted with a kiss that melted her womb.

Still, she was quite unprepared for the vortex of desire

that beset her body as Jace, watching her with an expression of absolute reverence, slowly separated her thighs and stepped between them. His focus was solely on her as he drew her, oh, so *slowly* towards the edge of desk. Of their own accord her legs lifted to close around his hips . . .

'Don't close your eyes.'

There was no time to respond for the command coincided with his warm, slick possession of her body and his invasion of her soul. The raw emotion radiating from him seemed all-consuming. She tried to speak, tried to verbalize her thoughts, but instead his existence personified every one of them. *Jace . . . Jace . . .* His face rapidly became a watery blur even as his hands drew hers nearer.

'Ah . . . gypsy . . .' he said brokenly. 'I've missed you so damn much . . .'

And then there were no more words. No more thoughts. Nothing but him and the heat he built and built inside her until it became an almost pleasurable pain . . .

'Easy, Tate . . . I'm with you, gypsy . . .'

She heard his promise through a kaleidoscope of sensations too beautiful to describe and accompanied by a strangled cry of glory which in another world might have been hers . . .

Jace clamped his teeth together but to no avail, what remnant of control he'd had disintegrated at the specular sight of Tatum, head flung back, breasts thrust towards the ceiling, quaking in pleasure as she cried his name.

Tatum discovered she wasn't so much clinging to Jace as slumped against him. Her arms were slackly wrapped around his upper arms and she was pretty sure only her linked fingers kept them there; her chin resting on his right shoulder afforded her an unobstructed view into the outer office.

'We didn't even shut the door.'

Jace chuckled. 'Guess that ought to prove this wasn't premeditated.'

'The presence of a nice soft sofa, less than three feet away, also supports lack of forethought.'

'Not to mention the fact we didn't use any contraception.'

At the tense tone in his voice Tatum stiffened and sat back. 'You won't catch anything from me. I've practised *very safe* sex.' It was impossible to miss the defensive note in her voice. 'I lost my virginity to a guy wearing a condom when I was – '

'Tate, I don't want the history of your sex-life. I – '

'Too late.' In one quick move she was out of his arms and off the desk. 'You just got it.'

'You mean *this* was only the *second* time for you?'

With a nonchalant shrug she continued picking up her clothes.

'Shit, Tate, why didn't you say so? If I'd known that . . .'

'You'd what? Have shut the door? Used the sofa?' She made no attempt to cover herself as she stood there in high heels, with her clothing casually slung over her arm. A teasing smile crawled across her face. 'Relax, Jace,' she said gently. 'It's okay. I'm not about to start complaining. I mightn't have much personal experience with sex, but I'll go out on a limb and say what we just had was pretty good.'

Pretty good? Good? Astonishment left Jace speechless. It

was one thing to be blasé about sex, but either he was watching a corpse casually dressing herself or Tatum's expectations of what constituted *great* sex, exceeded the realms of even miraculous probability!

'You better get dressed,' she advised, checking her watch. 'Dawn'll be here soon.'

'Tate,' he said. 'Look at me.'

'What?' She spared him only a brief glance before she began hunting furiously through her handbag. A satisfied expression lit her face seconds before her hand came out holding a hairbrush. Moving to the etched mirror in a panel of the bookcase, she began tidying her hair.

'Tatum! Damn it, will you stop for a minute and talk about this?'

His tone slowed her hand, but she met his gaze via the mirror. 'Jace, Dawn will – '

'I don't give a stuff about Dawn! I want to know what the hell you're feeling about what just happened between us!'

Striding across to her, he spun her round to face him. The shadowed confusion in her eyes doused his irritation somewhat. She wasn't anywhere near as composed as she was trying to make out.

He spoke softly. 'What we just shared went *way* beyond being "pretty good" sex. We *both* know that; previous experience can only be used as a gauge, it doesn't alter what happened.'

Her acceptance of the fact came in a resigned sigh.

'Look, Tate, about you starting work – '

'I'm not about to back out of this job because of – '

'I don't want you to. The question is . . . what happens *now*?'

Her shoulders stiffened and her chin shot up. 'If you're worried about me getting all clingy and dependent on you and generally making things difficult – *don't be*.'

'I'm not. My question was, What happens *now*? Do we . . .' He smiled. 'Stay here and try to explain to a very experienced private investigators' secretary why your jacket's torn and I'm wearing my shirt *sans* buttons? Or . . .' He slipped a hand under her hair to the back of her neck and drew her towards him. 'Do we get out of here *fast* and spend the rest of the afternoon in my bed *trying* to achieve *incredible* sex again?'

His kiss was slow, sensuous and persuasive. When he pulled back Tatum's heart was thumping fit to burst. Knowing she was ignoring all common sense, and tempting fate beyond the boundaries of sanity, she still answered, 'I guess every girl should do it in a bed at least once.'

She blinked several times, adjusting to the dusk-dimness of Jace's bedroom, then turned her head to discover him propped on an elbow watching her. His hair was uncombed, still damp in patches from a shower they'd shared at some point during an afternoon of torrid love-making, his jaw was shadowed by the lateness of the day, and his eyes . . . so blue and seductive they shouldn't have been legal. Tatum decided Jace Benton was the most gorgeous man ever created.

'Still want to stick to your assessment of "pretty good"?' he asked her, drawing a feather-soft finger down her nose and making her smile.

'How does *pretty bloody terrific* sound?'

258

'Only slightly less understated.' He dropped a quick kiss on her lips and sat back. 'I'm going to order a pizza. What would you say if I offered you a super supreme with extra cheese?'

'That you're getting kickbacks from heart surgeons.' She smiled. 'Thanks, but I'll pass. Besides I'd better be going. Judy's expecting me for dinner.'

As she blithely rose from the bed and headed for the bathroom Jace suddenly found himself consumed by the sensation of being totally pissed off! He didn't know why he was so irritated, except he was. His temperament was only marginally improved when she arrived in the kitchen twenty minutes later, mumbling concerns about what she was going to say when Judy asked how her first day at Bentag had gone. Jace had excused their absence to Dawn with a note saying that he'd had to go out and, not wanting to leave Tatum alone in the office in case Dawn got delayed, he'd told her not to bother starting until the next day.

'Tell her the truth,' he suggested.

'What? That I spent the afternoon in bed with you?'

His look chided her. 'That we spent the afternoon together, catching up on things. She'll assume as much anyway when I take you home.'

'You don't have to take me home. I'll get a cab.'

'I said I'll take you home, and I will. Don't worry, I'm not going to think of you as *clingy* if you give in gracefully.'

'It's not that. It's . . . well, your mother's very astute. No matter how hard we try not to act differently, she'll sense things have changed between us.'

He was amused by her comment. 'I don't see how.

259

Unless, of course, you start getting all *clingy* and calling me things like *sweetiepie* and *snookums*!'

Tatum tried to look stern. 'I'm trying to be serious here, Jace. If your mother found out we were . . . er . . . um . . .'

'Lovers? Having an affair?'

She shrugged. 'Whatever. I don't think she'd approve.'

'Tate, my mother wasn't born yesterday. She *knows* people have sex outside marriage. Hell, she's got friends *I know* are having extra-marital affairs and she doesn't pass judgement on them.'

'Still, I can't help thinking she'd be disappointed. She expects better of me – '

'Expects better! I'm her *son*, for crying out loud! She has a maternal obligation to think I'm wonderful!'

Tatum rolled her eyes. 'That's not what I meant and you know it.

'Well, it's no secret she adores you. I sometimes think she wishes you were really her daughter.'

'And *there*,' Tatum exclaimed, 'lies the problem! How are *you* going to handle it if she decides I'll make the perfect daughter-in-law?'

Jace visibly paled and Tatum felt half-amused and half . . . *Not hurt*, she told herself quickly. But a part of her felt . . . *miffed*! Yeah, her pride was *miffed* that just the idea of marriage to her should be so abhorrent.

'Chill out, Jace. I've got about as much inclination to get married as I do to enter a convent. Less. But Judy's a born romantic. Hell, she even thought Ethan and Donna could make it work, and look at the shit *he's* going through.'

Jace knew Tatum wasn't exaggerating the difficulties Ethan was experiencing. His marriage to Donna had been a disaster from day one, and his idea that accepting a partnership he didn't want but that Donna did, in Melbourne, would help things hadn't borne fruit. Currently they were separated, with Ethan having to fight tooth and nail just to see his daughter. The thought of his niece, LaTasha, who was newly three, jolted him.

'What are you going to do if you're pregnant?'

'*Pardon me*?'

'We didn't use a condom in the office. You might be pregnant.'

Tatum pushed aside the pinch of pain in her heart and forced a dry laugh. 'If I'm pregnant, it'll be what a gynaecologist in Paris would call the ultimate miracle. I've had endometriosis since I was fourteen, Jace,' she explained. 'Recently it's got worse, which is why I came home. If I've got to have a hysterectomy, I'm having it in a hospital where the nurses will *know* I'm swearing at them!'

Strangely, it hadn't been until Tatum was told she couldn't have children that she'd actually stopped to think whether she *wanted* them. And of course she'd realized right away she didn't! She'd long ago decided she'd never marry and risk becoming emotionally and financially dependant on a man. And she sure as hell wasn't going to be responsible for putting a kid through what she'd gone through as the child of a single mother. But the thought of a part of her being surgically removed and rendering her less a female than she'd been born had shaken her. Shaken her deeply.

At the time Kaylee had been wonderfully supportive and compassionate, but Tatum had found herself needing more. What, exactly, she wasn't sure, but it had been then that she'd started to acknowledge how much she missed Jace. Perhaps it was purely sexual – a need to experience complete sexual gratification while she was still a complete woman – or perhaps it was the need to be with someone who *expected* her to be strong and wouldn't smother her in sympathy; she didn't know. All she was certain of was that the notion of going home had suddenly become going home to Jace.

So why, now that she was here, with Jace, and in the wake of a sexual pleasure she'd never even begun to imagine was possible, did acceptance of her condition seem harder rather than easier?

Jace won the debate about seeing her home and glibly told his mother he'd spent the entire afternoon with Tatum 'chewing his ear'! At Tatum's choking gasp, he grinned and tacked on, 'Sounds like she really enjoyed herself . . . while she was gone.' Of course, instead of sitting opposite her at the dinner table, so she could have kicked him, he'd taken the seat beside her, and he took devilish delight in teasing her legs with his roaming fingers at the most inappropriate times. Fortunately Brian's distress over the current public inquiry into police corruption kept Judy's concerned attention centred on her husband.

Likewise, Jace's unexpected departure to Adelaide the next morning to pursue a lead on a case also proved fortunate. His four-day absence from the office allowed Tatum at least some chance of concentrating on all Dawn was trying to teach her. Not that he wasn't capable of distracting her long-distance anyway. Just answering the phone when he rang daily to check in with Tag was enough to make her blush and to plunge her hormones and imagination into sensual overdrive . . .

'Bentag Investigations. May I help you?'

'*Oh, yeah, gypsy, you can help me* . . .' His deep, suggestive voice sent goosebumps skittering down her spine. 'Go in my office, sit on the desk and – '

'Jace!' She practically yelped his name.

'What's wrong? What's happened to him?' Tag demanded, slopping coffee on the carpet as he dashed to her desk.

'Tell him I'm suffering severe withdrawal and need a fix of incredible gypsy sex.'

Praying she wasn't as red-faced as she felt, Tatum tried to focus on Tag. 'Er, nothing's wrong, Tag. He's just fooling around.' She smiled at him before saying into the phone, 'Do you harass all new employees like this, or is it just me?'

A warm male chuckle met her ear. 'Just you, gypsy. You've spoiled me for anyone else.'

Though she knew he was only teasing her, she couldn't help the warm softness his words stirred in her chest. 'I wasn't aware they had a Blarney Stone in Adelaide,' she said. 'Now, do you want to talk to Tag or not, because he's standing right next to me.'

'Lucky bastard!'

She cast a furtive glance at Tag, trying to gauge whether he could hear what came through the phone. Though he was frowning, it appeared to be more with impatient curiosity than offence.

'Do you miss me, gypsy?'

'Ja – '

'*Do you?*' he persisted.

'Yes. Okay?'

'How much?'

'Enough.'

'How much is enough?'

'Enough is enough!' she said. 'Get the message?'

He laughed. 'Enough to take my spare set of car keys out of the top drawer of my desk, get my car from my place and meet me at the airport at eight forty-five tonight?'

Her heart lurched with joy. 'Y-y-yes.'

His sigh could only have been described as relieved. 'In that case, you can put Tag on now. Oh, and gypsy?'

'Yeah?'

'*I've missed you like hell . . .*'

That night Tatum lay snuggled in his arms and, though she knew a man's lovemaking wasn't an accurate gauge of the truth, a portion of her heart tried to convince her otherwise.

Though she reluctantly insisted on returning to Judy's in the predawn hours of Saturday morning, the sight of him sitting in his parents' kitchen when she rose a little before nine filled her with a sensual pleasure she could only attribute to too much bed and not enough sleep the night before.

'Hi, Tate,' he said casually, though there was nothing casual in the heated glance that crept over her robe-clad body. 'I remembered you said something about going shopping this morning, so I thought I'd tag along and get your help on replenishing my abysmally stocked kitchen.'

She was actually in the process of walking over and

kissing him when Brian's voice reminded her of his presence at the breakfast table.

'I'd think twice if I were you, son,' he said, looking up from his paper. 'She got bitten by the health food bug while she was away. A man could starve for want of a decent meal with her around.'

Jace's grin was salacious enough to knot her stomach. 'Only if he wanted *food*. So, Dad, think I can scab a cup of caffeine while the health nut is getting dressed?'

Much as she didn't want to arouse the Bentons' suspicions that her relationship with their son had moved a step beyond what they perceived it to be – more like it had taken a blind leap off a cliff! she mentally amended – there was something deliciously exciting in having Jace drop reckless hints all over the place. But on Sunday evening, after a morning at the beach and an afternoon of slow, languid sex at his apartment, both she and Jace agreed to keep things strictly businesslike at work.

But, after two weeks, Tatum discovered it was an arrangement that the very nature of the business they were involved with made impossible . . .

CHAPTER 15

In the early evening silence of Bentag's offices Tatum closed down the main terminal on her desk and leaned back in her chair with a sigh that was as weary as it was frustrated.

Jace should have been here more than an hour ago. When he'd phoned this morning he'd said that the investigation that had kept him absent for the last three days would be, if not completed, then at least at a stage where he could manage the evening off and that they'd go out to dinner together. Tatum, starved of the luxury of having more than the brief glimpses she'd caught of him since last Thursday night, when he'd fallen asleep on her after a physically satisfying but too short session of love-making, at the end of a long day, had said she'd be equally happy with a pizza at his place. Jace, though, had insisted she deserved a slap up dinner and named an exorbitantly expensive restaurant where he wanted her to make a reservation for them.

Since not even Superman could have got them across town in the fifteen minutes that remained before the maitre d' was scheduled to seat them, Tatum reached for the telephone to phone the restaurant and cancel. Her fingers hadn't even touched the receiver before her handbag emitted the bleep of the mobile phone she'd inherited along with Dawn's job. Hurriedly she answered it.

'It's Tag, Tatum . . .' Disappointment again weighted her stomach. 'I s'pose it's too much to hope that partner of mine turned up before you left the office?'

'Er, no. He didn't. He's not back yet.'

'Not back yet? Are you *still* at work? It's almost eight-thirty . . .'

'I'm about to leave,' she said. 'I had some insurance company details to update, so I thought I'd work back and bum a lift home with Jace.' She laughed. 'Only now it looks like I'll be cabbing it again. I assume you've had no luck getting him on his mobile?' she asked, knowing *she* hadn't.'

'Hah! It'd help if he turned the bloody thing on occasionally! I understand him turning it off at certain times on a surveillance, but geez, Tatum!' Exasperation tightened his voice. 'If he's contactable on it even once a month I rush out and buy a lottery ticket! If *you* can train him to use it, you'll be doing better than Dawn and I have in the past.'

Tatum laughed. 'Maybe you should get him one of those new models where the sound can be turned off but they vibrate when a call is coming in,' Tatum suggested.

'I would if I believed he even *carried* his phone; but I doubt he'd feel it vibrating shoved under the seat of his car.' He paused, then said, 'Listen, Tatum, you pack it in and get yourself home. If by some remote chance you hear

267

from Jace, have him call me at my folks' place; for a change I thought I'd indulge myself in a home-cooked meal and catch up on the latest gossip on that sister of mine.'

'Sure, Tag. Oh, and say hi to your parents for me.'

'Say, if you're not doing anything, why don't you come over? Mum and Dad would love to see you.'

'Thanks anyway, Tag, but I have plans.' At least, I *did*, she thought miserably. 'I'll see you in the morning.'

'Okay. And Tatum . . .' a serious edge entered his tone '. . . when you call that cab, ask them to have the driver come to the office door and get you. Do it any time you work back alone in the office. In this business you can't be too careful.'

After promising to do as he said, she slipped the tiny phone into her bag and reached for the one on her desk. First she hit redial, and again heard the familiar recording of '. . . The mobile, telephone you are calling has not responded; please call again shortly. The mobile – '

Severing the connection, she punched in the cab company's number and ordered a taxi as per Tag's instructions. Then she rang and cancelled the restaurant reservation before settling in for what she knew would be at least a fifteen-minute wait for a cab.

Though it was a long-standing joke with the Benton clan that with Jace work came first, last and all positions in between, to the exclusion of all else, Tatum was worried by his non-appearance. And what worried her most, once she'd discounted the idea that anything serious had happened to Jace, was how three days could suddenly seem so much longer than three years . . .

★ ★ ★

He was at the coffee machine when she arrived at work the next morning, but the sight of him didn't bring the rush of excitement she'd expected; instead, shock and distress flooded through her. 'Oh, my God, Jace! *What happened*?'

He grimaced. 'Would you believe I roughed myself up shaving?' His attempted smile was little more than a grimace that had her blindly tossing her bag in the direction of her desk as she hurried towards him.

Tatum doubted losers to Mike Tyson came off looking this bad. His bottom lip was swollen and bore evidence of having recently been split, his right eye was blackened and all but closed, and an ugly three-inch gash ran along the left side of his jaw.

'Oh, Jace . . .' He winced as she tenderly touched his blackened eye. 'How?' she whispered, her voice sounding as if the pain was hers.

'Couple of guys who didn't like the idea of me tailing their boss.'

She swore.

'Look on the bright side – at least I didn't need stitches.'

Her eyes flashed disapproval at his lame humour, before softening as they again reviewed his mangled appearance.

God but *she* was beautiful! Jace thought. He felt better for merely looking at her.

'You sure you're okay?' she asked.

'I've had worse.' It was a statement of fact, not a boast or an attempt to be macho, but had Jace known the added distress the comment would bring to her sad brown eyes he would never have made the admission.

She lifted a hesitant, trembling finger to his lips and

slowly stroked them twice, before looking up into his eyes. 'Is Tag here?'

Jace had barely started shaking his head before she rose on her toes and her lips gently took over her finger's task. Lifting his left arm as far as his bruised and battered shoulder would allow, he slipped it around her hips to hold her steady as she sprinkled butterfly kisses over his war torn face.

Under Tatum's unique approach to healing, the pain of his injuries quickly receded, and it wasn't long before he was no longer confident of passively resisting his body's urging to respond to her deliciously sweet brand of first aid. On a reluctant, ragged sigh, he determinedly set her from him.

'Easy, gypsy,' he said. 'You're in danger of activating me to personal mode in a professional environment.'

She sighed. 'Only because we're seldom in a personal environment at the same time.'

'I know. And I'm sorry.' He reached out and tested the softness of her hair. 'But it'd be a bit easier if you'd agree to stay the night at my place occasionally.'

Even though she knew he was right, Tatum was loath to agree to an arrangement that exclusively required *her* to fit into *his* lifestyle, while he wouldn't have to make any adjustments to his. Had she lived alone, they could have alternated the nights when Jace wasn't working between his place and hers; that way she would have felt he, too, was willing to be inconvenienced for the sake of their relationship.

It might be a selfish, utterly juvenile way of looking at things, but as Tatum found herself redesigning her individual pursuits to accommodate him, such as rescheduling or even *cancelling* her gym sessions and once-weekly basketball games – and *happily* doing it, at that! – for the sake of grabbing even a half-hour with him, she wanted some sort of evidence that she wasn't making a fool of herself over a man. While she was perfectly willing to react to his shout of 'Jump', she wanted at least to know that his feet were leaving the ground at the same time!

Feeling a bitch for thinking that way when he was obviously in pain, she smiled at him. 'Take your poor mutilated bod into your office and I'll bring you some coffee. I'll even pamper you and forgo making it decaf – '

'Don't let him milk you for too much sympathy, Tatum.' Tag's dry-voiced intrusion pulled their attention to the front door. 'His face is an occupational hazard. In a *bad* month you might find yourself fetching and carrying for him every second day!'

'Shut up, Taggart,' Jace said, discreetly increasing the distance between him and Tatum. 'A little genuine sympathy is overdue in this place. *I* wouldn't be envious of *you*, if our positions were reversed.'

Tag laughed. 'And I'll bet you wish like hell they were! What happened?'

Jace recounted the story. He'd been following a guy whose wife, in the process of divorcing him, had come to Bentag because she believed her husband was understating his income in settlement discussions.

'The guy's scum,' he said. 'And I'm not crazy about the two heavies he sicced on me either.

'Was it just being followed that he took exception to, or did you find proof he's trying to scam his wife?' Tag asked.

'He's scamming more than his wife,' Jace said. 'I think he's running a sideline in pharmaceuticals.'

'He's dealing dope?'

Jace shook his head. 'It's my guess he's running a backyard pharmacy. And from what I can gather he's manufacturing in a big way: speed, ecstasy – you name it.'

Tag whistled. 'So, even though she didn't know the source of their extravagant lifestyle, the wife's hunch was right; the bloke was fudging the figures.'

'Like hell she didn't know!' Jace spat. 'It's my bet she knew *exactly* where the money came from. The only reason she came to us was to make her old man think she had a few heavies of her own. The guys who nailed me thought I was hired muscle, nothing more.'

'So, how do you want to handle this?' Tag asked him.

'*I don't*. We hand everything we've got over to the cops and let them sort it out.'

Tatum snorted loudly. 'Assuming you can find one who isn't up to his eyeballs in the drug scene!'

'Gee, Tatum.' Tag laughed. 'You've only been here three weeks and already you sound as cynical as a hardened investigator.'

She gave him a long, level look. 'I was cynical about cops long before I started working here, Tag,' she said tersely. 'Besides, haven't you been reading the reports on the corruption inquiry? Outside of Brian, I wouldn't trust one enough to ask them the time.'

Although Tatum had conscientiously tried to put her past behind her, and worked hard to keep it there, on odd occasions it still managed to creep into her thoughts. At odd moments images of Fantasy or Lulu, or even Christopher and the people she'd grown up with, would pop into her head and she'd find herself tormented by irrational insecurities. Usually she had no trouble banishing both the memories and their accompanying unease. Usually. But in the wake of detailed newspaper reports of the police inquiry, the past had started encroaching more often into her mind. She'd told herself she wasn't going to read the daily press reports any more, but she did. Compulsively.

The arrival of two of the investigators Bentag subcontracted work to brought a fresh round of macho jokes and sarcastic comments about Jace's 'improved' looks. Tuning them out, Tatum gave her attention to her work, determined not to think about either the past or how long it would be before she could get some time alone with Jace.

Her dismissal of the first matter from her mind was easy, the second wasn't, thanks to the sexy, provocative smiles Jace threw her during his constant forays to the coffee machine between clients. How could a man possibly look *sexy* when his face was a puffy mass of bruises and cuts? She was still pondering this question when the phone rang mid-afternoon.

'Bentag Investigations. May I help you?'

'Jack Cooper, here. Put me through to Tag or Jace.'

'I'm sorry, Mr Cooper, they both have someone with them at the moment. Can I take a message or have them – ?'

'Just tell 'em to ring Coop, ASAP.'

Before she could even repeat the message the phone went dead. 'Rude bastard,' she muttered, turning at the sound of Jace's voice as he ushered his client from his office.

'I'll contact you in about a week and let you know what we find out. But if you think of anything else that might help us, Mr Dalton, call me.'

Tatum gave the agitated-looking gentleman a reassuring smile, waiting until he'd left the office to speak to Jace. 'I'm not sure you instil a lot of confidence looking like that,' she teased.

'Sure I do!' He hitched himself onto the edge of her desk. 'The client assumes I'll go through hell to get to the bottom of their problems.'

'Well, you sure look like you stopped through there recently. Is your face bothering you?'

'Not as much as yours is. Any chance of getting you into my office for a bit of dictation?'

'I don't take dictation.'

'What . . . about,' he said, angling himself across the desk towards her and speaking in a drawn-out whisper, '. . . if . . . I . . . promised . . . to . . . go . . . *real* . . . slow?

A sensuous tingle slid down her spine. 'I thought we decided to keep things strictly professional during working hours.'

'We did. What we do on our afternoon tea break is our own business.'

'You don't drink tea.'

He grinned. 'So I'll –' He swore and straightened as the troubleshooter from a large insurance company exited Tag's office, with Tag in tow.

While Jace got to his feet to greet the man with familiar

274

ease, Tatum bent her head and began shuffling the stack of messages by the phone. She resented Jace's ability to switch instantly into cool businessman mode, when she was certain her face had 'caught in the cookie jar' written all over it. She didn't even want to *think* what was written on it when, closing the front door behind the man, Tag said, 'Came damn close to getting caught with your pants down then, Benton!'

'Baker's a jerk. He likes trying to rattle my cage. The evidence we supplied them is watertight.'

Thank God! They were talking about something else! With utter relief, Tatum let out the breath she hadn't even been aware she'd been holding and automatically reached for the ringing phone.

'Bentag Investigations. May I help you?'

'Jack Cooper again. I want to – '

'Apologize for your rudeness during your earlier call?' She ignored the puzzled male frowns directed at her. *No one* hung up in her ear and got away with it!

'Listen sweetheart, I'm in a hurry. I – '

'I am *not* your sweetheart, *Mr Cooper*. Nor do I appreciate having phones slammed down in my ear. Do you – ?'

Jace, looking as if he was about to explode with mirth, took the receiver from her as Tag leant on the door shaking with laughter.

'You giving our new secretary a hard time, Coop?' Jace asked through a grin. 'Nah! Dawn was a pussycat compared to Tatum,' he continued with wry amusement. 'You'd better come prepared to apologize when you meet her *or . . .*' he paused '. . . heavily armed.' He chuckled

275

and in a loud aside said, 'Coop says he's sorry . . . Will a box of chocolates square things for him?'

'Hand-made Swiss ones might have a *chance*,' Tatum said, gathering an armful of files and walking to Tag's office. '*But*,' she tossed over her shoulder, 'it'd have to be a big box.'

Jace had to go out that afternoon, but his departing words of, 'Not even an AK47 will keep me late today, gypsy,' left Tatum in no doubt they'd be leaving the office together that evening. Nor was there any question that, once they did, they'd head straight to the bedroom of his waterside Drummoyne apartment and tumble as one onto his futon.

The pure carnal bliss of being naked in Jace's arms was worth the strain of an afternoon of trying to act like a calm, efficient secretary to Tag while practically hyperventilating from lustful anticipation. Now, watching satiated from the bed as her naked lover opened his briefcase, she wondered how she'd managed it.

'What's this?' she asked, when Jace returned to the bed and dropped a gift-wrapped package beside her. 'My birthday's not until tomorrow.

'I know. They're an apology for not being able to make dinner. I'm sorry.'

Wrapping dispersed with, she smiled at the familiar logo on her favourite chocolates. 'Thank you. But you don't have to apologize for getting beat up; I'm not *that* hard-hearted.'

'They're for missing dinner *tomorrow* night, not last night.'

Her head jerked up before she could hide her disappointment. '*What*?'

Wearing nothing but a rueful expression, he sat down on the bed. 'I'm sorry, gypsy, but I've got to work. We're investigating an insurance fraud. A woman who's been receiving workers' compensation for an injury which *supposedly* prevents her from standing or working for longer than thirty minutes at a stretch. But we suspect she's supplementing her insurance pay-out by working as a part-time hairdresser. We have to get video evidence for the insurance company.'

After working at Bentag for three weeks, her mind instantly recalled the case he was referring to, but that didn't mean she was flooded with immediate professional understanding. 'Couldn't Tag do it?'

'Tag's flying to Port Macquarie tomorrow afternoon, remember? And either we act tomorrow night or it'll be a week before we get another crack at her.'

'How come? Obviously you're talking about the Milstat case, and according to what the insurance company report says they got tipped off the woman was working four or five days a week.'

Jace knew he shouldn't have been surprised at how quickly Tate had acquainted herself with the firm's current cases. She'd always been naturally intelligent, but his problem was that in the last few weeks he'd been more focused on her *physical* attributes than her mental ones. Not that it would be smart to admit that to her!

'Yeah, but we don't know the names of any of the salons, except for the one she's at on Thursday nights.'

Her pensive expression indicated that she was considering what he'd said. 'So what are you going to do? Walk in with a concealed video and get her to cut your hair?'

'Pretty much, but Jennifer Trayber is going to be the one in the chair. All I'll be doing is sitting back pretending to read a magazine while I wait for her and angling the bag with the video so we get the maximum value from it.'

Tatum was only half listening to what he was saying, her mind stuck back on the name of Jennifer Trayber. Trayber was one of two women Bentag used when the circumstances of a case called for a female investigator. Tatum had met the tall, striking redhead only once. It had been the second or third day after Dawn had left, and the woman's condescending attitude to 'the new secretary' hadn't gone far towards endearing her to Tatum. Nor had the way she'd batted her big green eyes at Jace.

'So why Jennifer? Why not the other woman?'

'Brenda O'Brien?' At her nod, Jace shrugged. 'Jennifer was the first one I phoned; as it turned out she was available and happy to do it.'

'I'll bet!' The vehement remark earned her a curious look. 'I mean, what woman wouldn't jump at the chance of a free haircut if she was getting paid for her time into the bargain?'

He lunged at her and rolled her beneath him in one smooth move, before plunging both hands into her hair. 'Promise me *you'll* never get your hair cut, even if someone offers you a million dollars to do it.'

She laughed. 'Are you nuts? For a million bucks, I'd shave my head!'

He scowled. '*Do not*,' he said, winding her hair around

his wrist and drawing her face near, '*even think about it*! I *adore* your hair.'

She grinned. 'I thought it was my body you adored.'

'Mmm,' he agreed, suckling hard on her neck and making her squirm. He lifted his head and brushed his thumb over the area where his mouth had been. His satisfied smile, told her she bore his mark. 'Shave your head, gypsy, and you'll have to spend the rest of your life wearing polo-necked sweaters.'

With hindsight Jace knew he shouldn't have expected Tatum to take being stood up twice in a couple of days graciously, regardless of whether it was her birthday or not; but he hadn't expected her revenge to be quite so bizarre. Or that Tag would support it.

'No way, Tag! It's just not on!' he told his partner. '*No* friggin' way!'

'Jace, you – '

'*You*!' he said, swinging round to face Tatum at the sound of her voice. 'Keep quiet!'

'I will not! What right – ?'

'Shut up both of you!' Tag's voice was louder than Tatum had ever heard it. 'In case you've both forgotten, this is an *office*, not a damned sideshow.'

He ran a frustrated hand through his hair and looked from one to the other. His eyes finally settled on Jace. 'If you can form a more articulate objection to this than simply "no way" I'd like to hear it. You both know I'm flying out of town this afternoon, but I'd like to be reasonably certain you pair aren't going to start chucking furniture at each other the minute I'm out the door.'

'The solution to that,' Jace muttered, 'would be to cuff her to her desk.'

The comment earned him a narrowed-eyed glare from the woman leaning against the doorway of Tag's office. 'I hardly think *I'm* the one he's worried about!'

'Make that *gag* her and cuff her to – '

'Will you pair give me a break, here?' Tag implored. '*Now*,' he continued, when silence had reigned for ten continuous seconds, 'it seems to me that Tatum's suggestion makes sense. With Jennifer being sick and Brenda not available, why not use Tatum tonight?'

'Because, *you* – ' Jace put an accusing emphasis on the word ' – hired her as a secretary. She's not trained to do what we need.'

'How much training does it take to get a haircut?' Tag asked drily.'

'Don't be a smartarse, Tag!' Jace snapped. 'You know as well as I do investigative work can get dangerous; in case you've forgotten; take another look at my face.'

'All she's got to do is walk into a hairdressers and start a conversation with the woman who's doing her hair, Jace.' Tag grinned. 'If she's anything like Kaylee, it'll be second nature.'

Jace grabbed at Tag's reference to his sister. 'I'll bet you'd be objecting if I was suggesting we use Kaylee in something like this?'

'No.' Tag was unfazed. 'If you recall, we *did* use her a couple of years back. Remember, when that woman wanted us to bait her fiancée to see if he'd cheat on her?'

'Oh, that's right. I'd forgotten you were the type of guy who *encouraged* his little sister to pick up blokes in bars!'

Behind him, Tatum chuckled. 'Like Kaylee *needs* encouragement.'

Tag smiled. 'Jace, you know damn well if Dawn was still here you'd have no hesitation in getting her to do this. And you also know *I* wouldn't back *anything* I thought would put Tatum at risk. Hell, if this was anything more than an insurance scam, or if she was going out there with anyone else but you or me, I *would* veto the idea.' He frowned then. 'Unless you think there's more to this than a simple insurance fraud? Jace?' Tag said when he got no immediate response. '*Do you?*'

Jace almost wished he could lie. 'No.' He knew he was backing the loser in a two-horse race, but he stubbornly gave it one last shot. 'Look, there's no real urgency on this Milstat thing. Waiting another week won't hurt. Besides, it's Tate's birthday; she'll have to cancel her plans – '

'No, I won't, Tag,' Tatum cut in. 'My plans *fell through* last night. My date had something *urgent* come up.' Her brown eyes fairly scorched Jace when he turned to her, but she was the first to look away. 'You guys decide what you want to do. I just thought my offer might've been helpful.' Pivoting, she walked out and closed the door on both men.

At her exit, Jace dropped into the nearest chair, propped his feet on his partner's desk and stared at the ceiling. 'I will never forgive Dawn for getting married. *Or* Jennifer-bloody-Trayber for allowing her appendix to burst.'

At Tag's laugh, Jace lowered his head to glare at him. 'And you're no certainty to stay on my Christmas card list either, *mate.*'

'I guess it must be my curse in life to be the voice of reason.'

Jace grunted.

'She'll handle it on her ear, Jace, and you know it. I've got to say, I'm damned impressed with the way she's adapted to things here.'

'Wonderful. The next thing I know you'll be encouraging her to apply for a sub-agent's licence and a gun permit.'

'Why not? I think she'd make a great investigator.'

Jace's feet hit the floor with a thump. 'The last thing I need to worry about is Tatum Milano running around with her in-your-face attitude and a gun, taunting bad guys!' The comment was a slight exaggeration, since Tag and Jace refused to hire agents who carried guns and only on the rarest occasions carried them themselves. 'I'll be lucky to stand the stress of working with her tonight.'

'Okay, now, since we've got that peacefully settled . . .' Tag merely grinned at the scowl Jace sent him '. . . have you given any thought to what we'll give Dawn for a wedding present from the firm?'

Jace shook his head. 'And, given how I'm feeling about her for deserting us, at this particular moment anything I suggest would be against the law.'

'Seriously, Jace.'

'I haven't thought about it. Dawn's wedding's been the last thing on my mind.'

'Well, start thinking, 'cause we've only got two weeks to come up with something.'

'You taking that model you've been seeing?' Jace asked.

Tag grinned and shook his head. 'Uh-uh. I'm not doing anything that'll give her ideas. The last time I took a woman I was involved with to a wedding, she started planning ours! Nope, I'm going to find a nice platonic escort who won't mind if I decide to try my luck with the bridesmaids. Actually, I think I'll ask Tatum.'

Jace straightened in his chair. 'No, you won't.'

'Huh?'

'I said, *No, you won't* ask Tatum.'

'Why not? Ah, shit!' Tag's face contorted. 'Now I get it! Bloody hell, Jace! You've known her for ten years – '

'Nearly eight.'

'And *now*, when she's working for us, you suddenly decide you've got the hots for her? Geez, mate!'

Tag paced the length of his desk twice, muttering under his breath, before stopping to glare at Jace. 'Do you have any idea how complicated this could get? Of course you do! Hell *you* were the one who said, *'let's make sure Dawn's replacement isn't pretty, because we don't want the hassle of an office romance.'*

Jace shrugged and held his palms up in innocence. 'So why blame me for the complications? *You hired her.*'

Try as she might, Tatum couldn't identify one single reason why she should be angry with Jace, so she spent the day furious with him for a huge combination of them! The importance of celebrating her birthday varied in accordance with what *he* wanted to do! One day he couldn't wait to get her into bed, the next he treated her like a child! It didn't matter which way she looked at it – and unlike Jason Benton she was fair-minded enough to look at things from *both* perspectives! – Jace Benton had insulted her! Either he'd cancelled their date because he'd preferred Jennifer Trayber's company to

283

hers, or he'd acted as he had in Tag's office because he considered her totally incompetent!

Until Jace had gone ballistic, Tag hadn't had any problems with her filling in for Jennifer. And she'd only made the offer because last night Jace had convinced her that it was vital to act on their information tonight. She'd *thought* she was doing him a favour. Well, the devil would ice-skate before she'd make the mistake of trying to help him again!

'You glare any harder at the keyboard and you'll warp it,' Tag said, dropping his overnight bag onto her desk and bee-lining to the coffee machine. 'You want one?'

She nodded. 'Thanks.'

'Decaf, right?'

'Yeah.'

'Will you be coming into the office tomorrow when you get back?' she asked, nodding her thanks as she took her cup from him.

'That depends if I think I'm up to walking into a war zone.' He watched her over the top of his cup. 'The tension gets any thicker in this place and we'll have spray a defoliant just to breathe.'

Tatum tried to keep her response honest, but emotionally bland. 'If I'd known he was going to carry on like a lunatic, I wouldn't have opened my mouth. Then again, it's not like lunacy hasn't featured heavily in his life before.' She swivelled her chair around and gave Tag an earnest, determined look. 'I'm *not* going to stuff up, Tag.'

He smiled. 'Relax. I know that. And so does Jace. The . . . er . . . *circumstances* have just made him a little over-protective towards you.'

'*Over-protective* towards me?' She gave a dry laugh. 'Try *homicidal*.' Belatedly her brain registered Tag's awkward use of the word 'circumstances'; rage ejected her out of the chair. 'He told you we'd slept together! Why, that – '

Hastily Tag grabbed her arm. 'Now, Tatum, he said no such thing.'

The appeasing tone had no effect on her. 'If I'd wanted to own up to being stupid enough to sleep with that jerk, I'd have told you myself!'

'Well, now you have.' Tag fought a grin. 'Honestly Jace didn't say *anything*. I guessed.'

'Damn!' She sank back into her chair. 'We agreed we wouldn't let things affect our professional relationship . . .'

'Yeah, well, you were both being naïve if you thought you could manage that. But now that it's out in the open – '

'Out in the open? Oh, no!' She shook her head. 'Oh, no, Tag! It's not in the open – *it's over! Finished! Finito*! Great sex isn't worth this much hassle! If – '

'I keep telling you gypsy,' a smug voice interrupted her, 'what we have is *incredible* sex.'

Tag chuckled. 'On that *fascinating* note, I'll take myself off to the airport. Oh, and *children* . . . remember what I said about the furniture.'

CHAPTER 16

The fury smouldering in her eyes reminded Jace of the way she'd looked the first night he'd met her. At the time he'd whimsically called her a witch, and wondered if she wasn't trying to hex him; more than seven years later he was beginning to understand why it was often said that fact is stranger than fiction.

It irked him, though, when she reverted her attention to the computer, resuming her tasks as if he'd left the room with Tag. The fast, angry clicks of the keyboard under her fingers were the most grating sounds he'd ever heard. The urge to walk over, haul her out of the chair and kiss her senseless almost overwhelmed him, but he knew that to do so would mean he'd again be putting his personal feelings ahead of his is professionalism.

Tag had been right; Jace would never have had a problem with asking Dawn to cover for Jennifer Trayber; yet, even now he was still unsettled knowing Tatum would be doing it.

He would have liked to think it was because, while he was able to successfully contain his personal feelings for Tatum between the hours of eight-thirty a.m. and five o'clock p.m., he didn't want to put himself under the strain of extending them. That was what he'd have *liked* to think. The reality was he was failing miserably at shelving his need for her for any measurable period of time.

He moved with slow, deliberate strides to stand by her desk. Her hands didn't pause in their movement over the keyboard; her eyes never wavered from the monitor.

'I've managed to reschedule the appointment at the hairdressing salon for eight,' he said, fingering the birthday note on the huge arrangement of native flowers Tag had arranged to have delivered prior to her arrival at the office. It read: 'Happy Birthday to a great secretary. Love Jace and Tag.' It was the same safe, generic message Dawn had received for years.

'That'll allow time for us to have dinner at Mum's before we go. When I phoned to tell her that because of work neither of us could make dinner at the club, she said she'd organize something for you at home. You got any problems with that?'

'Yes,' she said, finally looking up. With narrowed-eyed annoyance she flicked her hair over her shoulders and jutted her chin. 'I'll probably throw up if I have to eat at the same table as you.'

'Okay,' he said. 'Objection noted. But if you *do* get sick that'll mean I'll have no option but to call off our plans for tonight.' He smiled at her. 'Can't risk having an investigation blown because of an ill operative, can we?'

The moment Jace pulled up at his parents' house Tatum dashed from the car and hurried to her room. Her excuse of wanting to shower and change before dinner went unchallenged by both Brian and Judy, but she doubted they'd remain ignorant of the silent hostility between her and Jace for too long. Especially not if she went with her urge to hit him over the head with a heavy blunt object! She swore. Jace Benton was the most infuriating person she'd ever met, and right now he had her so wound up she'd probably explode if he so much as asked her to pass the salt at dinner.

Tatum swore again, then sighed. *This wasn't doing her any good*. It was imperative she calm down or her emotions might jeopardize what they had to do tonight. She was determined not to make a single mistake while investigating the Milstat case. Not because she gave a rat's backside about winning Jace's approval, but because she refused to give him the satisfaction of saying she screwed up!

Head bent, hands braced against the wall, she let the hot, hard spray of the shower pour over her neck and shoulders in the hope it would draw some of the tension from her body. Employing a meditation technique she'd learned when she'd first started judo, she drew a deep breath and held it for as long as she comfortably could before slowly exhaling. She continued the procedure until her breathing was steady and rhythmic. The next step in the technique was to close her eyes and empty her mind of all tumultuous thoughts by focusing on something that had generated happiness and tranquillity in her life.

'Eeek!' she screamed. 'Get out of my head, Jace Benton!'

Jace joined his father in the family room as the older man watched the sports wrap at the end of the news, but his mind was only half-tuned to the interview with the young blond spin bowler who'd captured six first innings wickets in the cricket test match against Pakistan. Indeed, he wasn't even aware the news had finished or that his father had turned off the TV until he realized his dad was regarding him with a concerned expression.

'Er, sorry, Dad,' he said, straightening in the armchair to look more alert. 'What was it you asked?'

'I don't approve of you encouraging Tatum to take an active role in surveillances.' Grey eyebrows pulled together to add further disapproval to his tone. 'Her features won't hold the black and blue colour scheme of your face quiet so well.'

'I know that, damn it!' he snapped.

'Good. Then I'll assume what you have planned for tonight isn't tied in with whoever did that to you.'

'*It isn't. I'd never* put her in a situation where she might be in danger,' he said tersely. 'All we're doing tonight is getting video evidence of a claimant suspected of scamming an insurance company!'

'So how come you're so edgy?' his father countered. 'You've been like a cat on a hot tin roof since you came in the door. And you keep looking towards her room, like you're worried about her.'

Cursing himself for being so transparent, Jace schooled his features to blandness. 'I'm no more worried about her than I would be about anyone else doing their first surveillance,' he lied. 'Plenty of sub-agents mess up first time out; the thought of a stuff-up always makes me uneasy.'

'He's lying, Brian.' Tatum strolled into the room, wearing a black ankle-length singlet dress and a radiant smile that was pointedly directed away from him. 'He's *beside himself with worry*. He's convinced I'm so totally brainless that an empty beer can is brighter than I am. If it wasn't for *Tag's* high opinion of me and my capabilities, I wouldn't be going at all.'

Brian Benton laughed, rising to slip an affectionate arm around Tatum's shoulders. 'Well, I'm with Tag, Birthday Girl! I think you're bright enough to put power companies out of business. You just ignore my son.'

Huh! thought Jace, following the laughing pair into the dining room. Like she needed *that* advice! She hadn't said one word to him during their entire trip home.

'Judy, that was delicious.' Tatum smiled as she set her empty dessert plate aside. 'You shouldn't have gone to so much trouble.'

'Well, since Jace messed up our plans for dinner at the club by making you work – '

'It wasn't Jace's idea to have me work tonight,' Tatum said quickly, before the man under attack could. '*I* suggested it to Tag,' she explained. 'Jace is completely opposed to the idea. He's convinced I'm going to screw everything up.'

'Damn it, Tate!' He slammed his fist on the table. 'Will you stop saying that? I never said you'd screw anything up.'

'I didn't say you *said* it,' she said coolly. 'I said you thought it. And you do.'

'I do not!' She gave him a sceptical look. 'Tatum, I *do not think you're going to screw up.*'

She turned to Judy. 'That's what he says now. Today, at

290

work, he acted like letting let me do this was a risk to the reputation of the entire agency.'

Jace swore. 'I'm not worried about the agency's reputation, you idiot! I'm worried about *you*. About the consequences of having *you* there!'

'Tatum!' Judy gasped.

And at the same time her husband said, 'I thought you said this *wasn't* dangerous!'

Choosing to ignore the startled comments of his parents, Jace responded only to Tatum's mystified, '*Me?*'

'Yes, *you*, damn it!'

'*Jason*,' his father said insistently. 'Is this, or isn't this thing safe?'

He sighed. 'Yeah, it's safe. In everything except my professional concentration.'

The way he said the words triggered every sensual nerve-ending in Tatum's body.

'You won't be able to concentrate?' Judy sounded genuinely puzzled. 'Why not?'

Tatum watched his eyes turn smoky with desire.

'Because, I'll be watching gypsy over there – '

'*Gypsy?*' Judy's echo made no impact.

'And I'll get so caught up thinking about her, I'll forget all about positioning the video. All about the fact I should be observing things about the claimant . . . All about everything except how much I want her . . . and how long we'll have together before I have to drive her home, so you won't think any less of her because she's having an affair with your son . . .'

* * *

Tatum waved at the two figures standing on the front veranda of the Benton house as Jace backed his car down the driveway. 'I still can't believe you actually said that,' she murmured.

'I didn't know I was going to till I heard the words coming out of my mouth,' Jace said.

Within the limits of her seat belt, she turned to face him. 'I did,' she whispered. 'I saw it in your eyes, a split second before you spoke.'

Smiling, he reached for her hand and clasped it on his thigh. For several kilometres they drove through the early evening traffic towards the city in a silence so attuned and natural it reminded Tatum of the times they lay quietly satisfied in each others' arms.

Jace must have chosen that instant to look at her, for he said, 'You're looking very satisfied with yourself, gypsy.'

'I was just thinking how good it feels not to have to keep things from your parents.

'You have to admit, they took it well. I told you they wouldn't make a fuss.'

She laughed. 'Jace, they were in *shock*. It took your mother almost five minutes to work out *I* was gypsy. You know,' she said in a more serious tone, 'your timing could've been better.'

'Better for them, or better for you?' he asked knowingly.

'*Both*. I, for one, feel like I'm suffering emotional whiplash. It's not easy to go from wanting to kill you with my bare hands one second to being willing to die for the feel of *you bare in my hands* the next!'

'Guess which mood I think suits you the best,' he teased.

'If I was ever in doubt, I'd only have to ask your father,' she retorted. 'Poor Brian went from looking like he was afraid we'd come to blows, to looking as if he was afraid he'd have to hose you down to stop us doing it on the dinner table!'

'Now, there's food for thought!' He grinned across at her. 'We haven't done it on a dinner table . . .'

To Jace's way of thinking, Double Bay seemed to exist for no other reason than to give people with money somewhere to flaunt it. Yet, despite its pretensions of grandeur, in reality it was little different from any other suburban shopping area. Teenagers cruised the streets for the sheer pose value of showing off their wheels – albeit in late model sports cars purchased by cashed up parents rather than rust-infested Commodores, or Falcons hotted up in their backyards on weekends – and parking spaces close to the subtly understated but outrageously priced boutiques, restaurants and trendy coffee lounges were at a premium. Not that Jace wanted to park too near the hairdressing salon; they'd already driven past twice.

'Judging by the way the two women who just walked out are dressed, this Milstat woman is probably earning more in tips than I do in a week,' Tatum said.

Jace manoeuvred his low profile, six-month-old Falcon into a space between a maroon Rolls Royce and a state-of-the-art four by four that looked as if the roughest terrain it had been over was a supermarket speed hump.

'Remember, we were told she's using the name *Crossby*, not Milstat.'

Tatum nodded, watching silently as he reached into the

293

back seat for the hessian carry-bag that held a miniature video camera creatively concealed by bags bearing the logos of two well-known stores. When he was satisfied everything was as it should be, he expelled a 'here goes' breath and looked across at her.

'You sure you're comfortable doing this?'

'More than you are,' she said. 'I can tell you're still got doubts about my being able to handle it.'

He shook his head. 'No. I know you'll handle it.' He reached over and rubbed her hair between the tips of his fingers. 'It's the thought of you having this cut off that bothers me.'

'I'm not having it cut – '

He sat back. 'Tate, you have to. A trim isn't going to keep her on her feet long enough. She'll – '

'I know. That's why I'm going to have it shampooed, conditioned, then set into some elaborate and time-con- suming style.'

He leaned over the console and pulled her close for a quick hard kiss. 'That's incredibly smart of you, Mrs Mitchell.

He glanced down at the matching wedding bands they wore to convince the suspect that they were a wealthy married couple.

'I know.' She smiled. 'So, are we going to get this show on the road or sit here and neck?'

Staring into her beautiful brown eyes, feeling the light touch of her fingers grazing the back of his neck with promised magic, the question didn't strike Jace as the least bit teasing. With a groan, he grasped her wrists and, having freed himself, opened his door.

'Don't,' he told her, 'ask such things at a time like this! It's considered very unprofessional for an investigator to conduct an investigation with a hard-on!'

Though he'd been half joking when he'd made the comment, sitting watching Tate getting a shampoo was decidedly more uncomfortable than he would have imagined. Her head being angled back over a basin only emphasised the long, smooth column of her throat, and lifted her breasts that much closer to the scooped neck of her dress, which, given its thin straps, told him she wasn't wearing a bra. The knowledge tightened his gut and he groaned softly. The blue-rinsed matron beside him looked up from the *Vogue* she was reading to give him a frosty frown, her eyes widening as she noticed the fading, but multi-hued bruises on his face.

Jace couldn't resist having a little fun with the uptight snob.

Grimacing, he groaned again, then gingerly clutched his neck and rolled one shoulder. 'Put my neck out playing polo,' he muttered in a confidential tone. 'I'm afraid if that pony throws me one more time I'm having him put down.'

Stark horror registered in the woman's face. '*Put down?*' she said, with exaggerated vowels that led Jace to believe she probably had a video collection of the Queen's Christmas messages since the Coronation. 'My goodness, how many times has it happened?'

'Just the once.' Jace kept his face deadpan. 'But it's costly enough to keep a decent string of ponies, without paying upkeep on a hack.'

Her eyes flicked, discreetly, of course, to his clothes, and in case her mind was having trouble reconciling faded jeans with the ownership of a string of polo ponies Jace casually looked at his watch, to draw attention to its distinctive Rolex design. Almost instantly she relaxed.

'I do appreciate what an expensive hobby polo can be,' she said. 'My late husband was quite a supporter of it. But would it not be better to *sell* the horse and recoup *something* of its original price, instead of *shooting* the animal? I have a number of friends who might be interested,' she said.

'Thank you, but I've already turned down a number of offers for the beast,' Jace said, with just the right amount of uninterest. 'Regrettably, shooting it is my only option. The horse was a gift; I consider it quite bad form to sell a gift, no matter what the circumstances.'

The woman was still slack-jawed with disbelief when a fresh-faced young girl ushered her towards the seat Tatum had just vacated. Unobtrusively, Jace angled the bag at his feet to capture the claimant, walking briskly, in high, chunky heels, no less, from behind the row of basins to direct Tate to a chair in front of a wall of mirrors. He sent her an encouraging smile, which she returned via the mirror. The exchange caused the woman with her to turn and look in his direction.

Nothing in the casual glance or the plastically polite smile she gave him made him think she thought Tate anything but just another customer, whose husband had nothing better to do than hang around hairdressing salons waiting for her.

According to the data supplied to Bentag by the insurance company, Carole Milstat was a divorced mother of two who'd filed a workers' compensation claim three years

296

ago, after slipping on a wet floor in the salon where she was working at the time. Despite their best efforts, the company's doctors had been unable to disprove medical evidence provided by her stating that, due to irreparable soft tissue damage, she was no longer able to work.

Well, she was currently doing a damn fine job of faking it, Jace noted as she pivoted on her platform shoes to snag something from the mobile tray being pushed by another staff member. Wearing trendy wire-rimmed glasses and with short-cropped vermilion hair, she matched the description Jace had been given, although he'd have judged her to be in her late twenties rather than the reported thirty-four. Her face suddenly became animated, and she stopped fussing with Tatum's hair so her hands could assist in what she was saying.

He was too far away to pick up any of the conversation and could only hope Tate was taking advantage of the woman's chatty nature to get the name of at least one of the other salons where the woman was supposedly working. If she managed that, he'd arrange for someone else to get video evidence of her working there as well; then it would be up to the insurance agents to decide whether they wanted to extend the fifteen hours of surveillance they'd authorized Bentag to carry out or not. Bentag hadn't done much work for this particular company, so Jace was hoping a good, fast result might lead to some additional work from them.

Because private investigation wasn't cheap, and only about three out of every ten enquires Bentag handled ever actually turned into paying jobs, steady insurance work was important to the firm. Insurance cases might, on the whole, be dull, boring and time-consuming, but the up side was that they were safe, well-paid and so far hadn't involved Jace having to identify teenage corpses in the morgue. The cynical thought sent his gaze to Tatum.

Despite her easy, relaxed body language, the mirror revealed a bright edge of excitement glowing in her big brown eyes and it bothered him. Regardless of how well she did tonight, Jace wasn't eager to expand Tate's involvement beyond the office again any time soon; there were some sides to this business he never wanted her to see.

It was almost two hours later that she came rushing towards him, with a beaming smile and hair that looked like a cross between a beehive and a laundry basket.

'Oh, darling,' she gushed, 'hasn't Carole done the most divine job on my hair? I'm so pleased with it, I'm going to have her do it again for the party next weekend!'

Before Jace even opened his mouth she was chiding him. 'Now, don't say it, darling! I *know* you think this is an *awfully* long way to come just to have my hair done, but we don't have to!'

'We don't?' Given the skyscraper style of her hair, he could only marvel that she could shake her head so vigorously and not overbalance.

'*No!*' she said excitedly. 'Carole actually works on Fridays in a salon at St Ives! Isn't that wonderful?'

'It's certainly more convenient,' Jace said, only now looking directly at the woman who was the reason they were here. 'Looks like you have yourself a new customer.'

Her smile was completely without guile as she led them towards the cash register and, as they'd planned, Tatum asked for a business card for the other salon.

'I'm sorry,' Milstat said, reaching for a card from a perspex holder on top of the register. 'I haven't one with me. How about if I write the phone number on the back of this? You can call any day to make an appointment, but, remember, I only work there Fridays.'

Jace made sure the video captured her scribbling down the number and passing the card to Tatum.

'Thanks *ever so much*, Carole,' she said. 'I'll call early in the week, so you're not booked up. I'd *really* hate to miss out.' She patted her head. 'You've done such a marvellous job!'

Wearing a look that said his masculine patience was wearing thin, Jace pulled out his wallet and raised a questioning eyebrow at the woman. Though the cost would be billed to the insurance company, the figure she named staggered him. Obviously the reason wealthy men went in for polo was to keep the cost of their women's hairdressing expenses in perspective!

Tatum slipped her arm through his as they left the hairdressers and moved into the now thinning stream of late-night shoppers.

'So?' She looked up at him. 'I did good?'

'Yeah,' he said, smiling at her. 'You did real good. I even think you've got a chance of suing over what she's done to your hair.'

Tatum hid her face in the side of his arm and pretended to sob. 'Oh . . . *darling*, that's an *awful* thing to say! I . . . I . . . think she did a . . . a simply *marvellous* job.' She felt him chuckle.

'I can't believe that what they do in that place and the prices they charge for it doesn't qualify as extortion. You

299

could stick a screwdriver in a power socket and get the same results.'

'Actually,' Tatum said as they reached the car, 'she knows her stuff. Even if she is ripping off the insurance company, I have to say she's a very good hairdresser.'

Opening her door for her, Jace gave her a sceptical look. 'Then all I can say is . . . get in, Madge Simpson!'

As they drove back towards the city Tatum gave Jace a rundown of the conversation she'd had with the woman and her general impression of her. Overall, Carole had come across as pleasant and intelligent, although she'd been at pains to point out to Tatum that she wasn't working because she *needed* the money, but because she was bored with the social tennis and lunch scene.

'I don't know if she said that trying to project a non-frivolous image or because she doesn't want the salon's cashed up clientele to think they're better than her,' she told Jace. 'But she asked where I lived and when I said Killara, she started rattling off the names of women she thought I might know. A few I recognised from the social pages, but the others meant nothing. She could've been making them up.'

Jace frowned. 'So what did you say?'

Tatum grinned. 'I bluffed. If she said, say, Carmel Van Aston, or something equally snobby-sounding. I'd say, Wasn't she Carmel Pillington before she married? Or I'd say, The name's familiar, but gosh! I've been in Europe ever since I left Chelmsford Academy; I only got back a month ago. Then I'd start prattling on about things that happened overseas.'

'Good. Very good. Other than stressing she worked by

choice, anything else she said strike you as odd?'

'There was one thing. You said the insurance report had her address as Rozelle, right?'

Jace glanced across at her. 'Yeah, so?'

'Well, I'm almost positive she said she lived at *Roseville*.'

'No chance you misheard her?'

'Perhaps.' She sighed. 'I guess I should've pursued her on that point, shouldn't I?

His eyes remained on the road ahead. 'Why didn't you?'

She shrugged. 'I didn't want to push in case she thought I was overly curious. I tried to camouflage it by asking her what she liked best about the area, and she said she liked having a water view even if it was tiny. Which doesn't help much, because from certain areas of Rozelle you *can* see the water.'

'But *not* quite so spectacularly as you can from certain parts of Roseville. Maybe the Rozelle address is a dud and she only gets her mail forwarded from there.' Jace smirked. 'That'd explain why I didn't manage to see her entering or leaving the house when I staked it out the other day. Looks like you've saved Bentag a lot of possibly wasted time . . .'

Registering that her information might be far more important than she'd assumed, and that Jace was pleased by it, Tatum couldn't help saying, 'See! I said I could do this!'

'I never really doubted it for a minute.'

Though he realised he was being truthful, that deep down it had been impossible to underestimate the woman beside him, Jace expected the comment to earn him a sceptical if not a blistering comeback. But she said nothing. He slanted her a quick look. 'Tate?'

Even in the limited light of the car, when she turned her head from the window, it was impossible not to see her distress. 'Hey,' he said. 'What I said, I – '

'It's not that.' Her gaze reverted to the neon tawdriness of their surroundings. 'It's different,' she said softly. 'Different and yet exactly the same.'

It was then Jace realized she was talking about their location – Kings Cross. Because they'd been tight for time on the way to Double Bay, he'd driven the most direct route there through the city, but, coming back, he'd automatically detoured through the Cross. It had become second nature for him to scout the area any time he was in the vicinity, on the off-chance that he might spot a missing kid from Bentag's listings. He'd given no thought to the fact that the area held memories for Tatum.

'I suppose because I work up here a lot I don't notice the changes so much. But I know what you mean; the face stays the same, but the names of the clubs and strip-joints et cetera change all the time. I guess with you being away for three years it makes more of an impact.'

Tatum didn't tell him it was longer than three years. That in her late teens, when Kaylee and their other friends had been to 'check out the Cross' when the rest of the city had closed down, she'd never once gone with them.

And *impact* wasn't the right word to describe what she was feeling. Nostalgia didn't quite work either, because the bittersweet memories the sights and sounds enveloping her triggered were offset by a more unsettling sensation. One that had hit her the instant she sighted the

302

looming Coca-Cola sign. A sensation that the past had finally run the present to ground. And Tatum feared it was only a matter of time before it started overhauling the future.

She tried to shove the thought aside, but unwillingly she found herself trying to recognise the faces of the women working familiar street corners and feeling sad when she didn't. Eight years had produced a new generation of street girls; had it also produced a younger, prettier crop of employees for the more discreet, upmarket brothels? And, if so, what had happened to the older ones? *What*, she wondered, not for the first time but certainly for the only time without resentment, had happened to Lulu?

'Can we stop?' she asked. 'And just walk for a while?'

Though Jace's first inclination was to refuse, he didn't really understand why. It wasn't as if at this hour on a Thursday night they'd be in any real danger, yet a part of him was reluctant to agree.

'Sure,' he said. 'But is there any particular reason you want to do that?'

She nodded, the sad smile nudging her mouth giving him the impression that this wasn't so much something she *wanted* to do, but something she *had* to do. 'For me, having your roots in Kings Cross has a different connotation than it does for most people.'

He held her hand as they strolled amid the noise and colour of Australia's internationally famous red light district, but it was Tatum his eyes stayed on, not the cocktail of sad, funny, outrageous characters they passed. He watched a million different emotions from glee to tragedy cross her incredibly beautiful face, yet refrained from asking what prompted them. Somehow he sensed that, no matter what she said, for the answers to be anything but words Tatum would have to surrender them voluntarily.

Though he held her hand, Jace let her set the pace and direction they took. He indulged her demand for change for a busker who played pathetically bad sax as readily as her plea for a double mango ice-cream cone from the ice-cream parlour, but his docility balked when she she insisted on taking a tour of an 'adult' shop.

'Stop acting like a prude, Jace Benton!' she told him. 'I've *slept* with you, remember?'

'I know,' he muttered. 'But not today. And after abstaining for so long I doubt I can walk in there with you on my arm and not end up getting arrested for indecent behaviour.'

Laughing, she tugged him inside, and then promptly proceeded to torture him by recruiting his opinion of a pair of leather sheepskin-lined handcuffs!

'That's it!' he said. 'We're going home. *Now*.' Feeling *everything* but amused, Jace hauled her outside and practically dragged the giggling witch back to the car!

'Lady,' he said gruffly as he climbed behind the steering wheel, 'I hope you aren't counting on getting too much sleep tonight. 'Cause the way I feel right now, you don't have a chance in hell of getting *any*.'

'I don't need sleep tonight, Jace.' Her hand trembled on its way to touch his cheek. '*I need you*.' That was the absolute truth, she thought. Except she wasn't certain the need was entirely a physical one.

As they drove beneath it the brightness of the Coca-

Cola sign hypnotically drew her gaze again. No, she thought, for some reason tonight she craved more than mere physical closeness from Jace.

And the realization scared her.

CHAPTER 17

It was after midnight when they pulled into the basement parking lot of Jace's Drummoyne apartment block. Tatum lifted her overnight bag from the boot of the car, but when Jace would have taken it from her she shook her head. 'It's light; I can manage it.'

Following him into the elevator, she hoped she could. Right now the significance of the small nylon bag weighed much more than its meagre contents of a toiletry bag and the clothes and shoes she'd wear to the office tomorrow. She didn't know why spending the entire night with Jace felt like such a big deal, just that it did. In many ways the possible repercussions of this decision overshadowed those of having a physical relationship with him, and by the time they entered his apartment she was a mass of raw nerves.

'I better hang my dress up straight away or it'll be crushed,' she said, walking directly to the bedroom. 'I won't be long. You . . . er . . . you go ahead and set up the VCR,' she tossed over her shoulder, knowing Jace would want to check the quality of the video evidence.

Telling herself to calm down – hell, it wasn't like she'd

never slept with the guy before – she unzipped the bag and pulled out the dress. She cursed when she realized she'd not brought a hanger. Not that it was a real oversight, the truth was the dress she'd brought was crease-resistant, but she'd felt a lot more confident when she packed it than she did now. Now she needed to stall until she stopped feeling like a skittish virgin.

Drawing a deep breath, she looked at the wardrobe that stretched almost the length of one wall, but couldn't bring herself to open it. It was one thing to know that Jace had more wire coat hangers than a dry cleaners, but taking one out, slipping her dress onto it and then sliding it back to hang among his clothes was another thing entirely. Entirely too presumptuous. Entirely too personal. Entirely too *significant*.

'I owe you a birthday celebration.'

She spun round to find him watching her, his left hand capably holding a bottle of champagne and two glasses, his right an ice bucket. With slow, easy grace, he moved to the bedside table and set them down.

'I thought you'd want to watch the video first.'

Smiling, he shook his head and came to stand directly in front of her. 'I'd rather re-enact it.'

His hands went to her mile-high hair, but his gaze remained on her face even as he deftly began removing bobby pins and dropping them, one by one, onto the carpet. 'I've been fantasizing about doing this all night.'

The agility of his fingers against her scalp as they burrowed through the woven complexity of the lacquered tresses was made more arousing by the low-pitched words accompanying the action. 'I watched you in that chair

307

tonight, gypsy, having your hair shampooed,' he said. 'Your eyes were closed and you looked all loose and relaxed, with your head back over the basin, and all I could think about was, if I was doing it, you wouldn't be so relaxed. You'd be all tight and wired inside, the way *I was*, watching you tilt that long, elegant neck of yours back, so your beautiful, braless breasts could torment me.'

All pins dispensed with, his fingers raked through her hair from scalpline to ends, weakening her knees till she had to clasp the front of his shirt to stay balanced.

'And you wouldn't be dressed either,' he went on, sliding the thin straps from her shoulders to her bent elbows. 'Oh, no, gypsy, you'd be naked. Naked, so I could take my foam-covered hands out of your hair and lather you all the way to your toes.'

His hands moved back up her arms and desire trembled through her as they crossed bared shoulders and exerted a gentle pressure on her neck to bring her nearer. Instinct and anticipation lowered her lashes and parted her lips, but it was his thumb, not his lips that brushed her mouth. Desperate for the taste of him, she sucked it into her mouth and laved it with her tongue. But it wasn't enough.

'Kiss me,' she demanded, rising onto her toes and pressing her aching breasts into the hardness of his chest.

'Uh-uh.' Her eyes flew open at the refusal. 'I kiss you now and my fantasy goes up in smoke.' His voice was raspy, but determined. As determined as the way he unlinked her arms from his neck and proceeded to roll the dress's straps down her arms until her breasts, with their erect nipples, were exposed to the heat of his eyes.

'Beautiful,' he whispered, then slowly dipped his head.

Anticipating the cool touch of his mouth on her burning flesh, Tatum uttered a soft, encouraging, '*Yes* . . .' But, in lieu of drawing her deep into his mouth and offering some small respite from the desire clawing her insides, only his breath connected with her. 'Beautiful,' he whispered over one aroused peak, before nuzzling his way to the other. 'Exquisitely beautiful.'

Her hand grasped his head to pull him closer, but he didn't allow it; with his blue eyes dancing with devilment he blew across each peak, then whispered, 'Patience, gypsy, has its own rewards.'

Yet he gave her no time to be angry over his torment, for in the next instant he was guiding the stretch fabric of her dress down over her hips; his thumbs hooking into the lacy band of her knickers and simultaneously dragging them down too.

His leisurely actions were, she was sure, intended to drive her crazy, but in some distant region of her brain, Tatum was grateful for Jace's cool, calculated control of the situation. For, despite the fact he'd reduced her to a naked, quivering mass of desire, the sheer eroticism of what he was doing had her so focused on her physical response to him that there wasn't room in her mind to worry about what she was feeling emotionally.

By the time he carried her to the bathroom and laid her full-length on the vanity bench, her hair trailing into the sink, Tatum couldn't breathe. In fact she was incapable of doing anything but staring fascinated into his hypnotically handsome face. With a long drawn-out sigh of pleasure, her eyes closed as he angled the tap to deliver a warm stream of water to her head.

At the sight of her laid out as if she was a sacrifice on an altar Jace found he was having to fight to adhere to his original plan. He'd stripped off his shirt, unbuckled his belt and released the button on his jeans before he remembered that, much as he wanted to possess this woman, it was more important to prove he wasn't possessed *by* her. Therefore, for the sake of his rapidly plunging self-control, he forced himself to concentrate only on working the pearly yellow shampoo into a lather.

'Jace . . .' He heard his name as a breathy whisper, and gritted his teeth to strengthen his resistance to it. Too late, he realized he should have shut his eyes, for the peripheral sight of her squirming pleasurably in response to the movement of his fingers had his arousal meter soaring and his restraint level plummeting at an even faster rate.

'Oh, Jace . . . Touch me . . .' Her whisper became a plea. One, Jace told himself, only an excessively cruel man could ignore.

He lowered his head to hers, rationalizing that kissing her would also help relieve a little of the steaming pressure of his libido, but *that* theory was scorched to cinders at the first electric contact with her bewitching little tongue. For long, mind-numbing moments he allowed himself simply to drown in the unique taste of her, until eventually his lungs' innate need for oxygen freed him from the power of her sorcery.

Tatum's despairing groan when once more his hands went to her hair was premature, and it faded to insignificance compared to the one that broke from her when handfuls of thick white bubbles were lavished over her breasts, then down over her abdomen. Jace's hands continued their slick, soapy journey to her thighs, and under the direction of the most carnal hunger she'd ever experienced she drew her legs up and arched into his touch.

When his teasing shifted to concentrate on the sensitive flesh of her inner thigh, desire ricocheted her into a sitting position. Coherent speech beyond her, she clutched desperately at his wrists to still his hands.

Jace had never felt an onslaught of emotion such as that which hit him at the sheer wanton desire reflected in Tatum's face and body. Her breasts rose and fell in a quick jerky rhythm that he wanted to feel against his chest. Her lips were parted just enough to permit the tip of her tongue to moisten them with the nectar of her oral juices. And her brown eyes were fevered with a passion he knew only he had ever witnessed.

'Let go, gypsy, so I can get my jeans off.'

Her compliance led to her being deftly repositioned until her legs dangled from the counter. Stunned by the unexpectedness of the move, and entranced by the hot, hungry look in Jace's eyes, Tatum held her breath in anticipation as he separated her thighs and stepped between them. Belatedly her desire-clouded brain registered the brush of denim against her leg, and she verbally rebelled at further prolonged frustration.

'Oh, Jace! *Please*,' she begged. 'No more soap!'

'No more soap, gypsy,' he promised, assuming a semi-crouched position in front of her. 'I hate the taste of soap . . .'

In a solitary gush, Tatum's breath left her body . . .

★ ★ ★

311

Ensconced within Jace's loose-limbed embrace, Tatum watched the bedroom lighten with the dawn. She supposed that at some point during the night she must have dozed, but if so it hadn't been for long, for she'd spent long hours watching the darkness. She would have been happy if she could have blamed the exquisite lovemaking she and Jace had shared as the sole contributor to her lack of sleep, but other factors had been the culprits: a disorganized parade of disjointed thoughts and memories which had marched through her mind, and the tumultuous emotions that had simmered like an active volcano within her.

Beneath the sheet, she curled her right leg up and reached down to finger the fine gold chain adorning her ankle. It seemed ridiculous that something so light and delicate should weight so heavily on her mind. Sighing, she remembered Jace's words from the night before when he'd given it to her . . .

'I know I usually give you something practical,' he'd said, not long after his mouth had made the most soul-stealing love to her. 'But I figure every gypsy should have one of these.' Slipping the delicate bracelet from the pocket of his jeans, he'd tenderly clipped it around her ankle. 'Happy birthday, Tate.'

'Oh, Jace! It's . . . it's beautiful . . . Thank you.'

His smile as he'd drawn her into his arms had nearly broken her heart. 'No, gypsy,' he'd whispered. '*Thank you . . .*'

And somehow the bracelet shackled her more firmly to him than the mock wedding rings they'd removed when they'd left the hairdressers.

And now it was morning.

The morning of the start of her twenty-fifth year of life. The morning after a night when Jace Benton had not only slipped a chain onto her ankle, but also, she feared, shackled her heart for all the years to come. But it was also the morning after the night she'd heard the rattling of chains anchored in her past.

Tatum didn't want to risk putting what she felt for Jace into a word, even mentally; to do so would be to invite grief. Only a fool would dare believe the rusty old chains of her past could be weaker than the soft rose-gold of the one gracing her ankle. And Tatum was no fool.

She would take each day of her relationship with Jace as it came, and enjoy it for however long it lasted. It was her *present*, but not her future; she wouldn't allow herself to become dependent upon it, or *him*. When it ended, she would be prepared, and she'd comfortably file it into her past. Tatum acknowledged that she'd existed for the past twenty-four years without falling into the trap of imagining she'd have an idealistic future, and her emotional survival demanded she not start now.

Jace wasn't sure whether he was grateful for the hectic pace at the office over the next week or not. On one hand it ensured that during business hours things remained perfectly professional between him and Tate, and on the other . . . Damn it! It ensured, during business hours, that things stayed perfectly professional between him and Tate!

Fortunately he'd been able to swing the surveillance schedule so he and Tate managed to get one entire night together at his place, and on others they were able to snatch a few hours of bliss between each other's various commitments. For the most part he'd been pretty satisfied, but it peeved him that come Friday night, when he had an entirely free weekend ahead, something cropped up to prevent Tate and him going home together.

Last night he'd met her at ten-thirty, after working on a MP case. They'd spent four glorious hours in the throes of passion and the fifth arguing over why Tate should shouldn't stay the night. In the end he'd climbed out of bed and deposited her in his parents' kitchen some time around four in the morning, then turned around and driven back to his place. He didn't know why, but for some reason turning up a his folks' house in the morning to change before going to the office was as big an issue with Tate as going to work in the same clothes two days running. He'd figured that tonight, being Friday, neither argument could hold water, and he'd planned a quiet romantic evening and a torrid Saturday morning at his place. Then work had shot all his plans to hell.

'Actually, it's worked out well,' Tate told him, making him think she'd probably say earthquakes were a convenient way to loosen garden soil. 'I promised Brian I'd help out down at the youth club tonight.'

He frowned. 'You didn't mention that.'

Her shrug was blasé. 'You didn't ask.'

It hadn't occurred to him that he would have had to; prudently, though, he kept the comment to himself, asking instead, 'Any plans for tomorrow?' and praying she'd say no.

'Yes.' She grinned. 'To sleep late! I've been yawning all day, thanks to you!'

'In that case, stay at my place. I promise I won't let you out of bed before, oh . . . three in the afternoon.'

Laughing, she shook her head. 'I need *sleep*, not sex.'

'*Incredible* sex,' he corrected.

She rolled her eyes. 'I also want to do some Christmas shopping.'

'Okay, then, I'll pick you up at Mum's tomorrow and we'll go shopping. Fair enough?' She nodded and he grinned, grabbing her waist and pulling her into a gentle embrace. 'Good. And after all that you'll be tired, so I'll take you over to my place and tuck you into bed.'

She laughed. 'And after *that*, I'll be *totally exhausted*!'

'Mmm,' he agreed against her neck. 'Count on it.'

Jace rounded the side of his parents' house a little after ten the next morning to discover his father, bare-chested and wearing swimming shorts, skimming leaves from the pool.

'G'day, Dad. How's things?'

'Things'd be a whole lot easier if God hadn't created leaves, wind and crooked cops. If you're looking for Tatum, she's not here. Bring me that bucket of chlorine, will you?

'*Not here?* We're supposed to be going Christmas shopping together.'

His father straightened to give him a long, hard stare. 'And you're *worried*?' Jace was subjected to a look normally reserved for idiots. 'Struth. You got *any* idea what shopping with a woman is like, son?'

Ignoring the sarcasm, Jace unlocked the gate of the pool fence and picked up the chlorine. 'Where's she gone?'

'Flat-hunting.'

'*Flat-hunting!* Why, for God's sake?'

'Wild guess, I'd say she's looking for one,' his Dad said drily. 'But, hey, I've been wrong before.' He motioned towards the glistening water. 'Just chuck it in.'

Taking care to avoid getting his clothes splashed with the pungent-smelling bleaching agent, Jace emptied the bucket with the experience of too many years of Saturdays spent maintaining the pool. It was one of the few things he hadn't missed when he'd first moved out of home, and he'd long ago decided that if *he* ever had a house with a pool he'd hire someone else to do the upkeep on it.

'She didn't say anything to me about looking for somewhere else to live.' He spoke more to himself than his father, but that changed when, unbidden, a nasty thought popped into his head. 'Hey, you and Mum haven't been making her feel guilty on account of her sleeping at my place, have you?'

Indignity tightened Brian Benton's mouth. 'We've done no such thing! The guilts not *hers*.' His accusing glance and tone stunned Jace. 'You always were too damn selfish for your own good.'

Jace dropped the now empty bucket onto the ground, uncaring that it rolled from the non-slip decking into the pool. '*Selfish?* Okay, Dad, don't beat around the bush, spit it out! What have I done now?'

With a grunt of disbelief, his father snatched the bucket up and stalked towards the security gate. Jace followed.

'C'mon, Dad, out with it.'

Whatever his old man muttered under his breath, it was too soft for Jace to catch, but there was no mistaking the ramrod-stiff irritation of his back as he walked into the house, not caring that the screen door practically hit his son in the face.

'You want me to guess, is that it, Dad?' he asked. 'Okay, well, is it something I've done since I left uni, or some earlier transgression you've decided to rehash? I'll at least need that much of a clue, since you've blamed my self-ishness, my stubbornness or,' he went on, 'my stupidity for everything except the Crucifixion.'

The niggling worked. 'I've made it a point to stay out of you boys' personal lives since you reached the age of consent,' his father told him. 'I figured you were both responsible enough not to make any big mistakes in that area and smart enough to learn from any small ones. I've even managed to keep my mouth shut about all the crap Donna is putting your brother through . . .'

Jace had to admit everything his father said was true. He might have given him and Ethan a hard time about their studies and their career choices, but he'd never en-croached on their private lives. Which was why being on the receiving of his lengthy pause and glare was like waiting for the other shoe to drop.

'I'll say this once, Jace. If you were anyone else but my son I'd be warning Tatum against you. And I'll tell you this for nothing too . . . You hurt her and your mother'll kick your backside so hard your nose will bleed.'

Slamming his fist against the sink, Jace swore. 'What the hell do you take me for? I'd cut my own throat before

317

I'd hurt Tate. Damn it, Dad! She's gone out with bigger sleazeballs than me and you've barely batted an eyelash.'

'Yeah, well *those* sleazeballs didn't advertise she was sleeping with them!'

'That's because *she wasn't!*

His father lifted an eyebrow. 'Then maybe that says more for them than it does for you.'

With that ominous comment, his father went back outside. The next time the door opened it was to admit a laughing Tatum followed by his equally amused mother.

'I thought we were going shopping.'

His growled greeting caught Tatum off guard. 'Er . . . we are. Aren't we?'

'And good morning to you too, Jason,' his mother said.

'Sorry, Mum.' He smiled at her, searching her face for any of the animosity his father had hinted at. There was none. Relaxing, he stood and kissed Tate lightly on the cheek. 'Sorry, gypsy. I guess I got out of the wrong side of the bed. I get confused when I've got the choice of two.'

Recovering from both Jace's innuendo and the surprising unabashed show of affection in front of his mother, Tatum could only nod.

'Dad says you've been flat-hunting.'

'*Again.*' His mother inserted. 'It's been a regular Saturday morning thing since she got home. I swear, I'm at the stage where I know the first names of practically every real estate agent in a thirty-kilometre radius of Strathfield.'

It was news to Jace that Tate had been so actively involved with plans to move into her own place. 'Any luck?' he asked.

'Nope. The entire morning was an exercise in wasting time.'

'That's not true,' his mum objected, filling the kettle. 'She bought a nice cotton-weave rug. Show it to him, Tatum.'

Sending him an apologetic look, she tore open the roll of brown paper and unfurled the two metre by one metre rug. Against a grey background irregular, roughly hewn stripes in mauve, pink and black were woven through it.

'Nice,' Jace said. 'But I thought we were going to shop for gifts together?'

'We are. The rug isn't a gift. It's for when I eventually find a flat.' She smiled. 'Apart from that, the only thing I've bought in a depressingly unsuccessful morning is this.' She extracted a freshly baked apple tea-cake from a bag bearing the name of a local bakery for which Jace had an historic weakness. 'I suppose you'll be wanting some?' she asked, following his gaze.

'You bet!' He grinned. 'But I'll settle for some tea-cake for now.' Flushing, she sent a worried look in the direction of his mother, who was busy pulling cups and plates from a cupboard across the room before lowering her head and quickly slicing the bun.

Her seemingly embarrassed reaction bothered him. He moved closer to her and lowered his voice. 'Has Mum been giving you a hard time?'

'What?' She blinked then. 'Of course not. But I think we ought to give her time to get used to things before you start talking like you're ready to make out on her kitchen floor,' she said drily.

'Stuff her, then,' Jace said lightly. 'We'll do it on our own kitchen floor.'

'You mean *your* kitchen floor,' she corrected. 'And forget it! There's no way you're getting me naked on cold slate.'

He smirked. 'God, I love a challenge. Still, I have to admit that rug will look pretty good in my kitchen. Specially with you stretched out on it.' His eyes were seduction itself. 'With the rug under you and me on top of you,' he whispered, 'I can pretty much guarantee the cold slate wouldn't bother you.'

'Jace!' she hissed, darting a furtive glance at his mother. '*Behave.*'

'If you wanted me to behave, gypsy . . .' Pushing aside her hair, he drew a slow finger from her earlobe across her all but bare shoulder and down her left arm, creating a tremble that made the knife drop from her right hand. 'You shouldn't have left me here all alone with my fantasies, then walked in looking all sexy and soft.'

Summoning the little will power that didn't immediately desert her whenever she was within six metres of this man, Tatum planted her hands on his chest and pushed gently. 'Go sit down,' she instructed, adding for the benefit of Judy, 'No pinching cake until it's on the table.'

Rank amusement lit his blue eyes as he resumed his seat, and even as she busied herself arranging the sliced bun on a plate she could feel him watching her. Just that was enough to cause her pulse to dance about.

'So,' he said. 'Let's get back to discussing how this rug will work in the kitchen.'

Tatum groaned. 'That's *my* rug. But if you're so

desperate to have one,' she went on, placing the tray of cake on the table and slapping his hand as he reached for a piece, 'we can get you one when we go shopping.'

'Well, if you insist. But don't you think having two rugs in the kitchen seems a bit . . .' He frowned. 'Over the top?'

'You don't have a rug in your kitchen.'

'I will, once that one goes down.'

She glared at him, then laughed. 'Jace Benton, I don't care how much double-talk you throw at me, you're not getting that rug. I got it for *my* kitchen.'

'You don't have a kitchen.'

'I know that! But I will, when I move, and that's where the rug is going!'

'And, like I said, it'll look great in my kitchen.'

'In your kitchen . . .' She shook her head. 'Jace, aren't you listening to a word I say, or have you finally gone completely insane?'

'All things considered, I'm probably insane,' he said, his voice strangely rough. 'But *you're* the one who's not listening, gypsy; I'm asking you to move in with me.'

The timeliness of Judy dropping all four of the cups she'd been carrying to the table gave Tatum at least a few seconds to recover from the catatonic shock caused by his announcement.

Move in with Jace?

Live with him?

Wake up in his arms every morning?

'Well?' he prodded from the floor, sparing her a quick glance in between picking up pieces of smashed china. 'I mean, if you're going to move out of here, it's only logical you come to my place.'

Logical. *Logical*. He thought them living together was *logical*?

At that moment her peripheral vision picked up Brian's entrance from the backyard. 'What the devil happened here?'

'Mum dropped the cups.'

'Jason asked Tatum to live with him.'

Jace and his mother spoke in unison. Tatum remained mute. It was to her, though, that Brian turned his questioning expression. Under the penetrating gaze of the older man she lowered her head, fearful of what he might read in her eyes.

'That about explains it,' she said, trying for a teasing tone.

'And *what*,' he asked, his tone demanding, 'is going to be your response?'

Jace quickly got to his feet. 'I think I deserve to hear that first, don't you, Dad?'

'I know what *you* deserve,' he told his son. 'I also know what I think Tatum deserves.'

Jace's body tensed with rage. 'What you think doesn't come into this. This is between Tatum and me.'

Tatum could *feel* the suppressed aggression arcing between the two men. Its potency was disturbing. She couldn't guess at the cause, though clearly something must have happened before she and Judy had arrived home. She looked at the other woman, who'd frozen in the act of picking up the china, and sent her a silent plea for intervention.

'Brian . . .' Judy scrambled to her feet and moved quickly to her husband's side. 'Jace is right. This is something they have to talk about. *Discuss* between themselves. You can't expect Tatum to make a snap decision about this big a commitment.'

Tatum sensed Judy's comments were directed as much to *her* as to her husband. Apparently, Jace thought them aimed at him.

'*This big a commitment?*' He faced his mother with absolute astonishment. 'She's already decided to leave here, Mum. And, considering our relationship, how big a decision can moving in with me be?' He shook his head. 'Hell! It's not like I'm asking her to *marry* me, for God's sake!'

'God forbid you should bloody do that!' Brian snapped.

Tatum's laughter surprised everyone. 'Trust me, Brian, you've got no worries there!' she said, amusement lighting her face. 'I'd have said *no* to that, quick-smart!'

For some reason Jace didn't experience the rush of reassurance her statement should have brought. Although he hoped he didn't look as disappointed as his mother.

'You don't think Jason would make a good husband?'

Tate shrugged. 'If he's anything like his father . . .' she smiled gently at the man in question . . . 'he'll be *great*. And if there *is* a woman crazy enough to want to spend the rest of her life washing his dirty socks and raising his brats, then I'll gladly dance at his wedding.' Again she laughed. 'But I promise you it won't be the bridal waltz.'

'You'd never consider marrying Ja – *anyone*?' Judy asked.

'Believe me, Judy,' she said solemnly, '*suicide* is five spots higher on my list of "Things to Do" than marriage.'

★ ★ ★

323

At her wits' end, Tatum pulled to a dead stop and grabbing Jace's wrist, hauled him out of the bustling stream of Christmas shoppers. 'Look,' she said tersely, 'I said I'd think about it and I will! But I can't do that if you're going to keep asking, "Have you made a decision yet?" every five minutes!'

'Like I told Mum, I can't see what the big issue is. All that's going to change is I won't have to get out of bed and drive you home in the middle of the night, 'cause all your clothes will be in the wardrobe.'

Tatum wanted to hit him. Didn't he realize that from her perspective agreeing to live with him involved much more than simply transferring her clothes to his place? God, if it were that simple she'd have given in to her first impulse when he'd voiced the suggestion and thrown herself at him screaming, *Yes! Yes! Yes!* But it wasn't that simple. Moving in also meant eventually moving out. And she didn't need a crystal ball to tell her that, no matter how far or near that situation was, it was going to be painful for her. Agonizingly painful. But of course she couldn't tell him that.

'If you'd stop thinking so selfishly for a – '

'*What?*' Jace ignored her frown, ticked off at being called selfish twice in the space of a few hours. '*You're* the one who insists I take you home at all ungodly hours of the morning! And I do it. If I was as goddamn *selfish* as everyone seems to think, I'd make you get a bloody cab!'

'I'm not accusing you of *acting* selfishly; I said you were *thinking* selfishly. There's a difference.' She sighed. 'You don't seem to realize, my living with you has bigger ramifications for me than it does you.'

He scowled. 'How do you figure that? This isn't something I do on a regular basis, you know. I've never even been willing to *consider* letting any other woman to encroach so far into my life. Hell, I'm inviting you to share *my* apartment rent-free, I'm – '

'Exactly! You're providing me with *everything*.'

'That's *bad*? That makes me *selfish*?'

'Damn it, you're not selfish!' she snapped. Then she sighed, uncertain of how to make him understand what she was feeling. 'Jace, the thing is you don't expect me to contribute anything to this arrangement except my body. Do you?'

He grinned. 'You're forgetting the rug.'

'I'm being serious.'

'No,' he said, his hand cupping her jaw, 'you're being silly. But if you want I'll store half my furniture and you can replace it with stuff of yours.'

'I don't *have* furniture.'

'So I'll buy you some.'

She swore, hating his generosity. 'Jace, I'll move in with you on one condition – '

'That you get to choose which side of the bed is yours?'

She shook her head, causing a delicious friction between his palm and her face.

'That you get first shot at the bathroom in the morning?' He assumed a pondering expression. 'That I bring you breakfast in bed on weekends – ?'

'That you charge me a reasonable board.'

'Charge you – ' He snatched his hand away as if her face had erupted into flame. 'Shit, Tate, why would I do that? I own the place outright.'

'But I don't. I pay board to your parents – '

'That's different and you know it! I'm asking you to be my live-in lover, not a bloody flatmate!'

She'd known he'd be angry. And she knew he'd get a lot angrier with what she was going to say next, but this was something her pride demanded she say. 'Jace, it's like you told your mother; we aren't talking marriage here. And I don't want you perceiving me in either the role of a wife – '

'Oh, right! The dreaded dirty socks scenario you mentioned earlier!'

'*Or*,' she continued over his muttered sarcasm, 'the role of live-in whore.'

He reeled back as if she'd slapped him. She'd expected anger, but the momentary flash of unchecked pain she glimpsed in his eyes was unexpected.

'Jace, I'm sorry – ' He jerked away from the hand she lifted to his arm, and if it hadn't been for the fact that he'd been a split second slow in masking his initial reaction she might have thought him merely furious. Yet unintentionally she'd somehow hurt him. Knowing this brought a physically crippling pain to her gut.

'*Please*, Jace,' she implored. 'Let me explain. I . . . that . . . what I said wasn't a reflection on you.'

'You could've fooled me.'

'It wasn't!' she yelled, uncaring of the curious looks her denial drew from passing shoppers. '*Please*,' she begged. 'At least hear me out.'

But though he stood silent and completely motionless, she knew he wasn't ready to listen to anything she said. He was staring down at her as if he didn't know her, as if he hadn't ever seen her before. She told herself the excruciating pain in her chest was caused by her lungs' inability to draw breath, that it had nothing to do with how she felt about this man, nothing to do with knowing that any second now he'd push his rigid frame away from the wall, push past her and walk away. From her. For good.

During the lifetime of silence that stretched between them she repeated that thought over and over. It *was* simply breathing that hurt. Breathing, thinking, life . . .

'You know,' he said finally, and her legs nearly buckled with relief, 'if I do as you ask and believe that comment wasn't aimed at me – '

'*It wasn't!*'

He acknowledged her interruption with a minute nod of his head. 'I feel *more* angry, not less. Because it implies that's how you view *yourself*. Is it, Tatum?'

She sighed.

'*Is it?*'

'No. But I'm afraid I might.'

When he continued to look at her, she lowered her head, first to look at the floor, then to the high ceiling of the multi-level shopping mall. The brightly coloured decorations hanging from it seemed as far from her reach as any explanation she could produce with confidence that Jace would accept it.

'I know this is going to be difficult for you to understand, but it might help if you remember where I came from – '

'Tate, your past doesn't matter – '

'It does to me!' Forcing herself to modify her tone, she focused on her hands. 'I grew up in a world where sex was

327

a commodity and a serious relationship was a guy who slept over occasionally and didn't refer his friends to you.'

Jace swore, bringing her head up. 'I *know* this is different. I really know that, Jace.' She hit her chest with a closed fist. 'In *here* I know that. But in here – ' she tapped her temple ' – in here, sometimes the echoes of my past are really loud. Most of the time I can shut them out, because I live in a different world now and nothing they say applies to me any more, but I don't want to *ever* be in a position where they might have reason to taunt me. To make me doubt myself.'

'And you think moving in with me would do that?'

She shook her head. 'Living with you isn't a problem. But . . .' She paused and drew a long, steadying breath, before meeting his gaze squarely. 'Living with you on *your* terms, with me making no financial contribution, *is*. That comes too close to being paid for services rendered for me to be comfortable with it.'

'I see.'

It was a lie. Jace didn't see at all. While he'd always admired Tatum's pride, he wasn't so sure that was the case at present. In fact, he wasn't sure about anything, least of all whether he wanted to throttle her where she stood, somehow looking both resolute and vulnerable, or throw her onto the ground and make love to her on the spot. Since acting on either impulse in the midst of pre-Christmas shoppers would get him arrested, he folded his arms as a precautionary measure and leaned back against the display window of the shop behind him, feigning a casualness he was far from feeling.

'What would you say,' he said, 'to board of, oh . . .'

Though he named a ludicrously large figure, Tatum had to fight the elated temptation to say, *I'll take it!*

'I'd say,' she managed, once her heart had slid from her throat back into her chest, 'that'd necessitate me asking Tag, *the notably more money conscious partner in Bentag Investigations*, to triple my salary.'

His handsome face wrinkled in disapproval. 'Hardly a good, feasible idea, considering the increase in our liquid paper expenses since you've joined the firm. What about,' he said, ignoring her affronted gasp, 'if we settled on what you're paying my parents?'

'Double that. I've always felt they were taking too little.' She shrugged. 'But, since they refused to accept more, there wasn't a lot I could do about it.'

Jace had absolutely no idea what monetary arrangement she and his parents had arrived at, but he was tempted to ask why she was willing to pander to their generosity and not his! In view of their delicately positioned negotiations, he bit the remark back. 'Reduce that by twenty-five per cent and we could have a deal.'

He watched her fight down a smile and try to pretend she was considering the offer. Her expressive brown eyes doomed her to failure. 'Done. *Providing*,' she said, 'we take turns cooking dinner when we're both home and I get first call on the shower in the mornings.'

Snaking out a hand, he tugged her to him. 'Gypsy, I'm such a generous landlord, I'll even apply the soap for you. Satisfied?'

'Very . . .' She kissed him. 'Much . . .' She kissed him again. 'So . . .'

This time Jace didn't give her the chance to draw back.

Their ardour, however, was kept in check by the cat calls from a group of passing youths.

Tatum blushed, but made no attempt to escape his embrace. 'You really don't mind my . . . you know, *condition*?'

He shook his head, smiling through the lie. 'Nah! I was willing to go to any lengths to get that rug.'

CHAPTER 18

Living with Jace was nothing like Tatum had imagined it would be. It was better. Much better. Perfect . . . well, damn near perfect. *Near* perfect only because there were some nights when the erratic nature of his work meant she fell asleep alone in his huge empty bed. The bright side to these occasions was that he always woke her in the most tantalising fashion to let her know he was, in his words, 'home safe, sound and horny'.

She mostly used the nights Jace worked to do the, 'solo stuff' she weakly allowed to slide when he was home. She worked out at the gym, visited girlfriends who brought her up to speed with all the gossip she'd missed while she was overseas, or cruised shopping malls in search of the perfect Christmas present for Jace. To date, she still hadn't found one – well, she *had*, but a red Ferrari was a bit too extravagant for a cheque account that, as yet, wouldn't stretch to a car for herself!

Of course, some nights she didn't feel like sweating it out in the gym or socializing. Those nights she stayed home and did exciting things, like painting her nails or, as was the case tonight, her ironing, with her eyes focused on some mindless TV show and her mind focusing on thoughts of Jace and the hope he'd get back early. This was the third night in a row he'd had to work.

Sighing, she continued to work her way through the basket of clothes until it dawned on her that she didn't own an aqua silk shirt. Screaming, she threw it back in the basket, only a split second after the dangerous thought that it wouldn't really hurt to iron just one of his shirts fluttered into her mind.

'Damn it, Tatum!' she told herself aloud. 'You *should've* planned something!'

It was worrying to think missing him had become such a powerful emotion that she'd nearly succumbed to the urge to *iron his clothes*! At this rate, she figured, she was rapidly becoming a potential candidate for 'devoted little woman' syndrome! Deciding to act before she reached the degrading stage of looking for dirty socks to wash, she unplugged the iron and phoned Judy, with the ulterior motive of cajoling a dinner invitation out of her.

Since she'd moved out, she and the older woman had fallen into a pattern of phoning each other every few days, and Brian insisted she come to dinner at least once a week. And though she would have had to be less intuitive than a rock not to notice that Jace's father hadn't initially been thrilled by her's and Jace's living arrangements, after nearly five weeks he seemed to have adjusted to the situation.

'Gee, I really lucked out when I invited myself over,' she said later that evening, as she packed the last of the dinner plates into Judy's dishwasher. 'Better not tell Jace he missed out on a roast dinner or he'll sulk and stop me coming here when he's working.'

'I'd like to see him try.' Judy laughed. 'And you be sure and tell him he better be here with you Christmas Day or he'll be answering to me!'

Tatum turned around and fixed a disbelieving look on the other woman. 'If he so much as *contemplates* working and missing my first Christmas dinner at home in three years, he won't be *alive* to answer to you.'

'Oh, Tatum, you've no idea how much I'm looking forward to having everyone here for Christmas!' She beamed with pure pleasure. 'It'll be *wonderful*. You're back and Ethan's coming up with that precious granddaughter of mine! Have you seen the photo he sent last week?'

'Only ten or twenty times.' To describe Judy as a proud grandparent would be the grandmother of all understatements! What limited knowledge Tatum had of the little girl, who'd been born just after she'd gone overseas, had come via Nanna Judy's glowing letters and International Express Post. *Regularly. Complete with snapshots.*

'It'll be nice to finally meet her.' Tatum smiled, in case her ambivalent feelings on children in general told in her voice. As far as kids went, her experience of them was limited to the tantrum-throwing supermarket variety and the angelically cute species seen in television commercials. If one believed photos, Ethan's daughter would fall into the latter category. Again she smiled, and offered the noncommittal comment, 'She looks a real sweetie.'

'She *is* a real sweetie,' Judy insisted, her smile vanishing as she added, 'which only goes to prove her father's genes were mercifully dominant!' She sent Tatum a conspiratorial look and dropped her voice, even though they were the only two in the house, since Brian had popped over to a neighbour's.

'*She* phoned me the other day . . . with a whole list of what LaTasha was and wasn't allowed to do while she was here and I was looking after her.' Nothing in Judy's tone or demeanour left any doubt as to how she felt about *that*. 'When I reminded her that *Ethan* would be looking after *his* daughter, do you know what she said?'

There were too many derogatory remarks Donna was more than capable of making and *none* she wasn't for Tatum to narrow it down to one. She shook her head.

'She said, "Oh, Ethan's useless! Besides, he's a man; men don't understand how protective we mothers are towards our children." Can you believe it?'

'Of Donna?' She rolled her eyes. 'Easily. Her feet spend so much time in her mouth, they're equally foul. And her mind's worse.'

'Yes, I know. I've always prided myself on not passing judgement on her or sinking to her level, but I did when she said that. I said that while *most* mothers were protective of their children, some were just too plain stupid and selfish to do anything but use them as tools to gain their own way!' She sighed, worry and embarrassment creasing her brow. 'And then I hung up in her ear.'

'Good for you! She deserved it.'

Pursing her mouth, Judy shook her head uncertainly.

Hating the absent Donna more than ever for the anger and hurt recalling the incident had brought to the woman's previously glowing face, Tatum patted her shoulder. 'Don't let her worry you, Judy. She's not worth it. She's always been an out-and-out bitch.'

'It's not *her* that worries me. It's what she's doing to Ethan and my baby granddaughter. *And*,' she added, concerned eyes lifting to Tatum's, 'what she *will* do. What if because of what I said she refuses to let Ethan bring LaTasha up here? Or, worse, doesn't even let him see her at Christmas? Oh, Tatum . . .' She clutched the younger woman's hand. 'What am I going to do if that happens? Ethan will never forgive me. Why couldn't I have kept my mouth shut one more time? Why . . .?'

The only time Tatum had seen Judy cry had been at Bryce's funeral. She supposed it wasn't unreasonable to assume she'd also cried when her own father had passed away last year, but having been overseas at the time, she couldn't say for certain. But one thing she *did* know was that Judy Benton was the strongest, most rational woman she knew, which was why she was completely unprepared when Judy dissolved into a sobbing, trembling wreck before her eyes.

Never in her life had Tatum felt as homicidal towards Donna as she did at that minute. Nor quite so useless at offering comfort to a woman she owed more to than she could ever tell or show her. Acting purely on her instincts, she drew the distraught face into her shoulder.

'C'mon now, Judy,' she crooned, patting her shoulders. 'I'm sure it'll be okay. Didn't you say Donna was planning to spend the holidays cruising the Whitsundays with friends?'

The faintly greyed head bobbed against her breast.

'Then the only way she could prevent Ethan having

LaTasha for Christmas would be if she cancelled her plans or had someone else to take care of her.'

Tatum was drawing this conclusion by trying to think like Donna, and, had it not been for Judy's distress, she would have been thankful that she was floundering to come up with another suitably bitchy scenario. Not even a Satan would aspire to think easily along the same lines as that sow! Still, she tried.

'Donna's an only child, right? And, even assuming she *did* have a friend, how many people would be prepared to look after someone else's child for an extended period over Christmas? But just say Donna found someone,' she went on, 'Ethan's got the legal know-how to fight them, and if it came to a court order the ruling would favour the father over a non-blood relative.'

Though she injected a confident tone into her voice, Tatum was only surmising this, but she couldn't believe any *thinking* magistrate could possibly rule any other way. Not if a mother was prepared to dump her child with strangers while she flitted off on a cruise and – *Damn!* She cursed silently as a spanner she hadn't considered suddenly dropped into the workings of her head.

'Er, Judy,' she said hesitantly, hoping what had occurred to her wouldn't tip the scales in Donna's favour. 'What about Donna's folks? They wouldn't be likely to take LaTasha for her, *knowing* she was deliberately trying to spite Ethan, would they?'

'Pp – probably . . .'

Tatum swore softly amid the hiccup-dotted response.

'They . . . think . . . Don – Donna is p-perfect.'

'Shows where their judgement is!'

'But . . . but they're . . . a-way.'

'*Away?* For how long?'

Judy shook her head. 'They . . . went to . . . the States. They go ev – every few years to spend . . . Christmas in . . . Aspen or – '

Laughing, she eased Judy's head back so she could look at her.

'Judy, I *really* don't think you have to worry!'

'You . . . you don't?'

Grinning, she shook her head. 'Like you said, Donna's selfish; *way too selfish* to punish herself purely to score points off Ethan. And if her parents are skiing their little butts off in Aspen I hardly think they'll rush home and babysit, even if darling Donna *did* ask them.'

'I'd love to think you were right . . .' There was a wealth of doubt in Judy's tear-blotched face, before a spark of hope lit it up. 'You know, Donna booked this trip before Ethan told me he was going to have LaTasha.' A recollecting frown caused her to pause for a second before she continued. 'I remembered because at Easter he was upset because he thought Donna was going to take LaTasha with her and he wouldn't see her for Christmas.'

'Do you know if Ethan approached Donna about him having LaTasha or vice versa?'

'Ethan asked her,' Judy said positively. 'I know because he jumped on a plane and flew up here last Easter Sunday utterly miserable because she wouldn't let him have LaTasha that day. I was here when he phoned to wish her a Happy Easter, then he asked to speak with Donna. And *that's* when she told him she'd arranged a cruise for Christmas-time.'

'And Ethan asked if LaTasha could stay with him?'

Judy shook her head. 'No, he started calling her every name he could lay tongue to and then hung up in her ear. He was furious, Tatum, absolutely livid. It wasn't until that night he calmed down enough to ring and apologize.' She sighed. 'I told him it was necessary for LaTasha's sake; as a social worker, I know more than I care to about the repercussions of divorce. I don't want things unwittingly made worse for LaTasha by Ethan's stubborn pride – God knows, Donna's creating *deliberate* emotional carnage.'

'So that's when he asked about having her for Christmas?' asked Tatum quickly, fearful that Judy would become tearful again.

At Judy's nod, Tatum was unable to hold back a smirk. 'And even though, only hours earlier, the man she despises and considers useless, had verbally abused her and slammed a phone in her ear, Donna agreed to let her daughter – a daughter she's been scheming to keep away from him, I might add – stay with him for three weeks at Christmas?' She paused, before urging, '*Think about it,* Judy.'

It took a moment for the older woman's smile to appear, but a heartbeat later it evolved into a fully fledged laugh, and Tatum was swallowed up in a hug of bear-like proportions.

'Oh, Tatum! You're right! You're absolutely right! It suits *Donna* to let Ethan have LaTasha, so it wouldn't have mattered what I said; she won't change her mind, because that'd mean changing her plans.'

'Exactly! The only good thing I can say about Donna is

338

she's *consistent*. Consistently nasty, consistently selfish and consistently manipulative. She's also – '

'Oh, my Lord!' Judy's eyes widened at something behind Tatum, and automatically she turned to see.

'Hell,' Jace muttered from the back door. 'You're supposed to be at home.'

Too shocked by the sight of his right arm hanging limply at his side and the blood staining almost the entire front of his shirt, Tatum could only sit mute and watch as his mother guided him to a chair. Then she started to shake. 'Christ, Jace, there's blood all over you!'

'Calm down, gypsy,' he said quickly. 'It's not as bad as it looks.'

'I'm calling Kev Prendergast.'

Jace was so distracted by the fearful paleness of Tatum's face and the coldness of her hand enclosed in his that it took a moment before his mother's words registered. When they did it was too late. She was hanging up the phone as she said, 'He's on his way.'

'Mum, I've already seen a doctor. All I need now is a shower and a clean shirt.' Tatum's brown eyes were wide with both disbelief and incomprehension. 'Truly,' he went on, trying to reassure her. 'The arms' a bit stiff, but there's more blood than damage. It's just a little knife-nick.'

As horror propelled her to her feet Tatum felt the floor roll beneath her. 'Somebody *stabbed* you?' Nausea and fear rose in her throat to strangle her. 'Oh, God!' she gasped, clutching the bench for support. 'I can't – '

'Tatum!'

Jace sprang from the chair the instant she started to crumble, and instinctively his right arm bore most of her weight. Yet despite his injury the only pain he recognized as he caught her pseudo-lifeless body before it hit the floor was that in his heart.

The first thing she saw when she opened her eyes were six legs. A moment later they distinguished themselves as three separate pairs. Judy's, Brian's and a pyjamaed pair. Jace didn't own pyjamas.

'Wh – where's Jace?'

'Here, gypsy. I'm right here.' His inverted face appeared above hers, and for a moment she thought her vision was swirling again. Then she realized her head was on his knees and they were both on the floor.

'Are you okay?' she asked, pressing her own hand over the male one that cradled her face.

A silly upside down grin preceded his answer. '*I'm* not the one who fainted.'

'It wouldn't have happened if you hadn't lost so much blood.'

A chorus of laughter followed her accusation.

'Now, that's taking the theory of sympathy pains to new heights!' The pyjama-clad man she now recognized as Kevin Prendergast smiled down at her. 'He suffers the blood loss and *you* pass out.'

'Is he all right?' she asked the still chuckling doctor.

'I'd say so, since he says he's already been patched up at the local hospital.'

'*You mean you haven't examined him yet*?' Some doctor he was!

'Young lady, that would've been a bit hard to do with him cradling you in his lap – assuming he'd even been prepared to co-operate. According to him, *you're* the priority patient.'

'I'm fine,' she declared, pushing herself into a sitting position over Jace's pleas that she take it slowly. 'Jace,' she said gently, twisting to give him a reassuring smile, 'apart from having a *mild* reaction to seeing you covered in blood and admitting to being stabbed, I'm fine.'

'You're sure?'

'Yes. Really. Let me get up.'

'Okay,' he said, helping her to her feet with his left arm. 'But just for the record, so am I. And I wasn't *stabbed*. I simply picked a bad time to step between a guy flashing a knife and his intended victim.'

'And how did that come about?' Brian Benton, who had presumably come in while Tatum was out, wanted to know.

Tucking Tatum tightly against his side with his good arm, Jace explained. 'I'd tailed a subject to a pub at Ashfield and was waiting a few minutes before I followed him inside. A couple of teenagers were trash-talking each other outside. It seemed harmless enough, until one got careless with his arms and clipped the other's girlfriend on the side of the head.' He shrugged. 'Next thing I know, out comes a knife and instant chaos. I reached in to haul the guy out of the way and collected the edge of the blade.' His body absorbed the shudder that racked Tatum's.

'Gypsy, it wasn't that bad. If it was, I'd never have been able to restrain the guy until the cops got there. Although you'll be pleased to know, Dad, *four* of them showed up almost immediately. If nothing else, this inquiry is improving their response time. I gave my statement, the guy got charged and I took myself off to the hospital.'

341

'But why didn't you go straight home from the hospital?' Tatum asked. 'Why drive all the way out here?'

His lips curled into an ironic smile. 'Because I wanted to have a shower and borrow a clean shirt from Dad.'

The frown she raised to him was as beautiful as it was bemused. 'What for?'

'So I wouldn't scare you witless by arriving home looking like this!' He tweaked her nose. 'Only *you* weren't where you were supposed to be.'

'Jace, you let Kev take a look at that arm,' his father instructed. 'I'll leave a shirt in the bathroom for you.'

'Thanks, Dad, but since the damage is done we might as well head off home now.'

'No, you won't!' His mother looked aghast. 'You aren't taking Tatum anywhere till she's had a cup of tea and time for her nerves to settle!'

Her tone filled Jace with renewed guilt about what he'd put Tatum through and increased worry that perhaps his mother sensed she was far more shaken than she appeared. He took the time to peruse her face again. Though the colour was coming back to her cheeks, there was a fragility in her eyes robbing them of their usual sparkle.

'Maybe it'd be better if we stayed here tonight,' he suggested gently to her, turning her face this way and that to study it better.

She rolled her eyes and pulled her head back. 'Jace, stop fussing! I'm fine. Really. I *want* to go home.'

'Okay,' he agreed, finding her resilience a godsend. 'But a cuppa is a good idea, so you have one while I clean up. A shower and a change of clothes will at least make me *look* a hundred per cent better than I do now.'

342

'Don't believe him, Tatum,' his father said, winking at her. 'There's only so much water and a shirt can do. It'll take a team of plastic surgeons to improve the look of that big lug, and all we've got on hand is Kev.'

Tightening her arm around Jace's waist, she laughed. 'That's typical of your modesty, Brian. Anyone can see Jace inherited his incredibly handsome looks from his father, and in one of your shirts, why, you'd pass as twins.'

Judy groaned. 'I don't think tea will cut it. Best check her out again, Kevin. Poor child obviously hit her head when she fainted!'

In the quiet darkness of their bedroom, Tatum gently fingered the white bandage concealing the ugly eight-centimetre wound running down Jace's arm. When Kevin Prendergast had removed the bandage to inspect it, the sight of stiff black thread criss-crossing the vicious cut had made her gasp, despite the doctor's observation that the emergency room doctor had done 'a real nice sewing job'.

'Twelve stitches,' she said, 'Does not constitute a *nick*.'

'It's nothing,' Jace dismissed, able even to overlook his phobia about needles when his body was pressed against hers. 'The chick who stitched me was simply into embroidery. Now, *changing the subject* . . .' He nuzzled the the skin below her ear. 'Have I told you recently how much I adore those cute little noises you make when we make love?'

Tatum couldn't accept his cavalier attitude towards the incident any longer. 'No! You've been too busy getting yourself *stabbed*.'

'Thoughtless of me.' His blasé tone made her want to

scream. 'However, now that I'm home . . . safe, sound and horny . . .' She stiffened and he chuckled. 'Okay, scratch two of those.'

'And, naturally,' she said drily as he nudged a knee between her thighs, 'they'd be the first two.'

'Naturally. I could be six feet under and twenty years dead and I'd still ache to be inside y-Ouch!'

Her elbow was driven hard into his sternum as she rolled away from him. Instinctively Jace touched her shoulder to ease her back, but she resisted.

'*Tate*,' he said, trying to work out what he'd done between the time they'd arrived home, ten minutes ago, and now that had annoyed her. She'd been fine on the trip home; laughing, chatty – hardly letting him get a word in edgewise.

It was then he recalled the bad bout of cramps she'd suffered last weekend. When they'd hit her Saturday afternoon, she'd doubled up with pain and he'd been on the verge of calling an ambulance. But she'd stopped him, sarcastically explaining that it was 'one of the joys of endometriosis' and that she knew how to handle it.

Jace had had his doubts, even as he took himself off to the health food store and bought the bizarre list of herbs and potions she'd asked him to get. And, though she'd recovered by Sunday night, she'd refused to listen to his pleas that she stay home Monday and rest, so it had been a relief to him, with his conservative approach to medicine, when she'd told him she'd made an appointment with a gynaecologist. But that was still two days away –

'Tate, are you having cramps again? Do you want me to

get you something . . . call a doctor . . . *what*? Just tell me and – '

A weak, ironic laugh cut him short. 'I don't need a doctor, Jace. I'm not *sick*. I'm. – ' Her voice broke then faded right away.

'Tate, *please*. Tell me what's wrong.'

Her response was slow to come, and so soft he had to strain to hear it.

'I don't understand how, after what happened, you can use death jokes as a lead-up to getting laid. All I can think about is how easily that knife could've *laid you out* . . . permanently.'

It was the plaintive, bemused quality of the admission as much as the admission itself that knocked him sideways. Never had he felt more of a jerk. 'Aw, hell, gypsy, I didn't think about – '

'I can't *stop* thinking.' In the darkness, her words were more an observation than an interruption. 'Not just about what did happen . . . but what could've. Would . . . would you just *hold* me, Jace? Just hold me real tight – '

Heedless of the protests of his arm, Jace did as she asked and pressed her delicate trembling frame against his own.

How? he asked himself. How could he have been so blind as not to recognize she was deliberately toughing it out?

With hindsight, it was blatantly obvious . . . The way she'd made bad jokes and initiated light-hearted conversation on the most inane topics at his parents'. How on the way home she'd made not a single reference to what had happened, but treated him to an animated, detailed and rapid-fire monologue of what had transpired between his mother and Donna. She'd talked on and on and on . . .

Jace had been surprised at how quickly she'd bounced back from the fainting incident, but he'd been too grateful for the fact to question it, because, he realized now, it had reassured *him*. Her vibrancy, albeit forced, had eased the terror residing within him. A terror not stemming from the moment when he'd realized he couldn't avoid the knife's blade, but the gut-wrenching, RichterScale-registering terror which had gripped him as Tatum's fragile frame had crumbled before him.

He'd deluded himself into believing Tatum's charade that she was fine because he'd wanted her emotionally and physically sound; *needed* her warmth, her passion, her body.

He had no idea how long he lay there trying to compensate for his self-centred disregard by holding her and stroking the smooth length of her back, with no other thought other than to console her to sleep. But though she lay still, her breathing even, he wasn't surprised by the alertness in her voice when she spoke.

'Jace . . . is your arm hurting you?'

'No. My conscience is. I should've realized how upset you were. That you were putting on an act.'

She squirmed around to lie flat on her back. 'I didn't want you to know.'

'Why not?'

'Because if you'd acknowledged it I knew you'd say something, and then *I'd* have had to acknowledge it too.' She laughed. 'That doesn't make any sense to you, does it?'

It didn't . . . and yet the words broke the thick darkness of his guilt like a flare illuminating the night.

'Close your eyes,' he whispered as, straining his right arm, he reached for the bedside lamp and flicked it on.

Lifting himself onto his good elbow, so he could better study her face, he watched her open her eyes and blink at the sudden brightness of the room. It was impossible not to marvel at the picture of sheer perfection she made lying there.

Her dark hair streamed out across the cream-coloured pillow, creating a contrast almost identical to that which her deep brown brows and lashes made against the immaculate smoothness of her skin. A casual observer would have noted nothing beyond the unimaginable beauty of her classically shaped features, but Jace had long passed the point of regarding Tatum casually. He saw the confusion and uncertainty in her half-smile, the hint of tension in her brow and jaw and the faint shadow of fear lingering in her eyes.

'Talk to me, gypsy,' he said, stroking her neck.

'Oh, Jace . . .' Her hand trembled as he lifted it to his cheek, and the tremor reverberated through his body. 'I've never felt so scared as I did when I saw you all messed up and bloody. It was a thousand times worse than when you got beaten up – '

'That's only 'cause the blood made it *look* worse,' he said quickly, wanting to alleviate her heart-wrenching distress. 'Honestly, babe, truth be known, one swipe of a blade is a picnic compared to two guys alternating their fists on your face.'

'Maybe. But it wasn't the blood that frightened me . . .

It was realizing I could've lost you.' Unshed tears shimmered in her eyes. 'If you'd died tonight, Jace, part of me would've died too. I've never cared that much for another person . . . I didn't know it was possible.'

Emotion rose in his chest, expanding swiftly until he thought it would suffocate him. It didn't, yet it impaired his vocal cords so much that when he tried to speak they simply wouldn't function. That was probably a blessing; mentally he was incapable of formulating a phrase that would adequately convey what he was feeling. Hell, his mind couldn't even manage to produce a single word he recognized amid the kaleidoscopic images of the woman he held. Verbally and mentally paralysed beyond articulation, he lowered his mouth to transmit his feelings in the only way left to him . . . with his soul.

At the first touch of Jace's warm, gentle kiss, Tatum felt the tiny icicles of fear bumping through her veins start to thaw and her blood begin to flow again. Flow freely, faster, febrile. Not with passion, but with *life*.

Jace's life. *And her existence in it.*

Her hands lifted to his neck and her fingers felt the strong, vibrant beat of his pulse. When they shifted to splay themselves over his broad shoulders and back, his muscles danced beneath them. Under the weight of his chest her heart felt, and matched, the flamenco tempo of his own. To touch him was to touch life.

The generosity of his kisses grew to meet her ever-increasing hunger for their sweetness and their sustenance. His hands scouted her body with both recklessness and reverence, searing her flesh, flaming her blood and melting her bones. But even as desire mounted to passion, and her brain became fogged from the carnal inferno erupting within, her emotional vision had never been clearer . . . She, Tatum Milano, felt *loved*! And in the wake of that awe-inspiring revelation she crested a wave of such sensual majesty that she . . . cried . . .

As he kissed her face dry Jace couldn't distinguish between the salty taste of her tears and his own. He shifted slightly, so as to reduce the weight of his satiated body on hers, and immediately her hands clamped on his buttocks and her eyes flew open.

'Don't leave me yet!'

'Not if my life depended on it.' When she smiled, Jace decided it *did*, for surely it was only the beat of *her* heart pumping the blood through *his* body.

Her fingers grazed his lower lip. 'That was incredible.'

'But it wasn't sex.'

'No,' she agreed softly. 'It wasn't.'

Dipping his head, he kissed her. Then grinned. 'Just making sure you noticed.'

She laughed. 'Oh, I noticed!'

Sliding two hands under her buttocks, he flattened himself against her and whispered in her ear, 'Roll with me.'

The manoeuvre looked as if it might succeed, until Jace's body jerked and apt four-letter words tumbled from his lips. Instantly Tatum moved off him to kneel beside him, a wry grin on her face.

'I love it when you talk dirty, Jace, but the grimace of pain is a turn-off.'

'Damned arm,' he muttered. 'Hey! Where are you going?' he demanded as she scrambled off the end of the bed.

'To get those painkillers Kev Prendergast gave you.'

'I don't need painkillers,' he called out as she left the room.

Tatum returned a few minutes later with the pills and a glass of water. And, after putting up only a token resistance, Jace took them. A few minutes later the arm that held her to him spoon-fashion began to slacken.

'Night, Jace,' she whispered.

'Mmm, 'night . . . gypsy,' came the sleepy reply. 'I love . . . you.'

She closed her eyes as her heart exploded in her chest. 'I know . . .'

CHAPTER 19

According to the smartly dressed doctor now sitting across the desk from Tatum, the spike-haired, bib-and-brace-overalled feminist who'd been treating her prior to her years overseas had moved on from the unpretentious women's health clinic to marriage, motherhood and a more conventional private practice. 'I can, of course, refer you on to her if you wish', she said. 'You may be more comfortable with someone you know.'

Tatum produced a wry smile. 'For the last few years I've been poked and prodded by so many different doctors, in so many countries, my idea of continuity was two successive appointments where the doctor spoke halfway recognizable English.'

The doctor laughed. 'Then I'll watch my enunciation.' She glanced at the file on her desk. 'You've suffered endo since you were sixteen?'

'I've had the symptoms since I was fourteen. It wasn't until my first visit here that I was given a name for it.'

Nodding, she reverted her attention back to the notes. After a moment she made a 'Mmm-hmm' sound, then looked sympathetically at Tatum. 'It says here you took yourself off the prescribed medication. Because of the side-effects?'

'Bingo. None of the multitude of pills I tried did a damn bit of good for the pain and I couldn't handle the mood-swings. I figured I had a better chance of enduring the pain than I did my homicidal stroke suicidal moods. I decided to try naturopathy.' She waited for the disapproval, a scowl or a comment about witch doctors; surprisingly nothing like that came.

'Several patients of mine have found that quite successful,' she said. 'You didn't?'

'Yes and no. It seemed to work for a while, until seven months ago when I had a bad attack while in Paris.'

'How bad?'

'I was hospitalized.' That pretty much said it all, without going into graphic Technicolor. 'One French doctor wanted to do a hysterectomy on me the minute I put my foot in the door.'

'Male, I'll bet!'

Tatum smiled at the woman's mutter of knowing disapproval. 'That's when I decided to come home. If parts of my body are going to be extracted, I want the surgeon doing it to be able to comprehend every obscene name I call him.'

An understanding smile rose on the woman's face. 'Well, you can hold onto your abuse for a while yet. There's a lot of options *I'd* consider before I'd perform a hysterectomy on a childless twenty-four year old. Laparoscopy, laser treatment – but for now . . .' She stood up and moved to the examination table. 'We'll start with a pelvic exam.'

'Oh, great,' Tatum mumbled drily. 'My least favourite camera angle!'

The doctor smiled. 'With your history, you knew what to expect when you made this appointment.'

'Yeah, but hope springs eternal, and all that stuff . . .'

Judy watched her son's bent head fondly and waited for him to tell her what was troubling him. She'd known something *was* the minute she'd heard his voice on the phone, a couple of hours ago, when he'd called and asked her to meet him for lunch.

During the entrée and main course he'd kept their conversation family-orientated – what he should get his father for Christmas, whether Ethan would mind if he asked to have LaTasha spend a few days at his place, so Tatum could get to know her. He'd talked a lot about Tatum; *a lot*. When he had, his voice had taken on a softer, almost whimsical quality, that left his mother in no doubt about how he felt about her, even if he didn't know. She smiled to herself, feeling quietly smug and positively delighted that her suspicions of nearly four years ago had proved right.

She could count on one hand the number of times Jace had issued a spur-of-the-moment mid-week invitation to lunch, but she was generously patient as she sugared her third cup of coffee and waited, in silence, for Jace to reveal the reason behind this one.

'Mum,' he said eventually, his voice rough with emotion. 'Tell me everything you know about endometriosis.'

Though she knew it was Tatum who'd motivated his words, they weren't the ones Judy had hoped to hear.

* * *

A week after her visit to the women's health clinic, Tatum was still giving thanks that Christmas and the holiday season meant that the earliest she could arrange to undergo the laparoscopy the doctor wanted her to have was late January. The procedure was as unsettling as it was necessary, but she determinedly tried to push it from her mind and wallow in the ever-increasing pre-Christmas cheer. There was certainly no lack of it in the Benton clan, with Ethan and the much idolized LaTasha due to arrive shortly from Melbourne.

'I know!' Jace exclaimed, his hip resting on her desk as she opened Bentag's mail. 'We could get her a push-bike!'

Tatum didn't bother to look up from her task. 'She's not three until February, Jace, and I'm not sure Ethan would appreciate transporting a bike back to Melbourne.' The bike was only a marginally less impractical gift suggestion for his niece than the play-house and pedal powered scaled-down Porsche he'd considered 'perfect' last night, when he'd insisted on dragging Tatum into Toys, Toys, Toys & More Toys.

'We could keep it at our place, for when she comes to visit,' he said.

That *did* get her attention. Setting the letter-opener aside, she sat back in her chair. 'Jace, I really don't think it's a good idea to have LaTasha stay with us,' she said, as she'd *been saying* ever since he'd told what he wanted to do. 'We don't *know* how to look after a baby.'

'She's not a baby, she's three. Mum says she doesn't even wear nappies any more, *or* wet her pants.'

She fought a smile. 'Impressive as that is, Jace, I'm not used to kids. I'm not even sure I *like* them.'

'Well, you'll *adore* Tasha the second you meet her! She cute, pretty, smart as a – '

'*Jace,*' she interrupted, then paused to get her terse tone under control. 'I'm sure your niece is every bit the angelic, talented, extremely gifted little girl you, Judy and Brian say she is . . . But taking care of her is *a big responsibility*. One neither of us have any experience with – ' She halted at his violently shaking head.

'Not true! I babysat her one time, when Ethan had to go to the shop for more disposable nappies and didn't want to wake her.'

'My mistake,' she said. 'You're an expert on watching a baby sleep for twenty minutes. *I*, however, *don't* have any such brilliant recommendations.'

A smug smile spread over his face. '*Exactly!* And . . .' he grinned '. . . you can't beat hands-on experience as a learning method. You'll do fine. LaTasha will do anything you say, simply from blind adoration.' He winked. 'Just like I do.'

'Then that'll be a case of the blind following the ignorant.' Sighing, she raked her hair, then launched another appeal for reason.

'Jace, you're not thinking sensibly about this. Disasters strike even perfect parents. *No* child is accident-proof; accidents happen to kids all the time. It's why we have emergency rooms in hospitals and warning labels on poisons. *This is not a good idea, Jace.*'

Standing, he rounded the desk and swooped to plant a kiss on her pursed mouth. 'Relax, gypsy. Trust your maternal instinct. I do.'

Which, she decided as he merrily headed to the door,

only proved how misplaced trust could be. She didn't have a maternal bone in her body and, come the result of the laparoscopy, the odds were she'd be minus one of the internal organs necessary for motherhood. She recalled the doctor's parting words as she'd left the clinic . . .

'Tatum, if you're confident of the relationship you have with your partner . . . Jace? I'd seriously advise you to consider trying to fall pregnant. Given your condition, you'd only have a slim chance of conceiving, but it might be the only one you get.'

Tatum had automatically repeated the response she'd given in the past, when other doctors had suggested the same thing. 'Kids aren't a major priority in my life.' Subconsciously she'd been pleased at hearing Jace described as her 'partner'; the word seemed so much more permanent than 'lover'. But it was becoming more and more evident to her that Jace genuinely *wanted* kids some day.

Don't think about it! she told herself. Just don't think – Her thoughts skidded to a halt at the sight of a letter personally addressed to her, rather than Bentag. Checking for a sender's address on the back of the envelope and finding none, she quickly slit it open and unfolded the elegant cream notepaper enclosed . . .

Dear Tatum,

When I heard you worked for a private investigator and realised there was someone I could turn to for help I was overwhelmed with relief. I know it's years since we've seen each other, but, as an old Chelmsford girl, I know I can rely on you to help me and to be discreet.

It's imperative that I speak with you as soon as

356

possible, as I don't know where to turn next. I've made a dinner reservation at the Centrepoint Tower restaurant for eight-thirty on fifteenth December. Please meet me there or, failing that, make another booking in my name for a time which suits you and I'll meet you then.

Please come, Tatum . . . You're my last resort.

Sincerely,

Nicola Ashton-Bradfield.

Tatum stared at the signature, trying to put a face to the double-barrelled name. Not even the reference to Chelmsford Academy was much help, since hyphenated surnames had practically been a condition of enrolment and to Tatum they'd all sounded alike.

She went back and reread the letter. It clearly indicated that Tatum's connections to Bentag had been a crucial, if not the prime reason for it being sent; whatever this Nicola's problem was, her connection with a private investigation firm was evidently a plus.

Frowning, she again tried to conjure up an image of the mysterious Ms Ashton-Bradfield and failed. None of the time-faded mental photographs of classmates from her years at the exclusive college seemed to fit. She put the letter aside. Perhaps it would come to her later in the day . . .

It didn't.

But the next afternoon, after Jace announced he'd received news on a case that required him to fly to Adelaide for the weekend, Tatum decided a free meal and pandering to her curiosity was a good way to delay the start of two boring, lonely days.

* * *

The table reserved for Ms Ashton-Bradfield was in a prime position in the luxurious rotating restaurant, and, knowing she was ten minutes early, Tatum ordered a glass of wine and settled back to enjoy both it and the spectacular views of Sydney by night.

Twenty minutes later she was still sitting there alone and no closer to putting a face to the name of the woman she was supposed to meet. She toyed with the idea of ordering an entrée, but the realization that in the wake of her Christmas shopping her credit card would be lucky to cover the one glass of wine in a place this expensive stopped her from acting on it. She'd give the tardy Nicola Ashton-Bradfield just ten more minutes and –

'Hello, Tatum.'

'*Shit.*'

'Still swearing, I see. I'd hoped you'd have become a little more eloquent.'

Given her body's catatonic state, that her vocal cords had managed any sound seemed a miracle.

'My apologies for being late,' Tatum heard her say as the maitre d' seated her. 'But getting a taxi on a Friday night is a disaster.'

As the words rolled from the woman's tongue Tatum was instantly transported to another restaurant a lifetime ago when she and this woman had been interrupted by a dizzy blonde schoolgirl . . . *Nicola Ashton-Bradfield*.

'*You* sent the letter.'

'Yes. If you haven't ordered yet, may I suggest the smoked salmon?'

'Why?'

'Because it's really quite excellent, Tatum.' Turning to

the wine waiter, she ordered a bottle of wine. When he had departed she returned her attention to Tatum. 'You'll enjoy the label, Tatum. It's light, yet . . .'

The perfectly pleasant smile combined with the perfectly modulated tone jerked Tatum from her disbelieving daze.

'Let's cut the crap, Lulu. Why send a letter to me pleading for help under someone else's name?'

For the first time since she'd materialized from the past, Tatum was alert enough to note the changes in a woman she'd neither seen nor heard of in eight years. The natural vivid russet of her hair had toned down to a rose-gold, due to the addition of a considerable amount of grey, its style, though, remained a precision-cut bob. The nails on the hand she raised to her throat were short and painted a soft coral, in contrast to the cardinal-red talons of Tatum's memory, and, while her make-up was as impeccable as ever, it couldn't disguise the wrinkles that had gathered in her once flawless skin, nor the haggard hollows of her too thin face.

'Do I pass inspection?' she asked.

'You wouldn't walk out your bedroom door unless you were convinced you couldn't look any better.' Tatum ignored her amused laugh. 'Answer my question. Why the charade with the letter and bogus name?'

Lulu fiddled momentarily with her cutlery, before lifting her eyes; they, too, Tatum noted, had changed. They were no longer bright emerald-green, but drab olive and lifeless. Physically, Lulu had . . . The only word Tatum could think of was *faded*.

'I was afraid you might not want to see me,' she said.

'Would you have come if I'd simply phoned and asked?'

Would she have? Tatum had to think about it. But not for long. 'No,' she said. 'I wouldn't have. My face stung for a long, long time after you slapped it goodbye, Lu. And I'm not just talking days.'

'I'm not going to apologize for leaving you with Christopher. I did what I thought was best for you, Tatum.'

Bitter bile rose in her throat as the name evoked ugly memories she'd fought to suppress. She cursed the curiosity that had led her to respond to the letter – the same curiosity stopping her, even now, from getting up and walking away from the table, from her past.

'Why now, Lu? Why, after all these years, have you decided to look me up?'

'Because until a few weeks ago I had no idea where you were.'

'You should've gone to Christopher. He has a contact number for me.' Actually, when he'd requested it Judy had given him her business number as a precaution, should Robin decide to get hold of Tatum. It hadn't mattered in the long run. Christopher had evidently been no more anxious to keep in touch with her than Lulu was, back then.

As the other woman picked up her wine glass Tatum noticed its slight tremor, but before she could speculate on it Lulu was speaking again.

'I did try to contact Christopher, but he was dead.' Her voice was devoid of any emotion. 'Apparently he committed suicide in 1991. From what I can gather, his lover, a fellow called Robin, died of AIDS; Christopher, grief-stricken, killed himself three days later.'

All Tatum heard was the sound of her heart pounding in her brain. Dear Lord, what might have happened had she not fled from the party that night? 'Oh, God . . .'

'Yes, it's hard to believe, isn't it?' Lulu said. 'Christopher was always so vibrant and cheerful.'

If Lulu had phoned even once during those days after she'd first left Tatum might have explained now that it wasn't Christopher's death which most disturbed her, but how close she'd unwittingly come to her own. But Lulu hadn't cared enough to call her eight years ago and Tatum didn't want her pretending retrospective concern now. Fleetingly, an image of Christopher, complete with his handsome blond good looks and charm-your-socks-off grin, strutted through her mind, its poignancy forcing her to blink quickly.

Then she reminded herself. Her past was *over*. Done with and packed away! How dared Lulu barge back into her life and drag it out again? She didn't bother trying to hide her resentment. 'So how *did* you find me?'

Amusement lit her face, but did little to reduce the effect of time on it. 'In the end I hired a private investigator.' She chuckled lightly. 'Ironic, isn't it? It took him eight months to locate you.'

Professional interest made her ask, 'Who'd you get?'

'A fellow by the name of Vincent Corso. Do you know him?'

'I know his reputation. He wouldn't have come cheap.'

'I've invested.' Lu's shoulders shrugged, lifting her breasts beneath a dress that seemed a little too large. 'I wasn't concerned about the money.'

Tatum produced a laugh heavy with superiority. 'You

should've been. Vince Corso overcharges, isn't licenced, and I wouldn't hire him to locate his own mouth.'

A flame of pure, bitchy satisfaction shot through her when the other woman scowled; revelling in it, Tatum smirked. 'You got taken, Lulu. A halfway decent investigator would've been able to tell you in a matter of days that I've been out of the country for nearly three years.'

'You, I gather, consider yourself a better than "halfway decent investigation"?'

'Yes.' It wasn't a real lie. With the knowledge she'd picked up from Jace and Tag, she *did* consider herself a better than half decent investigator and, licenced or not, she'd run rings around a cowboy like Corso!

A speculative gleam came into Lulu's eyes, and a moment later a very satisfied grin widened her mouth. 'I think we should order now, don't you?'

Tatum was still too disorientated by the position she found herself in to make any major decision right now; the best she could do was nod. Maybe with some food in her stomach she'd be able to start collating and filtering through her scrambled thoughts. Yet by the time they'd finished ordering she realized she couldn't simply sit here and share a meal with Lulu as if the last eight years hadn't happened.

Once she'd been an insecure, uncertain young girl who had aspired to be like this woman; now she was a mature, independent adult. An adult who realised that if it hadn't been for Lulu's act of abandonment eight years earlier she could all too easily have become just that. Exactly what Lulu had been eight years ago: one of Zeta's 'girls'.

Lulu had taken her in when her mother had died and in

her own misguided way had tried to protect her. For that, Tatum conceded, she owed the woman her thanks, but *not* her future. And she wanted that made clear. Crystal-clear.

'Lulu,' she said, using her courage while she had it. 'If I'd had a choice, I'd never have agreed to meet you. Not because I hold the fact that you left me against you, but because you remind me of a time in my life I want to forget.'

Some emotion she had no chance to name flickered in the tired green eyes, but it had the effect of nullifying the go-for-the-jugular vindictiveness that only seconds ago had consumed her. Impulsively, Tatum found herself reaching across the table and placing her hand lightly on Lulu's.

'All in all, the last eight years have been happier than I'd ever imagined my life could be. The truth is, you *did* do me a favour when you left me with Christopher.' She sighed. 'But it was only God's intervention that prevented it ending up a disaster.'

A frown formed under the rose-pink fringe. 'How do you mean?'

For a moment she was tempted to recount every disgusting, sickening detail of the ugly incidents with Robin, but what was the point? Shock value?

'It doesn't matter now. But what I want you to understand is that while I appreciate what you *tried* to do for me back then, and after Fantasy died . . .' She paused before continuing. 'While I can appreciate all those things enough to remain here and have dinner with you, I'm not so grateful I'll let you waltz back into my life.

'What I'm saying, Lulu,' she added, when the woman

remained mute, 'is that while I can live with knowing my past, I can't live with reminders of it.'

Lulu turned her hand so that she held Tatum's, and placed her other hand on top to enclose it completely. The gesture was so like Judy's it startled Tatum as much as the sadly sweet, understanding smile she'd never have credited Lulu with possessing.

'You won't have to live with the reminders for long, Tatum,' she said softly. 'I am dying of AIDS.'

For half a heartbeat Tatum had the crazy urge to laugh – Lulu always had had the knack of sitting you on your ass, in the most gracious of tones! Two heartbeats later the full impact of the words gripped her. Acid tears rose to burn Tatum's eyes and throat, blurring the beautiful understanding smile as guilt, pain and remorse bombarded her from all sides.

'I . . . Are . . .?'

Unable to both breathe and speak at the same time, she concentrated only on filling her concrete-heavy lungs with oxygen. With each hard-drawn breath she took a warm reassuring squeeze was delivered to her hand.

'Come now, Tatum,' Lulu urged. 'Don't – don't fall apart on me. That's it, honey . . . nice deep breaths.'

Gradually the sheer ludicrousness of the picture they must have made summoned a grudging smile from her. While *she* was practically hyperventilating Lulu, with her voice pitched as if negotiating with a crazy gunman, was trying to console her with her right hand while sipping intermittently from the wine glass in her left. She felt as if she was in a scene from a very dark comedy.

364

'Much better!' Lulu said, taking her hand from Tatum's and looking relieved.

'Lu . . . I . . . I don't . . .' Shaking her head, she tried to get her scrambled thoughts into a logical sequence. 'I don't know what to say . . . I . . . *You were always so careful.* You – '

'I guess that's what pisses me off the most.' The bitterness in Lu's voice poisoned her effort at a smile. 'All those years on the game . . . and in the end it came down to nothing more than a case of me being in the wrong place at the wrong time.'

'Lu?'

'I was living in Wagga and leading the respectable, low-key life of a hard-working cosmetic consultant in a department store.' She paused, refilled Tatum's glass and then her own, and took a sip before continuing. 'One night, after attending a staff-training seminar, I stopped at an all-night service station to pick up a carton of milk and I walked into a hold-up. Except the guy doing the hold-up wasn't armed with a shotgun or a knife . . .' Her voice started to break and she cleared her throat. 'He had a blood-filled syringe instead.'

'Oh, Lord . . .'

'I was walking with my head down, hunting in my handbag, when he came running out with the cash. We collided . . . fell . . . and I ended up with the syringe sticking into my calf.'

Anguish and rage raced simultaneously through Tatum's body. It wasn't fair! *It was too, too cruel!*

Picking up her glass, Lu peered at its contents. 'Four months later I tested HIV positive. Now, three years later, my life expectancy is twelve months, tops.' In a calm, almost blasé manner, she took a delicate sip of the wine. 'At the risk of sounding pathetically common, *life sucks*. Regrettably for me, my death isn't going to be any picnic either.'

With her next breath she greeted the waiter, who had appeared with another bottle, with a smile and a frivolous comment, leaving Tatum veritably speechless. Lu's completely *natural* behaviour was so . . . so *un*-natural! How could she look and act as if everything was normal when Tatum felt as if she was in the middle of some warped out-of-body experience? Twice she tried to speak, and twice nothing came out. With a complete absence of any of Lulu's elegance she grabbed her glass and drained it.

'You'd appreciate it more if you sipped it,' Lu chided her.

'Apppre – ! Lu, *how* can you be so calm? Act so . . . so unfazed?'

Lu arched one eyebrow. 'I've already passed the panic, hysteria and denial stage, Tatum. I'm now into the "getting my house in order" stage. Which,' she said, 'is why I needed to find you. I'm making my will and I want – '

'*I don't want anything!*'

'*I want,*' she repeated, 'to name you legal guardian of my daughter.'

'*What?*' Tatum gasped. She was hearing things. She had to be.

Except that wouldn't explain why Lulu was looking as if she'd just played the right bower in a deciding euchre trick.

'I have,' she said, 'a four-year-old daughter. Her name is Alira-Jayne. And when I die I want you to raise her.'

'No.' Panic fought with shock for supremacy within Tatum. 'I . . . I can't. I won't. You can't expect . . .'

'I *do* expect it, Tatum. I'm dying and there's no one else suitable.'

Staring at the ceiling of the bedroom, Tatum wished she could pretend the previous evening had been nothing but a dream. And, considering the state of her life *prior* to last night, her feelings for Jace, his absence and the worry of her up-coming laparoscopy, a shrink would have found such a dream *understandable*.

For starters, Jace was away and she was lonely. But even knowing that he'd be back in a couple of days was no consolation for the fact he'd one day be absent from her life for good. Sure, she could *pretend* not to think about it, but the truth was she did; sometimes when he was with her and constantly when he wasn't.

More and more she saw evidence of his inherent need to replicate his parents' middle-class normality and settle down to marriage and children. It had started with his idea to have LaTasha stay a few days and progressed to where he now pointed out houses that were for sale when they were out driving, passing comments on their potential and the practicality of real estate as an investment for the future. When he did this Tatum made comments like, 'Talk to me after I make my first million' or 'Don't ask me for investment advice. I can't even afford a car.' She could just as easily have said, Houses are designed for people with children, and there's little hope I'll ever have one. A problem which, in a dream, could be neatly solved by Lu willing her a child; something she knew Jace craved, but she couldn't provide.

Oh, yes, last night could quite feasibly have been a dream . . . except *it wasn't*.

'God, why are you doing this to me?' Tatum asked aloud. '*Why?*'

She wasn't a religious person by any means. The sole extent of Fantasy's spiritual guidance had begun and ended when she'd had Tatum baptized. Officially she was Roman Catholic. Unofficially she'd come to believe in God because it seemed handy to have someone to ask the impossible from, credit for the unexplainable and blame for things beyond her control. Right now, *nothing* was within her control!

Lu's words echoed through her head. 'I want to name you legal guardian of my daughter . . . I'm dying and there's no one else suitable.'

In the early-morning solitude of her bedroom, Tatum allowed herself a bitter laugh. 'Shows how dumb you are, Lu! God thought I'd be so unsuitable a mother he didn't even give me working parts!'

Leaping from the bed, she ran naked into the bathroom, and, flicking the taps on in the shower recess, she stepped into it. Under the shower she wouldn't have to acknowledge the water washing down her cheeks as tears.

CHAPTER 20

Jace stood at the door of his office observing Tatum. She was staring off into space, her brow wrinkled with worry and her teeth gnawing at her bottom lip, completely oblivious to the insistent ringing of the phone at her elbow. He would have liked to believe that her concern stemmed from nothing but indecision over what to buy him for Christmas. If he had his way, Tatum wouldn't ever have to face any thing more problematical than that. Unfortunately he couldn't make her life that simple.

'If you pick that up, it'll stop ringing,' he said, causing her to start. She recovered instantly, her voice typically efficient but pleasant as she identified the firm and began dealing with the caller.

Jace crossed to the coffee machine and proceeded to pour two cups. Since her visit to the gynaecologist's, he'd tried at least a dozen times to get her to discuss her treatment options and how she felt about them, but to no avail. Well, no, he corrected mentally, that wasn't entirely true. The first time he'd asked, she had supplied a breezy summary: 'I've got to have a laparoscopy in January. It's no big deal, just an exploratory thing to find out how quickly I'm falling apart inside.'

On the second occasion she'd rolled her eyes at him and said, 'Jace honestly! Stop going on about it! There's no reason for you to be concerned. I'm not!'

But, damn it, he *was* concerned. And angry. Bloody angry, because he knew she *was* worried! That despite her roll-with-the-punches attitude it was tearing her apart! What was more, it hurt like flaming hell that she wouldn't confide in him!

He didn't pretend to have any great understanding of complex female medical conditions, but he knew enough to realize Tatum was facing a woman's worst nightmare. His mother had told him the only thing he could do was be supportive, let Tatum know he'd be there for her no matter what. But how was he supposed to do that when she kept shutting him out? Not physically, but emotionally.

Once he would have been pleased to be involved with a woman who was passionately unrestrained in the bedroom yet self-contained enough not to burden him with her personal problems, but not any more! When it came to Tatum he wanted her to share *everything* with him: her joys, her disappointments, her frustration, her anger, her fears, her heart . . . the future. He swore silently. Hell, he couldn't even pin Tatum down to give a definite answer on anything as long as a month away!

When she hung up the phone he crossed to her desk and deposited a cup of coffee on her coaster, inscribed with 'PARK IT HERE'. And he refused to let himself be sidetracked by the brilliant smile she gave him. 'Okay, gypsy. What's up?'

'Up? Nothing!' Her eyes widened with confused innocence.

He shook his head. 'I'm not buying that, Tate. You've been distracted and edgy ever since I got back from Adelaide. One minute you're all sunshine and the next – '

'You're imagining things, Jace. Apart from the fact Christmas has put a dent in my car budget – '

'It's more than that, Tate. Even Tag's noticed it.'

She straightened in her chair. 'Tag said something to you about me?'

'Not about you, exactly. He asked me if we were having problems.'

'What did you say?'

'I said none that I knew of, unless he counted your hesitation about LaTasha staying – '

She jumped to her feet. 'God, will you shut up about her? All I hear every time you open your mouth is LaTasha this! LaTasha that! What'll we buy LaTasha?'

'Tate, I – '

'I don't give a stuff what you get her! Buy her a friggin' 747, for all I care! Hell, get her three wise men and a couple of shepherds of her own. You might as well! The whole damn Benton clan think Christmas *belongs* to her anyway!'

Her outburst stunned him so much she'd snatched up her bag and was half out the door before he could react. 'Tatum! Tatum, where're you go – ?'

'Lunch! I'll be back in an hour! *Maybe!*' The door slammed shut on her last word.

'*What is going on out here?*'

Jace didn't bother to turn in response to Tag's question.

'I'm *trying* to be supportive.' It was more a comment to himself than an explanation, but Tag took it literally.

'Couldn't you do it more quietly?'

Jace sent him a despondent look over his shoulder. 'I don't think it'd make a difference *how* I did it.'

Shoving his hands in his pockets, Tag leaned leaned against the wall. 'Okay, what's happened?'

He shook his head. Tatum wouldn't appreciate him discussing her medical problems with Tag. He stared at the door, willing her to come back through it and throw herself into his arms. To tell him she loved him, that she needed him as much as he needed her . . .

'Look, it's quiet here,' he heard Tag say. 'Or, at least, it seems that way *now*. Why don't you go find her and talk out whatever's bothering her? I'll hold the fort.'

For a moment Jace considered taking the advice, then grunted negatively. 'She won't talk about it. Not to me, not to Mum, not to *anyone*.' He knew because he'd asked his mother to invite Tatum out on a shopping excursion with the intention of trying to find out what was bothering her. At first his mother had been irritated by the idea.

'Jason, I *will not* be used as a *spy*. You can't ask me to pump Tatum for information and report what she says back to you!'

'Mum, that's not what I'm asking! If Tatum doesn't want me to know what's going on in her life . . . well, fine. I can accept that.'

'Can you?' His mother's voice had been sceptical.

'If that's what she wants,' he'd replied. 'I'm not saying it doesn't hurt to know that's how she feels, but I'm not going to add to her woes by pushing her. But, damn it, she *needs* to talk to someone. I know she does. I was hoping maybe she'd open up to you. Please Mum,' he'd implored. 'I'm not asking you to tell me what she says, just listen to her.'

In the end his mother had agreed. True to his word, he hadn't asked for a report, but nevertheless his Mum had given him one.

'You're right, Jason,' she'd said. 'Emotionally she's wound up tighter than a spring, but she didn't let on what was bothering her. In fact all she talked about was *you* and what she could get you for Christmas!'

'I hope you told her to giftwrap her trust and give it to me,' he'd replied wearily.

His mother had produced her most sanctimonious expression and tone. 'I'd have thought you'd have realized you received that long ago. Perhaps, not recognizing its worth, you overlooked it at the time, hmm?'

These days not even his mother made sense; suddenly his bloody life had become a cryptic crossword!

Sighing, he brought his mind back to his conversation with Tag. 'Going after her isn't going to do any good.' He picked up the contents of the tray marked 'In – BENTON' and headed back towards his office. 'If Tate wants to discuss what's hassling her, Tag, she'll do it if and when she's ready. No one can make a person talk when they don't want to.'

He was in the other room when he heard Tag laugh and say, 'I've got a kid sister who'd prove you wrong there, mate! Hell, Kaylee could make a rock talk!'

Tatum relished the anonymity of sitting amid the lunch-time crowd that milled around the pedestrian mall. The

373

people passing the bench where she sat were all inter-changeably ordinary, and the few who might have have noticed her aimlessly sitting there would probably have thought the same of her. And that was all she'd ever wanted to be – *ordinary*.

She'd never wanted the attention or adulation that being famous brought. She'd never aspired to owning multiple cars or properties. She'd never wanted anything that wasn't accepted as being so totally ordinary and *normal* that it protected her from the raised eyebrows, behind-hand whispers and vile taunts which had haunted most of her childhood and adolescence. There had been nothing ordinary in her life until the rain-lashed night Jace Benton had crash-tackled her on his mother's front lawn. A half-laugh broke from her.

No, that wasn't quite accurate. That night represented the *extraordinary*, the turning point in her life. It hadn't been until Bryce Benton had invited her to share his home and the rest of the Benton clan had accepted her as family that she had truly sampled normality. On the heels of that a chatty, vivacious girl by the name of Kaylee Taggart had extended her friendship, and gradually Tatum had come to believe she was just like everyone else. Ordinary.

And then Bryce had died.

His death had shattered her. Not just because of how fond she was of him, but because it had threatened her in ways she didn't really understand. As she'd packed her belongings for the move back to Judy's, a move everyone else treated as 'natural', she'd experience an eerie sense of *déjà vu*. She hadn't been able to help seeing parallels between then and after Fantasy's death, when she'd packed and moved in with Lulu. Or when Lu had left her with Christopher and how she'd ultimately fled from Robin.

She'd told herself she was being silly, but she had never been comfortable with her transition to Judy's home from Bryce's. There had been nothing different in the way Judy and Brian had treated her, and yet Tatum had always sensed her time there was only temporary, despite the fact very little had changed in her daily life. She'd still worked at the gym, helped out at the youth club, still had Jace quizzing her about her boyfriends every couple of days. But it hadn't been the same. She'd felt crowded and yet lonely at the same time. When Jace had started to pop in late at night for a chat, as he'd often done when Bryce was alive, she'd felt awkward. She groaned, remembering the night she'd told him to stop it . . .

It was late, well after eleven o'clock, and Judy and Brian had been in bed for ages. Tatum was all but asleep on the couch when she heard the kettle whistle in the kitchen. She couldn't remember putting it on, although she'd vaguely thought about making herself a cup of tea. When she walked into the kitchen and found it occupied she barely managed to stifle a scream

'Shit, Jace!' she hissed. 'You scared me half to death. What the hell are you doing here at this hour?'

'I've just finished a surveillance shift out Liverpool way. I saw the light on and I felt like a cuppa and a chat. So . . .' On cue, as usual, he produced his teasing grin and pointed to two cups on the bench. 'As you can see, I've provided the tea. Therefore it's only fair *you* provide the chat.'

'*What*? Are you crazy? It's the middle of the night! I was nearly asleep!'

'I know. You looked real cute curled up on the sofa in my old school basketball singlet.'

'It isn't yours. It's one of Ethan's, and – '

'You can't sleep in *Ethan's* shirts!'

'Oh, for God's sake, Jace! You're carrying on like I was sleeping *with him*. Not,' she added, 'that it'd be any of your business if I was!'

'It wouldn't be hard to spot if you were. You'd be walking around with Donna's hands grasping your throat.'

'Like hell! I don't let that bitch within touching range.'

'Mmm,' he said, rubbing his chin in a considering fashion. 'I wonder how Dearest Donna will react at dinner on Sunday night when I tell her you're sleeping in her husband's clothes. Not that I'd be likely to do that,' he said quickly. 'I loathe Donna.' He grinned. '*Nearly* as much as I hate drinking tea alone in the middle of the night . . .'

'You wouldn't dare!'

Laughing, he handed her a cup of hot tea, and resignedly she let him manoeuvre her into a chair. Despite her earlier protests, they sat there talking about God only knew what until long into the morning. As usual, he insisted on her walking him to the back door, where he'd wait outside until she reset the deadlock.

'You're asleep on your feet,' he told her as she started to close the door.

'Gee, I wonder why? Could it be that some inconsiderate person keeps dropping by at ungodly hours and insisting I entertain them?'

'Hey? Can I help it if I find you scintillating company?'

'You only find *my* company scintillating,' she said drily, 'because none of your multitude of preferred companions will let you barge into their home unannounced in the middle of the night, Jace Benton.'

'Not true.' He sounded sincere until he added, 'I bet I could call, oh . . . five or six, and they'd all be agreeable to a – '

'Wonderful! Well, you go right ahead and do that the next time you feel like a cup of bloody tea at midnight! Because in future *I'm not* going to be agreeable. I hate it when you keep turning up like this all the time!'

She recalled now how he'd frowned and looked genuinely hurt. 'You never complained when I use to do it at Bryce's.'

'That was . . . different. Besides, I didn't trust you and Bryce alone in case you started plotting to sabotage my love life.'

A tiny smile had played at his mouth. 'Someone's got to watch out for you – '

'I can look after myself! I don't need you checking up on me constantly. Or barging in on me when I'm sleeping! Now, go home and don't come back! I'm banning you from my home *and* my life!' She had slammed the door in his face and clicked the deadlock. Instantly he'd knocked.

'Er, Tate,' he'd said, his voice dripping with amusement, 'I have to point out you don't have the right to ban me from coming here any time I like; this is *my* family home. If you're not nicer to me I'll have to tell my folks, and they'll turf you out on your pretty little ear for upsetting their precious son.'

Now, sitting in brilliant daylight years later, Tatum recognized the teasing for what it had been, but back then, when she had already been unsettled by Bryce's death and fearing that her wonderfully normal life could suddenly be whisked away from her, it had only upset her more. Adding to her confusion had been the realization that she was angry with Jace when he was around and she missed him when he wasn't.

Then, just when it had seemed she was drowning in doubts and confusion, that there wasn't one thing she could count on in her life, Kaylee had come to her rescue, just as she'd done that day years earlier in the school corridor.

'Oh, c'mon, Tatum! You'll love Europe. It'll be good for you! Besides *everyone* does it!'

So in January 1993, exactly a year and eight weeks after Bryce's death, she'd walked through the departure gate at Mascot airport with nothing more than her passport and a backpack. Kaylee had said the magic words: – '*everyone* does it.' Nothing and *no one* had been more important to twenty-one-year-old Tatum Milano than being as mainstream as everyone else.

Now, a twenty-four-year-old Tatum studied the people surrounding her in the city mall and wanted to scream at her past naïvety and present stupidity! For eight years she'd believed that by acting 'ordinary' and pretending her past didn't exist she could truly *be* 'ordinary'. But *ordinary* people, *normal* people, didn't pretend the first sixteen years of their life didn't exist. Or try to make other people believe it. *Normal* people didn't shy away from the responsibility, commitment and risks of everyday life; they didn't reject love.

But that was what she'd been doing.

She loved Jace. She loved him with every fibre of her being, but she was afraid to put that love into words because she wasn't sure her love was enough for him. She wanted Jace to have *everything* he wanted . . . and she knew he wanted a family. No, that wasn't true . . . She *sensed* he wanted a family. Yet, while it was highly unlikely she'd ever be able to give him children, she was insulting the most wonderful man she'd ever known by *assuming* he'd dump her the minute it was confirmed she'd have to have a hysterectomy. That wasn't fair – to him or her.

Her. What about what she wanted? What she *really* wanted.

Propping her elbows on her knees and her chin in her hands, Tatum focused on the question for all of a second. 'Besides him, you idiot!'

'Excuse me?'

Realizing she'd spoken aloud, she smiled at the frowning woman beside her. 'It's okay. I'm talking to myself. I should have done it ages ago.' Unconcerned by the woman's puzzled expression, she returned her attention to her thoughts.

Kids? *That was a toughie*. She wasn't sure when she'd started telling herself she didn't want kids, but she knew the first time she'd said it to someone else. It had been the day Judy had taken her to the women's clinic. She'd been sixteen years old and her only real understanding of endometriosis, once the spike-haired feminist gynaecologist had put a name to it, was that it hurt like hell and was inconvenient! Sometimes her periods would be virtually non-stop for months, then non-existent for the same length of time.

But that day she'd learned that pregnancy, while providing a 'cure' for the condition, was almost impossible to achieve for someone with it. On the way home Judy had consoled her by saying she shouldn't worry about not being able to have children, since that only happened in extreme cases.

Automatically Tatum had quoted the words she'd heard Lulu say countless times. 'Men and kids are both more trouble than the're worth but at least you can count on a man being gone inside a month. I don't want kids. Ever!'

Now she wasn't sure whom fate had played the biggest joke on; her or Lulu. But that wasn't the issue, she reminded herself. *Did she really want children*?

'Yes, if Jace is their father!' Amazement at how instinctively and confidently she'd said the words overpowered any embarrassment she felt at again speaking aloud. But acknowledging the truth in them, and knowing their futility, almost ripped her heart out.

Okay. Okay, she told herself. Get a grip! Leave Jace right out of the scenario for a second. Do *I* want a child?

The question ran rampant in her head until she thought it would explode. There was no answer to it because *any* child she had she'd want to share with Jace, and given a choice she'd *never* take on single parenthood! It wasn't that she didn't believe she *couldn't* be a good mother, but growing up as she had convinced her that every child deserved *two* parents. They –

Her idealistic thoughts jerked to a halt. Every kid might *deserve* two parents, but the reality was not all of them got what they deserved. Some, like her, only got a mother. Yet she'd had Fantasy for fifteen years; Alira-Jayne would have Lulu for only a third of that. *If she was lucky.*

Oh, God! Hot tears welled in her eyes as she recalled what she'd said to the woman who'd taken her in and done her best to keep her from ending up with the same tragic life she and Fantasy had had. Refusing to raise the little girl was one thing, but Lu's request that Tatum keep in regular contact with the little girl, so that in years to come she'd have someone to answer her questions about her mother, wasn't asking that much! Tatum groaned. Had she really become so shallow and selfish that she'd refused ever to meet the child and maintain minimum contact with her after Lulu died?

If it had been Kaylee who had come to her announcing she had a child and wanting her to raise it, Tatum knew she'd have agreed without a second thought. Because Kaylee was part of the idealistic, 'ordinary' world she'd created for herself. Lu wasn't and, in turn, neither would her child be. Dear Lord, had she, in her obsession to become a 'normal' part of society, become too good for the people who'd cared about her when no one else had? Had she turned into one of those people who'd whispered behind their hands and stopped their children from playing with her because of who and what her mother was?

The truth was she'd come damn close; too damn close. The knowledge made her stomach churn.

From the public phone box she dialled the Wagga area code and then the number written on the piece of paper she'd pulled out of her purse, read and then screwed up a hundred times with the intention of throwing it away. The hand holding the receiver trembled as she waited for it to be answered at the other end. When it was, the voice was instantly identifiable.

'Lu,' she said quickly. 'I've changed my mind about meeting Alira-Jayne. If you bring her to Sydney in January . . . I . . . I'll arrange to meet with you both. Oh! But it can't be be the week of the fifteenth.' She didn't say that was the week she had to have the laparoscopy, because Lu's health problems made hers rank only marginally higher than a head cold.

'*Thank you, Tatum.*' The relief in Lu's voice was at odds with the cocky way she'd shoved her phone number at Tatum as she'd left the restaurant and said, 'Call me when you change your mind.'

'Thank you with all my heart! I can't tell you – '

'Lulu!' she cut in, feeling a rush of panic. 'At this stage I'm only agreeing to *meet* her. And . . . and stay in touch occasionally. Beyond that . . . Well, I'm not making any promises.'

Lu's chuckle came down the line. 'I've never put my faith in people's promises, only in my instincts. I'll call you when we get to Sydney.'

Tatum sighed. 'Okay. Oh, and Lu . . . you and Alira-Jayne have a nice Christmas.'

There was a moment's silence on the line before Tatum heard the response. 'We will. In fact I'm going to make it so damn good, she'll *never* forget it . . . or me.'

'Oh, Lu – ' The line went dead in her ear, and for a long time Tatum's vision was too blurred for her to move.

* * *

'Do I still have a job?'

Jace spun his chair from the view he'd been staring at without seeing for the last ninety minutes. Hovering in the doorway, she looked so damn forlorn it fair snapped his heart, yet at the same time the relief of seeing her had him smiling.

'It's company policy not to sack breathtakingly beautiful staff members merely because they snap their boss's head off and take extended lunches.'

A weak smile tugged at her mouth as she stepped slowly into the office. 'I know I owe you an apology and an explanation for being – '

'The apology isn't necessary and you don't have to explain anything you don't want to.'

'I want to,' she assured him. 'It's just, I'm not sure where to begin except to say . . .' She let her shoulderbag slide from her arm onto the floor, then came to stand directly in front of him.

'Jace, I don't want you to say anything until you hear *everything* I have to say. Okay?'

The determination in her words didn't quite gel with the uncertainty in her beautiful brown eyes and the evidence that she'd been crying. But her resolute air filled Jace with dread. *He couldn't lose her. He couldn't!*

'Jace,' she said, her hand going to his forearm to shake him gently. 'Not a word. Until I've said all that needs to be said. *All right?*'

Reluctantly he nodded. 'All right.'

'First off . . . I love you. I – ' A squeal replaced her words as Tatum was bodily lifted into the air. For a split second she glimpsed cosmic joy in the male face below hers. Then she tasted it.

His mouth moved over hers and she was gripped in an embrace that even as it forced the breath from her lungs poured life into her soul. She felt his hands in her hair, on her neck, her face, and it was gloriously long minutes before he lifted his lips from hers. His breathing as ragged as her own, he rested his forehead against hers and let his radiant blue eyes burn his emotions into hers.

She felt her smile rise-straight from her heart. 'You were supposed to wait until you knew everything.'

'I heard everything I've ever wanted to know in three words, gypsy.' Her heart went into overdrive. 'I've never known you to be so concise, but I'm glad you were just then. I was dying from the minute you said you had something to tell me,' he said, his voice rough. 'I thought you were going to say you were leaving me.'

Touching the perfect line of his jaw, she traced both sides of it. 'I'm not that strong.'

He shook his head. 'You're the strongest, bravest woman I know, Tatum Milano. And I love you more than I ever imagined it was possible to love someone.'

She sighed and rested her head on his chest. *That* was strong. As strong as the man it belonged to, as strong and dependable as the heartbeat beneath her ear. Tightening her arms around him, she closed her eyes and tried to absorb the courage flowing through his veins.

'I'm *not* a strong person, Jace,' she said, at length. 'Not *inside*, where it counts. I've been too terrified of my past to face the future. I've lied to myself about the things I really wanted because I was too afraid to deal with the thought of not getting them. I've deliberately been an under-achiever emotionally because I feared failure. And worst of all . . .'

She paused and drew a long breath. 'I let the bad things that happened in my past poison the good. I wouldn't acknowledge that Fantasy was the best mother she knew how to be. That she loved me enough not to put me in welfare, that she'd made a will and named a legal guardian for me *nine years* be – before she died!'

Her tears arrived in a torrent and burned Jace's skin through his shirt. Bracing himself against the desk, and wishing he could relieve her of her distress as easily as he could her insignificant physical weight, he stroked the back of her head and her shoulders; alternately whispering words of consolation and love.

After a time her anguished crying eased to sobs, but even then Jace continued to hold her; willing the warmth of his love to travel from his body into hers and dry her tears for ever. She was the most precious thing in his universe. She'd possess his heart and soul beyond the grave.

When he felt her body vibrate against his he thought she was crying again, so it was as if the room had taken on a celestial radiance at the sound of a tiny chuckle.

'You're drenched. You'll have to take this off to let it dry.' Her palm patted the front of his shirt as she tilted her head back to look at him. Even with red eyes and a pink-blotched face she did the most exquisite things to his body.

'And you're beautiful. If the shirt comes off, it won't be the only thing.' He kissed her briefly, but thoroughly, then smiled and asked gently, 'Feeling better now everything's off your chest?' She stiffened slightly before producing a smile, albeit a rueful one, and nodding.

'Yes,' she said. 'But there's more to come. I think it might be an idea if you sat on the sofa to hear the rest.

He raised an eyebrow. 'First you want my shirt off, now you want me on the sofa?' His eyes twinkled. 'Either you give me the concise version while I'm standing here or it'll have to wait. 'Cause, gypsy, under those conditions over there – ' he inclined his head towards the black leather settee – 'you're not going to get a chance to *talk* much!'

'Okay,' she said, after looking momentarily as if she was going to protest. 'But when you collapse with shock, don't say I didn't warn you.'

Her shoulders rose on a heaved breath. 'A former prostitute who took me in when my mother died is dying of AIDS. She has a four-year-old daughter and she wants me to be her legal guardian.'

Tatum saw surprise, shock and disbelief all flash across Jace's face as he physically started at her words. Then they vanished, to be replaced by love, understanding and a teasing smile. 'As you can see, I haven't collapsed. But you're obviously desperate to get me on that sofa, so – '

He scooped her into his arms and sat down still cradling her. Gazing up into his smiling face, Tatum couldn't believe how wonderful this man was. 'You . . . aren't shocked or . . .? You wouldn't mind if . . . if I agreed to it.'

'*If* you agreed to it? Oh, gypsy!' He laughed. 'There's no way you'd have ever said *no*.'

'But I did! I said no right off!' she confessed, ashamed that she didn't deserve Jace's impossibly high opinion of

386

her. 'I know I owe Lulu – big time – but . . . even today I only agreed to *meet* the little girl in January.'

He frowned. 'Why wait until January?'

'Well . . . Well, because . . . because they live in Wagga and won't be up until then.'

'Dumb reason!' Dropping her unceremoniously, he strode to the phone and pushed the button that connected him to Tag's office. He spoke almost immediately. 'Mate, you're holding the fort on your own for the rest of the day and tomorrow. Tate and I are about to hop a plane to Wagga.'

'*What*?' Tatum leaped to her feet. Tag's response must have been the same, because Jace answered her question into the phone.

'I said we're going to Wagga on the first flight we can get,' he replied. 'There's a lady there who helped Tatum through a bad stage.' Turning, he gave her a look that melted her heart. 'I need to see her and thank her for it.' He hung up.

'Jace . . .' she said, nonplussed. 'You haven't even heard the whole story.'

He winked. 'Save it for the plane.'

She had no choice. Because the next minute he was booking their flight, and from then she was sucked into a hectic whirl of emotion and travel preparation.

Mere hours later she stood nervously holding Jace's hand on the front veranda of a pleasant weatherboard cottage in rural New South Wales, waiting for Lulu to answer her doorbell. When she did, it was a Lulu Tatum barely recognized!

387

She was wearing *jeans and an oversized T-shirt*! But even more amazing was that for the first time in Tatum's memory her face was completely devoid of make-up – and slack-jawed with surprise as she stared at Tatum.

'Ah . . . hi, Lu. I guess I should've called, but – ' She stopped, noticing Lu's eyes had moved from her and were now studying Jace. 'Oh, this is Jace. Jason Benton. He's my er . . . my er . . . um . . . partner.'

'Partner? *Tag's* my *partner*,' he muttered, scowling at her before producing his most brilliant smile for Lulu. 'What Tatum means, Lulu, is that I'm going to be filling the role of your daughter's *male* guardian. Unless, of course,' he added, 'you have any objections?'

Tears filled Lulu's eyes as she shook her head. 'I'd trust Tatum's instincts with my life. More importantly, with my daughter's life.' She extended her hand. 'I'm very pleased to meet you, Jace Benton. So very bloody pleased!' And then she did the most un-Lulu-like thing of all – she burst into tears.

CHAPTER 21

Christmas 1995

The next morning Jace sat on the back veranda with Lulu, sipping coffee and watching Tatum and A.J. – his less cumbersome title for Alira-Jayne – try to convince an uninterested border collie that fetching a ball *was* fun. Seeing the joy their antics brought to the face of the woman beside him, he wondered if he was being cruelly selfish to be contemplating asking her what he was about to. Then the dog finally bounded to its feet and retrieved the ball, and the sound of delighted childish laughter triggered memories of the boyhood antics of himself and Doug Russell.

'You know, Lulu, until yesterday Tatum hadn't told a living soul about you. Never so much as mentioned your name.' He waited for her response.

'You can hardly blame her for wanting to put the past behind her. My name isn't exactly going to carry a lot of weight on a character reference.'

'It wasn't that. When she was pressed to prove the jewellery she had was hers, she told us about Christopher and that bastard . . .' He spat the name. '*Robin!*'

Lulu sat bolt upright. 'She didn't tell me she knew Robin – '

'*Knew him!*' Jace swore graphically as he told Lulu of what Tatum had endured.

'Oh, dear God!' Pure anguish tortured her face. 'No wonder she never talked about me! She must hate me. She – '

'No, Lu!' Jace reached and took her bony hand in his. 'She doesn't hate you. If she did she wouldn't have shielded you all these years. Wouldn't *still* be trying to protect you by not telling you about what Robin tried to do.'

'But the danger I exposed her to – ' She clenched her fists against her forehead. 'Dear God, she could have been infected with the same death virus I am – '

'Lulu, stop it.' Jace moved from his chair to crouch beside the distraught woman. '*You did what you thought was right*. She accepts that. Hell, *you* know that. You didn't know Robin was going to enter Christopher's life and become a threat to Tate. But you did know Zeta already was one.' He squeezed her hands in both of his. 'You successfully removed her from the dangers you *saw*; don't blame yourself for something you couldn't possibly have predicted. Neither of *us* do.'

Though she looked unconvinced, Lulu nodded. Then slowly smiled. 'I like you, Jace Benton. You're the most decent man I've ever met.' She gave him a salacious grin. 'And, honey, I've met them *all*!'

'You haven't met my old man yet.'

'If he's as good-looking as you, Jace, I'll go to my grave regretting it!' She laughed, but only momentarily. 'Unfortunately it's a little late for you to be matchmaking for me, because *I am* going to my grave.'

Jace ached for her. 'I know. And that's why I'd like you to meet my father.'

I don't understand.'

Jace was mentally struggling for the best place to start when the sound of Tatum's laughter gave him poignant direction.

'I'm the one person who knows exactly what Tatum felt the day she found her mother dead, because in early 1988 I found one of my oldest friends almost exactly the same way; he died before the ambulance I called arrived. When I call him my oldest friend, I'm talking in terms of friendship, not years. We were both only twenty-three at the time.' He waited as the chill of the memory lessened a little before continuing.

'As a private investigator, a lot of my time is spent checking Kings Cross for missing persons, and I get to hear all sorts of interesting bits and pieces of street gossip. Because of what happened to Doug, I've always listened extra hard to rumours about dope dealers.'

Lulu's face was showing nothing beyond polite interest. Jace was looking for something more.

'About eighteen months after Doug's death there were a lot of street murmurs about a guy who'd been recruiting pharmacy students to produce speed, but had dropped the project when a couple of bad batches, *lethal batches*, had hit the streets. The first was around . . .' Jace paused to ensure he had Lulu's attention. 'Around Easter of 1987.'

Evidence of the impact of his dramatic revelation came via her hard, sharp gasp and widened eyes.

'Yeah,' he said. 'The same time Fantasy OD'd.'

She nodded, as if he'd been waiting for her to confirm

the fact. He hadn't, but it gave him hope that she hadn't automatically dismissed the two occurrences as coincidence.

'The second batch apparently went at wholesale prices, way below what was considered good street value at the time, in November of the same year. That was four months prior to Doug's death from a heroin overdose, but I've never been able to rule out a connection.' He sighed, hating what he had to say next. 'Mainly . . .' he swallowed '. . . because my mate Doug had been a pharmacy student.'

'So were two of Fantasy's clients when she died.'

Jace's body physically jerked in his chair. '*What?*'

'You heard me.' Lu's eyes were flint-hard. 'Now tell me why you told me all this.'

Standing up, he walked to the edge of the veranda before turning to face her. 'The reason Tatum never mentioned you was that you'd led her to believe you knew who'd supplied Fantasy's drugs and could identify them, and that you were leaving Sydney because you didn't trust the police enough to go to them.'

'I see.

'Not yet.' His voice hardened. 'The reason Tatum never even dropped a hint about you was because *my father's a cop*. He's been in Internal Investigations for over ten years and is currently heavily involved in the state-wide investigation into police corruption.'

The apprehension and fear he read in Lulu's eyes and body language made Jace soften his tone. 'Lulu, my father is as straight as *anybody* comes, with or without a uniform. He loves Tatum as much as if she were his own child.' He laughed. 'The way he's been looking at me lately, *more*! The thing is,' he went on, 'if I give you the initials of the man who *I* think is responsible for what went down back then and they're the same as the one you know . . . I'd like you agree to talk to Dad.'

He gave her a minute to digest what he'd said. She sat statue-still, her back straight, her hands on her knees, weighing the pros and cons of what he was asking. And Jace knew he was asking a lot. At the most, she had a year to live. A year when her already frail health would take a rapidly downward spiral. It was a year when most women would want only to spend every precious second they could with their child. He was asking her to spend days, possibly hours, being examined and cross-examined in a police inquiry.

'All right,' she said at length. 'I swore to Fantasy I'd take care of Tatum, and I let her down there. I – '

'Lu! You didn't let her down.'

She ignored his objection. 'I swore to myself I'd get even with the bastard who killed her if I could. So . . .' She looked at him. 'Let's see if I can. Give me the initials,' she ordered.

Jace sucked in a deep breath. Crossed his fingers. Sent up a silent prayer for Doug and Fantasy. Then he opened his mouth to speak –

'No! Wait!' Lu looked panic-stricken. 'Jace, you have to be sure this is what you want. Because . . .'

Lulu's pause was even more attention-grabbing than the one he'd tried on her.

'Because if the man we're talking about is one and the same it means your friend Doug *could've* produced the drugs that killed Fantasy.' Worry tightened her features as she asked, 'Have you considered how Tatum will feel if that's proven true?'

Jace had. Long and hard. He nodded. 'I discussed the possibility with her last night. She understands Doug was as much a victim of addiction as her mother. Tate's only request was that I not push you into doing anything you don't want to do.'

Lulu smiled. 'That girl's heart must be bigger than she is.'

'It is.'

'Give me the initials, Jace Benton.'

Jace turned to face the backyard, not wanting to find himself searching Lu's face for signs that she was lying if she said she didn't recognize the initials.

'X.W. *Correction!* S.X.W. *My* scumbag has a knighthood for service to the national community!' Disgust flavoured his mouth just saying the words.

Behind him, Lulu remained utterly silent. Without turning around, he waited for her response. Then she was at his side.

'So when do I meet the man who sired you?'

Jace exhaled hard, until that moment unaware that he'd been holding his breath. He grabbed the veranda railing behind him as relief and gratitude flooded through him. 'I've already got four seats booked on this afternoon's flight to Sydney.'

Her laugh was loud, clear and genuinely delighted. 'You're a cocky bugger, Jace Benton.'

'Modesty prevents me saying that Tatum hasn't complained.' He winked cheekily, then smiled. 'Truth is, Lu, I was praying the plane tickets wouldn't be wasted, regardless of your decision. I kind of hoped you and A.J. might like to spend Christmas checking out all the relatives she's going to inherit.'

Her eyes drifted to where Tatum and Alira-Jayne were stretched out on the grass, chattering away. When she again looked at Jace it was with an expression of complete serenity. '*Both* my girls are remarkably lucky to be having your love in the future, Jason Benton.'

'No luckier than they are for having had yours in the past . . . Louissa Grant.'

Tatum awoke on Christmas morning to the best present of all . . . the loving attention of Jace's mouth on her neck. Purring her pleasure, she linked her arms around his neck and brought his mouth to hers and showed him how much she cherished both him and this, their first Christmas as lovers.

'Much as I'd love to carry you outside and ravish you under the Christmas tree, I'm afraid it's out of the question now,' he whispered. 'A.J. and Lulu are already out there, impatient to see what Santa brought them.'

In a flash, Tatum was off the bed. 'Ooh, me too!' She snatched up her robe and hugged it to her bare breasts, not in modesty but excitement. 'I can't wait to see what I got!'

He chuckled at her childish glee even as he admired her womanly curves. 'Well gypsy, you'll have to wait for my present. It's at Mum's place.'

'Judy's? Why?'

'Too hard to hide it from you here.'

Her hands went to her hips. 'You didn't buy me a car, did you? I told you, I didn't want – '

'I swear, it's not a car! And other than that,' he said, patting her on the bum to steer her out of the bedroom, 'I'm not giving you any more clues.'

'That wasn't a clue! That was a denial! C'mon, Jace, just one iddy-biddy clue . . .'

The two packages Jace had left under the tree to placate her – a jade silky negligee and the largest available box of her favourite Swiss chocolates – did their stuff for as long as it took them to get in the car to go to his parents'. By the time they were within only two blocks of their destination Tatum had pretty much driven everyone crazy!

'Tatum, give it a rest,' Lu moaned from the back seat. 'I've only been here a couple of times, but even *I* know it's not that long before you'll be able to find out for yourself.'

'Thank you, Lulu, on behalf of my tired eardrums.'

'Oh, c'mon, Jace,' Tatum cajoled again. 'I only want a *hint*.'

'A hint, huh?' Catching Lulu's eye in the rearview mirror, he gave her a furtive wink. 'Okay. Never put your coloureds in with the whites.' A glance to his left showed her wide-eyed with disbelief.

'You bought me a *washing machine*?'

He gave her a horrified look. 'You *wanted* a washing machine?'

'No! Of course I didn't.'

'Phew! That's a relief, 'cause I didn't get you one.'

Her expression was one of absolute cluelessness. 'So if it's not a washing machine why are you going on about mixing whites and coloureds?'

'A laundry hint Mum gave me when – Ouch!'

'You can't hit Jay at Christmas,' protested a tiny voice from the back seat.

'You tell her, A.J.'

Tatum turned to peer at Jace's defender. 'It wasn't a *hit*. It was just a *big* love-pat.'

'Fibber!' Jace whispered, so only Tatum could hear, but she ignored him.

'What's with this *Jay* stuff?'

Green eyes widened beneath a mass of shoulder-length strawberry-blonde curls. 'He calls me A.J. so I'm gonna call *him* "J".'

Lu chuckled. 'We were practising the alphabet last night and she decided then,' she explained.

'Oh.' Tatum smiled, but turned back to face the front as they swung into the Benton drive.

'I can't wait to show LaTasha my doll!' the child exclaimed as she raced up the driveway ahead of her mother.

'Use the front door today, Lulu! And be sure A.J. rings the doorbell. Brian rigs it to play carols this time of year.' As she said the words it struck Tatum how much a member of the Benton family she'd become. All year they entered the house through the kitchen, but come Christmas Day it was always 'Front door only'.

'Happy?'

She turned to find Jace leaning against the open car boot, smiling at her. 'Happier than I can ever remember being.' She walked into his arms and locked her arms around him. 'I love you.'

She felt his kiss on the top of her head. 'Hold that

thought when you see your Christmas present.'

They walked in, laden with presents, to a house that welcomed them with a cacophony of festive greetings and the excited noise of two little girls throwing paper in all directions in front of a huge tree in the family room.

Because Lulu and A.J. had been staying with Jace and Tatum since they'd flown up from Wagga three days ago, and Ethan and LaTasha had arrived from Melbourne the day after that, all the adults were at ease with each other. As for four-year-old A.J. and almost-three LaTasha, as far as Tatum could see they got along fine together. Although she still thought LaTasha was a tad spoilt by the Bentons in general. Then again, she decided, looking at Ethan, who'd become bitingly cynical in the time she'd been away, who wouldn't tend to overcompensate a kid with Donna for a mother?

As was tradition, the Taggart family arrived for a celebratory drink, and Tatum hardly had time to greet them before she was despatched to the kitchen for more ice. She was wrestling with the ice tray when Tag came to her rescue.

'How are you finding your first summer Christmas in two years?'

'Wonderful! Not that the weather has anything to do with it.' It was true. It was families that made Christmas special. 'Have you phoned Greece yet and wished Kaylee a Merry Christmas?'

'I spoke to her first thing this morning.'

'How was she? I was going to try and call this morning, but Jace said it's better to ring at night, when the international lines aren't so congest—'

'Hey! Hurry it up, you pair,' Brian yelled from the hall. 'A man could've had ice imported from the North Pole in the length of time it's taking you! Tatum, Jace said to tell you to come get your present from under the tree before the kids tear it apart.'

'Oh, God! I clear forgot it in all the excitement.' Hurriedly she began tipping the ice cubes into a bucket.

Tag stopped her. 'You go rescue your present. I'll fix this.'

She hurried down the hall and into the family room so fast that she nearly barrelled into Tag's parents, who were chatting with Lulu. Jace, Ethan and Brian were standing around the tree, their backs to her, while Judy was trying to shush the girls.

'You wanted me, Jace?' she asked, trying not to look as expectant as she felt.

'Yeah,' he said, pivoting to face her. 'All my life.' The comment brought approving sighs from the assembled women and groans from the men.

Tatum felt a blush begin to rise, but in that instant Jace stepped to one side saying, 'Merry Christmas, gypsy . . .' And there, sitting under the tree, was a grinning blonde who was supposed to be thousands of kilometres away.

'Kaylee!' she yelled joyfully.

Her friend bounced to her feet. 'Merry Christmas, kiddo!'

Hugging each other, they laughed, their words tripping over each others'.

'What are you doing here? You said you were too broke to come home yet.'

'I was. But Jace said bringing me home was his present

399

to *you*.' Tatum spun to hug Jace. 'Oh, thank you! Thank you!' she said, unable to stop grinning. 'Where'd you get the idea for such a fabulous surprise?'

'Tag reminded me that Kaylee could get a rock to talk.'

She blinked. 'Come again?' she asked, then waved a hand saying, 'Oh, I mean, *I know* she's persuasive!'

'A *much* nicer way of putting it,' Kaylee endorsed.

'But why did that give you the idea?'

Smiling, he pulled her closer. 'That day you stormed out of the office I was worried you were bottling things up inside yourself. I figured if *anyone* could get you to confide in them, it'd be old Havachat over there.' He motioned towards her best friend. 'I'd already phoned her in Greece and told her I was telexing her air fare home when you arrived back and explained everything.'

Tatum touched his cheek. 'But you were too kind-hearted to tell her you didn't need her anymore. Oh, Jace—'

'Kind-hearted, nothing! I figured her verbal powers of persuasion would still come in handy when I gave you . . .' He reached into his pocket and with one hand pulled out a small green leather box and flipped it open. 'This.'

Tatum stared at the beautiful solitaire diamond set in a wide gold band. In the hushed silence of the room all she heard was her own heart thumping. Emotion welled up in her, tightening her throat and weakening her limbs until she was incapable of speech or movement.

Tatum's catatonic reaction wasn't the one he'd expected, and the longer it lasted the harder it became to handle the expectant silence engulfing the room. He searched his head for something to say that would break its painful monotony but wouldn't make her feel pressurized. Hell if she didn't want to marry him that was fine – so long as she never left him!

'Listen, if it'll make you feel better,' he said, 'I'll increase your board.'

Her eyes lifted to his.—

'*Board*?' Someone murmured in disbelief, but he was interested only in what the woman he loved had to say.

'All right,' she whispered.

The box snapped shut in his hand. '*You want me to put your board up?*'

'*Board*!' One hand went to her hip while the other grabbed the box from him. 'Jace Benton, if I'm going to have to wash your dirty socks there's no way I'm *paying* to do it!'

His cheer, Tatum figured, should have lifted the roof. But then again he threw her so high before catching her safely she thought her head would! Not that she would have cared! What was a minor concussion when the most caring, considerate, generous, loving guy in the world wanted to marry her?

'Excuse us, folks,' he said, carrying her in the direction of the bedrooms. 'But I want five minutes alone with my *fiancée*.'

'Take ten, son,' his father called. 'We've waited this long for you to *produce* a ring; it's not gonna kill us to wait another few minutes to see her wearing it!'

They left the room amid cheers and congratulations.

'Goose!' Jace chided gently as he lowered her to the floor in his old bedroom. 'You're supposed to say *yes*, not "all right" when you get a proposal. For a second I thought you were knocking me back.'

'And when have I ever said no to you, hum? Oh, Jace!' She laughed. 'I was still reeling – you'd produced Kaylee from nowhere! And then the next minute . . . *Whammo*! again.'

'*Whammo*?'

'Yes, *whammo*! You can't blame me for messing up on the response part when *you* didn't give me the right cue. You're supposed to ask 'Will you marry me?' not just flip open a box and blind me with a rock the size of a paperweight.'

'Why not?' He grabbed a handful of her hair and brought her mouth into kissing range. 'You dazzled me the day you first walked into my office.'

The unique blend of passion and tenderness his mouth stirred was irresistible to her as always.

'I wish I could put into words how I felt that day. It was . . .' She smiled. 'It was as if I'd loved you for years. And I think I have.'

His fingers stroked her throat. 'All I care about is that you keep loving me for all of them to come.'

'I will.' Rising on her toes, she kissed him lightly.

He grinned. 'It's a relief to know you won't muff those words up.'

'Speaking of muffing things . . .' She opened the hand that still clutched the ring box. 'Are you going to put this on me or do I have to carry it round in the box for the rest of my life?'

Taking the box from her, he opened it and removed the ring. Tatum was certain that if his smile didn't split his face as he slipped it on her finger hers would. She'd never been this happy.

'Like it?' he asked.

'How could I not?' she replied, moving her hand as he held her fingers. 'It's the most exquisite thing I've ever seen.'

'Gypsy, *you're* the most exquisite thing I've ever seen.'

This time their kisses left Tatum groaning as they pulled apart. But then so was Jace. He leaned back against the door to support them as they recovered their breath and cherished the quiet moment together.

'Do you realize that you always seem to drop bombshells about our relationship in front of an audience?' Tatum mused. 'You announced we were having sex – '

'*Incredible* sex.'

He felt her silent amusement. 'Right. *Incredible* sex at dinner with your folks. You asked me to move in with you in front of your folks. And today you proposed to me in front of your parents and a room full of people.'

'Yeah, but I think Dad's starting to take my announcements *much* better,' he said. 'Don't you?'

'Much,' she laughed. 'But I should warn you, if you're intending on our honeymoon night being open-house, well . . .' She shook her head. 'It could cause him to regress.'

'I'll keep that in mind. *And now* . . .' He eased them back into an upright position. 'We have to rejoin the throng. Ready?'

'Answer one question for me first . . . Does it bother you that you won't have kids of your own?'

'Oh, gypsy . . .'

Sighing, he put his hands to her shoulders, gave them a light shake and brought his face very close to hers. She was so beautiful it was hard not to lose himself in the luxury of just looking at her, but once his gaze had admired the rest of her perfect features it was trapped by the bewitching brown eyes that had hexed his heart eight years ago.

'Listen to me. The verdict isn't in yet on whether or not you'll be able to get pregnant. If knowing for certain one way or the other had mattered to me I'd have only had to wait a few weeks to find out. *It doesn't matter to me, Tatum*. All that matters is *you*.'

'I love *you* Tatum. If we do have children of our own, I'll still love you. If we don't have children of our own, I'll still love you. I'll love you till I die. I'll love you beyond the grave. If all the stars fall out of the heavens, *I'll still love you*.'

He straightened. 'Am I making myself clear here, gypsy?'

And Tatum only loved him all the more for the trace of humour he injected into his voice.

Smiling, she stepped into his arms. 'Yeah. Crystal-clear.'

THE EXCITING NEW NAME
IN WOMEN'S FICTION!

PLEASE HELP ME TO HELP YOU!

Dear *Scarlet* Reader,

As Editor of *Scarlet* Books I want to make sure that the
books I offer you every month are up to the high standards
Scarlet readers expect. And to do that I need to know a
little more about you and your reading likes and dislikes. So
please spare a few minutes to fill in the short questionnaire
on the following pages and send it to me. I'll send *you* a
surprise gift as a thank you!

Looking forward to hearing from you,

Sally Cooper

Editor-in-Chief, *Scarlet*

QUESTIONNAIRE

Please tick the appropriate boxes to indicate your answers

1 Where did you get this Scarlet title?

Bought in Supermarket ☐
Bought at W H Smith or other High St bookshop ☐
Bought at book exchange or second-hand shop ☐
Borrowed from a friend ☐
Other _____

2 Did you enjoy reading it?
A lot ☐   A little ☐   Not at all ☐

3 What did you particularly like about this book?
Believable characters ☐   Easy to read ☐
Good value for money ☐   Enjoyable locations ☐
Interesting story ☐   Modern setting ☐
Other _____

4 What did you particularly dislike about this book?
_____

5 Would you buy another Scarlet book?
Yes ☐   No ☐

6 What other kinds of book do you enjoy reading?
Horror ☐   Puzzle books ☐   Historical fiction ☐
General fiction ☐   Crime/Detective ☐   Cookery ☐
Other _____

7 Which magazines do you enjoy most?
Bella ☐   Best ☐   Woman's Weekly ☐
Woman and Home ☐   Hello ☐   Cosmopolitan ☐
Good Housekeeping ☐
Other _____

cont.

And now a little about you –

8 How old are you?

Under 25 ☐   25–34 ☐   35–44 ☐
45–54 ☐   55–64 ☐   over 65 ☐

9 What is your marital status?

Single ☐   Married/living with partner ☐
Widowed ☐   Separated/divorced ☐

10 What is your current occupation?

Employed full-time ☐   Employed part-time ☐
Student ☐   Housewife full-time ☐
Unemployed ☐   Retired ☐

11 Do you have children? If so, how many and how old are they?
_____
_____

12 What is your annual household income?

under £10,000 ☐   £10–20,000 ☐   £20–30,000 ☐
£30–40,000 ☐   over £40,000 ☐

Miss/Mrs/Ms _____
Address _____
_____
_____
_____

Thank you for completing this questionnaire. Now tear it out – put
it in an envelope and send it before 31 December 1996, to:

Sally Cooper, Editor-in-Chief

SCARLET
FREEPOST LON 3335
LONDON W8 4BR
Please use block capitals for address.
No stamp is required!   PAPAS/6/96

Scarlet titles coming next month:

MARRY ME STRANGER Kay Gregory
Being newly married is difficult enough, but when the couple concerned are strangers . . . difficult becomes impossible! At first, though, it seems that Brand and Isabelle will make their marriage work, until, that is, real life intervenes . . .

A QUESTION OF TRUST Margaret Callaghan
Billie is everything Travis Kent claims to despise in a women: she's an impetuous tomboy, who lives in a ramshackle cottage with a mischievous cat. Throw in Travis' suspicious fiancée and the outcome is anyone's guess. But one thing is certain . . . passion is the most important ingredient!

DECEPTION Sophie Weston
Ash believes that *all* men should be treated as enemies, Jake has other ideas: he wants something from Ash . . . something she isn't prepared to give! Jake sets out to melt her resistance and, against her will, Ash begins to turn into the sensual woman she was always meant to be . . . until she remembers the saying 'Once bitten, twice shy!'

IT TAKES TWO Tina Leonard
No woman has ever dared to refuse Zach Rayez . . . particularly when he decides he wants something! So when Annie says 'no', Zach is determined to win his battle of the sexes with this feisty lady. Annie can't believe that a successful man like Zach is interested in a country mouse like her, but if he isn't, why does he keep finding reasons not to leave her?